WHISTLE

Also by Linwood Barclay

WHISTLE

A NOVEL

LINWOOD
BARCLAY

wm

WILLIAM MORROW
An Imprint of HarperCollins*Publishers*

WHISTLE. Copyright © 2025 by NJSB Entertainment, Inc. All rights reserved. Printed in the United States of America. No part of this book may be used or reproduced in any manner whatsoever without written permission except in the case of brief quotations embodied in critical articles and reviews. For information, address HarperCollins Publishers, 195 Broadway, New York, NY 10007.

HarperCollins books may be purchased for educational, business, or sales promotional use. For information, please email the Special Markets Department at SPsales@harpercollins.com.

FIRST EDITION

Designed by Diahann Sturge-Campbell

Library of Congress Cataloging-in-Publication Data has been applied for.

ISBN 978-0-06-343603-9
ISBN 978-0-06-345712-6 (simultaneous hardcover edition)
ISBN 978-0-06-344790-5 (international edition)

25 26 27 28 29 LBC 5 4 3 2 1

For Neetha

WHISTLE

PROLOGUE

Christmas 2001

I t was starting to look like Santa hadn't come through for Jeremy. All the presents that had been placed under the tree had been unwrapped and there was no PlayStation.

Goddamn, he thought.

Jeremy was only seven and shouldn't have been using words like that, even when it was only in his head and not out loud, but his older sister, Glynis, who was nine, had brought him up to speed on forbidden vocabulary. Not that he didn't already know most of the words. He'd heard kids using them on the school grounds. He could have thought something much worse than *goddamn*.

He also knew it wasn't Santa Claus who'd failed him; it was Mom and Dad. Glynis had set him straight on this score, too. "There is no Santa," she'd told him while he was sitting in the basement watching an episode of *Bob the Builder*. "There's no guy at the North Pole who's going around on a magic sleigh to every house in the world, in one night, delivering presents. What kind of baby believes in stuff like that? And while we're on the subject, the Tooth Fairy and the Easter Bunny are bullshit, too."

Glynis not only knew all the swear words, she knew how to use them effectively. And she knew other stuff, mostly from watching

Sex and the City at her friend Sally's house because they had it on VHS. Sally's aunt lived in Boston and had HBO and taped the episodes for Sally's mom. If Jeremy's parents knew Glynis was up to speed on the sexual antics of Carrie Bradshaw and her friends, they'd have a double stroke.

Jeremy knew his sister was less interested in his knowing the truth than she was delighted to shatter his most treasured illusions. If there was something she relished more than tormenting her little brother, he couldn't think what it was.

This particular Christmas morning, in a year when it was hard to imagine that anything good could happen, Glynis had done quite well. New clothes, new shoes, and one of those Bratz dolls, kind of like if Barbie went full Goth. And, sure, Jeremy got a Lego set based on Harry Potter stuff, and he supposed that was okay, but it sure was no PlayStation.

But then Jeremy's father said, "Wait right there. There's one more thing. Didn't have a chance to wrap it."

Oh yes! This had to be it. Dad was saving the PlayStation for last. *Well played, Father.* Just when Jeremy thought it was game over, no pun intended, Dad was coming through.

Jeremy's father slipped out of the living room, went out the front door without bothering to close it, allowing a wintry wind to blow into the house. There was the sound of a car trunk slamming shut, and seconds later, Dad was back, nudging the door shut with his body because his arms were full.

He was carrying a cardboard box large enough that his chin was resting on the top. Printed boldly on the side of the box was the word TIDE.

Was this some sort of joke?

Had Dad bought him a year's supply of detergent? This was no PlayStation box, that was for sure. But Jeremy continued to hold out hope that there might be such a box *within* the Tide box. Dad was trying to fake him out here.

His father leaned over, set the box on the floor, and let out a long, exhausted breath. "Lotta stuff in there." He got down to unfold the cardboard flaps, but then motioned for Jeremy to scoot over and do it himself.

"Go for it," Dad said.

Jeremy did, feverishly. He pulled back the four cardboard flaps and before he saw what was inside said, "I knew you'd get it! I knew you'd get me the Play—"

He stopped.

There was no video game system in this box. What would Glynis say right about now if she were him? *What the fuck?* The box was filled with . . .

Trains. Stupid, dumb toy trains.

Jeremy looked into his father's face, unable to disguise his disappointment.

"No, no, you're gonna love this," his father said quickly because the kid looked like he was on the verge of tears. "This is way better than some stupid video game system. Tons more fun, believe me. I had trains when I was a kid, Lionel and American Flyer, and they're still making this stuff, and—"

"Trains are lame," Jeremy said.

The words were a dagger to his father's heart. "Give it a chance. Look what we've got here."

He pulled out a boxcar and then a caboose and then a heavy black metal steam locomotive. None of the pieces was in its original packaging, but carefully wrapped in newspaper. One shred of masthead—showing the *Burlington Free Pr*—offered a hint of where these trains had come from.

"It's all *used* stuff," Glynis said derisively.

"Where did you get all this?" Jeremy's mother asked her husband.

As Jeremy continued to bring out more cars and accessories—a tanker car, a flatcar with a helicopter perched on it, a train station, a water tower—his father said, "You know that new guy at work? Wendell? Wendell Comstock? Met him the other day at the Tops?"

She tried to remember, and when she did, her face fell. "Is that the poor man who just moved here? Where was he from?"

"Just across the border into Vermont." He paused, lowered his voice. "Lucknow."

"Oh God, *Lucknow*. He sure got out of that town just in time."

"Yeah, moved away before it happened."

"His wife was one of the vic—"

"No," he said, lowering his voice to a whisper so the kids wouldn't hear. "She got electrocuted a week or two before. But he grew up around here. Got a sister in Fenelon. Decided to sell the house, move back. Hell of a thing, what happened back there."

He gave his head a sorrowful shake. "Anyway, he brought this box in, and I thought he was selling it, but he was giving it away to the first person what wanted it, he had no need for it, said the movers packed it without him realizing. And I said, hey, I know just the boy who'd love this." At this point, he gave Jeremy a big smile. "Give it a chance, won't you, sport?"

He reached into the box, pulled out several sections of track, then a heavy black boxy item about half the size of a loaf of bread.

"This here's the transformer, brand-new," he said. "Wendell didn't have the original one that came with the set, so I picked this one up at a hobby shop in Binghamton." He grinned. "Train won't run without it."

He set down the transformer and brought out from the box a shiny red boxcar with the SANTA FE logo printed on the side. He held out the car, about a foot long, to his son. "Just 'cause it says SANTA on the side doesn't mean it has anything to do with Santa Claus. Santa Fe is a very important railway in the history of America. And check this out. The doors open and close and the couplers work and it looks like the real thing."

With limited enthusiasm, Jeremy allowed his father to place it in his outstretched hands for a closer examination.

And something happened.

Jeremy felt a . . . what, exactly? A shock? No, couldn't be a shock. The transformer wasn't even plugged in. But there was something . . . like a tingle. He could feel it running all the way up his arms, if only for a millisecond.

He brought the toy boxcar close to his face, studying it. Ran his fingers along the sides, feeling the raised bumps meant to replicate rivets. Opened and closed the side doors, spun the thick metal wheels with his finger.

"Pretty neat, huh?" said his father.

Jeremy, feeling his earlier indifference shifting into something approaching enthusiasm, said, "Can we make it go?"

"Let's make a circle of track around the bottom of the tree."

Each track piece had a third rail that ran down the middle. "That carries the electric power and the outer rails are the ground," his father said. "Keeps it from short-circuiting. But don't worry, it can't shock you."

Once the track sections had been made into a continuous loop, Jeremy pulled out more items from the Tide box and started to carefully place them onto the track, making sure the wheels' flanges were set within the rail edges. All that remained to make the train operational was the engine.

Jeremy picked up the weighty locomotive and the attached tender with PENNSYLVANIA emblazoned on the side.

"The tender's where they kept all the coal that they had to keep feeding into the engine to keep it going," his father said. "You don't see anything like that these days."

Inside the locomotive cab, sitting at the controls, was a tiny engineer, dressed in overalls and a striped cap, his head no larger than a pea. Jeremy leaned in for a closer look.

"Pretty realistic, huh?" his father said.

"He winked at me," Jeremy said, and his father laughed. He turned the engine around, grasping it with both hands, and looked straight into the headlight mounted on the front.

"The light'll come on when we get it on the track and turn the throttle," his father said, which struck Jeremy as an odd thing to say, given that he could already see a faint glimmer in the bulb.

Glynis, stroking the hair on her Bratz doll, bored and annoyed that this dumbass train set was getting so much attention, asked, "Are we gonna have breakfast or what?"

As Jeremy set the locomotive onto the track, there was that tingle again. It was hard to describe, but it felt a little like that old gag gift his friend Ricky had tried on him. A joy buzzer he'd found in his own father's box of mementos. You slipped it into your palm and when you shook hands with someone they got a zap. But this was like a tenth of that. Subtle, pleasing almost.

Jeremy's father ran two wires from the underside of the track to the two terminals on the transformer, screwed down the threaded connectors to ensure good electrical conduction, then plugged it into the wall. There was a handle on the top of it, which he explained was the throttle.

"Crank 'er up!"

Jeremy turned the throttle, and as if by magic the locomotive made an electrical humming sound, the headlight illuminated, and as he moved the handle farther to the right, the wheels began to turn. Feathery wisps of smoke puffed out of the steam engine's smokestack. And what a glorious sound it made.

Chuff. Chuff. Chuff.

Jeremy gave the throttle another turn. The wheels spun more furiously.

Chuffchuffchuffchuffchuffchuff

Jeremy's father pressed a red button on the transformer to activate a whistle on the engine. "There's so much more stuff you can get. Buildings and trees and little people. One boxcar has a trapdoor on the top and a giraffe sticks its head out and then drops it back just in time, and . . ."

Jeremy wasn't listening.

He lay down on his side, ear to the floor, the train's vibrations reverberating through the tracks and into the hardwood, buzzing their way into his skull. Every few seconds the train raced past, the engine chuffing furiously, the various cars in tow, the red caboose trailing, the glorious chorus of metal spinning on metal, the smell of ozone in the air.

Jeremy was mesmerized. He could lie here like this for hours, imagining himself in the cab of that locomotive, shoveling coal from the tender into the firebox, elbow on the window ledge, head poked out to view the track ahead, a red kerchief tied around his neck blowing in the wind, the world flying past.

It felt . . . magical. As though he and the engine had somehow become one and the same, fused together. He remembered that book his mother read to him when he was two or three, about that little engine that could. Jeremy was that engine now, and he could do anything.

"Have fun," his father said, and went to the kitchen with Jeremy's mom.

Jeremy tentatively touched his finger to the track, pulling it away a millisecond before the train swept past on its latest loop. He felt a small charge, that tingle again. He knew that wasn't supposed to happen, but he definitely felt *something*. Maybe this train was different. Special, even—

"Oops," said Glynis, kicking over the red boxcar and sending the entire train off the tracks.

Jeremy was so transfixed that the derailment hit him as though he'd been awakened from a dream. He looked first at the fallen train, then slowly turned his head to look up at his sister.

She said, "You got a *used* secondhand gift. Somebody's old junk. My Bratz doll is *new*. I'm gonna eat your Cinnabon." She set her doll on the living room couch and disappeared into the kitchen.

Jeremy pondered his sister's history of villainy as he looked at the devastation she had wrought, this scale train wreck. Telling him the truth about Santa and the Easter Bunny. The time she put rabbit turds in his ice cream. Stuffed a dead toad into the toe of his runners. Told everyone at school he'd wet the bed. That time she stole three dollars from their mother's purse and, when it looked as though she might be found out, slipped the bills under Jeremy's pillow. Their mother found them when she was changing the sheets. Jeremy's protestations of innocence were to no avail.

Glynis was a very, very bad sister.

She was his tormentor. He was her victim. It had always been this way. He'd considered retaliation before, but anything he attempted would bring serious blowback from his parents. He couldn't just hit her or pull her hair or put a snake in her underwear drawer. He wished he were more creative, that he could find a way to teach her a lesson without anyone tracing it back to him.

Then he rolled over and eyed the Bratz doll Glynis had left sitting on the couch, staring into the room with its dead eyes. And there, on the floor, were discarded strands of green ribbon that had secured some of the now-unwrapped presents.

An idea was forming.

One day, his father had shared some old tapes of cartoons he'd loved as a kid. One was about a dumb Royal Canadian Mounted Policeman named Dudley Do-Right who was forever saving a girlfriend when she got tied to the railroad tracks by the nasty Snidely Whiplash.

Jeremy took the Bratz doll from the couch. Placed it across the track and secured it with the green ribbon. Then he put the locomotive and cars back onto the track.

See how Glynis liked it when her *new* toy got run over by his *used* train.

He cranked the throttle so hard the engine's wheels spun as they sought purchase on the track. Only half a loop to go to make contact. There was no Dudley Do-Right coming to rescue Glynis's Christmas present.

For a second there, as Jeremy looked into the face of the doll, he thought he saw the face of his sister.

That was not possible, of course. He blinked, and the doll went back to being a doll.

Chuffchuffchuffchuffchuffchuffchuff

Jeremy hit the whistle button.

Woo-woo!

Rounding the turn. Almost there. The moment of impact a millisecond away.

Chuffchuffchuffchuffchuffchuffchuff

And then, *whomp.*

What wonderful chaos. The doll was catapulted across the room, the flimsy ribbon cut by the loco's wheels before the engine bounced off the track and landed on its side, taking the attached cars with it. It was, Jeremy thought, an epic derailment as good as any he had ever seen in a movie.

And then, from the kitchen, the sound of something shattering.

Followed by a bone-chilling scream.

Jeremy sprang to his feet and went to the kitchen doorway to investigate.

His mother, father, and sister were crowded around the sink, Glynis in the middle, holding her hand over some dishes that had been left there to soak.

On the floor by their feet, the shattered remains of a glass.

Blood was dripping furiously from Glynis's hand.

"My God!" Jeremy's mother shrieked. "Call an ambulance!"

Jeremy's father said there was no time for that, he would wrap the detached finger in a cloth with ice cubes around it and drive Glynis to the hospital and maybe they could reattach it and how in the hell did this happen anyway and then Jeremy's parents were yelling at each other while Glynis continued to wail.

Jeremy went back into the living room.

He found the Bratz doll. The right hand was missing, as if neatly cut off with a pair of shears. After a brief search, he found the hand between two of the metal ties that supported the train. He tucked the tiny hand deep into the pocket of his jeans.

Once the locomotive and cars were back on the track, Jeremy set the throttle to a nice, steady speed, got on the floor again, propped up on his elbows, head resting in his hands, and watched the train go around and around and around and around.

Chuffchuffchuffchuffchuffchuff

Part I

ONE

"I think I need to get out of the city for a while," Annie Blunt said, taking a long sip of her cocktail.

"Like, what, a vacation?" asked Finnegan Sproule, glancing about for a waiter. He could see that Annie was nearly ready for another drink.

Annie shook her head, her long, frizzy, weeping-willow hair swaying across her shoulders. "A change of scene. A month, two months, maybe. Part of the summer, for sure. I'd pack us up and go today, but I don't want to pull Charlie out of school before the end of the year. Someplace out in the country. A small town, I don't know."

"But you'd come back, in September."

She shrugged. "We find someplace we like, we could stay there."

"You've always lived in New York." Finnegan smiled. "You'll go nuts in a small town. Where will you get bagels?"

"We'll eat Wonder Bread. It's wonderful with peanut butter. There's a world beyond Manhattan, you know."

Finnegan appeared thoughtful. "Actually, I'm not sure there is. Sure, it can get so hot in the summer your shoes stick to the pavement. But come fall, when the leaves in Central Park start to change?"

"A reporter was waiting for me when I came out of my building this morning."

He frowned. "Shit."

"Said she was from *Vanity Fair*. She'd emailed me a few times and

I hadn't answered, so she decided on the personal ambush. Wanted to know if there'd ever be another book."

"What did you tell her?"

"I told her fuck off, that's what I told her."

"There've been some stories in the trades, speculating," Finnegan said.

"Let them speculate. It's nobody's business."

"Well," he said hesitantly, "that's not exactly true."

Annie gave him a look. "I know. I owe you one more book."

Finnegan raised his palms. "All I'm saying is, a lot rides on your decision. You've sold nearly fifteen million books and have an ever-growing fan base. One generation gets followed by another and then another. Those Sandra Boynton board books never go out of print. Look at *Love You Forever* by Robert Munsch. Came out in the eighties, continues to sell a shitload every year, and still will long after we're dead and gone."

He inwardly winced at his choice of words. Not the kind of phrase you wanted to use with someone who'd had the kind of year Annie Blunt had had. If she'd taken offense at his language, she did not show it.

Finnegan pushed on. "You're in that league. Your books are timeless. There's no reason people will stop buying them."

"They'll have to be content with the backlist," she said. "There just won't be any new ones."

The next Pierce the Penguin book was in the spring catalogue. The division's entire budget had been built around it. But Annie had not delivered, hadn't so much as sketched out a single page. To be out by May, the book would already have to be in-house.

Finnegan leaned back in his chair and took in the room around him. "This was where we had our first meeting, when I acquired *Pierce Goes to Paris*. Nine years ago."

The Gramercy Tavern was barely a thirty-minute walk from Annie's place on Bank Street in the West Village. More convenient for her than for Finnegan, whose Langley House Books office was way up Broadway near 60th. Langley, a division of one of the biggest publishing conglomerates in the world, had the better part of the twenty-third floor.

Annie wasn't about to admit her editor might be right about going mad in some small town. She'd never lived anywhere but New York, unless you counted that month she'd spent in Paris when she was twenty, doing the whole becoming-an-artist thing. She'd grown up in Brooklyn, had first lived on her own in a dingy apartment not far from the Guggenheim, then a slightly less rat-infested place in SoHo while she attended the School of Visual Arts on 23rd Street in Manhattan where, in an animation class, she met John.

John.

Fellow nerd, best friend, around-the-clock support system, love of her life.

When unimaginable success hit, she and John and, before long, Charlie, moved into their Bank Street brownstone. John Lennon and Yoko had lived on that street once. Sid Vicious even died there. Talk about a neighborhood with character.

Yeah, New York was in her blood, its taxi fumes in her lungs, even if more of them were going electric. But that didn't mean she wasn't capable of change.

Picking up on Finnegan's observation that they were back where it all began, she said, "And I probably don't look much different than I did that day." She half raised her arms, showing off her shapeless knit sweater. She glanced down. "These might be the same jeans."

"It's one of your charms. You've never let success go to your head. You almost bailed on the Newbery Awards because you didn't want to get glammed up. I almost wish you *had* skipped it. I could have accepted the award on your behalf."

"John talked me into it," she said, smiling sadly at the memory. "When I came out of the bedroom in that Dior gown he asked who I was and what I'd done with his wife."

Her eyes wandered the room.

"You're not liking the halibut?" Finnegan asked. He pointed to the mostly untouched piece of fish on her plate. "Send it back. Get something else."

"It's fine."

"Really. You were going to get the chicken. Send it back and get the chicken."

"I don't want the chicken. But I wouldn't say no to another one of these Garden Gimlets."

She indicated her cocktail glass. She'd already had two. Finnegan waved a hand in the air, caught the eye of a waiter, pointed to Annie's empty glass, and nodded. The waiter nodded in return. Message received.

"There are two women at that table over there who've been looking this way," she said. "Christ, don't turn around."

"I wasn't going to."

"This is what I'm talking about," Annie said. "People sneaking glances, whispering. Even Charlie's dealing with it at school. Kids teasing. Asking him if he's taking flying lessons."

Finnegan grimaced.

"I'm no A-list celeb," Annie conceded. "Not even C-list. But I do get recognized occasionally. I want to go where no one knows me."

"So take a break. Three months, six. A year. Whatever. Whenever you're ready, we're here. No pressure."

"I can pay back the advance for the next one."

His palms went up again. "There's no need for talk like that."

The waiter arrived with her cocktail, took the empty glass away. Rather than pick it up and have a sip, she simply stared at it.

"I see him every night," she whispered.

Finnegan waited.

"I'm afraid to go to sleep because he always visits me."

"John," Finnegan said.

Annie bit her lower lip. "Him, too. But I welcome those visits."

Stupid me, Finnegan thought. Of course she was talking about Evan.

"Every time, I try to talk him back inside. He's on the ledge and I'm doing everything I can to persuade him that his goddamn cardboard wings won't hold him aloft. He won't listen. He looks so happy."

Annie's eyes misted. She looked away again, trying to hold it together. She picked up her drink and took a sip, felt its warmth work its way through her body.

"I know you've heard this a hundred times, but it wasn't your fault," he said. "No more than if some kid thought he was Superman. Did you know there were actually incidents related to Peter Pan? When it was first published, kids got hurt trying to fly, jumping off their beds and worse. Originally, J. M. Barrie had Peter and the Lost Boys flying without any kind of help, but when he heard about kids injuring themselves, he amended the story, that you could only fly if you had pixie dust blown on you. Trying to make the point that the flying was magical, that regular kids couldn't do it."

She still couldn't look at him as he continued.

"Look, we've reached this point where you can't do anything without legal stepping in and saying, well, that warrants some sort of caution. You want to reprint *Goldilocks and the Three Bears*? Maybe we need a disclaimer, that in the real world bears should not be approached because they can be very dangerous. If creative people hold back because there's one chance in a million someone will interpret their work in a totally irrational way, what will we end up with?"

Annie slowly fixed her eyes on her editor. "He wasn't some nut with a gun who went on a rampage because of social media. He was six, Finnegan. He was six years old."

"And where were his parents? Why hadn't they explained that not everything in a book is real? That just because a penguin in a book can learn to fly, it doesn't mean a kid can jump out an apartment building? Why'd they leave that balcony door unlocked? Who was supervising? Annie, you can't beat yourself up forever."

"You sound like John," Annie said faintly. "He said all the same things. I feel like . . . I can't shake the idea that what happened to John was some kind of karma. The universe trying to even the score."

"Annie."

"I killed that boy, and then someone killed John." She forced a sardonic smile. "Maybe I should let it go. My punishment has been meted out. The gods have spoken."

Finnegan couldn't think of anything to say to that. He scanned the room again for the waiter, wondering whether he should just ask for the check, if they should get out of here.

"Oh shit," Annie said.

"What?"

"One of them's coming over here."

A slender woman, late thirties, early forties, looking like she'd walked off the page of an Ann Taylor catalogue, approached, looking apologetic.

"I'm so sorry," she said, smiling awkwardly. "I don't do usually do this. I really don't. I was here one day and Al Pacino was sitting at that table and I was dying to say hello but I didn't, but you're Annie Blunt and I just had to tell you how much our family has enjoyed your books."

Annie forced a smile onto her lips. "That's kind of you to say."

"We got your books when our daughter was little and read them to her every night and even though she's older now we always get the new one and she has them all on the shelf in her room. I so wish I had one of them with me that you could sign for her. Her name is Emily."

Annie continued to smile but said nothing, thinking that maybe if she didn't speak, the woman would go away.

"We think Pierce would make a great animated series. Do you think they'll ever do something like that?"

Finnegan stepped in. "There have been offers, of course, but, and I think I can speak for Ms. Blunt here, we think Pierce works best on the page and in the reader's imagination. But rest assured, you're not the only one who's mentioned it."

"Well, anyway, that's all I wanted to say," the woman said. "Enjoy your lunch!"

Annie heaved a quiet sigh of relief as their visitor returned to her table.

"Thank you," she said quietly to her editor. "I'm just not up—"

The woman had stopped, as if forgetting something. She turned and came back to the table, looking directly at Annie.

"I just wanted to add—I didn't know whether to bring it up a moment ago—but I just have to say that, of all your books, our favorite has to be *Pierce Takes Flight*. It's simply wonderful, and I'm here to tell you, *our* Emily was certainly smart enough not to go jumping off a balcony." She smiled broadly. "You have a wonderful day."

TWO

When John Traynor landed his first real live job at an animation studio in New York after graduating from art school, he decided to mark the occasion by getting himself a Mickey Mouse watch. It just seemed like the right thing to do.

"No, no," said Annie. "Not Mickey. Too cliché. I'll bet half the people who work there have a Mickey Mouse watch. Go for something a little different."

They wandered in and out of shops in SoHo and Greenwich Village, including a stop at an animation gallery—not because it sold watches, but because it carried framed, original animation cels from early Warner Bros. cartoons and more recent shows, like *The Simpsons*, all out of their price range. As a couple in their mid-twenties, they squandered any money they had left over after paying the rent on pot and lattes.

But now that John had the prospect of a regular income, a minor splurge did not seem inappropriate. They were at that age when they felt they had everything they could ever want because they had each other. Who cared about fancy cars and penthouse apartments and dinner at the Rainbow Room?

They'd finished school and were trying this whole being-an-adult thing, even if their take on being grown-ups involved creating entertainment for children. At least, that was John's goal. Annie was less sure where she was headed.

Her dream had always been to write and illustrate books for young readers, but what chance did she have against the millions of others pursuing the same dream? So she'd put her résumé into several web and graphic design places. Being creative with a screen, a mouse, and a keypad was not her first choice, but you had to make a living, right? It beat waiting tables or being one of those poor bastards hawking umbrellas on a street corner when it started raining.

"This one," Annie said, pointing into a display case.

They'd found their way to a comic book store that sold much more than adventures of Aquaman and Wolverine. It carried action figures, models of ships from *Star Wars* and *Star Trek*, and every version of the Batmobile Bruce Wayne had raced through Gotham City in pursuit of the Joker.

And it had watches.

"Let's have a look," John said.

The kid behind the counter unlocked the cabinet and placed the watch in John's hand. On its face was not Mickey Mouse, but that oddball character whose goal of blowing up the earth was thwarted at every turn by Bugs Bunny.

Marvin the Martian.

He had his arms folded across his chest and an annoyed expression on his face, like, *Every time I want to kill all of humanity I can't, and I am soooo angry.*

John hooked it around his wrist and admired it. "What do you think?"

"What do *you* think?" Annie replied.

"I think it's perfect. Quirky."

He didn't bother to take it off so that it could be placed in its factory packaging. Paid for it and wore it home, where they dined on macaroni and cheese made from a box, killed off a bottle of the cheapest sparkling bubbly the local wine shop carried, then screwed their brains out before watching *Letterman*.

God, it was a great life.

One day, the two of them sitting at the breakfast table, John said, "You wanna get married this week?"

Annie took a sip of coffee. "I got nothin' planned. How's Friday?"

They called family and friends, keeping the number to under twenty, since that was the number of guests you could invite to a city hall ceremony, then invited everyone back to their place for wings and beer.

They weren't the kind of couple to get all corny about it, but they truly believed they'd been destined to find one another. They'd met in the art school's animation class, Annie doodling oddball creations more than she took notes, John leaning in, whispering how much he liked them. Not the most gorgeous guy Annie had ever dated. Already, in his twenties, starting to lose his hair. Had a little roll of fat over his belt, looked at the world through thick glasses, but, hey, this was art school, with a heavy nerd enrollment and light on jocks, and if she were honest with herself, she was no pinup model. Big frizzy hair, heavy through the hips, bought most of her clothes at "vintage" shops, which was a nice way of saying someone else had had the pleasure of wearing them before she did, and she didn't spend a lot of time, or money, at the makeup counter.

Fuck all that. She wasn't put on this planet to have others gawk at her. She wanted to *create*. She wanted to make *art*. Even as she sat at her workstation picking out fonts and background colors and creating links, there was always a fine-point Sharpie and a sketch pad on the desk next to the mouse pad.

She filled one entire notebook with sketches of an adorable polar bear she christened Barry. Barry traveled the world to warn people about the melting polar ice caps. She moved on from sketches to put together a prototype book. Twenty pages, words and illustrations on every one of them. Annie also, as was her custom, created a six-inch-tall, three-dimensional model of Barry so that she could picture what he looked like from any angle. She started with a wire arma-ture, bulked up the body with crumpled tinfoil, then used plasticine to make his body, limbs, and head.

Annie sent the book off to multiple publishers. Few responded, and those that did took a pass. Too preachy, they said. Nothing wrong with a message, but you don't have to hit the kids over the head with it.

Annie put aside her dream for a time and continued to design websites. John went into the animation factory every day. Life had settled into a routine that bordered on the mundane. They made a living that would have been decent had they lived someplace other than New York, but rent was a killer. They had no car. They rarely took cabs and relied on public transportation, or they hoofed it.

John's one extravagance was his smartphone, which he used to connect to the Internet so he could watch animation clips on You-Tube and elsewhere. It was his addiction, he freely admitted, to the point that even as they walked down the street, he'd be looking down at his phone, laughing at some snippet of a Daffy Duck car-toon or a politically incorrect *Family Guy* moment. Annie repeatedly warned him his obsession would be the death of him. She'd showed him online surveillance videos of people falling into open sidewalk cellar doors, which were all over the place in New York.

He paid no mind.

One day, eyes fixed on his phone's screen, watching the Loo-ney Tunes classic Bugs Bunny cartoon *Rabbit of Seville*, he walked right into a streetlight pole, hard enough to raise a bump on his forehead. Annie felt bad about laughing, but, honestly, he had it coming.

Bottom line was, as long as they didn't have any unexpected expenses, they'd get by. And God forbid one of them got sick, because neither of them had a decent health plan.

And then came a surprise.

"Oh shit," John said when she came home from the doctor's office and gave him the news that she was pregnant.

Not exactly the words she was hoping to hear.

But he did some fast backpedaling. "We can do this," he said, and then, unexpectedly, began to laugh. "I have no fucking idea how, but we can do this."

And they did. Seven months later, Charlie was born, and despite them now being down a salary, it was joyous. John took a part-time second job in the evenings working in the kitchen of an Italian restaurant around the corner. (At least he got to score the occasional free pizza.) John's parents—Annie's had both passed by the time she was twenty-three—sent them checks when they could, but they were working-class folks who had their own financial worries.

There were no websites to design, at least for now, but even when Annie nursed, Charlie in her arms, the pen and sketch pad were not far away.

One night, up for a feeding when the baby was seven weeks old, so tired she could barely keep her eyes open, Annie thought about a penguin who wanted to explore the world beyond Antarctica.

When Charlie napped, Annie would sketch out her character in more detail. She made up another wire armature and created a three-dimensional model, just as she had done with Barry the Bear. She would name her penguin Pierce. He would ask his fellow penguins why the hell (okay, not *hell*, but why on earth) they had wings if they couldn't use them to become airborne. They were about as useless as those forearms on a *T-Rex*. He wasn't going to let his superfluous wings keep him from traveling, so he saved up his money from his bookshop job (a store that sold mostly thrillers, and was called Chillers) to buy airline tickets. He always took off from Antarctica International Airport, where the jumbo jets were fitted with skis.

The first book Annie put together was *Pierce Goes to Paris*. He visits the Eiffel Tower, the Louvre, buys himself a beret, and damned if he isn't the jauntiest-looking penguin who ever walked the Champs-Élysées. He returns to the South Pole with tales of his adventures, but decides he won't be staying long. There is so much more to see!

One of the editors who had rejected her eco-minded polar bear book had said some nice things about her drawings, so she decided to send a copy of her first Pierce Penguin story to him.

A week went by. Then two. A month without any response. She was getting ready to send the manuscript to another house when her cell phone rang.

It was Finnegan Sproule.

"You know the Gramercy Tavern?" he asked.

Well, she had *heard* of it. But she had never stepped inside the doors.

Over their first lunch, he said to her, "This is very special. It has tremendous potential. Do you have an agent?"

"An agent?"

"A literary agent. Look, I could make you an offer right now, something you'd jump at that might seem like a lot of money to you but would be lunch money for my publisher. You need someone in your corner. I'm going to suggest a few to you, all reputable. Or you can ask around, find someone else. But I want this, and I'm prepared to do a preempt."

"A who?"

"A preemptive offer. An agent will explain."

Annie found an agent. A deal was made. Was it a fortune? No. But it was enough to calm some nerves, to allow Annie and John and Charlie to move to a slightly larger apartment in a better neighborhood.

The book came out. It did nothing.

Okay, not exactly nothing. It sold in the low four figures. Annie signed at a couple of Barnes & Nobles in Manhattan to thin crowds. There was no tour.

"Not to worry," Finnegan told her. "Get cracking on the second one."

That book became *Pierce Goes to London*. The penguin met with the Queen; this was before her passing, of course. Toured Buckingham Palace, went to the Victoria and Albert Museum, rode around in a London cab. Ate fish and chips.

After the lukewarm reception to the first book, Annie didn't get her hopes up for Pierce's sophomore outing. She'd been thinking of a third book where Pierce went to Tokyo, but was there any point?

Turned out, there was.

A New York morning show host happened to mention the book. Said she'd read it to her son, who loved it. Sales spiked for a couple of days on Amazon. The publisher's publicity team reached out to the host, said, "The author lives just a few blocks from your studio. Maybe you'd like to have her on to talk about her world-hopping penguin?"

And that was how Annie got on the *Today* show.

The London book edged onto the children's books bestseller list. More stores invited Annie to do readings for young audiences. The publisher sent her on a six-city tour.

The Tokyo book entered the children's bestseller list at number one.

Then the merch offers started coming in. Pierce the Penguin notepads and stickers. Very basic, simplified tales that could be made into board books for infants. A Pierce the Penguin plush toy. There were TV offers, and while the money was tempting, Annie turned them all down. Pierce was not a TV star. He would not sell out.

But even without the TV money, what was coming in was more than Annie and John could ever have imagined. They vowed they wouldn't let the money change them, but despite their best intentions, it did. The Bank Street brownstone was proof of that.

John continued working his animation job, even though what he brought in was a fraction of what Annie's books were making, but he still enjoyed it. Charlie was growing up, changing every day, and they'd enrolled him in a private preschool program, mysteriously jumping ahead of countless other parents in the queue. (Fame did have its benefits.)

Things could not have have been more perfect.

Annie began to think Pierce deserved to more fully realize his flying ambitions. She would make him a penguin who could *really* fly. It would be a book about ambition, about being who you wanted to be, about not letting others hold you back.

Yes, Pierce was going to fly.

First, he tried working out. Figured if he could bulk up some, his wings would be strong enough to support him. But, try as he might, he couldn't do it. Pierce's research led him to Leonardo da Vinci's attempts to create a flying machine, particularly his bat-winged glider. A person would slip his arms into the wings, and off he'd go. Leonardo might not have perfected a working model, but that was no reason for Pierce not to give it a go.

It was, for Annie, the most wonderful project she'd ever undertaken. It allowed her to do some of her most ambitious illustrations. Not just of the device that Pierce would build, but of the views he would take in as he soared over such places as the Grand Canyon, the Golden Gate Bridge, the Empire State Building. Finnegan Sproule said it was her best Pierce book yet.

The book came out with great fanfare. A full-page ad in *The New Yorker*, for fuck's sake. If that isn't making it, Annie remarked to John one night, I don't know what is. *Pierce Takes Flight* sold nearly thirty thousand copies in its first week. And continued to sell at that pace for seventeen straight weeks.

One of the lucky children to receive a copy was six-year-old Evan Corcoran.

He already had all the other Pierce the Penguin books. And a Pierce the Penguin notepad. And Pierce the Penguin stickers. And a Pierce the Penguin doll that he clutched every night when he went to bed.

Evan was inspired.

Of all the Pierce books, he loved this latest one the most, and had his parents read it to him again and again and again. Evan was a bright kid, and when his mother or father wasn't reading the book to him, he was racing through the pages himself. What fun it would be to see the world as the birds do. Pierce had decided this was something he wanted to do, and by gosh, he did it.

If Pierce could fly, then why couldn't Evan?

One day when his parents were both at work and his nanny was busy in the kitchen preparing dinner, Evan made himself a set of cardboard wings, taped them to his arms, opened the unlocked balcony door of the tenth-floor apartment on the Upper West Side, pulled a chair over to the railing to stand on, and off he went.

Annie, who was not an iPhone doom scroller or news addict, had no advance warning when Finnegan called to say he was fielding calls from media outlets about the tragedy. Seconds later, she looked out the third-floor window of their Bank Street brownstone and saw the gathering crowd. Two news vans, people with cameras.

She collapsed to the floor of her brownstone studio where she was already at work on what would have been the next Pierce volume. She was sobbing, shaking uncontrollably. She couldn't get up. John, arriving home with Charlie after picking him up at school, had to fight his way through a cluster of reporters, managing to get a sense of why they were there, that something truly horrible that involved Annie had happened. He found her in a heap on the floor, nearly catatonic.

An ambulance was called.

THREE MONTHS PASSED.

Consumed with guilt, Annie descended into a deep depression. It didn't matter how many times John told her she was not at fault. She could almost understand, at some intellectual level, that she could not be blamed for what had happened. When an artist—author, songwriter, moviemaker, whatever—created something, put it out there for the world to critique, to love it or hate it, it was impossible to control how people would react. There were as many ways to respond to a creative work as there were people who read it or watched it or listened to it.

But rational arguments didn't help much.

Even in those moments when Annie could accept that she was not directly responsible, she could not shake the fact that she'd had a role to play in Evan's demise. John did his best to shield her from much of the fallout, good and bad. Emails and letters from fans who still loved her and Pierce. Emails and letters from the lunatic fringe who believed she was an evil sorceress out to poison children's minds. There were op-eds in the *Times* and other publications, debates online, about whether the incident would spark a round of self-censorship by creators, particularly those whose audience was made up of children. Would there be a chill factor? Would they second-guess every single thing they produced, wondering whether it would be the spark that made some child, somewhere, do something that might end up hurting them? The *Washington Post* even ran a front-page story: "Will Fear Kill Creativity?"

John showed none of it to Annie. And her agent and editor passed along none of the requests for interviews. Annie went to a therapist by the name of Dr. Maya Hersh—she'd come highly recommended by Finnegan, who had sent other authors her way—to deal with what she was going through, one of the few times she was able to laugh during this period. "How is it we've lived in New York all this time without at least one of us seeing a therapist?" she asked John before going to her first session.

She did little work. She rarely entered her studio, which was on the top floor of the Bank Street residence, the walls decorated with oversized framed blow-ups of the Pierce book covers. It had been her second-favorite spot in the house, after the kitchen, but to enter was to be reminded of her creation, and what it had led to.

But as her third month of despondency was coming to an end, Annie started coming out of her funk. She'd had a dozen sessions with her therapist. She wrote a letter to Evan's parents expressing her sorrow, and they'd written back to tell her how much joy her stories had brought their son, adding that they did not need to forgive her, because there was nothing to forgive her for.

That brought tears to her eyes, but it had helped.

She returned to her studio for an hour or two a day, often sitting at her desk and staring at a blank sheet of paper, but it was something. Annie debated whether to create a new character, one who didn't fly. Maybe it was time to move on from Pierce the Penguin. Charlie, who was now seven and well aware of what his mother had gone through, said she should do a book about a camel who solves crimes.

Annie had smiled. "Let me think about that."

She and John began reappearing at their favorite restaurants. They went to the movies. They took Charlie on a trip to Montreal. Annie spent more of the day in the studio, sketching out ideas, putting down anything that came into her head. One day, to her own surprise, she found herself drawing a short, stout little guy who looked like a head-waiter with wings and a beak.

Pierce.

And then she drew a bubble above his head and inserted the words, *I'm sorry, too.*

"It's not your fault," Annie told him.

She thought she could hear him saying back to her, *Well, if it's not mine, then it's not yours, either.*

"I'd like to believe that. I really would."

Are you going to end me?

Tears welled up in her eyes. "I don't know. I need . . . time. But maybe. Things are . . . things are getting better."

And then John died.

He'd worked at three animation studios over the years, moving for money or to take on more challenging work. His latest job had been at Cliff Drop Animation, located on 18th Street between 5th and 6th Avenues. Its name was inspired by Wile E. Coyote, who, when he was tricked by the Road Runner into running off the side of a cliff, would spend a moment suspended in air while he assessed his situation. And then down he would go.

Cliff Drop was a few short blocks from Bank Street, so John always walked it, even in the worst weather. If it was cold, he'd throw on an extra layer or two beneath his coat, and if it was raining, he'd grab an umbrella, because the chances of scoring a taxi or an Uber in terrible weather were about as good as that coyote ever catching that crazy bird.

He was crossing 6th when a van, turning the corner, hit him.

And took off.

Which was kind of strange, because from the NYPD's reconstruction of the events, the driver was likely not at fault. They believed John had been looking at his phone and walked into the vehicle's path when he stepped off the sidewalk.

Of course he was, Annie thought. *Goddamn it, John, how many times did I tell you?*

When John was struck, the phone flew from his hand and landed on the pavement about twenty feet away. When the first emergency responders arrived on the scene, they heard something. Someone saying "What's up, doc?" followed by a familiar melody. There was a Warner Bros. cartoon playing on the phone's screen. John had been watching it on YouTube as he walked to work.

The paramedics were able to do nothing for him at the scene. He'd died instantly. According to witness reports, the van had stopped briefly, the driver jumped out and ran over to John, knelt over him long enough to realize he had to be dead, then ran back to his van and took off. He was described by the half dozen witnesses who saw what happened as "average." No one could provide any telling detail.

The vehicle itself was equally generic. No markings on the sides, no business name. No one noticed the license plate. Of all the surveillance video the police were able to acquire, none showed the plate clearly, or the driver behind the windshield.

The police promised to keep the investigation alive, to follow every lead. But as the days turned into weeks and the weeks turned into months, it was clear the driver of the van that killed John would never be found.

Annie was again plunged into despair. If Evan's death had felt like a cinder block on her shoulders, weighing her down, John's death was a Sisyphean boulder she could never get up the hill even once. His passing overwhelmed her, cocooned her in grief. And as much as she probably needed to emotionally, she could not wallow in her misery this time. She had to pull herself together. If she couldn't be strong, she at least had to present herself as such.

She had Charlie to think about.

Annie wasn't the only one who'd suffered a devastating loss. Charlie had lost his father, and his sadness was more than she could bear. She had to be there for him, be strong for him. She had all the love in the world for him, but she lay awake at night wondering whether that would ever be enough. Charlie'd lost more than a father; he'd lost a role model. How would she be able to provide the intangibles that a dad passed on to a young boy?

As gently as she tried to explain to him that his father would never be coming home, he still stood at the window most days, watching pedestrians pass by on the Bank Street sidewalk, occasionally calling out to his mother, "I think I saw him!"

There were days when it was more than she could bear.

Even more alarming, Charlie'd had, since his father's death, episodes of sleepwalking. Annie would hear padding about the house around midnight and discover Charlie wandering in a trance-like state. Once, she found him standing in front of an open closet door, peeing, as though he were standing in front of the toilet. She would gently try to wake him, getting on her knees and holding him by the shoulders and softly speaking to him. When he came out of it, he would be baffled to find he was not in his bed.

Annie believed his sleeping self was looking for his father.

She took him to the doctor, who advised her not to be alarmed. Many kids sleepwalked, and in all likelihood it was no more than a phase Charlie was going through. There were many factors linked to sleepwalking, fatigue and stress among them. The death of Charlie's father had certainly taken its toll on Charlie in those areas. Whenever Annie and Charlie were out, and Charlie spotted a white van, he would ask if that was the one that had killed his dad.

John's personal effects were eventually returned to Annie. They came to the door one day by courier. She was in such a daze when they arrived in a padded pouch she didn't know whether they'd been sent by the funeral home or the coroner's office.

Anyway, there wasn't much. He didn't carry a lot of stuff on him. There was the fucking phone, of course. There was his wallet. It still contained all his credit cards, plus eighty-five bucks in cash. There was his pair of glasses. There were two pens that he had tucked into the inside pocket of his sport jacket. There was three dollars and forty-five cents in change that had been retrieved from the front pocket of his black jeans.

When the package arrived, Annie brought it into the kitchen and set the various items on the table. She held each and every item as though she could draw some of John's life force through her fingertips. She took the eighty-five dollars in cash from the wallet and wondered what to do with it. Tuck it into her purse? Spend it? What do you buy with the last bills your loved one touched? No, she couldn't spend those. She couldn't do anything with that money. She put it back into the wallet. She brought out the Visa and American Express cards, realized she would have to cancel them. Same with the phone bill for his cell. God, the shit you had to deal with.

His glasses.

She unfolded them, peered through them for a moment, imagining John working on some project as he used them. She folded the arms back down, put them in the kitchen drawer where she tossed all the things she didn't know what to do with.

Something was wrong.

Something was missing.

Where was Marvin?

The Marvin the Martian watch was not in the pouch. He'd worn it every day since they'd bought it together years earlier. He always wore it to work.

Where was it?

Had the impact been of such magnitude that the watch was flung from John's wrist? If it had been attached to a flexible, stretchy band, maybe. But the watch was on a leather strap John had to pull taut and secure with a small buckle. It seemed unlikely it would have been thrown clear. And even if it had, why hadn't it been found? The phone had been recovered.

It didn't make sense.

There was only one explanation. It had been stolen. But by whom?

Annie considered the list of suspects. It could have been one of the paramedics. It could have been a cop. It could have been someone at the coroner's office. It could have been someone at the funeral home.

Annie made calls to all of them. "Where's my husband's watch?" she asked the funeral home director. "Someone stole his watch!"

The director said she would investigate and get back to her. When she did, she had nothing to report. Annie went down a voicemail rabbit hole trying to find anyone accountable with the various emergency services people. The paramedics knew nothing. The police knew nothing.

She even went, in person, to the coroner's office and demanded to speak to someone, *anyone*, who could tell her what had happened to John's watch. She was met with shrugs and a chorus of, "Beats me."

Her despair had morphed into rage.

How *dare* someone steal John's watch? What kind of sick fuck stole a watch off someone who'd just been run down by a van?

What kind of city was this, where something like that could happen?

What kind of city was it, where a kid could crawl out on a balcony and think he could fly?

What kind of city was it, where someone could mow down a total stranger in broad daylight and suffer no consequences?

All of which was to say, this was why Annie Blunt wanted to take a goddamn break from this goddamn city, and who the fuck knew whether she and her boy were ever coming back?

THREE

"Y ou won't believe this," Finnegan told Annie over the phone. "I found you a place."

She had been walking back from Charlie's school. There might come a day when she'd let him walk there and back on his own, but, hey, this was New York, and that day was a long time off. She was turning onto Bank Street when her cell started ringing in her purse. She saw Finnegan's name and took the call.

"Where is it?" Annie asked after he'd delivered his news.

"Upstate. Near Fenelon, which, I have to admit, I have never heard of. But it's near Castle Creek, in case you've heard of that."

"I haven't."

"Yeah, there's a gas station there or something. Anyway, it's about a three-hour drive out of the city."

Annie and John had gone several years without a car, but as their fortunes improved, they'd bought a small, sporty BMW SUV for errands and out-of-town trips. They kept it at a garage one block south on 11th Street.

Annie liked the idea but wasn't ready to commit. "Maybe Charlie and I will drive up and have a look at it on the weekend."

"About that," her editor said. "I hope I haven't overstepped here, Annie, but I've gone ahead and set it all up for you."

"What?"

"You were right, you need a break, we *want* you to have a

break, and I couldn't see you having to go to all the aggravation of looking for a place. It's all ready to go. I'll send you a link to the listing so you can check it all out, just in case you hate it, but I really believe you're going to love it. And if you don't, you're not obligated to take it. Christ, *I'll* take it. *I'll* spend the summer there."

"Fin, you really shouldn't—"

"No, I should. This is something we want to do for you. It's kind of northwest of Binghamton. There's places there where you can pick your own blueberries."

"I get my blueberries from Gristedes."

"Not for the next three months, you won't. And you're the one who said she wants out of the city, so don't be throwing Gristedes at me. Anyway, the larder's already full. Got someone local to stock the fridge. You got wine, you got beer, you got yogurt."

"Listing those things in order of importance? Charlie's not quite ready for beer yet."

"I didn't forget the milk. And cereal and peanut butter and whatever else he eats. So you should start packing and get there before all that stuff passes its best-before date."

"I don't know what to say, Fin. I wasn't expecting you to do anything like this."

"Oh, and the place has wi-fi. Already had the tech guys there. Everything's up and running. Netflix, Disney, Amazon Prime, Paramount."

"God forbid we should be without those."

She got off the call and as soon as she was home she fired up the laptop in the kitchen and checked the link that Finnegan had emailed her.

It was a two-story Victorian-style home, built sometime around the 1930s, but had been updated over the decades so that there probably wasn't much of the original house still around. Kind of like the Temptations and the Four Tops, Annie mused, whom she'd come to love, what with her mom playing them all the time when she was growing up. Still touring, but with all new singers. There were a couple dozen pictures to click through. The outside was painted powder-blue with white trim. A porch ran along the entire front of the house and about halfway down the left side. There were garden chairs placed on it with big flowery cushions, and Annie could already picture herself sitting in one of them, a tall glass of lemonade on the wicker table, the latest Ann Patchett on her lap.

"It does look wonderful," she said under her breath, now viewing photos of the home's interior. A large living room with overstuffed furniture and a fireplace. A big kitchen with everything she could possibly want. She zoomed in on one of the shots and spotted a Nespresso machine.

"Oh my," she said.

There were four bedrooms on the second floor, one of which had been converted into a studio. No wonder Finnegan had liked this place. A caption on the photo said that the home had previously been occupied by husband-and-wife photographers, that they'd used this space as an office and for shoots.

Thoughtful, Annie supposed, but also sneaky. She was willing to bet that studio was as well stocked as the kitchen, but instead of food and drink, it would come equipped with paints and brushes and markers and pencils and Sharpies and pads of paper and a drafting table with multiple height adjustments. Fin's motives were less than pure, but it was, she supposed, still a nice gesture. In the very unlikely event she might want to do some work, everything would be ready.

As she continued to look at the photos, another email from Finnegan landed in the inbox.

Just one extra pic. Wanted you to see there's a room all set up for Charlie.

She clicked on the photo. It was of one of the bedrooms she'd already seen a picture of in the listing, but it was all dressed. A single bed with a Spider-Man bedspread. A set of shelves with books and half a dozen rubber dinosaurs. Three framed Harry Potter movie posters on the wall. A large window afforded a beautiful view of green fields and trees and what looked to be, in the distance, a set of railroad tracks.

Jesus, Annie thought. *Charlie will love this.*

She clicked on REPLY and wrote a note to Finnegan that read, in its entirety, You are a crafty son of a bitch. She hit SEND. The email had no sooner whooshed away than she decided to send a quick follow-up: How on earth did you find this place?

While she waited for him to get back to her, she rose from the kitchen table and went up to the bedroom she once shared with John and began sorting through what she would take. When she was done choosing her own clothes, she'd sort out what she needed to take for Charlie.

Now that so much of the decision-making was done, Annie felt there wasn't a moment to waste. *We are gettin' out of Dodge*, she thought.

But there were things to do. Tell the neighbors she was going to be away. Have the mail held. Not that there was ever much. All her bills either arrived by email or were automatically paid. About the only thing she couldn't control were unexpected FedEx or DHL deliveries of foreign-language editions of her books. She never knew when they were coming, or who they might be coming from, so there was no way to intercept them. She could ask one of the neighbors to check the front stoop every couple of days to see whether anything was sitting there.

When she went to meet Charlie at the end of the school day, she said, "How would you feel if I pulled you out of school a week early?"

The last day of school before the beginning of the summer break was the end of the following week.

"Why?" Charlie asked, stepping on every crack in the sidewalk as they made their way home.

"You know how I've been talking about us taking a break from the city? Out in the country. Maybe upstate?"

"Yeah?"

"I found a place. Well, Fin did."

"Are there buildings there?"

"Are there *buildings*?"

Charlie nodded.

"Of course there are buildings. And we'd be living in a big house. Probably bigger than our house here."

"But you said it was in the country. I didn't think there were buildings in the country."

"You've been in the country before. Like when we went to Cape Cod."

He looked at her like she was short a few marbles. "That was Cape Cod. Not the country."

"Okay, the *country* is just something people say when we mean out of the city. There are *buildings* in the *country*. They're just spaced out more, and they're not twenty or thirty or seventy stories tall like buildings here."

"I like it here. My friends are here."

"Maybe you can make new friends there for the summer."

"I thought you said the buildings are all far apart. How would I meet anybody?"

Before she could come up with an answer for that, he proposed a solution. "I could get a bike."

"A bike?"

Another nod.

"You don't know how to ride a bike."

Even before what happened to John, the idea of a bicycle for Charlie had always been out of the question. Riding a bike in the city was to take your life in your hands no matter what your age, but for a little kid? Okay, maybe some parents were fearless—or reckless, depending on one's point of view—when it came to this issue, but Annie was not one of them.

But, yeah, having a bike in the country was a possibility and was something that might close the deal with an as-yet-unconvinced Charlie. Except, who'd teach him to ride it? Annie'd never had a bike, but she recalled John saying he'd had one as a kid. He could have taught Charlie. Yet one more thing to make Annie feel she wasn't up to the task. But she'd have to do her best.

"Yes, you could have a bike." He raised two small fists in victory. "But I can't promise that we'd bring it back to the city."

Charlie shrugged, figuring that was a battle for another day. He'd won the first round. "When are we going?"

Annie felt a small tingle run up her spine. She couldn't recall the last time she had felt anything close to excitement.

"Tomorrow," she said.

ANNIE COULD BARELY get to sleep that night, she was so wound up. She'd helped Charlie pack, and very early on gave up trying to get him to be selective about which toys he wanted to bring and decided to let him toss into his bags whatever he wanted. Annie did a sweep of the medicine cabinets and packed everything she might need for both of them. In the morning, with Charlie in tow, she would go to the garage and pick up the car, then bring it around and pray she could get a spot on the street near the front door. Sometimes miracles did happen.

She slipped into bed after eleven, and when she couldn't at first get to sleep, she turned the light back on and reached for one of several copies of *The New Yorker* that littered the top of the bedside table, taunting her because she could never get to them. She was halfway through a movie review when she felt herself nodding off.

Annie killed the light and put her head down onto the pillow.

At some point, she felt a stirring beside her. A familiar feeling. One she had not experienced in several months.

She turned over in bed and opened her eyes. It was dark, but the streetlamps' glow filtering through the blinds allowed her to see.

John was in the bed next to her, his head propped up on his palm, elbow dug into the mattress.

He smiled at her and said, *"Don't go, Annie. Don't go."*

Annie woke up, sat up in bed, put her hand to her chest, and felt her heart beating so quickly she thought it might burn out.

FOUR

Annie had the car loaded shortly before eleven, and after advising Charlie to go to the bathroom one last time (good advice for Annie, too) they hit the road. It took the better part of half an hour to get out of the city, heading south and picking up the Holland Tunnel that took her under the Hudson River and into New Jersey. She followed without question the verbal instructions from her in-dash GPS companion, a woman Annie had, in her head, named Sherpa because she was such an excellent guide.

Annie was not the most confident driver. Having grown up in the city, she had never held a driver's license and never learned to drive when she was in her teens. Her father had an old Ford, but, what with taxis and buses and subways and the nightmare of trying to find a place to park, Annie had figured if she did have a license, she wouldn't make use of it. But when the money started coming in, and they moved into the Bank Street address, John thought it was finally time to have some wheels. With a car, they could head out of town on weekends. They had friends who lived out in the Hamptons. They could rent that Cape Cod beach house they'd always dreamed of spending part of the summer in. Annie said fine, okay, I'll get a license, I'll learn to drive, but don't ask me to like it.

And she didn't. But she could do it. It was the downtown driving she hated most. Once she got out of the city, hit the interstate, and could put the BMW on cruise control, wander the Sirius dial, sampling everything from Springsteen to punk, well, then she could endure it.

What she missed was having someone up front with her.

Charlie was still, for safety reasons, riding in the backseat on a booster seat that allowed him a better view out his window.

When she and John traveled, regardless of who was sitting behind the wheel, all she had to do was turn her head if she had something on her mind, something she wanted to talk about.

But these days, all conversations were conducted over her right shoulder.

"How's it going back there?" she'd ask, turning her head slightly so that Charlie could better hear her.

"Fine."

"Whatcha doin'?"

"Nothin'."

"You need a juice box or anything?"

"No."

"You need to make a pit stop?"

"No."

There were times when he would talk your ear off, and times when he had very little to say. Although the truth was, on this particular trip, Annie didn't actually have that much to say herself.

She couldn't stop thinking about the dream.

Because, of course, it *was* a dream. John had *not* come back from the Great Beyond to give her a little snippet of advice.

Still, it had been so real. She'd sensed that familiar stirring in the bed next to her. Even though she was generally a pretty sound sleeper, she could always tell when John was getting out of bed. It could be three in the morning, but no matter how carefully he might slip back the covers to head to the bathroom, she would know, and ask dreamily, "You okay?"

"Gotta pee," he'd say, and she would go back to sleep.

So it had to be that she'd *dreamed* the stirring in the bed next to her. And *dreamed* turning over in bed to see what it was. And *dreamed* seeing John there, head propped up on his palm. And *dreamed* what he had said to her.

"Don't go, Annie. Don't go."

She'd woken with a start, her heart hammering, her nightshirt drenched in sweat. She had flicked on her bedside lamp, turned and put her bare feet to the floor, and sat there a moment, catching her breath, letting her heart rate settle down to something more normal. She went to the bathroom, had a small drink of water, then returned to bed, unsure whether she would be able to get back to sleep, but after about half an hour, she did.

In the light of day, traveling along 280 West, waiting for Sherpa to tell her to bear left or bear right or take this mountain pass, she wondered what to make of the dream, if anything. She imagined herself as her therapist, what she would make of it: *Well, maybe you're giving yourself a warning here. Perhaps you don't want to leave the city as much as you thought you did. Maybe you don't want to go to the country for the summer.*

"What do you know," Annie said aloud.

"What?" Charlie asked from the backseat.

Annie glanced in the rearview mirror, caught a look at him. She thought he'd been sleeping. "Nothing, honey. Just talking to myself."

"What about?"

"Nothing. You getting hungry?"

They had been on the road for coming up on two hours and even though they'd had a late breakfast, they were due for a lunch break. When Annie had proposed making sandwiches to eat along the way, Charlie had made the face of a child who'd just been told they were having worms for dinner and asked if they could they stop at a McDonald's somewhere.

Back in the day, she and John had been organic this, organic that, wheat germ shakes, protein bars. But having a kid changed all that, and before long her child's tastes became her own, to the point that there were times when she would kill for a Chicken McNugget.

Charlie said he was, indeed, hungry, and so Annie hit the voice command button and asked Sherpa if there was a McDonald's coming up. The very next exit, she informed Annie. They got off the highway, had something to eat, used the bathrooms, and, after topping up the SUV's gas tank, were back on the road.

According to Sherpa, they would reach their destination in another two hours.

WHEN ANNIE TURNED off a state-maintained road onto a narrower county artery, Sherpa informed her that her destination was less than a mile away. Before reaching it, the car rolled gently over a railroad crossing. The fading round yellow sign, the letters R and R separated by a black x, was acned with what looked like BB-gun shots. She looked in the rearview mirror to see what Charlie was up to, whether he was comatose. She hadn't heard much out of him the last hour, not since she had turned off the interstate and passed through Castle Creek, which really was little more than a gas station with a convenience store and a couple of churches. Sure enough, he was in dreamland.

"Hey," she said. "Hey, Charlie. Wake up. We're almost there."

Slowly he opened his eyes, took a moment to orient himself, and looked out his window. "Where?"

"Soon."

She was reading names and numbers off mailboxes. The house she was looking for was 11318 Scoutland Road, and there remained the faded name of one of the previous occupants: SMITHERTON.

She said the numbers out loud as she passed them. "Eleven-two-fifty-eight . . . eleven-two-eighty-six . . . eleven-three-twelve . . . hang on. I think this is it."

"Why are there boxes beside the road?" Charlie asked.

"Those are mailboxes. You've seen those before. In Cape Cod."

The things you'd assume everyone, even a kid, would know, but when they'd grown up in the city, the country turned out to be full of surprises, even totally mundane ones.

She slowed the car to a crawl and put on her right blinker, spotted a mailbox with 11318, and turned into the driveway.

The house sat back a good hundred feet from the road on a slight rise, making it look taller than its two stories. It was, in fact, imposing, like something off a postcard. It was everything Finnegan had promised. Stately, but also charming, with its dormer windows, wraparound porch, a forest backdrop, painted in a shade of blue that matched the sky. Annie felt a hopeful swelling in her heart, that this was everything she had hoped it would be.

The driveway was circular, allowing Annie to bring the car right up in front of the house, at the base of the steps up to the porch. Charlie was trying to disconnect the seat belt that held him and his booster seat in place but couldn't reach it.

"Let me out! Let me out!"

"Hold on, pal."

She put the car in park, killed the engine, got out, and came around the other side to free Charlie. He leapt out and ran up the three steps to the porch, wide-eyed.

"How much of it is ours?" he asked.

That made Annie laugh. Another city-vs.-country perception. In

New York, you got part or, in their case, maybe most of a building. But even they rented out the basement, which was a totally self-contained unit.

"All of it," she said.

"Seriously?"

"Seriously. I mean, we don't *own* it, we're just renting, but we can use every single room if we want to." Annie couldn't imagine that they would. There was probably twice the square footage of their home. It had three floors, and this house had but two, but the brownstone was narrow, tall and skinny, and this house spread out, like it was trying to use up as much of the land as it could.

Annie said, "See if there's a key under the mat."

That was equally mystifying to Charlie. He knew about keys, even though their brownstone was accessed via a keypad, but he was not familiar with the notion of leaving a key where anybody could find it. But he did as he was told, lifted up the corner of the mat, and shrieked, "It's here!"

Annie reached the porch, took the key from Charlie, unlocked the door, and let it open into the house.

"Wow," Charlie said.

They stepped into a spacious front hall. A few steps directly ahead of them was a broad staircase leading to the upper floor. To the right, a large living room with a wall-mounted big-screen television. To the left, a dining room. Alongside the stairs, on the right, was a hallway that led to the kitchen.

"Where's the bathroom?" Charlie asked with some urgency.

Annie shrugged.

"Never mind, I'll find it." Charlie ran down the hall to the kitchen, vanished, then reappeared in the dining room, having done a loop of the first floor.

"Find it?"

"No!" he shouted somewhat frantically.

He went running up the steps while Annie headed for the kitchen, wanting to know if that Nespresso machine was really there. Not only was it sitting on the counter, but there was a box of pods next to it in a variety of flavors. If it didn't get any better than this, that was fine with her. But in fact the fridge was well stocked—even with milk and cream that had not yet reached their expiration date—and the pantry as well. Plus, on the kitchen island was a gift basket overflowing with high-end jams and cookies and caramel corn and God knew what else, with a note from Finnegan that read: "Enjoy."

Charlie came running into the kitchen, breathless.

"Did you find the bathroom?"

He nodded. "Just in time. I nearly exploded. And I found my room."

"Spider-Man bedspread?" He nodded. "Yep, that's your room."

And then he was off again, investigating. He rounded a corner and shouted, "I found another bathroom! A little one!"

Annie smiled to herself as his footsteps carried on. She climbed the stairs, checked out what would be her bedroom, then wandered into what had been the photographers' studio. There was a height-adjustable worktable, an Aeron chair, a small table already kitted out with paper and pens and brushes and tubes of watercolor paints.

"You bastard, Finnegan," she said under her breath. Just as she had suspected.

Shaking her head, she turned away to start bringing stuff in from the car. She was at the bottom of the stairs, about to head outside, when she realized Charlie was around the corner, picking up a remote on a living room coffee table and pointing it at the wall-mounted TV. The set came alive.

"The channels are all different," he said. "I can't find Nickel-odeon."

"I don't know what the setup is here," she said. "Could be satellite, could be cable. Maybe it's just antenna."

"What's an antenna?"

"I'm gonna start unloading. You helping?"

Charlie shook his head. "I'm figuring out the channels."

Any other time she would have insisted he pitch in, but he was happy. His instant acceptance of their new, if temporary, home had so exceeded her expectations that she didn't want to be a buzzkill.

She stepped out, descended the three steps from the porch, and happened to look toward the road. She hadn't seen any other traffic since their arrival. Not a car, not a truck, not so much as a motorcycle, and that was fine by her.

Across the road was a white story-and-a half house in what Annie believed was modeled on the Arts and Crafts style, with its broad porch pillars supporting an overhanging roof.

There was an old woman sitting on that porch in an oversized wicker chair. Annie was guessing she was maybe in her eighties, thin, with silver hair pulled back tightly. She peered in Annie's direction through thick-framed round glasses. On a small table next to her sat a cup of coffee or tea or, who knew, maybe something a little stronger.

Annie figured it was never too soon to introduce herself. This wasn't New York, after all, where you could live next door to someone for years and never know their name. Time to make more of an effort.

But when she raised her hand in a friendly wave, the woman did not respond. Annie surmised those glasses she was wearing weren't for distance, so she strolled down to the foot of the driveway and called out, "Hello! My name's Annie and my son and I are taking the house for the summer and I just wanted to say—"

But the woman was putting her hands on the arms of the chair, slowly pushing herself up, and turning her back to Annie. She went inside and closed the door with enough force that Annie could hear it from across the road.

She stood there a moment, slightly dumbstruck, then shrugged and turned around to start unpacking, thinking maybe it would be easier to get used to her new surroundings than she might have first thought.

"Just like New York," she said under her breath.

FIVE

There was some settling in to do.

Despite being told that the kitchen was well stocked, Annie had brought a few things, including Charlie's favorite cereal, the chocolate chip cookies he liked, a dozen authentic New York bagels that she put into the freezer to get them through the first week until she found something nearby that might fill the void. She got her clothes and Charlie's unpacked and put away in their respective bedrooms and set up their toiletry items. There was a bathroom attached to the larger bedroom, which Annie took, and a smaller one in the hall that would be for Charlie.

It was late afternoon by the time she had all that done. She was going to propose heading into nearby Fenelon, the closest town, to see what it had to offer, but an exploratory trip like that could go on indefinitely and turn into a dinner out, and they'd already had a fast-food feast at lunch, so Annie decided that could wait a day. Whoever'd stocked the place to Finnegan's specifications had loaded the freezer with several prepared entrées. Annie found a meat lasagna in there, and a bag of salad in the fridge that would serve nicely for a first meal in their new digs.

CHARLIE, HAVING GIVEN up trying to find his favorite channels on the living room TV, had resumed his exploration of the property. He checked out the books in his room, which included several Dog

Man and Wimpy Kid adventures. While they would have been perfect for any other kid his age, Charlie had already moved on to what was known in the business as middle grade and young adult books. Few, if any, pictures, and multi-chaptered. His teachers had said his reading skills were well ahead of any of the other kids in his class. The room had also been stocked with an assortment of plastic dinosaurs, several toy cars and trucks, and a couple of Lego sets, still in the original packaging. There was an Arctic explorer ship and a car wash that was part of the City series.

Nice.

As much as he was tempted to rip both boxes open now, he decided to wait. Maybe tomorrow, or maybe some rainy day.

He wandered into the room that the previous residents had used for a studio, all set up if his mother wanted to get back to work. He hoped she would. She seemed happier when she was working. He was tired of her being sad. He was tired of being sad himself.

Charlie found a door that led to the basement. He brushed away some cobwebs as he descended a set of wooden open-backed steps. They led to an unfinished room with cinder-block walls and a beam ceiling that allowed a view of the underside of the floor above. There was a furnace, a hot water tank, a circuit breaker box, and lots of tubes and ducts and wires going here and there and everywhere, and up against one wall, an empty pegboard and a big wooden table that probably served as a workbench at one time. There were four shallow drawers built into the table, and Charlie inspected each of them. One was empty, a second contained a few sheets of glossy paper with black-and-white pictures of people on it, and the last two were filled with odd screws and nails and pipe clamps and other junk.

Curiosity satisfied, Charlie decided to head back upstairs and go outside.

The outside was so *big*.

Not Central Park big. That was, as its name kind of suggested, a *park*. It was supposed to be big. It was supposed to have lots of trees and shrubs and rocks and stuff. You could run flat-out for ages and not run into anything if you watched where you were going. You could fly a kite in the park. You could play Frisbee in a park. But this was a private yard that went with the house. You didn't have to share it with other people. Charlie had heard his mother say it was four acres of property, and a lot of that was just woods. Charlie didn't know what an acre was, but he figured it had to be huge.

Charlie was right to have raised the issue of getting a bike. He *needed* a bike here. If he had wheels he could ride it around and around the house and down to the road and back again.

There was one item of interest in the backyard.

It was a small building tucked almost out of sight behind a couple of trees, about ten-by-ten-feet in size, with a wide door at one end and a small window on the left and right sides. It would, Charlie thought, make a neat fort. A place just for him. He could read comics back here, play video games, set up a table and chair and build his Lego sets. It could be like his own office. If his mom could have her own studio, shouldn't he have a place, too, to do what he wanted to do? Of course, much would depend on what was in there to begin with and if he could make some space for himself.

He wasn't going to find out by opening the door. It was secured with a padlock, which he pulled in the unlikely event it hadn't been snapped into place, but it held firm. He went around to a side window, where a pile of firewood leaned against the shed, for a peek inside. Climbing on top of the woodpile, he used his hand as a visor and put his nose up to the glass to peer inside. There was stuff in there, that was for sure, although the glass was so dirty—on both sides—that it was hard to make anything out very clearly. He thought he saw a wheelbarrow, maybe a lawn mower, some lawn chairs that had been folded up, and several boxes.

He hopped off the woodpile, tried the lock once again without success, then wandered off into the trees. He was hoping he might see a bear, or a fox, or maybe even a kangaroo, although he had heard those lived in Austria or someplace like that.

THE LASAGNA AND salad hit the spot. Annie also found two cartons of Ben & Jerry's ice cream—Salted Caramel Almond and Chocolate Chip Cookie Dough.

"I gotta hand it to Fin," she said as they ate their dessert. "He did think of everything."

"What's in the backyard?" Charlie asked.

"I don't know. Trees and stuff. I haven't been out there."

"There's a little building. It could be a fort."

"Probably a garden shed. Did you look inside?"

"It's locked."

"Then I guess we're not meant to go in there."

Charlie looked disappointed. "I was going to make it my head-quarters."

"I see. Military, or have you set up a corporation?"

"What?"

They watched some TV after dinner, but not for long. Annie found herself ready to pack it in at half-past eight, which was Charlie's normal bedtime.

"I'm done like dinner, pal," she said, hitting the OFF button on the remote.

They both got ready for bed, Annie promising to come in and see him before he turned out his light. About a year earlier, Charlie had announced he was too old to have a bedtime story, but since his father's death, he'd offered no protest when his mother offered to sit on the edge of his bed and read to him.

He was under the covers and had a selection in his hand when Annie came in. Rather than sit on the edge, she got right on the bed. "Scootch over," she said, settling in, her back on the headboard. Charlie handed her the book, an old, weathered paperback, yellowed along the edges.

"What's this?" Annie asked. It certainly wasn't one of the books Finnegan had arranged to have put on the shelf in Charlie's room.

"It's one of Dad's," he said. "I grabbed it from home." The book was *The Golden Apples of the Sun* by Ray Bradbury.

"Your dad loved Bradbury. He'd had this book since he was a kid. It's a collection of short stories."

Charlie nodded, suggesting he already knew. "Dad read me some."

"He did?"

How did she not know this? A range of emotions washed over her. Sadness, guilt, regret. Had she been letting Charlie down, not exposing him to more of his father's interests?

"Can you read me 'The Destrian'?" he asked.

"The what?" She started thumbing through the book, looking for the story. "You mean 'The Pedestrian'?"

"Yeah," Charlie said.

She read aloud the classic story about a man who draws the attention of the authorities because he prefers to take an evening walk over staying home and watching television, which is what everyone else does. She asked Charlie why he liked it.

He had to think. "I don't know. Because it's weird?"

"I think it was one of your father's favorites because it was about a man who didn't want to follow the crowd."

"What crowd?"

"He didn't want to do what everyone else was doing. He wanted to do his own thing. Your dad was like that. His parents weren't crazy about him becoming an artist, an animator. All the kids he knew got so-called normal jobs when they grew up, like accountants or car salesmen or plumbers, and those are all good jobs because we need all those people doing what they do, but when you say you want to be an artist or a writer or a singer, parents get worried you won't be able to make enough money to survive."

"You make lots of money."

Annie smiled. "I do okay. But it wasn't always like that. I'm just saying your dad didn't let other people, even his parents, stop him from pursuing his dream. Let me put it another way. Pretend every kid you know hates Lego. There's a new law that you're not even *allowed* to build Lego. What would you do?"

Charlie thought about that. "I would still want to play with Lego."

"There you go. You'd stick with it because it's what you love. And that's what your father did, becoming an animator when others weren't so sure it was a good idea."

Charlie nodded, getting it. "So no matter what I want to be when I grow up that would be okay?"

Annie felt herself about to be tested. What was he going to come up with? Rodeo clown? An astronaut? God forbid he said politician. "Probably. What do you want to be?"

"I just want to always be your son and stay with you when I'm old."

Annie gave Charlie's shoulders a squeeze and managed to hold it together until she got back to her room.

SHE'D PACKED SEVERAL books—she was saving the Patchett and instead was diving into a Stephen King novel from thirty years ago called *Needful Things* she'd always meant to get to—and soon found her eyes drifting closed. But once she settled under the covers and flicked off the light, she couldn't get to sleep.

There were no noises.

No sirens, no honking horns, no boisterous people walking along the Bank Street sidewalk, whooping it up. No distant sounds of jets coming into or leaving La Guardia or JFK. How the hell was someone supposed to get to sleep when it was this quiet?

But sometime after midnight, she finally drifted off.

And Evan came to her.

"Evan, come back inside. We're ten floors up. If you step off that ledge you'll be very badly hurt. Your mom and dad won't be pleased. They'll be angry. With you, and with me."

"It's okay. I told you. I can fly."

"Six-year-old boys can't fly. You don't have feathers. You don't have wings."

"Yes, I do. I made them."

"Those are cardboard, Evan. Held on with tape. They won't keep you up."

"Pierce Penguin can fly. And penguins aren't supposed to be able to fly."

"He's pretend."

"Pierce Penguin says you can do anything you put your mind to. Mom reads the book to me all the time."

"Evan, what Pierce's saying is, be the best little boy you can be, but it doesn't mean you can turn into a bird and fly or be a fish and live underwater or be a squirrel and climb trees."

"You're wrong. I can fly."

"Evan, just take my hand and come back—"

"Here I go!"

Annie woke with a start, sitting bolt-upright in bed, holding her hand to her chest. Her heart was pounding. She waited for the beats to slow down, then swung her feet to the floor and stood.

She had been prescribed Xanax after Evan's death, and had gone back on it after John's. She'd weaned herself off it, but had brought along the few pills she had left, just in case. She went into the bathroom, looked through the travel kit of various medications she had packed back in Manhattan, and found the plastic bottle. She gave it a shake. Only four pills left. She'd left in such a hurry that she hadn't thought to have the prescription renewed before coming here, but supposed that could be accomplished one way or another.

She uncapped the bottle and tapped one pill into her palm and was about to toss it into her mouth when she heard something.

A whistle.

A whistle and a low rumbling sound.

A train.

She recalled crossing a set of tracks only a mile before reaching the house. Was it a passenger train? A freight? It went on for more than a minute, so she was guessing a freight. A passenger train would undoubtedly have been shorter.

It was, in a strange way, comforting. She was almost tempted to run into Charlie's room and wake him so he could hear it for himself, but before she could decide whether to disturb him, the sound receded.

She looked at the pill in her hand, let it fall back into the bottle, and replaced the cap.

Annie went back to bed.

THE LEASING AGENT, who evidently also sold properties, came by just before noon. Her name was Candace Grove, she drove a black Lincoln Aviator, and was dressed smartly enough to suggest she made an annual pilgrimage to New York to raid Bloomingdale's.

"Wanted to make sure you'd settled in okay," she said when Annie answered the knock at the door, Charlie tagging along with her.

"Everything's great," Annie said. "If it was you who got this place ready, hats off to you."

Candace gave her a quick once-over. Annie knew the look. *You're a bestselling author and the best you can do is a ratty sweater, jeans, and would it kill you to slap on some lipstick or slip on some earrings?*

But the critical look vanished as quickly as it had appeared. Candace said, "Can't do enough for my daughter Stacy's favorite writer."

"Well, that's very nice to hear."

Candace said, "I don't mean to brag, and I know all parents think their little darlings are geniuses, but our Stacy is a pretty talented artist herself for a five-year-old."

"Is that so."

"She likes to draw kittens, mostly, although sometimes she draws other things. Would it be . . . I hate to ask . . . but do you think I could bring them by sometime, show them to you? You could tell me whether you think she really has a talent and if we should be considering some special art programs for her."

Annie felt a part of her die inside, but was careful not to let on how she felt. It was wearing, these hopeful parents who wanted you to tell them their kid was the next Charles Schulz or Ian Falconer, when in reality their work would never be displayed anywhere but on the fridge.

"Sure."

"Or, if it wasn't too much trouble, you could show her where you do your work."

"I'm not set up here for that," Annie said.

"Oh. Mr. Sproule wanted the studio all readied, so I assumed—"

"His expectations may be a little high."

Charlie, who'd been holding back behind his mother, stepped out and asked, "What's in the building in the backyard?"

Candace hadn't taken much notice of him until now. "Who's this young man?"

"This is Charlie. My son."

"There's a big lock on the door and I can't get in," he said. "I need it for an office."

Candace laughed. "I hope it's not a real estate office. I don't want any competition."

Charlie, thinking that adults said some of the dumbest things, did not have an answer for that. Candace said, "It's probably just a shed with garden tools and a lawn mower, but you don't have to worry about that because there's a landscaping service that comes around every week."

"Do you have the key?" Charlie asked.

"I'm afraid not," Candace said. She turned her attention back to Annie. "So, if and when you set up your workspace, maybe I could come by with—"

"Uh-oh," Annie said, touching the front pocket of her jeans, as though a muted phone had started vibrating on her upper thigh. She pulled out her cell, glanced at the blank screen, and said with feigned sincerity, "I'm so sorry, I really have to take this." She pretended to swipe the screen, put the phone to her ear, and said, "Hey, hi. With you in a second."

She flashed Candace an apologetic smile. "Thanks so much for everything," she whispered. "I'll call if I need anything."

Candace waggled her fingers and headed for her Lincoln as Annie and Charlie walked back into the house. Once inside, with the door closed, Annie lowered the phone.

Charlie said, "You didn't get a call."

She put a finger to her lips. "That'll be our secret."

He went to the window next to the front door to watch the Lincoln drive back down to the road. "Somebody else is coming," he said.

Annie took a look for herself.

An old man was glancing in both directions as he ventured across the road. He was coming from the house where the woman had rebuffed Annie the day before. Late seventies, maybe early eighties. Tall, thin, a few wisps of perfectly combed silver hair. Glasses. He was dressed in a black T-shirt and jeans that, even from this distance, appeared to have a crease in them. He gave a nod to Candace as she reached the end of the driveway and took off.

In one hand, the necks held between his fingers, were two bottles of beer. In the other, one beer.

Annie went back out onto the porch, descended the three steps, and stood near her car as the man closed the distance between them.

"Good day," he said, raising the bottles in his right hand. "Hope I didn't catch you at a bad time. I brought three. Wasn't sure whether it was you and your husband or just you."

"Me and my boy," Annie said, and realized that Charlie was on the porch. "That's Charlie."

The man nodded. "Good to meet you, Charlie." He grimaced and waved the bottles in the air. "I'd've brought a Mountain Dew or somethin' had I known. Don't think your mom's gonna let you have one of these." Then he eyed Annie. "And for all I know, you don't care for beer. I'm always assuming, and we all know what *assume* means. I'd say it if young Charlie wasn't standing there."

Annie smiled. "I'm Annie Blunt."

She took the one beer from him and then extended a hand. She felt the cold droplets of beer sweat on his palm.

"I'm Daniel. Daniel Patten. And the beers here is a peace offering."

"I'm sorry?"

"I know my wife gave you the cold shoulder yesterday. Not very neighborly and I wanted to try to patch things up."

"It was nothing," Annie said, and then motioning up the steps, said, "Why don't you come in."

It took him a moment to climb them. "My knees aren't what they once were," he said. When Annie held open the front door for him, he didn't move and looked dubious about crossing the threshold.

"Why don't we just sit out here?" he suggested. "Shame not to enjoy the lovely weather."

"Sure." She waved a hand toward the wicker chairs.

Daniel delicately set himself into one and Annie dropped into the other. She twisted the cap off the cold bottle in her hand and took a swig.

"So you do like a beer," Daniel said, grinning, exposing a couple of brown teeth.

"I do indeed," she said. "And it's hot enough out to appreciate one."

"A local brewery. About ten miles from here."

"Charlie, why don't you find something to do while I chat with Mr. Patten here."

"Daniel," he said. "You can call me Daniel, young man."

Charlie didn't look offended in the slightest to be dismissed, but he had a question for Annie before departing. "Can we look for a bike later?"

"We'll talk about that."

"You could try Jake's Hardware in town. They sometimes have bikes," Daniel said.

"We'll talk," Annie said again. Charlie got the message, and vanished.

Daniel said, "Dolores—that's my missus—isn't much for socializing. She came in, looked a titch flustered, and then I looked out and saw that you folks had moved in."

Flustered? Annie didn't see why saying hello would unsettle anyone. Had she given off some kind of New York vibe that rubbed this man's wife the wrong way? If so, she couldn't imagine what it was.

Daniel said, "She's really more of a homebody. Likes to keep to herself. Doesn't mean any offense by it. Just the way she is, the way she's been for some time now. And she moves even slower than me some days and doesn't like to cross the road. So, what brings you here? You moving in?" He chuckled to himself. "Dumb question."

Annie explained it was probably only for the summer. "It's been . . . kind of a stressful year and I wanted a break from the city for Charlie and myself. We live in Lower Manhattan. The West Village, if you know it."

"Can't say that I do. Never been to the Big Apple."

It always amazed Annie that there were people who had never been to New York City, but then, wasn't that just what a self-absorbed New Yorker would think?

"So," Daniel said cautiously, "it's just you and your boy."

"My husband passed," she said.

His face fell in genuine sympathy. He had his own beer open and took a drink, wiped this mouth with the back of his hand. "That's a shame. I'm so sorry. So, recently, then."

"Yes."

"He'd been sick?"

Annie slowly shook her head. "No," she said simply.

They were both quiet for a moment. Finally, Daniel asked, "What sort of work did he do?"

"He was an animator. You know, like cartoons." She guessed what he was thinking. Her husband was the provider. He wasn't going to ask what she did, because she was a woman and was content to run a household. She thought about telling him what she did, then decided she didn't need to make a point with this man. He seemed nice enough.

"Cartoons?" he said, and nodded. His expression grew wistful. "Our grandson loves cartoons." Daniel had another pull on his beer. "Although we don't see him too much. And he's in his teens now, anyway." There was a sadness in his eyes.

"So you obviously have grown children."

"Two. Son and a daughter. Son lives in Milwaukee. Him and his wife don't have kids. Daughter's in New Haven, mostly raising her boy alone. She got divorced a while back and her husband's not on the scene much."

"That's too bad."

"Oh well, what can you do? You bring them into the world, you raise them, then send them off on their own. Just wish they visited more. Offered to look after Thatcher—that's our grandson—a few times over the years so his mother could get away, but she's not been inclined to take us up on it."

So there was something going on there, Annie felt, but she didn't guess what, and wasn't sure she even wanted to know.

Another few seconds of silence. Finally, Daniel said, "You might have noticed I didn't really want to step inside."

She had, but didn't say anything.

"Dolores and me, we've lived in that house since 1961. That's . . ." and he paused, doing the math in his head, ". . . sixty-three years. Built that house with my father when I was eighteen. He was a carpenter, built houses all around these parts. And I worked with him since the time I was twelve. When I was seventeen, I met this girl."

He smiled, and a web of creases spread out from both eyes. He gave her a sly look. "We were young and kind of stupid, and I guess if we'd both known more we wouldn't have got into the situation we did. Dolores kinda got pregnant." He grinned at his choice of words. "I guess there's no 'kinda.' You either are or you aren't."

Annie smiled. "That's been my experience."

"So the pressure was on that we get married, and while Dolores's folks were ready to disown her, my mom and dad were more what you'd call supportive. Dad said we need to build you a house, and he bought that parcel of land over there." He pointed a long, bony finger at his place. "Your place was here. It'd been here a long time. Not fixed up nice the way it is now, updated and all. That fellow that lived here and his wife—they were both photographers of some sort—did some upgrades, but I think I'm wandering off topic here."

"Take your time."

"Me and Dolores got married right away and lived at my folks, and by the time she was ready to have the baby the house was done. Moved in, been here ever since." He suddenly looked proud, his chest swelling. "That's our house and it always will be."

But just as quickly his eyes seemed to mist over. He gazed out over the yard, not really focusing on anything.

"Dolores'd mostly been what you might call a stay-at-home mom, but she'd always been one to take the odd job here and there. For some time there, she baked out of the home and they sold her cakes and pastries at a place in Fenelon. She liked that. When our kids were in high school she got work at the IGA, cashier mostly. And she'd do housecleaning for folks. She wasn't proud. When the folks that lived here asked if she'd do that for them, I said, hey, do you really want to clean house for your neighbors? And she said, what are you talking about? You think they're better than us? A dollar's a dollar. I didn't have any argument for that. So that's what she did. Cleaned over here once a week for about three months before it happened."

Annie tensed, feeling that he was working up to something, but said nothing.

"I was home. Happened to look out the window, see Mrs. Anderson running over here fast as she can. I meet her on the porch and she's saying come quick, something's not right with Dolores. So I go running after her. I was younger then, in better shape—this was more than twenty years ago, what I'm telling you about—and was able to keep up with her, and even before I got to the house I could hear the screaming. Never heard a sound like that come out of my Dolores."

Just tell me what happened.

"I get in the house, and she's just standing there at the base of the stairs. Rigid, like she's at attention. Arms at her side, and she's got her mouth open and she's wailing. I'm standing right in front of her, sayin' her name, saying, 'Dolores, it's me, it's Daniel,' and it's like she's looking right through me, like I'm not even there. They called an ambulance, and the paramedics, they gave her something to calm her down and took her to the hospital, and the doctors, they say it was whatcha call some kind of a psychotic break and a bunch of other mumbo-jumbo, but the bottom line is I don't think they know what the hell happened."

Annie said nothing.

Daniel sighed. "A switch got flipped, and one moment she was fine and the next everything in her head went kablooey." He shook his head slowly. "Like there'd been this little time bomb in her noggin waiting to go off for years, and it just decided to do it while she was over here vacuuming and dusting. Like a heart attack, you know, but in her head, but not a stroke or one of those TIAs, either? If it hadn't happened there, I guess it would have happened someplace else. One doctor said, it was like if you opened a door and someone jumped out to surprise you. Like if that moment of shock never went away."

Annie thought about that. "Like if something scared her?"

Daniel shrugged. "Like if something maybe scared her in her *mind*. If that makes any sense. Anyway, because Dolores associates this place, and anyone living here, with her, whatever you call it, condition, she keeps her distance."

"Of course." Delicately, Annie asked, "How long did it take for her to recover?"

Daniel chuckled darkly. "Love to let you know when that day comes."

"All this time?"

"Well, it's not like she's been screaming for twenty years. It's more like a part of her got turned off. She takes her meds, and she doesn't talk much, and she watches *The Price Is Right* every day, and she likes to sit on the porch with a book that she won't read, and I don't really know how much of her is really there, but sometimes life throws you a curveball and you have to deal with it. I love my Dolores, and that's all she wrote."

He managed a grin. "So, welcome to the neighborhood," he said, and laughed.

Annie forced herself to smile. "Thank you."

"Do I know how to spoil the mood, or what? I'm laying all this on you, and that's just not right."

"No, it's okay. Really."

"I get talking and there's no stopping me."

"Really, I don't mind. So," she said slowly, trying to make conversation, "the people who lived here before were photographers."

"Yup."

"What kind of photography?"

Daniel screwed up his face. "Not sure, exactly. Think they did different kinds of things, whatever paid the bills. Weddings, nature stuff. Did a couple of picture books of the Hudson Valley, the Finger Lakes."

"Where'd they move to?"

Daniel slowly shook his head. "Don't know. They didn't even tell me they were moving. One day they were just gone. Didn't even pack up their own stuff. Moving truck came a few weeks after they left, cleared the place out without them even being there."

Annie had become curious. "When was this?"

"Five, six years ago. They never did sell the place. Well, they did, but they sold it to the real estate people, and they've been renting it out off and on since then. Been some seasons it just sits empty, which is a shame, nice house like that. But they've kept it up good. That woman who was just visiting you? She looks after it."

"I wonder why they left. The photographers."

A shrug. "People get restless. But not me. Built that house. Not leaving."

Annie smiled. Daniel was starting to grow on her. They were both quiet a moment. Daniel broke the silence. "I imagine, coming here from the big city, it's a tad quieter."

She managed a weak chuckle. "I could hardly get to sleep last night without all the sirens and garbage trucks and what have you. You get used to all that background noise, and can't manage without it. I'll have to get a white noise app for my phone or something."

Daniel looked puzzled, but didn't ask for an explanation.

Annie said, "I did love hearing the train, though."

"Train?"

"Woke me up, can't remember when, exactly. But it was . . . I don't know how to describe it. It was a *comfort*."

"You had to have heard something else," he said.

"Oh, I know what a train sounds like," she said. "Must have been on those tracks, just up that way." She pointed.

"Yeah, that would be the old A&B. The Albany & Bennington. Small railroad, went out of business some time ago. Nothing's run on those tracks for several years now. Have a look, you'll see the top of the rails are rusted. You got a train running on it, it keeps the rail tops shiny. There's been talk of pulling them up altogether and making it a hiking trail, given that it's fallen into disuse. You must've heard a truck."

Annie considered that. "Maybe so," she said quietly. It wasn't worth an argument. She knew what she'd heard. She might be from the city, but she wasn't an idiot.

"I best be off," he said, slowly rising from the chair. "It's been nice talking with you."

"A pleasure," she said, offering a hand. She stayed on the porch and watched until he had crossed the road and gone back into his own house.

SIX

T hat is one fucked-up story," Finnegan said. He'd phoned Annie not long after she had emailed him a thank-you for setting up the house, and listened to the tale of the man from across the road. "Now I feel like I should have found you someplace different."

"It's okay," Annie said. "I shouldn't even have brought it up, but it was too strange not to share. I mean, it happened a long time ago. More than a couple of decades."

"But still, if I'd had any clue . . . Candace certainly didn't mention it."

"Why would she? Someone had a medical event in the house. How many houses can you think of where something like that hasn't happened? That's life."

"I guess."

"I do kind of wish he hadn't told me. I came up here to get away from sadness, but maybe there's a lesson there. You can't escape it. You have to learn to live with it. For all I know, someone died in our Bank Street place." She laughed. "Maybe even Sid Vicious."

"You'd have wanted to put up a plaque or something."

"Actually, he died farther up the street, at number sixty-three. How'd you even get onto this house in the first place?"

Finnegan said, "Funniest thing. Someone new down in market-ing, there was a meeting, he dropped by, poked his head in the door, heard I was looking for a spot for you for the summer. He was from up this way, knew about it. I checked it out and it looked perfect."

"The studio space is very nice. Skylights and the whole deal. You stocked it well, you manipulative son of a bitch."

With forced sincerity, he said, "Only trying to help. My intentions were purely honorable."

"Of course they were."

Finnegan wrapped things up with, "If you need anything, anything at all, just call. Maybe I'll surprise you with a visit one day."

"Love you, Fin," she said, and once she was done, shouted, "Charlie! Let's go!"

When he didn't answer, she went to the front hall and called up to the second floor for him. When that produced no response, she went out onto the porch and called for him.

"Where the hell is he?" she said under her breath.

She started to walk down to the road, but before she'd gotten very far she decided to take a look around back. And there, sure enough, was Charlie, standing on a pile of wood, peering through the grimy window of that shed he'd been so curious about.

"Hey!"

Charlie's head turned.

"You want a bike or not?"

"One second!" he shouted.

Charlie waited for his mother to round the side of the house, then leaned in close to the window and whispered, "I'll be back. I'll figure this out."

ANNIE WAS AGAIN pretty wrapped up in her thoughts once she was behind the wheel and Charlie was belted in in the backseat.

Maybe, she said to herself, this was why John had told her not to go. Because this get-away-from-it-all house had been where some poor woman's mind had snapped. But so what? Like Daniel had said, if it hadn't happened here, it would have happened someplace else.

"For fuck's sake, stop it," she said under her breath, quietly enough that Charlie had not noticed.

John had *not* told her not to come here. She'd had a *dream* about John telling her not to come here. *Get a grip, lady.* She gave her head a shake.

It was about a five-mile drive to Fenelon, which was the closest town that amounted to more than a gas station, a church, and an antique store. It actually amounted to *much* more. With a population of about six thousand, it had half a dozen gas stations, a decent commercial strip as you entered with a Dunkin' Donuts, a Burger King, a Home Depot, and a Wegmans grocery store. The center of town had more charm, with a green that ran down the middle of the main street, lots of trees, and a couple dozen small stores and eateries, many of which chose to use the quaint spelling of "shoppe." There was the Card Shoppe and the Sandwich Shoppe and the Yarn Shoppe and, of course, Ye Olde Barber Shoppe.

Daniel had mentioned a place called Jake's Hardware (and not, refreshingly, Jake's Hardware Shoppe), where she might find a bike for Charlie. Annie thought they would make that their first stop, then scout a place for lunch.

"Keep your eye out for this Jake's place," Annie said.

As they cruised slowly down the main street heading west, Charlie called out, "Other side!" She made a turn at the next intersection, came down the east side, and nosed the BMW into an angled parking spot four shops past Jake's. Once they were out of the car, their walk to the store took them past a bakery, an antiques store, a card shop, and a shoe repair. Annie glanced into the antiques store as they passed. She'd spotted a tall, spinning rack of paperbacks in there, the kind supermarkets and drugstores used to have. Annie recalled the rack at her neighborhood Rite Aid when she was growing up, how it squeaked when she turned it.

A jingling bell over the door announced their arrival at Jake's. There were aisles of paint and tools and gardening gear and plumbing and electrical supplies and just about anything else someone might need for their household, but there were no bikes in sight.

A man in his early thirties, wearing a red shirt with JAKE's on the pocket, was working the till. "Sorry," he said when Annie asked if they carried bikes. "We usually bring in a few in the spring, but we're all sold out now. I doubt any place in town's got any. You might want to take a run to Binghamton."

"Is that far?" Charlie asked.

"About an hour," the clerk said. "Or check online, see if anybody's got anything in stock before you go."

Annie took a crestfallen Charlie out to the sidewalk. "Sorry, sport. I'll do some checking when we get back to the house. Hungry?"

He was. They decided to take a chance on the Bagel Shoppe, with that special spelling, expecting the worst. But the chocolate chip bagel Charlie wolfed down and the poppy seed with chive cream cheese Annie ordered proved borderline satisfactory.

On the way back to the car, passing the antiques store, Annie said, "Let's check this out."

"Do we have to?"

"You never know what you might find. Maybe some more old Ray Bradbury paperbacks."

Charlie offered a sigh of surrender and in they went, setting off another jingling bell. Annie quickly realized this was less an antiques store and more a hoarder's paradise. Old furniture, Sears catalogues from the 1970s, books, broken lamps, old model train buildings and other accessories, printers that hadn't been hooked up to a computer in twenty years, Beanie Babies that looked like they'd been gnawed by dogs, boxed jigsaw puzzles that Annie was willing to bet were missing several vital pieces.

Charlie wandered off toward the back of the store, while Annie had a glance at the paperback books, thinking that even if she found one that interested her, odds were it would not be mold-free.

"Look 'round long as you like!" said a voice. Seconds later, a heavyset woman with gray hair and wire-framed glasses emerged from between two aisles of junk. "We got just about everything you could ever want."

Provided your list consists of nothing but shit, Annie thought. "Thanks. Just thought we'd browse."

"Got some classic Teenage Mutant Ninja Turtle figures back there somewhere your boy might like. So long as he's not fussy about them having all their limbs."

Annie gave her a polite nod. For all she knew, there were great treasures to be found, but nothing was organized. Royal Doulton figurines were on a shelf with toy guns. Old copper pipe was in a box with wool mittens. A Cuisinart base with mixing bowl sat on a shelf next to an ancient Howdy Doody doll. The only reason to stay another couple of minutes was out of politeness. Once she'd rounded up Charlie, they'd be out of here, but he had vanished into the bowels of the shop.

She worked her way down an aisle and called out softly, "Charlie?"

She kept on going until she had reached the back end of the store, which was where she found her son, examining a bicycle.

"What about this?" he asked when he saw his mother standing there.

"That?" she said, unable to hide her lack of enthusiasm.

The bike was about the right size for a boy Charlie's age, but it was definitely from another era. The seat was one of those elongated banana seats, with the handlebars raised upward, like angel wings. The wheels and frame had rust spots, and the back tire looked flat. The bicycle was probably from the sixties or early seventies. And if all that weren't enough, it was a girl's bike, the center bars slanted down.

"It's perfect," Charlie said, swinging his leg over the seat, holding on to the handlebars and testing it out.

"The back tire's flat. Charlie, it's a piece of junk."

"Oh, it's still good," said the proprietor, who had materialized out of nowhere. "I got a pump to put some air into that back tire. It might look rough, but it works. I had a kid trying it out the other day. I know it's made for a girl, but, you know, these days we try not to judge, right?"

"Mom?" Charlie said pleadingly.

"Honey, we can go to Binghamton and find you one, or order it, like the man at the hardware store said."

"That could take *forever*. It might not even show up before we have to go home. And I need it right *now*."

"And why do you need it right *now*?"

"I got places to go," Charlie said.

"And people to see," said the store owner, laughing. "I can make you a good deal on it."

Annie thought, if anything, the woman should pay her to take it off her hands. "I really don't think it's the right one for him. He's never had a bike before, and it would probably need training wheels, and—"

"*Mom!* I don't need training wheels. I'm not a baby. I already know how to ride a bike."

"Since when?"

"I ride Pedro's all the time." Charlie's friend from school. "But in the alley, never on the street," he said, anticipating his mother's alarm.

"Ten bucks," said the shop owner.

"Pardon?" Annie said.

"I can let it go for ten."

"I don't think so," Annie said.

"I have it," Charlie said, digging into his front pocket.

He brought out a five, three ones, and some change. He was counting it out aloud, moving the funds from one hand to the other as he did so. "Six, seven, eight, twenty cents, thirty cents—"

"What you got there is just fine," the woman said, holding out her hand. Charlie put his money into her palm, Annie watching, shaking her head.

Okay, she thought, *maybe this will be a lesson learned*. A fool and his money are soon parted, her own mother used to say. When Charlie got this bike home and it fell apart before he reached the end of the driveway, he'd listen to his mother the next time she advised him against a purchase.

"A pleasure doing business with you," the woman said. "Let me get a pump for that tire."

Moments later she was back, hooking a hose to the nozzle on the back tire. "Why don't you do it," she suggested to Charlie. After she demonstrated how to use the device, he forced some air into the tire, then felt it between thumb and forefinger.

"Seems hard," he said.

"Tell ya what. I'll throw in the pump. If it gets soft again, you can pump it up at home."

Charlie beamed. As he wheeled it out of the store and toward the car, he asked if they could go back to the hardware store and get some special cleaner so he could get the rust off the rims.

"Why the hell not?" Annie said.

Once they were back at their temporary home, Charlie spent the rest of the afternoon with a rag and a tin of Brasso with the intention of making the bike look, if not brand-new, perhaps newer.

"When you're done cleaning it up, you call me before you start pedaling all over the place on it," Annie said. "There's some ground rules to go over."

"Like what?"

"Call me. Understood?"

"Understood," he said wearily.

While he worked on his bike, Annie went up to the second-floor studio. She stood just inside the doorway for a moment, sizing the place up. It appeared recently painted, judging by how free of marks the walls were, and the fresh coat of white made the room look bigger than it was. In the ceiling were two skylights that filled the space with sunshine. There wasn't a shadow anywhere except for under the chair and worktable Finnegan had arranged for.

She walked over to the chair, ran her hand along the back of it. Almost inexorably, she found herself sitting in it, giving it a little bounce, taking it for a test drive.

Nicer than her studio chair in the city, Annie thought.

She surveyed the items at the edge of the table. A large coffee can filled with markers and pencils and brushes. In another can, a rainbow's worth of tubes of paint. Plus, several large pads of art paper. Even some bricks of plasticine in a variety of colors, all wrapped in clear plastic.

Annie tore off a sheet of paper and secured the four corners to the table surface with short strips of masking tape.

A blank page.

She'd been good friends with an artist from *The New Yorker*, now passed on, whom she often met for lunch at Café Luxembourg up on West 70th Street near 10th Avenue. He was something of a fixture there, sitting in the corner, sipping on a scotch, always at the same table, where he had a view of the various neighborhood celebs who might wander in. He had said something to her once that had always stayed with her. "I never had a drawing that was as good on paper as it had been in my head."

Boy, did she get that. She could imagine so clearly what she wanted to create, but what traveled down from her brain, through her arms, and out her fingers onto the paper so rarely lived up to expectations. But then, that was the challenge, wasn't it? If it was easy, what would be the point? If anybody could do it, everybody would do it.

She knew this happened even more with novelists, and was something of a running joke among them, but she was often asked where her ideas came from. Like there was a store someplace, an Ideas R Us, where you could buy them by the dozen. She always just smiled and said she didn't know, that an idea would just pop into her head and she'd run with it.

The truth was, she did know, but was at pains to explain it. She'd tried more than once with John.

"Imagine an image on a pane of glass that's flipping slowly through the air," she'd told him. "Sometimes you can see it straight on, but other times, if you're looking at the glass from the edge, it's just a line, the image vanishes."

John had listened intently, trying to picture it.

"So, I'll see that line first, like it's slicing through the air, coming out of nowhere, a sliver almost, and then it starts to turn, and the image comes into focus. That's where I first saw Pierce. On that pane of glass."

"Cool," he'd said.

What she didn't tell him was that she'd been seeing those panes of glass slice their way into her world since she was a child, and they didn't always come through the air. Once, she saw one come right out of a person, like that time when she was eight, walking through Penn Station, holding on to her father's hand.

Annie caught sight of a tall, ordinary-looking man in a tan trench coat coming her way. Suddenly she had a vision of glass emerging from his head, hairline to chin, edgewise. The glass pivoted, becoming a mini-window through which she saw his face.

It had changed.

He was no longer ordinary. His features were covered with fur, his ears were pointed, and he'd grown a snout with a jaw filled with sharp teeth. His fierce eyes fixed on her for a fraction of a second.

And he smiled.

The glass flipped and vanished and the man was back to normal. As he passed, Annie turned and watched him walk away and be swallowed into the crowd.

Annie never said a word to her father.

So here she was now, waiting for that creative spark. Ideas didn't always have to come out of thin air, on a piece of glass. Sometimes you had to sweat them out.

She picked up a pencil, touched it to the paper, and started to sketch out the shape of a penguin.

She got as far as drawing Pierce's head, and then stopped.

"No," she said to herself. "Not yet."

Pierce had become that old friend you'd lost touch with and didn't have the nerve to pick up the phone and call. Maybe someday, but not now. She needed to try something else, be open to new ideas. Annie took a breath and allowed her mind to empty. Nothing happened right away, but she chided herself for being impatient. Tried to think of a cloudless blue sky.

After about a minute, her right hand began to move.

She deliberately looked away, casting her eyes up to the skylight, while her fingers sketched. It reminded her of when she and her childhood friends would rest the tips of their fingers on a planchette as it wandered a Ouija board.

After a couple of minutes, she lifted her pencil from the paper and looked down to see what she had done in her almost trance-like state.

"Oh my God," she said.

WHEN ANNIE STEPPED out onto the porch, she expected to find Charlie, still working on his bicycle. But he wasn't there, and neither was the bike.

And then he suddenly appeared, rounding the house from the right, racing past the porch, legs pumping furiously, before disappearing around the left corner. A few seconds later, he reappeared, again from the right. He was doing laps.

"Charlie!" Annie shouted.

But Charlie was oblivious to her cries and kept on going. One thing was clear. He had been right when he'd said he didn't need training wheels. He was handling the bike like a pro. Before he came around for a third pass, she descended the porch steps and positioned herself in what she expected to be his path. Sure enough, he came around again, saw her standing there, and cranked the pedals backward, engaging the brake. The bike skidded to stop two feet in front of Annie.

"Hi, Mom," he said, panting. There was sweat on his forehead, and his shirt was sticking to his chest.

"You were supposed to wait for me before you tried it out."

Charlie shrugged. "How's it look?"

She had to hand it to him. The chrome wheels and spokes that had been so rusty and grimy sparkled. There were still places on the frame where the paint was chipped or cancered with rust, but for a bike that had to be decades old, it wasn't bad. And if it bothered Charlie that it was a girl's bike, he showed no sign.

"I'm impressed."

"I used all the Brasso," he said.

"Not surprised."

"I've been riding around and around the house. I've already done it twenty-two times."

"You getting ready for the Tour de France?"

"The what?'

"You're a sweaty mess."

"I'm building up my enema."

Annie stifled a laugh. "Stamina."

"Yeah, that."

"And why do you have to build up your stamina?"

Charlie hesitated. "Just in case I ever had to ride somewhere far one day."

SEVEN

They had a quiet evening.

Annie opened up a jar of spaghetti sauce in the cupboard, warmed it on the stove, and slid some fettucine noodles into a pot of boiling water. A sprinkle of Parmesan, and voilà, world's simplest dinner. Charlie was at that age where he would take some cooked noodles—buttered or with tomato sauce—over just about any other food, and on this particular night Annie was content with the same.

After dinner they watched some TV. Charlie was right, the channels were all in different places than in the city, and there weren't nearly as many of them here, but the house was still equipped with wi-fi and there was always streaming. They watched *Galaxy Quest*, which had been one of John's favorite movies because it was such a great send-up of the whole Star Trek franchise, but Charlie took it at face value, as an exciting science fiction adventure with a few laughs. When Alan Rickman, in full alien garb, announces after a harrowing encounter with another spaceship that he's off to find the pub, Annie cracked up. It had been John's favorite line.

Uncharacteristically, Charlie turned down his mother's offer of a story, claiming to be too tired. And within seconds of tucking him in, Annie peered through a crack in the doorway and could see that he was out cold.

She tidied up the kitchen, watched Anderson Cooper on CNN, and when that was over she was ready for an early turn-in. But on her way to her bedroom she went back into the studio to take another look at what she had drawn that afternoon.

It was a messy sketch, not surprisingly, given that she had drawn it without actually looking at the paper. Even now, it was hard for her to describe where her mind had gone while she was drawing. She'd been looking up at the sky, through the two skylights, imagining, perhaps, that she was a bird, flying around up there, gazing down upon the house from the heavens. In the past, when she'd experimented with automatic drawing—clearing her head, letting her fingers seemingly work independently of her brain—she'd never had much to show for it.

Today had been different.

This was no adorable penguin she'd sketched.

She had drawn the man from Penn Station.

He was a kind of hybrid. Part rat, part coyote, with a dash of werewolf added to the mix.

He had a human-like figure, but with the rat-wolf head. Not some cute, Disney-like rat (or wolf), either. This was a nasty piece of work with piercing eyes and small, sharp, piranha-like teeth that could nibble off your fingers in an instant. He (she assumed it was a *he*) was dressed in a kind of long jacket, like a trench coat, and his feet were bare. They were oversized and furry, with long ragged nails. A bushy tail curled up from under the coat.

"*Good luck turning him into a bestseller,*" she heard John say in the back of her mind.

As rough as the sketch was, Annie had to admit that, from a purely professional standpoint, it was not half bad. If you were out to create a cartoon villain, you could do a lot worse.

But what in Annie's subconscious had led her to put this image on a sheet of paper? What had prompted her to dredge up a distant memory from childhood that might not even have been real? Sure, she'd endured the worst year ever. She'd suffered guilt, she'd endured loss. Was this how it manifested itself?

She sat in the chair, picked up the pencil, and refined some of the character's features. Made the teeth more individual, sharper. Worked some creases into the trench coat. Added some little hairs to the feet.

Were the creative impulses within her trying to send a message? Were they telling her to retire Pierce permanently? Was it time to abandon cute for creepy?

Take that pain. Take that hurt. Turn it into something.

Was that what was happening?

She put down the pencil and managed a smile. She imagined the look on Fin's face when she told him she was abandoning a cute penguin for this nightmarish character. He'd have a heart attack. Even if she had no intention of switching gears, it would still be fun to tell him.

Annie left the study, turned out the light, and retired to her room. Once under the covers, she plugged her phone into the charger cord on her bedside table, tried to read a few pages of her novel, but when she found herself unable to keep her eyes open, she hit the light and went to sleep.

CHARLIE HAD A dream.

Shortly after midnight, he saw himself on the front porch, in the middle of the day, polishing the wheels on his bicycle, when someone came walking up the driveway. At first the man's features were vague and ill-defined, but as he got closer, Charlie could see that it was his father.

"Hi, Charlie," said John.

Charlie came down the porch steps and said, "Hi, Dad. It sure is good to see you."

"Good to see you, too. I've missed ya."

Charlie was surprised he hadn't burst into tears. But it was like his dad had never actually died. He'd just been away for a while.

"Mom's going to be happy to see you."

"Oh, I bet, but it's you I've come to see," John said. "I've come to help you with something. To *show* you something."

"What?"

"May I come inside?"

Charlie nodded and led his father into the house.

"Let's go to the basement," John said.

Charlie noticed that he made no noise when he walked. It was almost like he was floating. Charlie opened the door that led to the cellar, turned on the light, and went down the steps, his father following closely behind.

"There's nothing down here," Charlie said. "I looked the first day."

"You missed something."

"What?"

His father led him over to the workbench and opened the drawer that Charlie had inspected before. The one filled with old nails and rusted pipe fittings.

"Have a look in there again."

Charlie moved around the various pieces of metal junk with his fingers until he saw something he had not seen before. He picked it up.

"What do we have there?" John asked.

"It's a key," Charlie said.

And just like that, his father was gone. There wasn't even a poof of smoke. He was there one second, and gone the next.

That was when Charlie woke up.

At first he wondered if he'd been sleepwalking, and really had

had a visit from his father. But Charlie was right in his bed. Then again, he could have sleepwalked his way back to his room, slipped under the covers.

He blinked a few times, rolled onto his side, and looked at the digital clock: 12:35 a.m. Charlie usually slept through the night, waking up around eight. But right now he felt every bit as awake as he would have when the sun was up.

He slipped out of bed, kept his pajamas on but pulled on his running shoes and laced them up. The house was dark except for slivers of moonlight streaming through the windows. He didn't want to turn on any lights for fear it might wake his mother. But he also needed to see where he was going. He crept quietly into his mother's bedroom. She wasn't snoring, but he could hear deep breathing, so he knew she was asleep. He tiptoed to her bedside and unplugged her phone from the charging cord, and, when he was back in the hallway, brought up the flashlight app.

Charlie descended the stairs and rounded the corner to the door that led down to the basement, shining the light ahead of him. Once he was atop the first step and had the door closed behind him, it was safe to flick on a light.

Even with the bare bulb illuminated, and the room largely deserted, the basement was not a place where he felt at ease. A little chill ran up his spine, the hairs on the back of his neck standing up when he reached the floor, although it might have been that Charlie was more excited than frightened.

Charlie walked over to the workbench, pulled out the drawer, and dug his fingers into the mix of rusty nails and pipe clamps and screws of varying sizes until he felt something small, smooth, and thin.

A key.

He grabbed it between his thumb and forefinger, lifted it out of the drawer, and brought it up to his nose for a closer inspection. It sure looked like a key that would open a padlock. Like the one on the shed door.

Charlie came back up the stairs, flicking off the light before he returned to the main floor and reengaged the flashlight app. He walked to the front door, opened it noiselessly, and stepped onto the porch. No security pad to worry about here. Nothing to disarm.

No bad guys in this part of the world.

He closed the door behind him and descended the porch steps. Even with his running shoes on, he could feel the dampness in the grass. Nighttime dew blanketed everything. Using the phone's light, he rounded the house and headed for the shed, the key gripped so firmly in the palm of his left hand that it was creating an impression in his skin.

Charlie reached the shed, set the phone on the ground, screen pointed up so the shed door was illuminated, and tried to insert the key into the padlock. He had it turned the wrong way the first time, figured out his mistake, and tried again. The key slid in nicely. Holding the lock firmly in his left hand, Charlie turned the key with his right.

The lock came undone.

Charlie slid it off the hook and opened the door. It was pitch-dark in the shed, and, feeling around the inside of the frame, Charlie could find no light switch. He picked the phone up off the ground and shined it inside.

As he'd already speculated, the shed was filled with various tools and garden-related items. Three rakes and two shovels. An old gas-powered lawn mower that, judging by the rust and the pull-cord that dangled from its housing, hadn't been fired up in a very long time. Three bags of fertilizer and one of grass seed, some of it leaking out a hole that had no doubt been made by a mouse. There were four folded lawn chairs with webbing so far into the disintegration process that no one could have sat in them without risking grievous bodily harm, an electric hedge trimmer, a couple of extension cords, gardening gloves, a seed-spreading machine.

None of this held any interest for Charlie.

He was focused on the box tucked into the back corner of the structure.

He stepped over to it, pointed the phone flashlight for a better look.

This was what had been calling to him. This was what had been demanding to be found.

A cardboard box about two-by-two-by-three feet. Probably had once held packages of detergent, judging by the word printed boldly on the side.

TIDE.

Part II

HARRY

EIGHT

No one could remember when, exactly, the shop had opened.

One day, there was nothing there. And then, one day there was.

People would say, it's like when you need your shoes repaired, someone recommends Mike's Shoe Repair, and you ask, where's that, and you find out it's right there on the main drag; you've strolled past it a hundred times but never noticed it because you never needed your shoes fixed till now.

This new shop was like that, except there wasn't a soul who could remember how long it had been there. A week? A month? Surely not longer than that.

Regardless of when it had opened, the town of Lucknow now had something it had not had before, at least not in anyone's memory. It had a toy train shop, somewhat anachronistic in a time when the electronic game systems—Nintendos and PlayStations and Xboxes—were ubiquitous. What chance did something as classic as a toy train stand, only a couple years into the new millennium?

Time would tell.

The place certainly had a catchy, if too-cute, name: Choo-Choo's Trains. It seemed designed to draw in the little ones, or at least prompt them to drag their parents in with them.

On this particular Tuesday morning, before the shop had even opened—the sign in the window said OUR HOURS OF FUN ARE 9:30–5:00!—two boys on their way to school had stopped to admire the window display: a loop of track about five feet across with a New Haven diesel engine and three passenger cars going around and around, disappearing briefly on each loop into a tunnel built into a mountain prop. Even when the store was closed, the train was left to run twenty-four hours a day.

The boys, both eleven years old, stared at the train, one more transfixed than the other. "It's kinda cool," one said.

"It's for little kids," said the other dismissively. "Slot cars are better. You can race them. You can't race trains."

"My uncle's got a big setup in his basement. He's got a station and a water tower and signals and crossings and all kinds of other shit."

"When'd this place open anyway?"

The other boy shrugged. They agreed the place was worth checking out on their way home once school was over.

One person who had, so far, shown not the slightest interest in the new shop was sitting behind the wheel of a plain white four-door sedan with a red light on the roof and the words LUCKNOW POLICE DEPARTMENT printed on the side. It pulled into an angled parking spot out front of the Lucknow Diner. There were two other diners in town, but, as they had come later, they lost rights to name themselves after the town in which they did business. Not unlike the train shop, no one quite remembered when the Lucknow Diner first started serving up bacon and eggs and French toast and the best coffee in this corner of the state, but they did know it had more or less been here forever.

The man behind the wheel of the police car killed the engine but took a moment before opening the door. Chief Harry Cook closed his eyes briefly, yawned, and put his head back on the headrest. Only nine in the morning and already he needed a nap. He'd been up since three, and hadn't gotten to bed until nearly one in the morning, so the fact that he was even operating on two hours' sleep was a minor miracle.

Harry allowed himself fifteen seconds to recharge. He knew if he took any longer he'd nod right off, and he didn't have time for that. But he would take time for a cup, or possibly two, of the Lucknow Diner's coffee. He didn't know what was in it—caffeine with a touch of nitroglycerine was his best guess—and it was just as well, because if he did he might have to arrest the manager. But Harry was confident it would give him strength to make it at least until noon.

Harry slowly eased his lean frame out of the car. He was a little underdressed when it came to small-town chiefs. A pair of jeans, a white shirt with an open button-down collar, and a dark brown sport jacket with a small star pinned to the lapel. Lucknow was small enough that everyone knew who he was. He didn't need a uniform to be recognized, although he did insist on it for the other members of the Lucknow Police Department. All six of them. When they called him on this double standard, he told them that when one of them became chief, they could wear tap shoes and a miner's hat, for all he cared.

Harry was headed for the diner entrance when he spotted a familiar face on a nearby sidewalk bench. A disheveled-looking man in his fifties with long stringy hair that came down to his shoulders, a three-day growth of beard, a ball cap with a faded Boston Red Sox logo, and a set of clothes that didn't look as though they'd seen the inside of a washing machine in some time. The man was staring vacantly at the traffic going by when Harry approached.

"How's it going, there, Gavin?" the chief asked.

Gavin slowly turned his head. "Oh, hey, there, Harry." He smiled awkwardly. "Gonna tell me to move on?"

Harry shook his head. "Just wondered how you were doing, is all. You spend the night on this bench?"

"Possibly."

"You know you can go to the shelter."

Gavin frowned. "I don't like it there. Place is full of losers."

Harry took a seat on the bench beside him. "But it gets cool at night. Gettin' down in the fifties." He waved a hand toward the towering trees that lined the main street. "Leaves are changin' already."

"It's pretty. Every fall it seems like a miracle, you know?"

"I do indeed." Harry paused. "I heard from somebody that there's a new inn opening up in Stowe and they're hiring. Not really your line of work, but it'd be something."

"I don't know. I like Lucknow. And my truck's hanging together with twine and Scotch tape. Can't be commuting all the way to Stowe and back every day."

"I think they'd put you up. They got living quarters for the staff. Won't be long before there's snow, and things'll really be hoppin' up there. Get your name in now and you might secure a spot." Harry scanned the street. "Not sure what might be keeping you here, save for this fine view."

Gavin nodded and said, "Well, that's something to think about. But if things get going again at Bergen's they're gonna want me back, and I'd hate to let them down."

If anyone had been let down, it had been Gavin Denham, and Bergen's, a furniture manufacturing company, had done it to him. This grand old year of 2001 had mostly been known for a recession and a stalled economy, but then along came September 11 and suddenly it was the year of the most audacious terrorist attack in history, which only made things worse at Bergen's, where orders for its finely crafted dressers and armoires and chairs were down sharply. Gavin had worked for them nearly two decades, but that didn't count for much when the bosses had to lay people off. Gavin started drinking, or, more accurately, had started drinking *more*, which prompted his wife to leave him and move to Portland to live with her sister. Gavin couldn't keep up the rent on their apartment and before long found himself on the street.

"Well, if I hear of anything a little closer to home, I'll let you know," Harry said.

Gavin smiled. "You know where to find me. Get all my mail sent to this bench."

Harry stood, reached into his pocket, and brought out a five. "Get yourself some breakfast or something."

Gavin shook his head forcefully. "Couldn't do that, Harry. Not looking for charity. Things'll turn around. You wait and see." He grinned as Harry slipped the bill back into his pocket. "Maybe you need another deputy or something?"

"These days I could probably do with an extra dozen."

"I tell ya, there's some weird shit going on, isn't there?"

"You could say that."

"For like a month now?"

"Give or take."

"You know what I think?" Harry waited for Gavin to tell him. "I think it's the terrorists."

"Oh yeah."

"They started with something big. Bringing down the Twin Towers, hitting the Pentagon. Freak us out, waiting for the next big thing, but now they got their operatives spread out all over the country doing smaller missions to keep us on edge."

"That's an interesting theory," Harry said.

"Just thought I'd mention it so you'd know what you might be up against. Osama's minions right here in Vermont."

"You have a good day, Gavin."

Harry stepped out of the way to let a woman in a dark green pantsuit exit the diner, then went in. Jenny had already filled his mug and had it on the counter in front of the stool closest to the cash register. Harry hauled his butt up onto the padded cushion, reached for the sugar dispenser, poured in a generous amount, and gave the black liquid a stir.

"You're an angel from heaven, Jenny."

"And you look like hell," she said.

Jenny had always been one to give it to him straight. She'd been slinging bacon and eggs and hash browns since Harry's dad brought him here for the occasional breakfast back in the seventies. Jenny was pushing that magic number herself, still working at an age when most had retired, but she showed no signs of slowing down, except for the odd complaint about her aching feet.

"Can I get a bacon sandwich or something for Gavin out there? He's not lookin' all that great. Put it on my tab."

"Tab? You gotta tab?"

"Just put it on there."

"How about you?"

"Just coffee."

"Bullshit. You need something to eat. You've lost five pounds this last month."

More like eight or nine, he thought. There was a tossed copy of the *Lucknow Leader* two stools over. Harry grabbed it, unfolded it to see the front page, ignoring the egg yolk stain across the banner. The lead story was not, for a change, about the two Lucknow men who had been missing for more than a month now. Angus Tanner, a fifty-two-year-old maple syrup producer, married thirty years, father of two. It had been a Tuesday, and sometime between leaving the factory and heading home, he vanished. And then a couple of days later, Walter Hillman, twenty-five, single, assistant manager of a Business Depot, didn't come to work one day. Someone finally went to his home—he lived on his own in a one-room apartment in a rooming house—and he was gone.

In both cases, there was no sign of foul play, but nor was there any indication that they had voluntarily walked away from their lives in Lucknow. No charges to credit cards, no withdrawals from cash machines. And in both cases, their cars—Tanner's 1996 Dodge minivan and Hillman's 1984 Toyota Celica—had been left behind.

But a story like that, of two town men disappearing, didn't stay on the front page of the local rag without developments. There'd been updates for the first ten days or so, then a story every couple of days, then maybe one a week. There were theories; chief among them, and without any supporting evidence, was that the two men had run off together. Hillman was gay, but if Tanner was, he'd kept that part of his life a secret.

Harry wasn't buying it. Not that he had a theory that was any better. And then came that call in the middle of the night—just a few hours earlier—about something suspicious being found in a ditch on one of the county roads about ten miles out of town. He didn't know how long he could keep a lid on that. Especially since there'd been a local in attendance who wasn't likely to stay quiet.

"I've been hearing some things," Jenny said, putting in front of him a plate with two pancakes stacked on it. She leaned in close enough to whisper. "Out Miller's Road way. Lots of flashing lights."

Well, there you go, Harry thought. Word was already getting around.

"People talk," he said, shrugging. "Thanks for the pancakes. Got some extra syrup?"

She reached down the counter, brought back a bottle, and set it in front of him. "I heard you found something. Or somebody. Emphasis on *body*."

Harry was about to reply when the woman in the green pantsuit, who had left moments earlier, came back in and asked Jenny, "Did anybody turn in a lipstick?"

"What's that, sugar?"

"A lipstick. Thought I left it on the table, but it's not there."

"Sorry. If somebody finds it I'll hang on to it, give it to you next time you're in." The woman left, and Jenny focused again on Harry. "You were going to tell me about a body."

"You *asked* about a body," he said. "I can neither confirm nor deny what you're saying." He lifted up the top pancake so he could pour syrup on the bottom one, then drenched the top one, too.

"When you say that, you're basically confirming it," she said.

"Not true," he said, cutting the pancakes with the side of his fork and taking a bite, then washing it down with coffee.

"Okay, suppose I asked whether it was true that Osama bin Laden is hiding out in Lucknow, serving ice cream down at the Frostee Freeze. Would you say the same thing, that you can't confirm or deny, when we all know it's a crock of shit?"

"Jenny, if you have information that bin Laden is working at the Frostee Freeze, you have an obligation to come forward with that. If you don't want to tell me, then you should get on the phone ASAP to Homeland Security. There might be a reward."

"Oh, forget it," she said, then grabbed the coffeepot and went to refill someone else's mug. On her way back, she pulled a bacon sandwich from under the heat lamp and set it next to his plate after slipping it into a white paper bag. He'd already killed off one of his pancakes and was downing the last of his coffee when he dug out his wallet. Jenny said, "You got a tab, *remember*? Just go. We'll settle up later. Go sort out that shit you can't confirm or deny."

He still left a five on the counter when Jenny turned away, then slid off the stool and went outside. He was heading toward the bench to give Gavin the sandwich, figuring he might not accept a cash donation but would find it hard to turn down something to eat, when he saw that there was someone already there, handing Gavin a paper cup of what Harry guessed was coffee.

"That's mighty decent of you," Gavin said. "And you remembered how I like it, too."

"Two cream, one sugar," said the man cheerfully. "You only have to tell me once."

Harry could not recall ever seeing this character before. A short man, almost pixieish. Bit of a tummy, probably bald on top judging by the lack of hair around his ears, which stuck out like handles, but it was hard to be sure because he wore a hat. One of those caps engineers on old steam engines wore. White with blue pinstripes. His jacket, or, more accurately, a vest, was railroad-themed as well, almost entirely covered with patches depicting various railroads. Santa Fe, Boston & Main, New York Central, Canadian National, and Canadian Pacific.

"Don't need the cup back," the man said. "Got plenty more just like it." As he was turning to go back across the street, he caught sight of Harry, gave him a quick, respectful nod, and said, "Chief." Then he made his way across the street, waiting for traffic to pass.

Harry stepped closer and handed Gavin the bag. He took it, peered inside, and said, "Aw, man, you shouldn't have."

"Ordered it along with some pancakes and couldn't finish it, so I thought, no sense wasting it."

Gavin dug out one half of the sandwich and took a huge mouthful of it in his first bite.

"Who's that?" Harry asked.

Gavin swallowed some of what was in his mouth. "That's Mr. Choo. Like choo-choo. Like a train. Look at the sign."

And that was when Harry noticed that there was a business in town he'd not been aware of until this very moment. "Choo-Choo's Trains," he said, reading the sign. "When did that place open?"

"Fuck if I know," Gavin said. "Nice enough guy, though. And I don't know much about him, before you ask. All I know is his first name. Edwin. I don't think Choo's his last name. He doesn't look like a Choo, if you get my meaning. It's probably a kind of, whaddya call it, stage name? 'Cause of his business."

"He looked like some kind of nut. That hat and the vest and all."

"Kinda nerdy," Gavin agreed. "Harry?"

"Yeah?"

"Thanks for the sandwich."

"No problem."

It was time to move on, get in touch with the coroner, and try to determine whether that body they'd found was Angus Tanner or Walter Hillman or even somebody else, and whoever it was, why this corpse was missing most of its bones, its teeth, and the hair on its head.

NINE

Edwin Nabler crossed the street, unlocked the front door of his shop, went in, closed the door, and set the lock again. He retrieved from a small pouch on the front of his vest a Waltham pocket watch and noted that the store was not due to open for another five minutes, and if there was anything Nabler believed, it was that if said you opened at 9:30 a.m., you didn't open at 9:29 and you didn't open at 9:31. You opened the store at 9:30, like it said on the sign. It was just like the railroads. They had schedules, and they were expected to keep them. Take that rail line that ran straight through the center of Lucknow, dividing the north side of town from the south. You could count on the Albany & Bennington passenger service to Stowe to blow its whistle every day at 2:23 p.m.

Without schedules, you had chaos.

He decided to spend these last five minutes quietly, contemplatively, thinking good thoughts about the day to come. The new people he would meet, the train sets he would sell. But it wasn't about the money. It had never been about the money. It was about making a difference in people's lives.

Oh yes.

There was a sheet of reflective glass behind the cash register, and Nabler used it to admire his vest, which was currently unbuttoned. There were still a few places for more railroad patches. He didn't have one for the Bangor & Aroostook Railroad in Maine, or Central

Vermont, or the north-of-the-border Ontario Northland. All in good time.

He buttoned the vest, wanting to look his most presentable when potential customers entered.

Choo-Choo's Trains was not a big shop, at least not the floor space that was open to clientele. Narrow, not more than twenty feet wide, some forty feet deep; it was a niche, a specialty store, but that didn't mean Nabler's ambitions weren't grand. He believed his offerings carried broad appeal, that there was something about toy trains that bordered on the intrinsic. In Nabler's experience, almost everyone was captivated by toy trains—men *and* women, despite the perception that the hobby was a largely male interest—even if they didn't collect them or set up displays in their home. People were entranced by worlds replicated in miniature. Toy soldiers, dollhouses, model cars and boats and planes. They marveled at the minutiae, how upon examining a simple steam engine they would suddenly discover that inside the cab was an engineer sitting at the controls, or a mom and her son sitting at a table in the window of a passenger train's dining car, sharing an ice-cream sundae.

And what set toy trains apart from so many other miniatures was that they *moved*. And as if that weren't enough, they made *sounds*. Once those wheels started turning, the train went *chuff-chuffchuffchuff*. Press a button, and a whistle would blow or a bell would clang. *Woowoo! Dingding!*

Who could resist such wonders? Nabler was confident that once word spread about his new shop—word of mouth was everything in this business—the train sets displayed so artfully on the shelves would be hard to keep in stock. Which was why Nabler had been preparing for several weeks to have sufficient stock before opening. Because Nabler was more than a straightforward seller and distributor of trains made by major manufacturers. No, everything that

Nabler sold had been customized by him personally. While the front of the store was small, the back end was grandiose, deceptively so. From the street, no one could have guessed the space taken up by Nabler's workshop, the place where all the magic happened. It was there that Nabler had been constructing, with his own innovative techniques, an elaborate model railroad with mountains and tunnels and bridges and stations, and it was on these tracks that every train Nabler sold was put through its paces to make sure it met his particular, exacting standards.

He pulled out his pocket watch again. It was 9:29 a.m.

Nabler walked to the front door, waited for the second hand to make one more sweep of the face, then flipped the switch to bring the neon OPEN sign to life and unlocked the door.

He had spied a couple of boys, on their way to school no doubt, looking at the window display earlier, and he had a feeling they might be back, but not until school was over. Anyone who ventured into the store through the day was likely to be an adult. There were many so-called grown-ups who enjoyed the hobby, plenty of dads who, fearing that their interest in toy trains might be mocked, used their children as cover.

"It's for my son," a man might say, handing over his money, but you could see the twinkle in his eye.

Ah, the joy of it. The setting of the hook.

But Nabler wasn't exactly reeling them into the boat like some fisherman out for bass. The Trojan Horse was a better analogy. The customer had to invite him in, take him into their hearth and home. That was when the *real* magic happened.

Five minutes had passed since turning on the OPEN sign. Mustn't get impatient. There hadn't been a lot of time for the townsfolk to notice he was here. *It will take as long as it takes*, he thought. Just as well that time was something of an abstract concept for Nabler.

While committed to punctuality when it came to hours and minutes and seconds, Nabler was vague on days and weeks and months. Was this his first day of business or his second, or third? He wasn't quite sure. Was this his fourth shop? His fifth? His fifteenth? Hard to say. He had set up shop in so many different places.

All he knew was he was here now, there was much he had already done, and there was much more to do.

It was a quiet morning until shortly after eleven, when a man in his late thirties wandered in. Slim, slightly balding. He was wearing a short-sleeved white business shirt even though fall was in the air. Dark brown pants with a perfect crease and a pair of Wallabees on his feet. In the pocket of his shirt was a plastic protector that held several pens. He stepped into the store hesitantly, briefly glancing over his shoulder, as though worried that someone passing by on the sidewalk might see him enter.

But once he was a few steps inside and confident he could not be seen from the street, he began to browse. Looking through the plastic windows on each of the boxes, picking up the occasional one for closer examination. When he got to the larger box sets, comprised of an engine, three or four cars, a power pack, and lengths of track, he stopped, checking them out, comparing one to another.

Nabler chose not to bother him, at least not yet. Didn't want to chase the man away by being pushy. Let the goods speak for themselves.

The man kept coming back to one set that had caught his fancy. It came with two boxcars that said SANTA FE on the side, a tank car, one flatcar with a small helicopter attached, and a second one whose load was a mini-submarine. There was even a red caboose. The most important item was a black metal steam engine and matching tender with PENNSYLVANIA emblazoned on the side.

The man held the box in his hands, contemplating. Nabler wasn't sure whether the man had even noticed he was there, so he discreetly cleared his throat.

The man turned, smiled. "Oh, hey. You the owner?"

"Mr. Choo at your service," he said, touching the brim of his engineer cap in a mini-salute.

"Mr. Choo?"

Edwin smiled. "My nom de plume, as it were. But you may call me Edwin."

"This is a nice train set."

"It's one of our biggest sellers," Nabler said, coming out from behind the counter. "And we sell all manner of accessories to go along with it." He waved a hand at his shelves. "Buildings and trees and crossing signals. Everything you could want to make your own miniature empire." He paused. "Thinking of something for a little boy or girl?"

The man looked sheepish. "I'm thinking of getting it for myself."

"Why not? We all need a hobby, don't we? And, to be honest, we're all still kids on the inside. We never outgrow the toys we had as children. I still have my Slinky."

"Oh God, I had one of those. What was the jingle?"

Edwin sang a couple of lines: *"Everyone knows it's Slinky, everyone knows it's Slinky."*

"Thing is, I always wanted a train set when I was a kid but my folks didn't have money for something like that. I had a friend, he had a super Lionel setup, and I would go over to his house and play with it. I was so envious."

"It's never too late," Nabler said.

"Can we open this up so I can get a better look at it?"

"Of course."

Nabler took the set from his hands and placed it on the counter by the register. He carefully opened the end flaps of the box and was starting to slide out the entire Styrofoam tray that held all the pieces securely when the man said, "That's far enough. I just wanted a peek at the engine."

"Have a gander. I've told you *my* name. What's yours?"

The man extended a hand. "Wendell Comstock."

"A pleasure to meet you, Mr. Comstock."

"Wendell."

"Of course, Wendell. Married, are you?" He had been looking at the gold band on the man's finger.

"Yup. Can't imagine what the wife'll think if I bring this home. She doesn't usually get into things I'm interested in." The man's face briefly fell.

Nabler, who would be the first to admit he was not particularly skilled in the areas of marital intimacy, decided to put on a happy face. "You might be surprised. She might take to it. Like a duck to water, as they say."

Wendell ran the tips of his fingers over the engine's surface. "You can actually feel the rivets. That's some nice detailing. And there's a little engineer in the cab and everything." He took his fingers away briefly, then delicately touched them to the engine again. "That's weird," he said.

"Yes?'

"I get . . . I get a little buzzing in my fingers when I touch it."

"I wouldn't think that's possible. It's not on a length of powered track."

"But I feel . . . something."

Nabler nodded with a sudden understanding. "I know what you're feeling. That's what we model train aficionados call the tingle of excitement."

TEN

Chief Harry Cook had seen his share of bad shit since taking the top policing job in Lucknow seven years earlier. Seen a lot even before that, too, when he was a regular cop and not the guy in charge.

Plenty of car accidents, of course. You had to have a strong stomach for those. First time he responded to one, he lost his biscuits. A tractor trailer with a load of lawn tractors ran a red and broadsided a woman in a little Corolla who'd already proceeded into the intersection. The impact sent the car flying a good hundred feet. When Harry looked into the Corolla and saw what was left of the woman, his stomach rolled over like an empty trash can in a windstorm. He ran over to the ditch to throw up, and, while he had his hands on his knees, had a very brief conversation with himself.

You are either going to be able to do this job, or you're not. Make up your mind.

He stood, took a couple of deep breaths, and resumed his investigation of the accident, which involved administering a Breathalyzer test to the truck driver, who blew so high he was basically a walking brewery.

There'd been plenty more stomach-churning scenes since then. A bar fight where a bouncer took the jagged end of a broken beer bottle in the neck. Nothing short of a miracle that he survived. Less fortunate was the fellow who worked in the service department of

Lucknow Ford whose wife took a baseball bat to the side of his head while he was eating a bowl of Cream of Wheat at breakfast. That guy never woke up, and based on what Harry had learned from the dead man's bruised and psychologically damaged wife, he had it coming.

And then there was that house fire on the north side of town.

Single mother with three kids under the age of five. No smoke detectors. Fire started in the middle of the night. Some kind of electrical fault. By the time the smoke woke the woman from a deep sleep, the flames had already overtaken much of the house.

No one made it out.

That had been the worst thing Harry'd ever seen in his career. Until last night.

Some six hours before he'd shown up at the diner and had that restorative cup of coffee, the cell phone on his nightstand started buzzing, only two feet from the pillow where he laid his head. He'd been to bed late, having had a meeting with all six of his staff to discuss whether there were any other possible leads they might pursue when it came to those two missing men. And as if that weren't enough, Dell Peterson, who had a dairy farm on the road heading south out of town but also had a few animals that were not cows, had called around ten to say his pet goat was gone.

This was not, in the overall scheme of things, a high priority for Harry. But he told Dell he would get back to him the next day, take a run out to his place. Maybe the goat had managed to get free, had gone exploring, and by morning he (she?) would be back.

Picking up his cell in the dark, Harry said quietly, "Yeah."

"Sorry to call at this hour, Chief. It's Stick."

His real name was Ben Bloodworth, but he was a skinny dude and topped out at six-foot-six, hence the nickname. One of Harry's brighter officers, who was more valuable dayside handling weightier responsibilities, but everyone had to take a turn working overnights, responding to the odd burglar alarm or car accident. Someone having too much to drink and rolling their pickup into the ditch was a weekly occurrence. Harry was not one to pine for a return to Prohibition—he liked a tumbler of scotch at the end of the day as much as anybody—but, honest to God, the list of mishaps that could be traced to alcohol was too long to compile.

"What's up, Stick?"

"Out on Miller's Road? Before you get to the cutoff? Guy coming home thought he saw a coyote in the ditch that had gotten into something?"

Harry said, "Yeah?"

The pause at the other end of the line was long enough for Harry to think the call had dropped out.

Finally, Stick said, "Looks like it might have been a person at some point."

Harry let that sink in for a second. "Be there soon."

He ended the call. From the other side of the bed, his wife, Janice, stirred.

"Duty calls?" she asked, her mouth pressed into the pillow, the words muffled.

"Stick's found something."

"Hope it's my Ray-Bans," Janice mumbled.

Even in the middle of the night, half-asleep, she could make a joke about a pair of expensive sunglasses she'd lost days earlier.

"I've got everybody on that," Harry said, as he leaned in and gave her a kiss on the cheek.

He made a pit stop in the bathroom, then threw on his clothes. He crept down the hallway and down the stairs, avoiding the creaks so as not to wake his nine-year-old son, Dylan, whose bedroom was only a few steps from his and Janice's. A minute later, he was in the car and on his way.

And seven more minutes later he was on Miller's Road, the flashing lights of Stick's car visible in the distance. There was a second vehicle there, a dark-colored Ford pickup, with a man leaning up against the back fender, baseball hat pulled low, arms crossed. Harry figured this was the guy who had spotted whatever had attracted the coyote's interest.

Stick had aimed his cruiser at the scene, headlights on. Harry parked behind Stick's car and, figuring he might need more than just high beams, grabbed a Maglite from the glove compartment.

Stick met him as he was getting out from behind the wheel.

"Janice says hi." Stick looked pleased. "Lead the way."

When they were two yards away, Stick stopped and pointed. Harry used the Maglite.

It was a body. And a naked one, at that. At a glance, male, about six feet, but it was in such a state that it was difficult to know much more. One thing that did stand out: this dead guy had no hair. And that didn't fit with the description of either of the two missing men.

As Harry moved closer, panning the Maglite's beam from one end of the body to the other, something unusual became evident. The legs, the arms, the torso itself, had the look of being deflated. Like a blow-up doll that had sprung a leak. No, not that, Harry thought. More like boneless chicken.

"Kinda weird, right?" Stick said.

Harry didn't want to contaminate the scene, but he had to get a better look. He took two tentative steps closer, knelt. The body had been sliced up everywhere, but not in the fashion of some fevered attack. The cuts were long and straight and precise, like slits, down the arms and legs and into the chest.

As best Harry could see, there were no bones in those limbs. And the way the chest was collapsed, he was betting much of the rib cage was missing, too.

The dead man's head was turned toward Harry, the mouth open an inch. Harry cast the light into the opening. The man had no teeth. Judging by the ragged state of his gums, the teeth had been removed recently, and not by a skilled dentist. But a coroner would be able to tell him more.

Before stepping back, he shined the light on the man's head. Harry had initially thought this man was bald, but there were some clumps of hair. The corpse appeared to be, among other things, the victim of a bad haircut. Harry was guessing the head had been badly shaved—by the man himself while still alive or someone else. There were three cuts in the scalp where the razor had nicked him.

Stick, standing behind him, said, "You think it's Tanner or Hillman?"

"Hard to say," Harry said.

Harry had been careful not to touch anything. Lucknow didn't have a crime scene investigation unit, so the state police would have to be brought in to assist. The coroner from the county seat would do the autopsy. Harry had calls to make right now. Once those were done, he'd see what else he could learn from the scene, and if he had to leave, he'd have Stick stand watch.

Harry tried to think it through. Most times, you found a body at the side of the road, it had been struck and thrown by a vehicle. But a body that had suffered that kind of trauma would have looked very different. Pulverized, yes, but not carefully sliced open down the limbs. Not even a Mack truck hitting you at a hundred miles an hour could knock bones right out of you.

In all likelihood, this person had not died in this location. Someone had dumped him here, and Harry was betting recently. The coyote hadn't made much of a meal of the corpse yet, and whoever'd left it here certainly wouldn't have wanted to do it in broad daylight and be spotted by a passing motorist.

Stick said, "That's the guy what called it in."

He pointed to the pickup. Harry nodded and made his way over. There was some spillover from the cruiser headlights, and as Harry got closer he could tell this was a young guy, mid-twenties, lean. He uncrossed his arms and took his weight off the truck.

"I'd really like to go home," he said.

"Appreciate you hanging in," Harry said. "What's your name?"

"Tracy. Bill Tracy. I gave the other guy my name and phone number and license and shit."

"And you were coming along this stretch why?"

"Heading home." He pointed in the direction of Lucknow. "Work a late shift in Bennington. Like, restocking shelves at the Price Chopper."

Harry thought he recognized him. "You ever eat at the diner?"

"Lucknow Diner? Yeah, breakfast sometimes. I got a second job at Jermyn's Lumber, start there at like ten this morning, so I'd really like to get home."

"So what'd you see?"

"I'm driving, and, like, I can see the butt end of this coyote pulling on something, and I didn't think much of it, like, maybe he found some roadkill and was having a midnight snack, like, you know, no big deal, what do I care, right?"

Harry nodded.

"But then he lifts up something that looks like an arm. And I'm like, holy shit, is that what I think it is? I was just about even with it at this point, so I stopped and turned to, like, shine the lights on it, which was when the coyote ran."

"You got out?"

Bill nodded. "I walked over and saw what was there and was like, fuck me, that looks like a naked dead guy, so that's when I called you. Well, not you, but, like, the police." He showed a Motorola flip phone that had been in his palm all this time. "Why would a guy be running around naked out here in the middle of the night? You think, like, a car hit him? Because he looked all smushed, you know?"

"You see any other vehicles as you were coming this way? Someone taking off in a hurry?"

"Nothing."

"You mind if I take a look in the back of your truck?"

Bill Tracy blinked. "What?"

"You could say no, and demand that I get a warrant, and we could hang around here for a couple of hours till we get one."

"You thinking I dumped that there?"

"I'm not thinking anything, Mr. Tracy. I just want to have a look in the back of your truck."

The man sighed, then waved his arms in a be-my-guest gesture. Harry turned the Maglite back on and shined it into the uncovered pickup truck bed. There wasn't much in there beyond some dead leaves. Nothing that looked like blood. Then he walked around to the front of the truck, shining the light into the grille, across the bumper. Finally, he opened the driver's door and had a good look inside. A couple of Big Mac containers, some candy wrappers, a torn condom wrapper.

"Okay, thank you, sir, for your cooperation," Harry said, backing out and closing the door. He fished out of his pocket a card. "You think of anything, you give us a call."

"I can go?"

"You can go. And if you wouldn't mind keeping what you've seen out here under your hat for the time being, I'd be most grateful." Harry didn't have high hopes here.

"Gotcha. Can I ask you something?"

Harry waited.

"You guys find lost pets?"

"I'm sorry, no."

"Okay."

Bill Tracy was heading for the driver's door when Harry said, "Why?"

"Uh, well, my girlfriend's cat, like, went missing about a week ago, but she does let it wander around the neighborhood, but the guy who lives next to her, his dog's gone, too, and he always keeps him tied up."

Which made Harry think about Dell Peterson's pet goat.

ELEVEN

It made sense to Harry that, several hours later, Bill Tracy would have been the one to leak the news about the body out on Miller's Road. He most likely popped into the diner before his next job just busting to tell someone—maybe Jenny—about what he'd discovered, how he'd been the one to call the cops, how he was right there when it all happened. How often did you get a chance to be a minor celebrity at the Lucknow Diner?

If Harry knew anything, it was that you couldn't count on people to keep their mouths shut. In this town, gossip was a brushfire. Once it got going, there wasn't much to stop it. Wouldn't be long before Rachel Bosma, that reporter for the *Lucknow Leader,* would be calling him.

After he'd given the bacon sandwich to Gavin and met, briefly, the owner of that train shop, he felt rejuvenated and went back to the scene. With the sun up, he'd be able to get a better look at things. He'd sent out one of his other officers, Nancy Clarkson, to relieve Stick, telling her to set up barriers about a quarter mile in each direction from where the body had been found. Not just to keep gawkers away, but to walk that stretch in case something might have been missed. Someone might have had more than just that one body to dispose of. After all, there were *two* Lucknow men missing.

"Hey, Nancy," Harry said when he walked up to her cruiser. She had the driver's-side back door open, her legs and butt sticking out as she searched for something on the floor.

She crawled back out, stood at attention, and made a brushing-herself-off gesture even though there was nothing on her. Looking sheepish, she said, "Hey, boss."

"Lose something?"

"My stupid Palm Pilot thing. With all my phone numbers and appointments and everything."

"When'd you lose it?"

"Haven't seen it in a couple of days. My whole life's in there."

Harry smiled. "I have this thing called a day planner. I write stuff in it with a pencil."

Nancy sighed. She been with the Lucknow Police for five years, and, lost Palm Pilot aside, she was as sharp as they came. Harry figured he'd lose her one day to someplace like Burlington or Mont-pelier, or maybe she'd make the jump to Boston or Albany. More money, more challenges. She was married, with a three-year-old son.

"Marty's been and gone, took the body with him," she said. The coroner.

"Okay."

"And I've walked both sides of the road, quarter mile in each di-rection, and didn't see a thing, but I can take another run at it, go a little farther off the road."

"Sounds good," Harry said. "You knocked on any doors?"

There were several houses along this stretch but spaced far apart and set back some distance from the road.

"No," Nancy said. "Needed to stay close, in case anyone drove around the barriers. Had one guy give me a hard time, said he was gonna be late for work. I started to get out my ticket book and he turned around. We don't know yet who it is?"

Harry shook his head.

"I had a look," Nancy said, looking grim. "You think an animal did that to him?"

He shook his head again. "No. You hang in, I'll ask around."

Harry went to the house closest to where the body had been left, a simple one-story with peeling white paint, several missing shingles, and a rusted tractor in the front yard tangled in enough weeds and grasses that it had become an integral part of the landscaping.

There was a battered Chevy in the drive that dated back to the seventies. The car looked familiar to Harry, who thought he'd pulled it over more than once. He rapped on the front door and waited for the sounds of footsteps within.

The door creaked open twenty seconds later. A man in pajama bottoms and a stained sleeveless undershirt, what Harry thought of as a "wife-beater," squinted at him.

"Yeah?"

Harry introduced himself, then pointed his thumb over his shoulder at the patrol cars stationed out on the road. "Had a bit of an incident last night and I was hoping you might be able to help us."

"What kinda incident?"

"Wondering if you saw or heard anything out of the ordinary last night between, say, eleven and two or three in the morning?"

The man continued to squint. "Don't I know you?"

"It's possible, sir. What's your name?"

"Darrell Crohn, Esquire."

Harry's eyebrows rose briefly. "Esquire. So, you're a lawyer, Mr. Crohn?"

He shook his head. "No, I just like the sound of it. Think you gave me a speeding ticket."

"It's very possible."

"Yeah, that was you. Give me a ticket for driving too fast near the school when it was ten o'clock at night and there wasn't even any kids around. You folks should be out catching terrorists, not bothering the likes of me."

"At the moment, sir, I'm not here to bother you, but to seek your assistance in an investigation. You notice anything unusual late last night?"

"Like what?"

"Maybe a vehicle parked out by the road. Some lights. Anything suspicious?"

Darrell Crohn slowly shook his head. "Nope. I was asleep. Went to bed around nine or so, got up maybe an hour ago."

"Okay, well, thank you for your time."

"Only woke up once, around two, because of the train."

Harry said, "Train?"

"The whistle. Why they have to blow the goddamn whistle in the middle of the goddamn night?"

"A train whistle woke you up."

"Isn't that what I said? But I got back to sleep pretty quick."

"What line of work are you in, Mr. Crohn?"

"Odd jobs. Salvage, mostly."

"Any chance you might have had something to drink before you retired last evening?"

Darrell smiled slyly. "That is a distinct possibility, Mr. Chief, sir."

The rail line that bisected Lucknow didn't come anywhere near Miller's Road. Darrell clearly had been awakened by his own imaginings.

Harry gave the man a tip of a hat that wasn't there and said, "I thank you for your time. You have a good day, sir."

HARRY HAD NO better luck with the residents of the other nearby houses. He'd hoped at least one place would have been equipped with surveillance cameras, that an image of a vehicle stopping briefly might have been captured. But not one house out this way had a security system. Sure, they locked their doors at night, but this was not what you would call a high crime area. If anything, they were more worried about the occasional black bears that wandered onto their properties and rifled through their trash.

Harry was on his way back to his car when his cell phone rang.

"Chief Cook," he said, taking the call. He always felt a little funny saying that, like he should add "and bottlewasher." Sometimes, some wise-ass would supply the words for him.

Not this time.

"Harry? Marty here." Martin Grist, the coroner.

"Hey, Marty."

"The fuck is going on in your neck of the woods?"

"You tell me."

"Never seen anything like this. Whoever did it, you'd want to take them on a fishing trip. He or she could debone a bass like nobody's business."

"Might sound like a dumb question, Marty, but have you determined a cause of death?"

"Well, he had a pretty nasty bump on the back of the head, but if that didn't kill him, something else did before he was sliced up. Asphyxiated, would be my best guess. And then largely bled out before all the detail work was done."

"Detail work."

"Taking out the humerus in the upper arms, the radius and ulna in the forearm. Tibia and fibula in the legs. That and the rib cage were the biggies. Didn't bother much with the little stuff. All the bones in the fingers were still there. And I have to say, very meticulously done. Must have had some very fine equipment. Maybe a Dremel."

"Why would somebody do that, Marty?"

"That, my friend, is your area. Something else. Those two missing people you've been trying to find?"

"Yeah. Angus Tanner and Walter Hillman."

"You know whether either one of them had a tattoo?"

Harry didn't have to think. He knew the answer. "Tanner's wife said he's got an eagle on his back. Served briefly in the Gulf War."

"There you go."

Harry sighed. He wasn't sure how he felt about this. He wasn't going to find Tanner alive, but at least he'd found him. And, while there was still nothing to directly connect Walter's disappearance to Angus Tanner's, it certainly didn't seem to bode well for the other man. He wasn't looking forward to the visit he was going to have to pay to the Tanner family.

"I've got some more to do here," Marty said, "but I at least wanted to give you that much."

Harry thanked him and dropped the Nokia phone back in his pocket. He went back to Nancy's cruiser.

"Tanner," he said.

Nancy nodded. "Figured it'd be him or Hillman."

"Yeah."

"I talked to a woman from that place." Nancy pointed to a house about fifty yards up the road. "She was driving to work, had to give her permission to go around the barrier to get into town. Nice Audi."

"Anything?"

Nancy shook her head. "Didn't see anything. She and her husband had that place built last year, nice house. Moved up from Boston. Both lawyers."

"They must love living near that guy." Harry tipped his head toward Crohn's yard full of junk.

"All she said she heard was a train whistle," Nancy said. "Woke her up around two. Since when is there a line around here?"

TWELVE

Edwin Nabler was settling into Lucknow just fine, thank you very much.

It always took a little bit of time to acclimatize to a new place. Over the last six decades—or was it seven, or maybe five, it was hard to say—he'd set up shop in a number of locales. There was Des Moines, which was nice until it wasn't. How long was he there, again? Two years, three? Something like that. And he had nice memories from Bradenton. Lots of retirees down there in Florida. Old guys looking for something to do. Even the geezers who'd traded a good-sized house in Rhode Island or Pennsylvania or Massachusetts for a cramped mobile home would find a way to set up a loop of track, maybe even a couple of sidings, in a bedroom that barely offered enough room to change your mind.

But, as charming as it was in Florida—the weather was, of course, much preferable to Des Moines, or the period he spent in Denver—Edwin chose not to stay that long. Less than two years. Not particularly challenging. Those folks were already in God's Waiting Room. They'd moved down there because they knew the end was near, that the land of palm trees and hurricanes was the last place they were going to wake up in the morning until the day came that they didn't. What kind of surprises could he really throw at them? What tragedy—big or small—would have the kind of impact he was looking for?

Philadelphia had its moments, no doubt about that. Hung out his shingle next to an ice-cream shop, which was good for bringing in the kids and their parents. But damned if he didn't gain ten pounds in the time he was there, and ice cream wasn't even something he'd thought he liked.

Sometimes he simply grew weary of a location; other times he felt an urgency to move on. There had been occasions when the locals started to get an inkling of what might be happening, who might be responsible. When all rational explanations had been exhausted, they considered the irrational, and that pointed them in Edwin's direction. Then he'd pack up and slip away into the night.

So now here he was in Lucknow, which seemed to be as good a place as any. Who knew how long he might stay? He'd met the local chief of police this morning, and while it was the briefest of interactions, Edwin did not get the sense this was a man he needed to be concerned about. He knew what the chief's current preoccupation was, and had little doubt he was out of his league when it came to solving crimes. After all, if he was any kind of policeman, why would he still be here in Podunk?

Yes, Lucknow seemed perfect to Edwin. He'd set up his own coffee machine—he'd brought a cup to that sad sack Gavin this morning—but he'd have to spend more time in that diner, not counting the few furtive visits he'd made, in and out so fast no one noticed. And he would want to get to know his fellow shopkeepers. Make himself known to the local business improvement association. Find out if there were any upcoming street fests when he could set up a display on the sidewalk. He'd heard talk about one coming up very soon.

He had always lived in his shop, regardless of which city he'd set up in. Threw down a mattress in the back to curl up on when he needed to recharge, but the truth was he didn't sleep much. Did some of his best work at night, in fact. He liked to be busy. Since arriving in Lucknow, he'd worked pretty much around the clock.

Although, if he was honest with himself, it was all starting to wear on him. More and more these days, his thoughts turned to the idea of retirement. If someone were to become privy to Nabler's secrets they might have guessed him to be ageless, immortal even, but such was not the case. Everyone ran out of gas eventually. One of these days—not too soon, but again, time was all somewhat relative to Edwin—he would turn his attention to a successor, someone he could mentor, but he hadn't reached that point quite yet.

He was in the back of the shop, where customers did not wander unless invited, working diligently on making the magic happen. If someone entered the front of the store, the door-mounted bell would alert him. With the exception of the visit by Wendell Comstock, it had been a slow morning, and Edwin didn't want to spend the day twiddling his thumbs by the cash register. He was not worried. Pretty soon he'd have all the business he could handle. He always did.

And, while Mr. Comstock had not made a purchase, Edwin knew the hook had been set, that he would be back, if not today then maybe tomorrow. The tingle had been particularly strong with that collection of trains Comstock had been examining. That had often been an issue for Edwin Nabler, maintaining consistent quality. Not everything he sold had the same potency. Oh, all his products looked the same. The paint jobs, the lettering on the sides of the various cars, the authentic logos of the various North American railroads, were all executed perfectly. The train wheels turned freely, the track sections went together snugly. But it was the indefinable *resonance* of the trains that most demanded Edwin's attention.

There was a lot that went into it, and that was why Edwin was in the back of the shop today, looking at what he had accomplished to date and what was left to be done.

It only stood to reason that a toy train shop proprietor would construct his own layout, display, whatever you wanted to call it. Certainly not a *diorama*. That suggested something small. What Edwin was building was nothing short of grand. A magnificent stage on which his trains were the players. Long stretches of track. Graceful curves. Mountains and valleys and rivers and lakes. Small towns with a post office and a gas station and maybe even a diner just like the one across the street. (Lots of opportunities for whimsy here. For example, Edwin's eatery was not named after the town, but featured a sign that read SAM 'N' ELLA'S EATS.)

Edwin loved to incorporate everyday items into his display, so-called "found objects." The arms from a pair of sunglasses could be fashioned into a railing, an antenna, or a streetlamp. A lipstick tube made a perfect culvert or exhaust chimney atop a factory. A Palm Pilot could be turned on its side and made to look like the screen at a drive-in movie theater.

Edwin realized he had been whistling a tune, the words to which would have been familiar to many:

"I've been workin' on the railroad, all the livelong day."

While enough track had been laid down to allow Edwin to run a train continuously while he puttered about—the constant *chuff-chuffchuffchuffchuff* was a soothing background noise, a Zen-like mantra—only about half of the layout was decorated with scenery. The tracks were affixed with short screws to narrow strips of plywood that ran across an open-grid network. Soon the spaces between these strips would be filled with hills and valleys and streets where the various buildings would be placed.

Edwin was about to configure some supports for a new mountain when he heard the bell above the door in the front part of the shop.

A customer.

Edwin set down his tools, slipped on his vest, and donned his engineer's cap. He slid open the door that separated the back room from the main shop, entered, and closed the door behind him.

"Hello!" he said cheerily to the woman who had just arrived. "And how are you this lovely day?"

"Oh, just great," she said, flashing a smile.

Edwin put her age at late thirties. Brown hair, plumpish, glasses.

"You're new, aren't you?" she asked. "The store, I mean?"

"Been here awhile," Edwin said.

"I saw the trains running in the window and couldn't resist." She cast her gaze wide, taking in the various items, then zeroed in on some steam engines in a glass case by the cash register. "These are just so cute," she said.

Ah, cute, Edwin thought. Women always thought the hobby was *cute*. Like these fine pieces of miniature machinery were Cabbage Patch Dolls or Beanie Babies. If she reached into her purse and brought out her wallet before departing, she could think these trains were the cutest goddamn things she'd ever seen.

"It's my son's birthday tomorrow," she said. "I already bought him a football, but somehow it doesn't seem like enough. He's going to be ten, and that's one of the special birthdays."

"Oh, you are right about that. Ten, thirteen, sixteen, those are milestones." He chuckled. "And so's thirty, and forty."

"Tell me about it."

"Feel free to look around, and if you have any questions, just ask. No hard sell here. If the appeal of my offerings isn't immediately apparent, nothing I could say will make any difference."

"Well, isn't *that* refreshing?" she said.

He smiled. "I'm Edwin Nabler, by the way, but I also answer to Mr. Choo. Just like it says on the sign over the window."

"Hello, *Mr. Choo*," she said, smiling broadly and tipping her head. "I love that. It's adorable."

God. Cute *and* adorable.

"I'm Christina Pidgeon. If you think I smell like a dinner roll, it's because I work down the street at Len's Bakery." She giggled. "My husband says work makes me smell better than my Calgon bath beads. Just finished for the day and was heading home, when I passed your store and just couldn't stop myself from coming in."

"Please. Look around."

And so she did. Before long, she had discovered the same packaged set that Wendell Comstock had admired.

"I love this. How much is it?"

"I'm afraid that one is spoken for. I mean, I'm pretty sure it's spoken for. There was someone eyeing that this morning and I'd feel terrible if he came back in before closing and wondered where it had gone."

"Oh, of course. How about this one next to it? Do you think a boy turning ten would like this?"

"A Chesapeake & Ohio steam loco and tender? How could he not? Comes with a tank car and a caboose and a two-bay coal hopper and—"

"A what kind of hopper?"

"A car that transports coal. A transformer and all the track you need to get started. It's one of the finest sets in the store."

Christina picked up the box in both hands and as she admired it, her cheeks slightly flushed. "Oh my," she said.

"Are you okay?"

"No, I'm fine, I just felt a little something wash over me, there."

"Maybe you've got the bug," he said.

"The bug?"

He grinned. "The train bug. Once the hobby gets hold of you, it's hard to shake."

"Well, I guess I've caught it, because . . . I'm taking this. Ring this up."

That was exactly what Edwin did. He held the door open for Christina as she departed, and then, not seeing anyone else on the sidewalk who looked like an immediate prospect, he returned to his project in the back.

This mountain was going to go over an existing track. There would be a tunnel, and portals at each end. But the mountain had to be strong. He didn't want the whole thing crashing down when a gleaming passenger train was running through it. And it had to support everything that would go on it. The rocks and trees and weeds and grass.

Edwin looked into the bin he kept on a worktable a couple of steps away from the layout. It contained various odds and ends that would be incorporated into the structure.

"Yes, let's start with this," he said, reaching in and pulling out an off-white stick with rounded ends, like a longer, thicker turkey bone.

Close at hand were an electric drill, a set of bits, and a box of screws. Edwin found everything he needed.

"Nothing beats a good, solid femur," Edwin said under his breath.

This time, instead of whistling, he sang. "Heigh ho, heigh ho, it's off to work we go . . ."

But he drowned himself out as he began to drill holes through bone.

THIRTEEN

It was never news Harry wanted to deliver, but he couldn't recall dreading it more than today.

Gloria Tanner, wife of the late Angus, was out the front door of her house before he was out of his car. Maybe she'd been sitting by the window night and day, waiting for the authorities to arrive with news about her missing husband. Or maybe something Bill Tracy had said at the Lucknow Diner had made it all the way to the Tanner household. Harry hoped it wasn't the latter. He didn't want the bad news to come from somebody else. Gloria Tanner deserved to hear it from him.

She must have known from the expression on his face that he didn't have anything good to report. As he opened his door wide, she began to crumple in slow motion, her legs weakening, and then her knees were on the lawn, her calves tucked under them, her right arm out to keep her from completely going down.

Harry got out of the car fast and was on his knees next to her, a hand around her shoulder, keeping her upright.

"Mrs. Tanner, why don't we get you inside."

"You've found him, haven't you?"

"Are your children home?" he asked. The Tanners had two grown kids. A son named Ivan, twenty-five, who worked the counter at a self-serve Sunoco station, and a daughter, Patrice, thirty-one, who worked for the town's tax department.

"No," Gloria whispered. "They both came by this morning."

"Let's go inside and call them. Get them back here."

Harry knew he couldn't wait for the children to arrive to break the news, but he wanted to know they were on the way. He didn't want Gloria Tanner to be alone when he departed.

"It's bad, isn't it?" she said as Harry helped her to her feet.

"Yes," he said. "Let's go in and put on some coffee. I know I could use a cup."

He walked her back into the house and guided her to the kitchen. She pointed to the coffee maker. The carafe was already full, the red light on.

"I must have had some kind of sixth sense," she said, sitting down. "I just made that ten minutes ago."

"What's your daughter's number?"

She told him and he made the call on his cell. He asked Patrice if she could come to her parents' house, and if she could pick up her brother on the way. Patrice didn't have to ask why. She said, simply, "On my way."

Harry poured himself a cup, sat down across the table from Gloria. Her hands were flat on the table, trembling. Harry moved them together and placed his on top.

"We found Angus very early this morning," he said. "South of town, on Miller's Road."

She seemed not to comprehend. "But he didn't take his car with him."

"He wasn't in a car, although we haven't ruled out that one might have hit him. He was off to the side of the road." He was going to say *in the ditch* but pulled back the words. They sounded too brutal.

"A hit-and-run?" she asked.

"We're in the early stages of the investigation," he said. There were things she would have to know eventually, details that would become painfully clear when her husband's remains were delivered to the funeral parlor. But did she need to know now that many of her husband's bones had been surgically removed from his body? No, that could wait.

"I know I asked you these kinds of questions when your husband first disappeared, but I need to ask them again. Did Angus have any enemies? Did he know anyone who might want to cause him harm?"

She shook her head. "He's a good man. He's in the Rotary Club, he raises money for the cancer drive. Everyone likes him."

It might be some time before she could bring herself to speak of him in the past tense, Harry thought.

"Where is he?" she asked. "I have to see him."

"Not yet," Harry said. "He's with the coroner. There has to be a full autopsy. When that's done, he'll be released to the funeral home of your choice."

"Do I . . . do I have to identify him?"

"There's a tattoo that matches the photos you showed us. When a further identification is needed, I'll let you know and we'll find a way to go about that."

Maybe one of her kids, he thought. But no member of the Tanner family should have to view what was left of Angus.

"Why are you asking about enemies?" Gloria asked. "Did someone deliberately do this to Angus? It wasn't an accident? Did someone kill him?"

If only it was just that, Harry thought.

"We are treating this as a suspicious death."

Suspicious, Harry thought. If that wasn't the understatement of the year.

HARRY STOPPED IN at the Hillmans', too, figuring once they knew Angus Tanner had been found, Walter might be next. He said they were still looking for Walter, and that there was, so far, nothing to link the two disappearances.

Then he went to the station and asked Mary Walton, who worked the front desk and handled various communications details, to come into the office so they could hammer out a press release on Angus Tanner. Mary was pushing sixty but could easily pass for seventy. Thin and wiry, she'd lost, two years apart, one lung and then a breast to cancer and kept on beating the odds, coming back after both operations and explaining that she was too mean to kill. Tough, without a doubt, but Mary was a sweetheart under her weathered exterior.

Harry told her what they could and couldn't say, and Mary went back to her computer and had something printed out for his approval in fifteen minutes.

"Press is gonna want a quote from you, so I made up a couple," she said.

Harry had a read of them. "Sounds like something I'd say. Let 'er rip."

"And this won't be enough. TV types are gonna want you in person, looking all chief-like."

Harry didn't enjoy going before the cameras but knew it was likely inevitable. "You can set it up for later today." He told Mary to fax the release to the usual list of media suspects while he headed off to the Lucknow Public Library.

He was relieved to have been able to put off, at least for now, telling Tanner's widow about the deboning of her husband's body, but he couldn't get the word out of his head. Was *deboning* the most accurate, the most *clinical*, way to describe what had been done to the man? Was there no more dignified description than what one would do to a brook trout or a chicken breast?

Maybe he'd find the answer at the library.

He was pretty much a stranger to the building, not being much of a reader himself, but Janice and their son, Dylan, were regulars. On an almost weekly basis, they were here to borrow reading materials or attend special programs. Dylan, unlike his father, went through books the way Harry went through bad coffee, primarily paperback novels based on characters from the *Star Wars* universe. Chewbacca was his favorite.

The librarian helped Harry find several medical reference books, and when she showed some curiosity about what he might be researching, he simply smiled and thanked her for her help.

He thought if he knew *what*, exactly, had been done to Angus Tanner, he might have a lead on *who* could have done it. Was there a murderous surgeon out there? A homicidal butcher?

He learned of a procedure called an osteotomy, but that involved cutting bone just enough to realign joints. It could be performed on jaws or knees or shoulders or spines or any number of other places on the human body. This struck Harry as more of a *trimming*, not a deboning. And then there was a carpectomy, the removal of carpal bone, designed to keep small, delicate bones in the wrist from rubbing up against one another and causing pain. Again, this did not involve slicing open a limb and removing a length of bone that ran from the ankle to the knee or the elbow to the shoulder.

As best as Harry could tell, the medical community wasn't spending a lot of time relieving individuals of their skeletal structure. It struck Harry that he'd have to come up with his own term to describe what had been done to Angus Tanner:

Sick.

What kind of sick, twisted bastard did that to another human being? And for what possible reason? This was new territory to Harry. Oh, he'd dealt with a handful of homicides in Lucknow over the years, but they were never what you'd called whodunits. No need to bring in Columbo. One drunk dickhead stabs another drunk dickhead at a tailgate party in front of twenty witnesses. There was that time a kid in a Chevy pickup cut off a guy in a souped-up 1970 Dodge Challenger. The guy in the Challenger then rammed the tail end of the pickup, running it into the ditch. Then he grabbed a gun from the glove box, got out, and shot the kid in the neck, killing him. When he got back to the Dodge, intending to flee, it wouldn't start, so he called Triple A for a jump.

You couldn't make this shit up.

But this Tanner case, this was different.

Harry made some discreet calls, to the state police, to the FBI, asking if they'd seen anything like this before. There was one agent at the bureau, Melissa Cairns, who said something about it rang a bell, a case out in Des Moines, maybe another down in Florida somewhere, and she'd love to help out, she really would, but ever since the eleventh of September, the bureau's focus had been on terrorism, and anyone with something less outlandish than a jet flying into a skyscraper would have to take number. But if she had a chance, she would look into it for him.

So, at least for now, Harry was pretty much on his own.

"Whatcha lookin' at?"

Harry had been sitting at one of the library's long tables, closing the last of the medical texts he'd been poring over, when he sensed someone standing behind him.

He knew that voice. Even before turning around in his chair, he said, "What can I do for you, Rachel?"

"Those are medical reference books," said Rachel Bosma.

"I'm thinking of switching fields," Harry said, turning around and getting to his feet. He bundled up the books under his arm. "Gonna lose the badge and start carrying around a six-pack of tongue depressors."

"You're funny," she said. "You should be writing for *Seinfeld*."

"What can I do for you, Rachel?"

Rachel was the top reporter for the *Lucknow Leader*, although, given the size of the town and the paper's circulation, that also meant she was the only reporter for the *Lucknow Leader*. They had a couple of other staffers who put together the births and deaths and wedding announcements and Little League scores, but when it came to writing about actual news, Rachel had that job pretty much to herself. Lucknow wasn't even large enough to have a daily paper. The *Leader* came out Monday, Wednesday, and Friday. Anyone who wanted a decent weekend read with plenty of sections went to the local smoke shop or convenience store and picked up a *Boston Globe* or *New York Times* or the *Burlington Free Press*. Where Rachel had it over them was, none of those papers cared what happened in Lucknow.

Rachel was in her mid-thirties, with two kids in elementary school and a husband who taught high school chemistry, and if she'd ever entertained thoughts of making it to the big leagues, she had abandoned them long ago. Harry didn't want to talk to her right now, but he liked her. She was tireless in her efforts to keep the good citizens of Lucknow up to speed on what was going on, and whatever the editor was paying her, it wasn't enough as far as Harry was concerned.

"I got the fax on Angus Tanner," she said. "Anything you'd like to add?"

"Nope."

"It was a little light on detail."

The phrase *bare bones* popped into Harry's head and he suppressed a grimace. "When we know more, you'll be the first person I call."

"Come on. Guy's been missing for weeks, and you put out something that's a basic hit-and-run story. What was he doing? Wandering Miller's Road all this time? Where's he been? What's he been up to? And was he hit by a car or dumped there or what? Is it officially a homicide? And I'm hearing stuff I can't go with until you confirm it, like his body was like rubber or something and that he was naked as the day he was born."

Harry had kept back the details for good reason. He didn't want to start a panic in Lucknow. If word got out that there was some nut on the loose who had a thing for removing bones, no one would answer their door without a gun in their hands. Vigilante groups would form. Nutcases who shouldn't be allowed anything deadlier than a peashooter would be carrying in public, guns slung over their shoulders and hanging from their belts, lining up for coffee at Dunkin' Donuts. Also, when they did bring someone in for questioning—and Harry prayed that would be sooner rather than later—they didn't want to poison the well. Fake confessions could be pretty convincing if the whole story was out there.

"What were you looking up, anyway?" she asked as Harry walked over to the counter, returned the books, and gave the librarian a nod of thanks.

"Maybe I've got hemorrhoids," he said. "I'm dealing with a real pain in the ass right now."

"Cut the bullshit, Harry. The fuck is going on? And what about Hillman? You still haven't found him."

"For all I know, Walter Hillman left town. There's no evidence of foul play."

Rachel had been whispering up to now, but her voice was growing in volume. "Except that he walked away from his Business Depot job without telling a soul, there's been no action on his credit cards, and his car's still parked at his place. Just like with Tanner."

The woman behind the counter shot her a look.

"Let's do this outside," Harry said, taking her by the arm and getting a nasty look in return.

Once they were clear of the building, and Rachel had shaken off Harry's grip, she said, "Do you even have a possible make and model on the car that hit Tanner? If a car even *hit* Tanner, because you've never said one way or another. You know I've talked to everyone who lives along there, probably the same people you did, and none of them heard anything like a car hitting somebody. No screeching brakes, nothing like that. The one who called it in was driving the pickup?" She dug a notepad from her pocket and flipped through the pages. "Tracy. Yeah. I know about him. He told me what he saw."

She paused to catch her breath. Harry said slowly, "You done?"

"No."

"Are you done for a *second* or two?"

"Okay."

"What I like about you is that you're a professional. You don't print rumors, you don't print stuff you can't substantiate, you don't go with sources unless they're reliable, and I am here to tell you, you can't put any stock in what Tracy told you. It was the middle of the night, he was tired, working two jobs, probably never seen a body in that state before, and is not what I'd call an experienced observer."

"I bet he's smart enough to know when someone's naked."

"Would you like to go ahead and print that? That you have new information, that Angus Tanner, fifty-two, married and a father of two, was naked. Just that. Would that answer a burning question, or prompt another dozen that you don't have the answer to? What will you do when Mrs. Tanner calls and asks what that's supposed to mean? Because she will. If you were her, wouldn't you call?"

"Christ, I'm not going to write a story that says nothing more than that the deceased had no clothes on. Give me some credit. And even if I did, and she called, I'd tell her to talk to *you*, and ask *you* what it was supposed to mean, and to give me a call back when she got a straightforward answer."

"Let me be as straightforward with you now as I can," Harry said, then added, "Off the record?"

Rachel considered the request. "Okay."

"There are . . . aspects to this investigation that make it slightly more complicated. I can't get into what those are yet. Releasing snippets of information's going to raise more questions I can't answer. So—"

Rachel was rolling her eyes. "Come on, Chief, give me a break here. At least you can tell me whether—"

The Nokia in Harry's jacket began to ring. Harry grimaced, brought out the phone, and put it to his ear.

"Yeah."

"It's Mary."

Harry turned his back to a scowling Rachel and walked three steps away. "What's up?"

"Dell Peterson found his goat. Thinks you're gonna want to have a look."

FOURTEEN

*H*appy birthday, dear Auden . . . happy birthday to you!"
Once they were finished singing, Christina and Darryl Pidgeon clapped their hands together in celebration as they sat around the kitchen table and watched their son, Auden, blow out the ten candles atop his birthday cake.

"Did you make a wish?" Christina asked.

"I didn't have to," said Auden cheerily. "I already got something better than I was asking for."

That, of course, would be the Chesapeake & Ohio freight train made up of a steam locomotive and several cars, which was already running nonstop on a large oval of track on the dining room table. The relentless din of metal spinning on metal, as the cars made loop after loop, reverberated through the table's wooden surface, making it even louder, but Darryl had argued that the engine needed to be broken in, and that having it run continuously for an hour or so would have the effect of fine-tuning the toy's mechanism.

Christina had chosen well. When her husband saw what she'd brought home from Choo-Choo's Trains, he argued they should open it up immediately, set it up, see if it worked, rather than wait two more days until Auden's actual birthday. "You know, to find out whether it's defective, in case we need to return it."

"Maybe I should have bought this for you," Christina said. "Boys and their toys. They never grow out of them, do they?"

So they waited until late afternoon Friday. Darryl left work early, and when Auden came through the door, tossing his backpack onto the bench in the front hall, his parents were standing there below a HAPPY BIRTHDAY banner they'd strung across the archway into the living room. And, still in its packaging, sitting upright, was the Chesapeake & Ohio train set.

Auden and his father set it up right then and there.

"Now we can't leave it here," Darryl said. "But I can get a four-by-eight sheet of plywood, or maybe an old door or something, set it up on some sawhorses, and put it down in the basement. How does that sound?"

Well, that sounded just fine to Auden. But that would mean a trip to the lumber store, and probably the better part of a weekend for his dad to get the set up and running, so for now, at least, he could have fun with his new gift right there.

"We've done this all backwards," Darryl said as his wife cut thin slices of cake for each of them and placed them on Happy Birthday paper plates. "I haven't even got the hot dogs on the barbecue yet."

"I don't think it matters what order we eat it all in," said Christina. "Eat a little bit of cake, and then a little later we'll have dinner."

Auden shoveled the chocolate cake frosted with white icing into his mouth in record time, then bolted from the table to check on his train.

"He loves it," Darryl said. "Good choice."

"I knew he would," Christina said.

Auden, back in the dining room, had his hand on the throttle of the transformer, slowly scaling back the train's speed until it came to a stop. Even at a standstill, it gave off a low-level hum, the electric smell of ozone hanging in the air.

A train set had never been on Auden's wish list. He'd been hoping for a football or a new catcher's mitt or a more up-to-date video game system. Every few months there was a better one with greater speed and more amazing graphics and infinitely more *bits*, whatever those were. But the moment he put his hands on this Chesapeake & Ohio steam engine, he realized that he cared little for the latest adventures of Mario or Zelda or Sonic. This was what he'd always wanted, even if he hadn't known it.

Before the singing of "Happy Birthday" and the blowing out of candles, while holding the engine in his hand as his father had put the lengths of track together, he could sense a . . . a what? It reminded Auden of putting his hand on the fabric covering of a speaker when the stereo's volume was cranked up, except in this case there was no sound. Only a slight trembling. It went up Auden's fingers and into his hands and traveled all the way to his elbow before ebbing.

He almost didn't want to have to let go of it to set it on the track. Before doing so, he'd looked deeply into the working headlight, putting his eye right up to it, as though he were peering into a telescope. He expected it to light up once it sat on the rails and the throttle was turned up, but was surprised to see a slight glimmer there already, almost as though the engine were looking back at him, winking.

What Auden needed now was a proper depot. A destination for his train. Where it could stop, pick up and unload cargo. Maybe an engine house, too, and a water tower.

His father, at the far end of the kitchen and about to step out onto the deck to fire up the barbecue, called out loud enough to be heard through the entire house, "How many hot dogs you want, kiddo?"

Auden, transfixed by his splendid gift, seemed not to hear his father.

"Auden!"

The boy blinked, as though awakened from a trance-like state, and shouted his reply: "Two!"

He gave the throttle a nudge, wanting to start the train at a crawl, the way it would begin moving in the real world.

The locomotive made a clicking sound, but failed to move.

Outside, his father opened the lid of the barbecue with his left hand, and clicked the wand lighter he held firmly in his right. A small flame appeared at the end.

Gripping the engine, Auden moved the train back and forth an inch, in case the electrical connection between the wheels and the track had momentarily been lost. He turned the throttle again. The train moved half an inch, and stopped.

There were four dials on the barbecue panel, one for each burner that sat below the grills. Darryl gave the one on the far left a quarter turn. There was a hissing sound of escaping propane. Darryl pointed the lit end of the wand down between the grills.

"What's your problem?" Auden said aloud to the train. He turned the throttle back and forth several times, trying to get the freight train to move. Each time it jerked slightly, but refused to maintain any forward motion.

The wand flame flickered and died. The burner failed to erupt in blue flame. "Damn it," Darryl said under his breath. He clicked it again as propane continued to hiss from the jets of the first burner. The wand did not light. He clicked again. And again. "This fucking thing," he said. The problem, it seemed, was not so much the barbecue itself as this useless lighter.

Auden turned the throttle as far as it would go. The transformer hummed, but the engine stubbornly refused to move. Leaving the throttle set to max, he put his hand on the engine and once again moved it back and forth, hoping that would somehow snap it back into action.

It did.

The train suddenly shot forward, like a stone from a slingshot, so quickly in fact that, as it reached the first turn only a couple of feet away, the Chesapeake & Ohio loco left the tracks and was airborne, flying off the end of the table, plummeting to the floor with the various freight cars trailing after it. As spectacular a railway disaster as the Pidgeon family's dining room had ever been witness to.

And outside, Auden's dad finally got the wand to light.

"Yes!" he said as the tiny flame emerged and ignited the gas that had been flowing from the burner and now filled not only the entire barbecue cavity but found its way back to a small leak in the valve atop the propane tank sitting underneath.

Kaboom.

The sliding glass doors to the kitchen shattered. Christina screamed and raised her arms defensively as double-paned shards flew past her. Auden, on his knees, assessing the damage to his brand-new train set, whirled around at the sound of the explosion and his mother's anguished cries.

Right up until the sun was setting, members of the Lucknow Fire Department were finding scraps of Auden's father more than a hundred yards away.

FIFTEEN

Edwin was gazing out the window of his shop when he saw Gavin walk past. Not so much walking, Edwin thought, as shuffling with no destination in mind.

He stepped out onto the sidewalk and went after Gavin. Moving at a regular gait, he caught up quickly, came up alongside him, and said, "Hey, how you doing today?"

Gavin glanced his way and said, "Oh, hey, how's it going, Mr. Choo?"

"Not bad, not bad. You?"

Gavin shrugged as he plodded along. "Taking it one day at a time. Getting my steps in. They say you should do a few thousand every day. You know they got those whaddya call 'em, pedometers, you can put them on your wrist, tell you how far you gone." He grinned. "I don't have one of those. When you're just walking around all day, you kinda don't need one. You know you're gonna get the steps in."

"Sorry I didn't bring you a coffee this morning," Edwin said. "You must forgive me. I was dealing with a few things."

"Oh no, don't feel bad about that. It's not like I'm sitting there thinking, *Where's Mr. Choo with my goddamn coffee?* That was a kindness you did me the other day, but you don't have to make it a regular occurrence."

"You mind if we take a seat? I just want to keep an eye on the shop in case anyone comes by."

"Oh yeah, sure."

There was a nearby bench and they took it. Gavin, in a pair of stained jeans and a threadbare pea coat that was probably once blue but now a mottled gray, peered curiously at Edwin from below the visor of his ball cap. His hair hung over his ears and touched the back of his collar.

"How long have you been out of work now, if you don't mind my asking?" Edwin said.

"Well, it's been a while. The days kind of all run in together. But I'll tell ya"—and he grinned—"I miss the weekends."

Edwin smiled. "I think I understand. What are you doing for a roof over your head?"

"I still got my F-150. Don't run it much unless I can scrape together a few funds to put half a tank in. But it's got a comfy front seat, and that does me most nights. If it's really hot and humid and doesn't cool down after the sun sets, there's plenty of benches to choose from here in Lucknow." He smiled. "The world is my oyster."

Edwin eyed the man sympathetically. "Not for a moment am I suggesting my situation is anything like yours, but you know, I live out of the back of my shop."

"Oh yeah."

"No home to go to every night, no little lady waiting for me. Have a hot plate to make my meals, a mini-fridge, a small bathroom where I can clean up, and a mattress. It's all I really need."

"Sounds like you've got a good setup," Gavin said, looking almost envious.

"Exactly. And I'm content. To each according to his needs."

"Who said that?"

"I believe I just did."

"No, no," said Gavin. "Originally."

"You're thinking of Karl Marx. It formed the basis of his socialist philosophy."

"Geez Louise don't say that word too loud. The townsfolk'll string you up. *Socialism*'s a dirty word."

"I think one can look at it in a broader context," Edwin said. "That, if we are content, we don't need to strive for more and more."

"I guess."

"Have you been looking for work?"

"Well, if the right thing came along, sure. The chief was telling me about some inn up in Stowe that's hiring for the ski season, but I'm not sure that's a good fit for me." He pursed his lips, as though reconsidering. "I wonder if they rent snowmobiles. I'm good with machines."

They were both quiet for a moment, watching others walk past in each direction.

"I would like to propose something," Edwin said. "An opportunity."

"What kind of opportunity?"

"Something I would prefer to discuss at greater length. But something that would put an end to your current situation."

"Oh?"

"Yes. Because, and believe me, I am not one to judge, but the way you are living is really untenable."

"Well, you might be right."

"I need to get back to the shop, but why don't you come by tonight, say around nine. And if you don't mind, please don't mention this to anyone, because then they're all going to want to get in on what I have to offer. Your discretion would be most appreciated. Just rap lightly on the door and I'll let you in. The lights'll be off, but I'll be there."

Gavin pursed his lips, considering the offer. "I s'pose I got nothing to lose."

Edwin smiled. "And can I just say, and I hope you won't take this the wrong way, because it's merely an observation, but you have a very nice head of hair."

"HERE HE WAS on the property the whole time when I was thinking he'd wandered off someplace," said Dell Peterson. "Poor Zeke. Poor, stupid Zeke. He deserved better than this. Gotta be some kind of animal, don't you think? A bear, maybe? I thought you should know about it, maybe warn others around here. More folks than me have cattle. Hendersons up that way got horses, although maybe a bear wouldn't want to tangle with a horse. Lot bigger than a goat. Anyway, hope I didn't bring you out here for nothing."

Dell and Harry were standing at the edge of a creek that ran through the Peterson farm, looking down at what remained of the goat known as Zeke.

"It was good you called," Harry said.

"Had Zeke a long time, since he was a kid. He was more than just a goat. He was a member of the family. Had the run of the house like he was a dog or a cat, he'd just come in, watch us eating dinner, hoping for a snack. I'd never known him to wander off before. Gonna break Donny and Brian's hearts."

"Your boys?" Harry asked.

"Yeah. They loved this dumb goat." Judging from Dell's expression, Harry was thinking he'd loved him, too.

Dell said, "I was thinking if not a bear, a coyote, although a coyote might be small to have taken on Zeke. But could have been a bobcat or a lynx. I know we got them in Vermont. They make themselves scarce, you don't see 'em much, but we got 'em."

Harry was nodding. "We do."

"But whatever it was, doesn't make any sense to me. Taking out most of the bones and leaving the meat."

Harry said nothing.

"You ever see anything like this before?" Dell asked.

Harry thought carefully before answering. "I can't say that I've ever seen anything like this happen to an animal, Dell."

Dell shook his head. "Damnedest thing. You figure an animal, it eats the meat and guts and leaves the bones, not the other way around."

"Yeah," said Harry, kneeling beside Zeke for one more look. He took from his jacket pocket a small camera, focused on the dead animal, fired off a few shots.

"What kind of camera's that?" Dell asked.

"Digital," Harry said. "Take the little chip out, put it in the computer, print out the snaps."

"I'll be damned."

Harry looked off into the distance and stood. "We're not far from the road here."

"Beyond that tree line," Dell said.

Harry said, "Thanks, Dell, I'm just gonna look around a bit."

"Yeah, sure, knock yourself out. If I was you, I'd maybe give the other farms around here a heads-up, you know?"

"Good advice."

He slowly paced the edge of the creek, then steered toward the tree line, looking to see whether anyone or anything had parted the tall grasses along the way. There hadn't been much rain this week, but there'd been a couple of overnight showers, so it was possible there might be some tracks left behind where the grasses gave way to open ground.

Harry stepped gingerly, not wanting to miss, or mar, anything. But as he moved slowly to the trees, he didn't see much that caught his eye. No impressions left by shoes. He did spot a short trail of some kind of animal footprint, and not one he recognized. It was nearly a foot long, and didn't look like a print from a lynx or a bobcat or a bear, either. He took a couple of pictures and continued on.

He worked his way through the line of trees and reached the road, a two-lane stretch of blacktop without a building in sight. Stood there a moment, thinking about what had been done to Angus Tanner, and now Zeke, and wondered what in the hell he might be dealing with here.

He turned, ready to retrace his steps and get into his car, which he'd left by the Peterson house, when something dark but shiny caught his eye. He stopped, bent over, picked up the item, and had a close look at it.

It was a cracked, tinted lens that evidently had become dislodged from a pair of sunglasses.

He was driving back into town, talking on the radio to Mary, when he learned that there had been an explosion over on Barrett Avenue. That was around the corner from Harry's house.

"One fatality," she said. "Darryl Pidgeon."

"Say that last name again?"

"Pidgeon. Like the bird but with a *d* in it."

"Rings a bell. I think Dylan hangs around sometimes with a kid named Pidgeon. Can't remember his first name. Wonder if it could be the same. What happened?"

"Some kind of barbecue thing. Blew up."

"Christ. I'll swing by on my way back in."

There were still emergency vehicles lining the street when Harry turned down Barrett. He parked his car a few houses away and walked up, spotted someone he knew from the Lucknow Fire Department.

"Jess," Harry said, waving the man over. "What happened here?"

Jess filled him in. "Poor bastard got scattered all over the place. Still finding pieces."

"Isn't that kind of over-the-top for a barbecue accident? I mean, I've seen people get burned up pretty bad, but, Christ, blown to pieces?"

Jess shrugged. "Early days yet. Got to do our investigation."

"Anybody else hurt?"

"Wife was in the kitchen, got hit by some glass, got a couple cuts. Paramedics patched her up here on the scene. Lucky thing the boy was in the dining room, far enough away that the glass didn't hit him. He was playing with his birthday present."

"It was a birthday? Were there lots of other kids here?"

"No. Just the kid and his mom and dad. Dad was cooking up dinner."

Harry sighed. "What's the boy's name?"

"Auden."

"Auden," Harry repeated. "Thought I recognized the name Pidgeon. Auden Pidgeon. Hangs out sometimes with our Dylan." Which gave Harry a moment's pause, thinking about what might have happened had Dylan been invited over to be part of the celebration.

"I'll have a word," Harry said, and walked up the drive to the front door, which was already open a few inches as the emergency workers continued to go in and out. No need to knock, so he tentatively went inside and found his way to the kitchen, saw the birthday cake with shards of glass sticking out of the frosting, felt more of them underfoot. There was no glass left in the doors that led to the deck, and all that remained of the barbecue were some scraps of metal bracing.

He heard voices nearby.

In the dining room, he found mother and son sitting in two chairs pulled closely together, their arms around each other, rocking slowly. Focused on the two, he barely glanced at what was on the table. Harry offered a solemn nod to the woman when she noticed he was standing there. She saw the badge pinned to his jacket, eyes narrowing for a moment.

"You're Chief Cook."

"I am."

"Dylan's dad," she said quietly, her face lined with dried tears.

He nodded. "That's right." He went down to one knee to be on a level with Auden. "I'm so sorry about what happened to your father. It's a terrible thing. I can't begin to imagine what you're going through."

Auden turned. His eyes were red and looked as though they had cried a thousand tears. "He was making hot dogs. I should have asked for something else. I should have said pizza. It's all my fault."

"Don't you be thinking that," Harry said, laying a hand on the boy's arm. "Not for a minute. This is going to be a tough time for you and your mom, and you'll need to do everything you can to help her get through it. But I know you can do that. You can be there for her, am I right?"

"I guess," he said, and his mother gave him a squeeze.

Harry noticed the train set atop the dining room table. "That's a nice-looking train you got there. You get that for your birthday?"

The boy looked over to it, as though he'd forgotten it was there, and nodded.

"When the time's right, I know Dylan would get a real kick out of seeing that. Looks like lots of fun."

"It wasn't working right," Auden said. "It sped up all of a sudden and crashed onto the floor."

Christina said comfortingly, "But we put it back on the track, didn't we, Auden, and nothing looks broken."

Auden didn't appear to care one way or another.

"Think it works now?" Harry asked the boy.

Auden shrugged.

"Why don't we see," Harry suggested.

Auden slid slowly off his chair, checked to see that the transformer on the the table was still plugged into the wall outlet, and then gently turned the throttle.

An electric hum emanated from the locomotive, and a second later it began to move. The black engine and tender, and the cars linked to the back of it, made one circuit of the table, and then another, and then kept on going.

"That's pretty cool," Harry said, his palm on the boy's back.

Auden appeared to take no pleasure in the train's flawless operation, and Harry could hardly blame him.

Auden said, with no enthusiasm, "It's working okay now."

SIXTEEN

I'm gonna do it," Wendell Comstock said earlier that afternoon.

He was Edwin Nabler's last customer of the day. He had been thinking it was almost time to switch the neon sign to CLOSED when the bell rang and in walked Wendell.

"That's great," Edwin said, and smiled. "I knew you'd be back. I just had a feeling. There was a woman in here a couple of days ago, and she had her eyes on that set, really wanted to buy it for her boy, but I said it was spoken for. When you've been in this business long enough, you know when someone's hooked."

"Yeah, well, I guess I am," Wendell said.

He found the set on the shelf where he had last seen it, picked up the box, and brought it to the counter.

"Have you thought about accessories?" Edwin asked.

"What would you suggest?"

"First, how much space do you have?"

"I've got a Ping-Pong table in the basement I never use. I'm gonna take the net down, set the train up there."

"I've got a roll of fake grass you might want to put over the table first, make it more realistic."

"Oh, I love that idea. Yeah, gimme one of those."

"And if you have that much space, maybe some buildings? A station? Maybe an industry or two? I have plenty of building kits."

"Load me up. I'm jumping in with both feet."

Edwin started pulling things off the shelves, Wendell saying yes to every one of them. Edwin said, "I bet your wife is going to be surprised when she sees you coming home with this."

Wendell let out a long sigh.

"Oh my," said Edwin. "That sounded ominous. You know, I have an instinct for these things. I believe your wife—what's her name?"

"Nadine."

"*Nadine.* What a lovely name. I believe you're going to be surprised by how much she loves this hobby."

Wendell shook his head skeptically. "I got my doubts about that."

"Let me help you get all this stuff to your car. It's like an early Christmas, isn't it? Except you're your very own Santa."

ONCE EDWIN HAD helped Wendell put everything into the back of his minivan, he returned to the store and turned on the CLOSED sign.

All in all, a successful day. And that wasn't even counting sales in the shop.

The incident over at the Pidgeon household had gone off well. Edwin hadn't needed to be there in person. He just knew. He would get that familiar tingling—not unlike the sensation his customers felt when they picked up his offerings—when an event was under way. He would take a moment, close his eyes, see his efforts come to fruition.

Not that he always had a perfect view. What he thought of as his remote eyes—the headlights on every diesel and steam engine he sent out into the world, or the tiny engineers sitting in the cabs— might not be pointed in the right direction, might not even be in the room where things went down, but he could still gain a strong sense of what was transpiring. This was not some piece of tech, not some miniaturized surveillance device. It was an organic extension of himself. He didn't need a viewing screen. The images were all there, playing in his head.

He looked at the clock on the wall. Still a few hours before Gavin was due to arrive. He would go into the back of the shop and see what he could accomplish in the meantime.

The time passed quickly, as it always did when he threw himself into his work. Reinforcing the hills with more plaster. Adding a pond. Laying more track. The work was never done, and this current project was not only far from finished, but Edwin was running low on some of the raw materials. It was easy enough to get more plaster and nails and screws at the local Home Depot, but the trains didn't hit the shelves with the necessary *resonance* unless they were run through a layout with ingredients more special than those. This was no ordinary testing track.

It was a finishing touch.

When he heard a rapping on the front door, he dropped back down into a Rubbermaid bin part of a rib—one of the last bone fragments from Tanner—that he had been using to reinforce some tunnel portals. He went up front to answer it. The store was in darkness, with but a single light on in the window to illuminate the one train that ran in a simple circle twenty-four hours a day.

It was Gavin. He unlocked the door, opened it quickly, and pulled the man inside.

"I hope I'm on time."

"Punctual!" Edwin said. "I like that. I like that very much." He glanced out at the street. "Did anyone see you?"

Gavin shook his head. "I waited till there was no one around before I knocked."

"Very good, very good, excellent."

"Kinda dark in here."

"Well, the shop *is* closed."

There was still enough light, however, from the street and the window display, for Gavin to see the items that filled the shelves. "Wow, this is some very cool stuff you have here. Really takes me back. There was a kid on my block, his parents were rich, and he had this monster setup in the basement with bridges and tunnels and everything."

"Wait'll you see what I'm working on out back."

"Can't wait, but I gotta ask, and I hope I'm not getting ahead of things here, but I've been wondering all day what kind of opportunity you have in mind for me. I don't know anything about this stuff you sell. I don't think I've got any experience that would be useful to you. I mean, I can fix machines, like I said, like snowmobiles, but the motors in the model trains are a lot smaller than what I'm used to."

"That's not going to be a problem," Edwin assured him. "I want you not for what you know, but for what you are."

Gavin smiled awkwardly. "I'm afraid these days that ain't much. When you get right down to it, I'm a homeless person, Mr. Choo. I'm down on my luck, and five years ago, if you'd told me this is where I'd be, I wouldn't have believed it."

Edwin put a comforting hand on the man's shoulder. "You're just who I'm looking for."

He held open the door to the back of the store and with a wave of his hand directed Gavin to walk in first.

"Holy moly," Gavin said. "I've never seen anything like this."

He stood openmouthed, staring at the display. Edwin could forget how impressive something like this could be to the uninitiated.

"There's a town and a bridge and—oh, that mountain looks amazing. And a river and—how long did it take you to build this?"

"Quicker than you might think. I don't sleep much."

"It would take me years to make something like this." The layout ran along two walls of the back room. Gavin inspected every foot of it, marveling at the details. A factory sign caught his attention and he laughed.

"The Flushing Toilet Company? Oh wait, this one's even better. A hair salon called Curl Up and Dye? I love it."

"Always fun to add a little humor to the scenes," Edwin said.

"How did you—this pond here, under the bridge? Is that like a hard epoxy?"

"Something like that."

"Is it supposed to look polluted?"

"What makes you think that?" Edwin replied as he stepped over to a transformer and powered up the track. He eased the throttle forward and a steam engine trailed by more than a dozen tanker cars began to roll out.

"Well, it's red. The water's *dark* red, like, well . . . You don't see that in the real world unless it's downriver from a chemical plant or something. And this little row of rocks, bordering this garden?"

Chuffchuffchuffchuffchuff went the train as it wound its way through the scenery.

"Yes?"

"They kinda . . . they kinda look like teeth, Mr. Choo."

"They do, don't they. Look what's coming your way."

Gavin gazed down the track at the approaching train. The steam engine's smokestack was furiously pumping out puffs of white vapor. A whistle sounded, followed by a clanging bell. Gavin, no longer focused on the blood-like water and rocks that looked like teeth, was briefly transfixed.

"Those tank cars look just like the ones that pass through town every day," he observed. The train sped past tall grasses that had been planted at the track's edge, and Gavin found himself running the tips of his fingers over them. "The grass is so . . . fine. What's that made of? Is that corn silk or something?"

"Look at the train, Gavin."

Chuffchuffchuffchuffchuff

Gavin, seemingly without realizing it, was twirling his fingers through his hair. "I was asking because it also reminds me of—"

"Look at the train."

Chuffchuffchuffchuffchuff

Gavin grew so mesmerized with the train's passage that he failed to notice when his foot bumped into the cardboard box with the last of the bones in it. A bit of Angus Tanner in there, as well as the still-missing Walter Hillman, one dumb goat, and any number of pets that were the subject of "Have You Seen . . ." leaflets staple-gunned to lampposts around Lucknow.

The steam engine had belched out so much faux-smoke that Gavin was waving his hand in front of his face, trying to keep it out of his eyes and nose. A layer of white mist was filling the room, making it look more like the venue for half a dozen nicotine-addicted poker players.

Gavin began to cough. The smoke was clouding Edwin's vision and working its way up his nose, too, although it didn't bother him in the slightest.

Chuffchuffchuffchuffchuff

As Gavin bowed his head, tucking his face into his elbow as he coughed again, he noticed for the first time the container of bones.

"Jesus, Mr. Choo, what the hell's this? If I didn't know better, I'd say those look like . . ." But Gavin, suddenly unable to breathe, could not finish his sentence.

Edwin did not bother to explain. Gavin was already dropping to the floor.

SEVENTEEN

Harry was wrung out by the time he got home.

He trudged through the door, took his weapon from his belt, and put it on the top shelf of the front hall closet, as was his routine. He walked slowly into the kitchen and grabbed a beer from the fridge, then went out onto the back patio, dropped into a chair, and twisted the cap off the bottle.

He killed off the first beer pretty quickly, went in for a second, and came back out. He'd been sitting there for a good ten minutes, struggling to unwind, hoping to clear his head, when he heard someone moving around in the kitchen. Seconds later, the door opened and Janice came out with a beer of her own, clinked bottles with Harry, took the chair next to his, and, without saying a word, had a drink.

Janice let another few minutes go by before she asked a question she already knew the answer to. "Bad day?"

Harry said, "Where's Dylan?"

"I think he's upstairs."

"Got something I have to tell him."

Janice sat up straight and set the beer on the broad arm of the chair. "What's going on?"

"I'd like him to hear it from me before he hears it from his friends, although it might already be too late. You know his friend Auden?"

"Is Auden in some kind of trouble?"

Harry quickly shook his head. "His dad." He told her.

"Oh my God," Janice said. "You stay. I'll find him." She slipped back into the house, and two minutes later Dylan was walking out onto the patio. "What's going on, Dad?"

"Have a seat."

"Did I do something wrong?"

"What? No. Why would you think you're in trouble?"

The boy went quiet. He needed a moment to work up the nerve. "I lost my skateboard."

"When'd that happen?"

Dylan shrugged. "Couple days ago. Went into Wilson's to buy some Ho Hos and left it leaning up against the front of the store, and when I came back out it was gone. So, like, I didn't lose it, exactly. Somebody swiped it."

Harry sighed. "That's a real shame, pal."

"I'd left it there lots of times before and nobody ever took it. So I'm sorry, and I'll save up money to buy another one."

Harry pulled him closer. "It's okay."

"I'm not in trouble?"

Harry, a hand on each of Dylan's shoulders, said, "Sometimes these things happen."

"I thought if the chief was your dad people wouldn't steal from you."

Harry smiled. "I wish."

"So why did you want to talk to me?"

"Sit."

Dylan sat.

"You know your friend Auden?" Dylan nodded. "Well. there was an accident this afternoon over at his place. Some kind of malfunction with the barbecue. A gas leak or something. It blew up. His dad was a little too close, and, well, it was pretty bad, and Auden's dad was killed."

Dylan's face went blank, as though he didn't quite know what to feel. "Oh," he said.

"Yeah."

"That's really awful."

"Did you ever meet him when you were over there?"

Dylan's head went up and down. "Couple of times. He was okay. Auden said his dad drank a lot. Is that what happened? Was he drunk when he was using the barbecue?"

"I don't know. But I wouldn't go around repeating a story like that because there might not be anything to it. Anyway, Auden's going to need his friends in the days and weeks to come. Pretty hard, losing your dad."

Dylan bit his upper lip. "I worry about that a lot."

"About?"

"About you. Being the chief."

"I'm okay. I'm careful."

Dylan cast an eye at their own barbecue. "We shouldn't use that anymore."

"Tell you what. I'll get it all checked out before we throw any more burgers on the grill. Check the gas connections and everything."

Dylan nodded slowly. "Okay." A pause, and then, "Is there anything else?"

Harry shook his head. "If you want to talk about it later, you know, we can."

The boy nodded and went back into the house as Janice was coming out. She sat. "How'd he take it?"

"I don't know what I was expecting. I thought he might burst into tears or something, but he seemed okay."

"It's a lot to process."

They were both quiet until Harry finally asked, "So, how was *your* day?"

Janice worked in the offices of Lucknow Power and Light, which supplied electricity to the town and the surrounding region. "SSDD," she said, short for *same shit, different day*. "They had the crew out again trying to track down that drain on the system."

"Have you told me about this? When I ask what drain on the system, are you going to give me that you-never-listen look?"

"I'm doing it now," she said, glaring at him.

"So tell me again."

"You know how last year around downtown, we replaced all the old low-pressure sodium lights in the streetlamps with induction bulbs? That use forty percent less energy?"

"If you say so."

"We were able to measure a drop in demand, which saves the town money, but in the last few days we've seen an uptick. Something drawing more power. So the new bulbs may work for a while, then they start sucking up more juice . . . and your eyes are glazing over."

"I'm sorry."

"Tell me what you were sitting out here pondering. I'm guessing it's more than what happened to Dylan's friend's dad."

Harry took a deep breath and let it out slowly.

"I might be in over my head, Jan."

"What are you talking about?"

"This . . . what's been happening. Something's not right."

"No kidding. Someone killed Angus Tanner. That other guy is still missing. I know that's on your mind."

Harry had not told her about what had been done to Tanner's body. There were some things he kept under wraps. Not just from Rachel Bosma, but from everyone. Even those closest to him. Not to protect Janice—she was as tough as they came—but because he didn't want there to be any chance of information getting out before it should.

But he did say this: "It's uglier than people know."

Janice let those words hang in the air a moment. "Okay."

"I've never dealt with something like this."

"You'll figure it out."

He smiled at her. "My biggest fan."

"Just because it's something you haven't faced before doesn't mean you can't handle it."

"Oh," he said, suddenly remembering something. He dug down into his shirt pocket and brought out the single lens from a pair of sunglasses that he had found earlier in the day. "You can use this like an eyepatch until you find the ones you lost."

"How thoughtful," she said as he handed it to her. The lens was dusty, with small flecks of dirt stuck to it. Janice brushed much of it away with her thumb. "Where'd you find this?"

"Doesn't matter."

She had a close look at it, held it up to the light. "Might actually be from the ones I can't find. See here?"

She pointed to the upper left corner of the lens. Written on it was the word "Ray," followed by a hyphen. "It's supposed to say Ray-Ban, but the 'Ban' part got worn off. Mine were like that."

Harry held out his hand, and Janice placed the lens on his palm.

"What? You've got a weird expression on your face."

"Any idea where or when you lost them?"

"As best I can remember, it was when I went in to pay for gas. Filled up, went inside, probably took them off when I was doing the credit-card-and-keypad thing, got back in the car, drove off, realized I didn't have them. I went back, but they weren't there and the cashier said he hadn't seen them." Again, she asked, "What?"

"Nothing," Harry said. "Nothing."

EIGHTEEN

G avin heard a buzzing.

At first he thought he was having a dream about a bumble-bee. No, not just one. Given how loud it was, it had to be a swarm of bumblebees. Hovering around his head. Wait, now some of them were crawling around in his hair. He wanted to swat them away, wave his arms around wildly to try to disperse them, but when he tried to do that, he found that his arms would not work, as if pinned to his side.

"Get off me! Get off me!"

He opened his eyes, blinked several times as they became accustomed to the bright light hanging over him. The buzzing ceased.

"You're awake," said Edwin, standing before him, something black and shiny in his hand.

Gavin kept blinking, struggling to focus. The world around him was blurry, as though he were looking at it through a dirty window.

"What's going on?" he asked sleepily.

"You nodded off," Edwin said. "You were under a little longer than I expected."

"What did you . . . I can't . . . I can't move my arms. Mr. Choo . . . Edwin, what's going on?"

Gavin looked down, saw that he was secured to a wooden chair by countless loops of duct tape. His arms, hanging straight down, were tight to his body, and his calves were held to the chair legs with more tape.

His vision began to clear, allowing him to make out what was in Edwin's hand. Electric hair clippers, like a barber would use.

"You're scaring me," Gavin said. "Come on, let me go. Get this goddamn tape off me."

Edwin smiled, put the clippers on a nearby workbench, pulled over a second wooden chair, and sat in front of Gavin.

"I take no pleasure in this," he said. "You seem like a nice enough fellow, Gavin. Down on your luck but a decent guy, in my estimation. I don't usually take time to chat in circumstances such as this, but it's so rare that I talk about my work. It's not as if I'm in an office somewhere and can shoot the shit for a while with someone at the water cooler. It's simply not the nature of my vocation, and if there's a downside to what I do, I guess it would have to be that."

A tear was running down Gavin's cheek. "Please. Just . . . I just want to go home."

"Home? What home?" Edwin chuckled. "Your truck? A park bench? What is this home you speak of?"

"Whatever it is . . . whatever it was you wanted me for, I'm not interested."

"Gavin, I really do need you. I hope you'll give me a chance to make my case."

Gavin said nothing.

Edwin sighed. "Here I am blathering on when there's work to be done." He stood, flipped a switch on the hair trimmer, and approached.

"Hey! Don't!" Gavin writhed about in the chair, struggling against the tape.

"Stop jumping about or you're going to hurt yourself," Edwin said. He came around behind Gavin, brought the cutting edge of the trimmer to the base of his neck, and cut a path upward. "You really do have excellent hair. It was one of the first things I noticed about you."

"You some kind of fucking serial killer pervert?" Gavin asked, spitting the words out.

Edwin clicked off the shears and came around to face Gavin, holding a long black lock of hair in his hand. "I take great offense at that, Gavin. Certainly the pervert part. My interests are much nobler." He draped the hair on the workbench. "When this has been dyed and cut into the proper lengths, it will look very realistic. Have a look."

He pointed to the grasses on a hillside on the railway. "See what I mean? Now sit still. The less fuss you make, the faster this will go."

He powered up the shears again and went back to it, cutting one path after another across Gavin's scalp, the man trembling throughout.

"You're a sick fuck, that's what you are," Gavin said.

Edwin faced him, smiled, and took a moment to reflect. "What I am, Gavin, is . . . I am happenstance."

"Happen what?"

"I suppose, more accurately, I am the opposite of happenstance."

"You're a fucking loon, that's what you are. In your stupid engineer hat and stupid vest with railroad badges all over it. A certifiable lunatic."

Edwin ignored the outburst. "You know how people will say something happened just by chance? Someone was in the wrong place at the wrong time. They were looking one way when they should have looked the other, and *wham*, the bus hit them. A hunter walking through the woods trips on a tree root and shoots his buddy in the head. Someone's walking along a slippery sidewalk and a sheet of ice falls off a building and slices their head off. What were the odds? What dumb luck?"

"Please . . ."

"And the truth is, in a lot of cases, that *is* what happens. Dumb luck. Fate. Their number was up. But it doesn't happen that way often enough. Bad luck sometimes needs a helping hand. It needs to be *enabled*. Hold still. Just a little more off the top."

He ran the shears over Gavin's head, more lengths of hair landing on the floor. He turned the shears off, stood back, and admired his handiwork.

"If I had a mirror I would hold it up for you," Edwin said, "but it's as neat a job as I've ever done, which is odd, considering that the others were in a more compliant condition at the time. It doesn't matter how long you've been at something. You can always improve."

"Are you going to kill me?" Gavin asked.

Without hesitation, Edwin nodded. "Yes. Yes, I am."

"If you let me go, I won't tell anyone. Nobody, I swear."

"But Gavin, I need you. You're material. It's a two-step process, you see, and it's ongoing. The layout there loses its potency without new material."

"What were those bones? In that bin?"

Edwin chortled. "Those are bones. In a bin." He frowned. "And, as you may have noticed before you nodded off, not nearly enough. There's more work to do. And I would imagine your bones are every bit as good as your hair."

"What are you talking about? What two-step process?"

Edwin thought about the question. "The first step in the process is to build my creation here. Sourcing the right materials. Like yourself, and others, or animals, or personal items I have liberated from people and worked into the project. The bones are like framing. The blood for coloring. The hair for grasses. A lost comb is fashioned into a miniature rake. A pen is an electric pole. That way, it all becomes very *organic*. You see what I'm saying?"

Gavin, trying to buy some time, but also, despite overwhelming fear, undeniably curious, asked, "Like a living thing?"

Edwin laughed. "Well, not quite. But made up of what *was* living, and what was *attached* to the living. That's what gives it its essence, and when it has that, then I can run the trains through it, so that *they* can absorb that essence. It's all very technical. I hope I'm not boring you."

"No, go on. Tell me more. I'm . . . I'm interested."

Edwin smiled, understanding that Gavin was trying to buy time. But he took pleasure in explaining what he did. "Quality control has always been something of an issue. It can be difficult to measure how much each train has absorbed, how much happenstance it carries, so you send it off into a household and you don't know what you're going to get. Will Mom get a simple paper cut, or will she fall down the stairs and break her neck? Will a toddler get his finger caught in a drawer or end up at the bottom of the pool? But something will happen, and that's what matters."

Edwin dropped into his chair again and crossed his legs. "I've been at this a long time. Have my own area of specialty. There are lots of us out there, working in the sliver. Finding our own ways to insinuate ourselves into people's lives." He smiled, waved an arm at his handiwork. "I chose this. It works for me. It meets . . . a creative need. Not that there aren't other ways to go about it. And I'll admit, I'm a bit tired. You might be inclined to think that someone—*something*—such as myself lives forever. That those of my ilk never die. That we have always been and always will be. Well, that's simply not true, my friend. I wouldn't mind turning over the business to someone else one day, but you need the right candidate. They wouldn't have to do it with trains. Art, perhaps. A lovely painting you could hang on your wall that made the magic happen."

Edwin ran his hand over his face wearily. "I've made some mistakes lately. Getting older. I was sloppy with Mr. Tanner. Shouldn't have left him at the side of the road where what was left of him could be found. I did better with Mr. Hillman. He's over there, by the way."

Edwin pointed to an outcropping of rock—about the size of a melon—that popped out of a hillside. It had, if this was possible, a kind of *profile* to it.

"Oh Jesus," said Gavin.

Edwin leaned in close so he was almost nose to nose with Gavin. "I don't expect this to give you a lot of comfort at a time like this, but you should know that you are part of something important. Something bigger than yourself. Something almost . . . cosmic. Am I getting through to you at all?"

"I—I could be your assistant. I could help you. Get what you needed. I could—I could work on the trains. I'm good at construction. Or—or I could be the one to take over for you. So you could retire. What about that?"

"As tempting an offer as that is, I'm afraid I'm going to have to say no. You don't have what it takes. One day, the right person will come along, but it's not you. I'm glad we had this chance to chat, but I must finish up."

The lights flickered briefly.

Edwin looked at Gavin apologetically. "Still a few glitches tapping into the town's network. Don't want an electric bill that attracts too much attention, do we?"

The lights stopped their flickering, then gave up altogether, plunging the room into complete darkness. A red-tinted, battery-powered emergency light tucked up into the corner of the room came on, casting a dim, blood-like glow for five seconds before power was restored and the lights came back on.

But during those five seconds, how Edwin Nabler presented himself to Gavin was altered. He was no longer that pixieish man in his silly railroad vest, but something else altogether. Silhouetted against the red light, he was a different shape. Taller, but round-shouldered. A face that seemed to have grown a snout, and were those . . . whiskers?

The lights flashed back on.

Edwin appeared just as he had before. But there was *one* thing different about him this time. He no longer had hair clippers in his hand. He was wielding something shiny. And sharp.

Gavin began to scream.

NINETEEN

That Saturday was the annual sidewalk sale.

This was the brainchild of the local business improvement association. Lucknow's main street was closed to traffic, half a dozen food trucks were allowed to set up, there were face-painters and jugglers and mimes for the kids, and last but not least, shop owners were encouraged to set up their wares on tables out front of their establishments.

By noon, the main street was thronged with adults and children. Some were out simply for something to do, to enjoy the fall air, to randomly run into friends and neighbors. And there were others engaged in doing what the town's boosters hoped they would be: they were shopping.

Featherstone's Men's Wear and the ladies' fashion shop, Yolanda's, had wheeled out racks of clothing. Mostly discounted stuff, outfits they hadn't been able to unload all year that were no longer in vogue, but a deal was a deal. Same with Smitty's Shoes, which was trying to unload sandals with winter only a couple of months away. The Different Drummer Bookstore had two tables stacked with remaindered editions. Len's Bakery wasn't offering anything different from what they usually had indoors behind glass, but having muffins and scones and cupcakes and cookies out on the sidewalk proved to be a brilliant marketing strategy.

At the Lucknow Diner, it was business as usual. But the lack of a table out front had done nothing to hurt their business. The place was packed, even busier than on a usual weekday morning. Inside, Jenny and her staff were run off their feet, showing people to booths, taking orders, wiping down tables the moment customers left so they could quickly seat people waiting in line, refilling mugs of their famous coffee. In the kitchen, the two cooks were furiously cracking eggs, frying bacon, and flipping pancakes.

Harry had been working the street since just after ten. Not only did he feel a need to be seen, he was making himself available to anyone who knew something that would be helpful to his investigation but had been keeping it to themselves. The odds were long, but you never knew.

As he passed the diner, he glanced at the bench out front where he would, most mornings, find Gavin. Today the space was occupied by two kids around seven years old who'd had their faces painted. Cheeks turned green, noses red, oversized black eyebrows. They were each working on a stick of cotton candy. Gavin had either surrendered his spot, Harry figured, or wanted to avoid the downtown altogether on a busy morning like this.

He went into the diner, bought a to-go coffee in a paper cup, and resumed strolling the main street, nodding and smiling as people said hello.

Harry had no interest in shopping, even with Christmas looming on the horizon. Well, hardly looming. It was more than two months away. He didn't usually start thinking about what to get Janice until around the twentieth of December. But just the same, he checked out what everyone was offering, paid his respects to the various merchants.

There was a small crowd in front of that new store.

What was it Gavin had said the owner's name was? Edwin or Edgar. Something like that. And he was out front of the store, looking as ridiculous as he had when Harry'd met him briefly that other morning, wearing his engineer's cap and vest adorned with various railway patches. Harry chided himself for his harsh judgment. Mr. Choo was in uniform. This was what he wore to draw attention to what he was selling, no different than Gary Featherstone down at the menswear store looking smart in a three-piece suit, or Len at the bakery in his hairnet and apron.

Harry staked out a spot out front of the store, a few feet into the street, folded his arms across his chest, and watched this Mr. Choo do his pitch in front of about ten kids, mostly boys, and several adults. On a broad table, he had set up two loops of track, one within the other, and was running two trains in opposite directions.

" . . . and believe me, it's not just the kids who love them!" Mr. Choo said, which sparked some laughs among the adults. One woman whispered into her husband's ear, and he nodded, gave her a look that seemed to say, *Guilty as charged.*

"Steam engines, diesel, I've got whatever you might want," Mr. Choo said. He waved his arm at a stack of packaged train sets. "You get one of these, and everything is included. An engine, some cars, lots of track, and a transformer to make it all go. And that's just the start! There's so much you can add! Switches and sidings and buildings. I've got it all. These trains are something you actually play *with*. Connect the track pieces, mix-and-match engines. It's not like some video game, where you just sit on the couch and press some buttons. That's not my kind of fun, let me tell you."

A boy was tugging at his father's sleeve. Another was pleading with his mother. Wallets were coming out.

As Harry watched, Mr. Choo sold five sets. They were going as fast as the bakery's chocolate chip muffins. The guy was a true carnival barker.

This, Harry thought, had to be where Auden's birthday present had been purchased. Not that Harry intended to mention to Mr. Choo how no train set, no matter how grand, would have been enough to lift Auden's spirits on that horrible day.

Harry was about to speak to Mr. Choo when he spotted a familiar face. Walking past was a man in his mid-thirties with his wife and young daughter, whose hand he was hanging on to tightly.

The family members' olive-like complexion distinguished them from most of the crowd. Vermont was, according to the latest census, the whitest state in America, running at about 90 percent. Mixed-race, Blacks, Latinos, and Asians made up most of the rest, but Ahsan Basher was almost statistically nonexistent. As a Muslim in Lucknow, he considered himself an *invisible* minority. But that didn't mean he hadn't attracted attention since September 11, and none of it welcome.

The self-serve gas station and convenience store he ran on the town's outskirts had been vandalized twice. The first time, after closing, someone had spray-painted OSAMA LOVER GO HOME across the front windows. The second incident occurred ten days later when Ahsan was inside behind the cash register. A brick came crashing through that same window. A red 1973 Ford Torino was caught on surveillance video speeding away.

Harry paid a visit to one Delbert Dorfman, to whom the vehicle was registered. A six-foot-four twentysomething asshole with one minor assault conviction who worked various shifts at Dexter's Bar & Grill. Harry couldn't prove Delbert threw that brick, or was even behind the wheel of the car, but he knew, and he told Delbert he knew, and put him on notice. If Ahsan's business got hit again, Harry was going to make him the sorriest son of a bitch Lucknow had ever seen.

"Mr. Basher," Harry said, tossing his unfinished coffee into a nearby waste bin and extending a hand.

"Chief," he said, smiling and returning the handshake. "I'd like you to meet my wife, Aisha, and this is our daughter, Maryam."

"A pleasure," Harry said, bending over to greet the little girl. "You having fun?"

"We've been to three food trucks," Maryam said. "I had a churro. I liked it, but I'm full."

Harry shifted his focus to her parents and asked quietly, "How have things been lately?"

Ahsan was hesitant. He said to his wife, "Why don't you get Maryam some cotton candy."

Aisha nodded, and led the girl away.

"She will have a stomachache for sure now," Ahsan said. He took a breath. "Nothing has happened, but I sometimes see this Delbert Dorfman driving by, slowly, like he wants me to know he's keeping his eye on me. It is a hard car to miss. And he came in once, to buy gas, and he had this grin on his face the whole time, like he knew that I knew but there wasn't anything I could do about it."

Harry didn't like the sound of that. "Okay. I'll pay him another visit. Anything happens, you know you can call me anytime, day or night."

"Thank you. You know I was born here. I am an American citizen."

"I know."

As Basher went to join his family, Harry turned his attention back to the town's new business. The crowd had thinned, some heading off with purchases. Harry stepped forward and offered a hand.

"Hello again," the chief said as Mr. Choo's hand wrapped around his and squeezed.

And Harry felt . . . something.

Something so fleeting, he almost didn't catch it. A half-second chill. If he'd even given it a thought, he would have blamed it on a cool gust of wind that coincided with the greeting. Fall was in the air, after all. The changing leaves were a cascade of color. It was a beautiful autumn day.

"And how is our chief today?"

"Good, thanks," Harry said. "We met the other morning. You brought Gavin a coffee."

"Right, right, yes. Haven't seen him today."

"He's probably around somewhere. Just wanted to welcome you to Lucknow, Mr. Choo."

He laughed. "Nabler."

"I'm sorry?"

"Not Choo. Nabler. Edwin Nabler."

"Well, welcome, Edwin. Looks like you're doing a booming business today. Amazing, for being so new to town."

"You know what the key to success is? Offering people something they don't need, because if they need it, they already have it. But offer something they might want? That's a different story. And word of mouth is everything." Nabler smiled. "Toy trains are such an iconic toy. They never go out of style."

"Trains were never really my thing, even as a kid," Harry said, "but I understand the appeal. My son would love them, I bet."

"Is Dylan here somewhere?"

"He's got a soccer practice this morning."

"You must bring him in one day. Open nine thirty to five."

Harry asked, "Have you had a shop like this in other places?"

Nabler nodded. "I'm a bit of a traveling salesman, to be honest. Hang out my shingle in a place, sell my wares until I've pretty much saturated the market, then move on."

"Has to be hard on a family, packing up and moving so often."

"It's just me, so I'm the only one inconvenienced. You've been eyeing my patches." Nabler ran a hand over the various railway logos stitched into his garment.

"They're quite something."

Nabler leaned in close and whispered, "I feel like a damn fool. The hat, the patches, the *woo-woo* and the *chugga-chugga*. But you have to get them into the tent, if you get my meaning."

"Sure. Salesmanship."

"Exactly. But it's worth it. Because there's a child within all of us, no matter how old we get. Did you know Frank Sinatra—bless his soul, three years now without him—was a collector? He had a separate building behind his house just for his trains."

"I'll be."

Nabler smiled slyly. "We're like a cult. Hiding in plain sight right in front you. You think we're normal, but in the privacy of our own homes, we get up to some very strange things."

Harry gave him a nod. "Nice meeting you. You have a great day."

He was turning to walk away, but Nabler had something else to say.

"That's a terrible thing that family's going through."

"I'm sorry?"

"Excuse my eavesdropping. This Dorfman man who's victimizing them for something they had nothing to do with? What's wrong with people?"

"Been doin' this awhile and I still haven't figured that out," Harry said, then added, "But you know what? Most of the folks in this town? They're good people."

His stroll took him to the far end of Main Street, past the temporary barriers, and he spotted half a block away the old pickup he knew belonged to Gavin. He made his way to it and peered inside, expecting to find Gavin sprawled across the seat, sound asleep. But he wasn't there, and when Harry tried the door, he found it locked.

He glanced down the street in both directions, hoping he might spot the man, but there was no sign of him.

Harry didn't know that he needed to be concerned. Gavin had probably been scared off by the crowds downtown today. But Lucknow'd already had two men go missing. And the one who'd turned up wasn't exactly in the best shape.

TWENTY

Wendell Comstock hadn't had this much fun since he was ten.

It had been several days since he'd made his initial purchases, but he'd returned to Choo-Choo's Trains a few times since. What he had accomplished in such a short time was, in his own estimation, pretty goddamn amazing.

His intention, as he'd told Edwin Nabler, had been to use his Ping-Pong table in the basement as the base for his model train empire. He put down a roll of grass-like carpet, staple-gunned it into place, then assembled a large oval of track with two sidings. With some sheets of black cardboard he created a street, which he lined with several assembled building kits. The transformer was notched into a corner of the table, two wires running between it and the track, plus the cord that ran to the wall outlet.

Wendell had been spending most of his time, once he had come home from work and shoveled dinner down his throat, in the basement. It was, he soon realized, just what he had needed, because Wendell had been looking for more than something to entertain himself. He had been looking for a refuge.

Things were not all that great on the home front. He and Nadine had been married almost ten years now, and whatever spark there'd been in this marriage had fizzled some time ago. The truth was, they were never really meant for each other. They'd gone out a few times while both attending Middlebury College, had a few drinks one night, and a few weeks later Nadine broke the news to him that she was pregnant. They were both from religious families, and even though it was the nineties, supposedly a time when young people felt liberated from so many social conventions, they felt under pressure to do the right thing and get hitched. Wendell left Middlebury before getting his degree and found a job in Lucknow. With financial help from Nadine's parents—her father ran a savings and loan— they bought a house. They had two cars in the garage and an apple tree in the backyard. A perfect couple, about to embark on life's great adventure. They had it all except for the picket fence out front.

And then, in her third month, Nadine lost the baby.

It was a devastating time for Wendell and Nadine. They were enveloped in a great sadness, but that gave way over time to resentment.

But, as it turned out, Wendell discovered that he enjoyed being a husband. There was a sense of fulfillment in having someone to care for, in being part of a union. And if he didn't love Nadine as deeply as he might have wished when they exchanged vows, he was hopeful that in time he would.

If only Nadine had felt the same.

She had married this man because she was having his child, and now she wasn't. She never said out loud what she was thinking. That she wanted out. That she didn't want to spend her life with this man if she didn't have to. Some couples, desperate to have a child, would have tried again, but Nadine didn't want to do that. But what could she do? Her parents had bought them this house. What would she say to them? She knew, at some level, she had disgraced them by getting pregnant, and to find a way to escape this marriage now would only make things worse.

Nadine resigned herself to this life. She would go through the motions, make the best of it. But she didn't have to love this man. She didn't even have to like him. She believed that she could *tolerate* him. Where was it written that you were entitled to be happy?

Wendell gradually resigned himself to a similar conclusion. It wasn't so much that he gave up on the idea of one day loving Nadine. It was as though love had given up on him. While they shared quarters, while they slept in the same bed, they were strangers to one another. They both went off to work in the morning and both came home at night. They each had their assigned duties and stuck to them.

It was a life.

Nadine kept herself busy most evenings. If it wasn't book club, it was a lecture series, or a Thai cooking class. Wendell would plunk himself in front of the television, eating microwaved popcorn, picking something from his library of VHS tapes, like *Ghostbusters* or *Jurassic Park* or the two Batman movies starring Michael Keaton. Movies Nadine had no appreciation for, movies she thought were, basically, stupid.

He was, he believed, living with a low-level depression, although he had not been clinically diagnosed. And he was pretty sure Nadine was, too.

Then came the trains. And the strangest, most wonderful thing happened.

Wendell had expected her to be, if not flat-out annoyed by his newfound interest, at the very least dismissive. *You're a grown man*, he'd figured she would say. *Am I married to a child?*

But she turned out to be *interested*.

She eyed him curiously the night he took his new purchases to the basement. She perched herself on the top of the stairs, out of sight, watching what he was up to. The second night, she came all the way down, pulled up a chair as he set about nailing track down to the table.

"You know," she said, "I don't know whether I've ever told you this, but I had a dollhouse when I was little."

"Did you?"

She nodded at the recollection.

"I loved it. Two stories, with gingerbread trim. A kitchen and living and dining rooms downstairs, two bedrooms, and a bathroom upstairs, and a staircase. I must have spent a million hours imagining I lived inside it, and now I don't even know what happened to it. Sometime in my teens, long after I'd stopped playing with it, my mother must have gotten rid of it. It wasn't like some pink Barbie house. It looked so real, and the furniture was the most exquisitely detailed stuff. Armoires and love seats and carpets and a little chandelier that hung over the dining room table. It had everything."

"That sounds like so much fun," her husband said.

"I'll be right back," she said, went up to the kitchen, and returned minutes later with a plate of saltine crackers and slices of Cracker Barrel cheddar. While they were having their snack, Nadine offered to assemble one of the building kits.

Wendell was hesitant at first. "It's okay," Nadine said. "You want to do it yourself."

"No, you know what? Go ahead." He found a box containing all the pieces for a post office. "Do this one. It just snaps together, I think. Doesn't need any glue or paint."

She had it built in twenty minutes. "Do you have any more?"

The third night, Wendell snuck down to the basement before dinner, making some last-minute preparations. Made sure all the electrical connections were good, the engine and cars sitting properly on the track, the throttle plugged in and ready to go. He went to the base of the stairs and called up: *"All aboard!"*

Nadine appeared at the top of the stairs. "It's ready?"

"We are good to go."

He gave her a thumbs-up and she came down the stairs at a gallop. In her enthusiasm, one foot got caught on the other and she tripped.

She let out a scream as she embarked on a headlong plunge down the stairs.

But Wendell was there, and he bolted up the first two steps, held out his arms, and caught her. She flung her arms around his neck.

"Oh my God," she said, panting. "I could have broken my neck."

Wendell's heart was beating as furiously as hers. "Are you okay?"

"I'm fine. That was close." And before she unwrapped her arms from around him, she looked into his eyes, put her lips to his, and kissed him. Their stairway embrace lasted for several seconds until Nadine finally loosened her hold on him and said, "Show me your engine, big boy."

"Which one?" he replied.

They shared a giggle, then he took her hand and led her the rest of the way down the steps. She took a seat while he went to the transformer and eased the throttle ahead.

The locomotive slowly began to move.

Chuff . . . chuff . . . chuff . . . chuff . . .

"I *love* the sound," Nadine said.

As Wendell gave the engine more power, its huffing and puffing grew more hurried.

Chuffchuffchuffchuffchuff

Wendell pressed a red button on the transformer.

Woowoo!

"A whistle!" Nadine said. "Does it make any other noises?"

Wendell smiled, pressed another button.

Dingdingding!

Nadine grinned. "I love the engine sound the most. That *chuff-chuffchuff*. There's something about it. It's almost . . . soothing, you know?"

"I do," he said as the train went around and around and around. He put his hand on the throttle and started to slow the train down.

"No," Nadine said, eyes locked on the train as it made its repetitive journey. "Make it go. Don't let it stop."

Wendell powered the train back to its original speed and looked with no small amount of wonder at how transfixed Nadine was.

They'd found something in common, something that brought them together. Something kind of *silly*, Wendell conceded to himself. Even he was willing to admit toy trains were an odd thing for them to bond over after all these years, but what the hell. For the first time in years, he felt something unfamiliar.

He was *happy*.

WHENEVER WENDELL WAS out, Nadine would slip downstairs, turn on the train, sit in the chair, and watch it go around. The times they spent in the basement together were not enough for her. She wanted more. She couldn't quite understand it, but she wanted to listen to the train travel around its loop all the time. She would be upstairs, watching TV or sitting at the kitchen table paying bills, when suddenly she would get up, go downstairs, turn on the transformer, and let 'er rip.

Chuffchuffchuffchuffchuff

The sound started boring into her brain, like the sound of a cicada on a hot summer's day.

Chuffchuffchuffchuffchuff

Just as she'd indicated to Wendell, it was a soothing sound. Intoxicating, even. Akin to some yoga-like mantra. When she listened to it, her stresses evaporated. She was in the moment.

So when Wendell said he would be gone all of Sunday, that he'd promised to help a friend from college who was thinking of buying a new house and wanted Wendell to have a look at it, Nadine could not have been more excited. On Saturday, at the sidewalk sale, she had gone to the bakery and bought a couple of chocolate chip muffins at Len's, and Sunday morning, moments after Wendell had departed, she made herself a pot of coffee.

Nadine felt an excitement unlike any she had ever felt before. And also, just a little guilty. It was like she was having an affair. She was going to play with the trains *alone*. Without her husband.

Was this cheating? And if it was, so what?

She took her coffee and a muffin on a plate and descended the stairs to the basement. She checked that the transformer was plugged in, turned it on, which brought up the headlight on the engine. Before turning the throttle, she leaned over so she could look directly into the light.

She stared for several seconds, not blinking.

The light stared back.

A few more seconds passed before Nadine quietly said, "Okay."

She cranked the throttle and the train began to move. She took her seat, had a sip of coffee, and nibbled on the muffin.

And watched.

And listened.

Chuffchuffchuffchuffchuff
Chuffchuffchuffchuffchuff

The more she listened to the engine huffing and puffing, she started to hear something . . . else. It was like listening to a song, where you think there are lyrics *behind* the lyrics. Hidden words. Or maybe, if you played the song backward, you'd pick up on something you'd never realized was there.

Chuffchuffchuffchuffchuff

She pulled her chair up to the edge of the Ping-Pong table, her ear so close to the track that it seemed to tingle with electricity. She felt the train pushing air out of the way as it flew past her head.

Chuffchuffenoughchuffenoughchuffchuff

Wait, what was that?

She held her breath, not wanting even the sound of her own breathing to interfere with what she was trying to pick up on. If she could have stopped her heart, she would have.

Chuffchuffenoughchuffenoughchuffchuff

Yes, there was definitely something there.

Chuffenoughchuffenoughchuffenough

It was becoming clearer. She took a breath, held it again.

Enoughchuffenoughchuffenoughenoughenough

Even clearer now. She felt a wave of expectation rush through her, as though she were on the brink of a great discovery. If she were to have looked at a clock, she would have learned that she had been sitting down here for more than three hours.

Enoughisenoughisenoughisenoughisenoughisenough

And there it was.

Enough is enough.

She sat back up in the chair, nodding to herself. The words were a revelation. No, not a revelation.

They were a *confirmation.*

They told her everything she already knew to be true. She'd been living this lie for far too long. This was no life. How could she continue such an existence? There came a time when you had to decide how much more you were willing to endure, how much more you were going to take.

Enough *was* enough.

She got up from the chair and turned back the throttle. The locomotive came to a stop. She flipped a switch to turn off the transformer, disconnected the wires that led from it to the track, then unplugged the unit from the wall, looping the cord about it. She took up to the kitchen the coffee mug and the plate that was now littered with chocolate chip muffin crumbs, put them into the dishwasher, and, seeing that she had a pretty full load in there, filled the detergent dispenser with some powdered Calgonite, closed the door, and hit the ON button.

She returned to the basement and found a short extension cord. She took it, as well as the unplugged transformer—which was heavier than she expected it to be—to the second floor of the house. She set them on the bed, then went into the bathroom, shoved the stopper into the bathtub drain, and turned on the taps.

She held her hand under the running water, adjusting the two knobs to get the temperature just right. She liked a hot bath, but not too hot. Once she had the water flowing into the tub at the desired temperature, she returned to the bedroom and disrobed.

Naked, she went back into the bathroom, taking the extension cord and the transformer with her. She set them on the counter next to the sink, then dipped her hand into the water to see how it felt.

Perfect. She turned off the taps, giving them both a good twist to make sure they would not drip.

Nadine knew the transformer cord would be too short for her purposes, which was why she had brought along the short extension. She plugged it into an outlet by the sink, the one she used for her hair dryer and curling iron and toothbrush charger. Then she plugged the transformer cord into its other end and set the transformer on the edge of the tub at the end close to the taps.

She turned the transformer on, then turned the throttle to the maximum setting. It made a low-level buzzing noise. The red light on top glowed brightly.

Nadine put one foot into the tub, then the other, then slowly lowered herself into the water. She stretched out, the water coming up to her neck.

The transformer continued to buzz.

Nadine raised her left leg out of the water and touched her big toe to the outer edge of the transformer.

"Enough is enough," she said to herself, then nudged the transformer slowly to the edge until it tipped and dropped into the water with a splash.

TWENTY-ONE

"What time did you get home, Mr. Comstock?" Harry Cook asked.

"Uh, I guess around five," Wendell said.

They were standing in the upstairs bedroom. Wendell's wife's clothes were on the bed.

"And you'd been where, again?"

"I'd driven over to Brattleboro. Got a friend there, he's thinking of making an offer on a house, and he wanted me to have a look at it."

"You do house inspections?"

"No. But I have a background in construction. Not lately, and I'm not the world's biggest expert, but I know a little."

"What's this friend's name?"

"Ron. Ron Hess."

"I'm going to need a number and address for him."

"Yeah, sure, I understand. You have to check my story."

Harry smiled wryly. "I'm not suggesting anything, Mr. Comstock. But I need it for the report. What time did you leave this morning?"

"After nine. Nine thirty, I guess."

"How long did it take you to get to Brattleboro?"

"About an hour. I stopped along the way and got a coffee. Nadine usually makes—Nadine usually made the coffee in the morning, and she hadn't yet and I was ready to go, so I said I'd get some along the way." He shrugged. "And a donut."

"Where was this?"

"At Dunkin's. You want to know which one?"

Harry nodded, and Wendell told him.

"So you got to your friend's around half-past ten?"

"Right. And then we went to look at the house, and we had some lunch and a couple of beers at his place, and then I left a little after four."

"Okay. And got home around five. Tell me about that."

"The front door wasn't locked. We don't usually lock the doors except at night, or if we're going out, like, shopping. When Nadine's here through the day, even if I'm not home, she wouldn't lock up. I mean, this is a good neighborhood. We've never had any kind of trouble."

"Right."

"So I parked the car and came in the front door and I called out for her, saying I was home, and she didn't answer, so I thought maybe she was downstairs or in the backyard. I was coming through the kitchen when I noticed the power was out."

"How'd you discover that?"

"Well, the little digital clocks on the stove and the microwave were blank, and then I flipped on a switch and the lights didn't come on, so I figured we'd had a power failure. You know how, when that happens, you think, is it just my house or the whole street."

Harry glanced up at the ceiling fixture in the bedroom. The light was on.

"Did the power come back on at some point?"

"Much later, after we found out . . . what caused it. So, even before I went looking for Nadine, I got a flashlight out of the drawer and went down to the basement where the breaker box is. Opened it up, saw that the whole house had been tripped. I flipped it back, but it kicked out again. Came up, looked to see if Nadine was out back. And then I came up here."

"Okay."

"I kept calling for her, still not getting an answer, and I came in here, and saw her clothes on the bed, and that was when I looked in there." He nodded toward the bathroom.

Nadine was still there. Her dead body in a tub full of cold water.

"I got down, put my arm into the water, around her, asking her what happened, wake up—I don't know what I said, exactly. But I could tell . . . I could see . . ."

Wendell choked on his words. He lowered his head, ran his hand over his mouth, tried to regain his composure.

"Take your time," Harry said, laying a hand on the man's back.

"I could see she was . . . she wasn't breathing, and her body was as cold as the water. But I called 911 anyway. I mean, I knew she couldn't be saved, but . . . The fire department and the paramedics came real fast, but they said that, you know, there would have to be an investigation and that they couldn't take her out of the bathtub."

"We're going to try to do what we have to do as quickly as possible, Mr. Comstock. I have to ask, had you and your wife been having difficulties lately?"

He had to ask, although Harry did not believe, at this point, that Wendell Comstock had murdered his wife. The coroner, who had made an initial assessment and was waiting downstairs, believed the woman had probably been dead since early afternoon.

"No. Things were fine."

"Had your wife been depressed lately? Had she made previous attempts to take her own life?"

"She'd never tried anything before, at least not that I know of."

"Do you know whether she was seeing someone?"

"You mean, like an affair?"

"No, sorry, I meant, was she seeing anyone like a psychiatrist, a therapist, to help her if she was feeling down?"

"No. I'd have known if she was doing that. But the truth is, we . . . we didn't have what you'd call a real happy marriage, at least not until lately."

"Lately?"

The man nodded. "We just discovered, after all this time, kind of by accident, that we had something in common. Things were looking . . . they were looking better. So I don't understand why . . . oh God, I'm going to have to call her parents. Jesus. This'll kill them." He bit his lower lip.

"I know," Harry said. "I'm so sorry." He paused, then asked, "Did she ever ask about, you know, questions about electrical things? Short circuits? What would happen if you dropped a toaster in a tub filled with water?"

"It wasn't a toaster."

"I'm sorry?"

"It wasn't a toaster."

Harry hadn't had a close look himself at what was in the bathtub with the dead woman. When he'd arrived, one of the firefighting staff had said the woman had died from knocking a toaster into the tub.

"Give me a second," Harry said, and excused himself. He went into the bathroom and looked at the black object down by the dead woman's foot. It definitely was not a toaster. It was slightly smaller than a toaster, and there were no slots in the top, but instead a little handle and a couple of buttons and lights.

He thought he knew what it was but wasn't certain.

He returned to the bedroom and asked Wendell what that device was.

"A transformer."

"What kind of transformer?"

"For running trains."

"Where would your wife get one of those?"

"Follow me," Wendell said.

He led the chief down to the first floor, then to a door off the kitchen, and finally down a flight of stairs to the basement.

He pointed to the train setup on the Ping-Pong table.

"It powered this," he said. "She had to have unplugged it, disconnected the wires from the track, and taken it upstairs. I can't . . . I can't imagine what got into her head." He looked at the trains and the buildings on the table. "I'm getting rid of all of this. I don't ever want to see any of it again."

As if struck by a sudden impulse, he crossed the room and grabbed a large cardboard detergent box that was in a far corner of the room. He brought it back to the table, picked up a caboose, and threw it forcefully into the box.

"Goddamn fucking things!" he said. Before he could grab another car, Harry reached for his arm.

"Mr. Comstock, please leave everything as it is for now, okay?"

The man stared vacantly at Harry, almost as though he couldn't see him standing there.

"Mr. Comstock?"

He blinked a few times. "Yeah, okay, okay. I'll leave it for now."

"These trains," Harry said. "You've always had these?"

"No, I bought everything this week. A few days ago. Nadine . . . she was really taken by them. I thought she'd think they were stupid but she liked them. She helped assemble the buildings and everything."

"Where did you buy all this?"

"That store on the main street. Oh God, I don't know what I'm going to tell her family."

Harry thought about that barbecue accident. That birthday gift for young Auden.

And then it hit Harry for the first time. The conversation he'd had with Nabler at the sidewalk sale. Nabler had known his son's name was Dylan.

Harry was sure he hadn't told him.

Part III

ANNIE

TWENTY-TWO

A little more than a week after moving into their summer place, things were really starting to click for Annie and Charlie.

She was generally up an hour or more before Charlie, in the kitchen by seven, putting a pod into the Nespresso machine, dropping a slice of whole wheat bread into the toaster while her coffee percolated, then taking her drink and her toast and jam to the table and savoring it while she read the *New York Times* on her tablet.

She and Charlie were only using one end of the kitchen table because half of it was covered with five hundred jigsaw puzzle pieces that, when done, would be a cover from *The New Yorker* magazine—this one featuring dozens of dogs in various comical activities—that she had brought with her from the city. So far, she'd only managed to put together the edges and part of the masthead ("The" and "ew" and "ork") and turned all the other pieces face up, clustering them by color. During the pandemic, she and John had ordered several puzzles to get them through their periods of isolation, but, after completing only one, had sworn off them. John said being hunched over the dining room table for hours on end was killing his back, and Annie began to feel she was wasting her whole day even when she had nothing else pressing.

But out here with nothing else to do, she was willing to give the pastime another chance, and so far enjoyed it.

When she heard Charlie stirring, she would take a break from reading the *Times* and set a place for him. Pour him a bowl of cereal, get the milk and orange juice from the fridge. Once he was down, they would discuss what they wanted to do that day. Go into Fenelon? Drive around randomly and see what they might discover? Hang out on the porch and read their books?

No, no, and no, Charlie would reply.

He had a project of his own that was as engrossing as his mother's jigsaw. Charlie was building an empire.

It had been several days since he had discovered, in the shed out back of the house, an old Tide detergent box filled with toy trains. And not just trains, but track and building kits and little trees. He'd told his mother he'd been racing past the shed on his bike when he decided, on a whim, to try that padlock one more time. He said he'd given it a good yank and it came apart. Just like that.

"I think it was rusted or something," Charlie said.

The box had been too heavy to carry, so he had been bringing the contents into the house a few items at a time. Before letting him get too far along in the process, Annie had put in a call to the leasing agent, Candace, to ask who the toys belonged to and if they should be returned to their rightful owner.

It was the first Candace had heard anything about a box of toy trains.

"Finders keepers," she said. "Let your boy have fun with them." There was a pause, and then she said, "Would today be good if I dropped by with Stacy? She's dying to show you her drawings."

"Why don't we revisit that later in the week," Annie said. "We're still settling in."

Charlie had been awaiting the results of the conversation anxiously. "Go nuts," his mother said, and he shrieked with delight. He had already brought in so many items from the box, including the heaviest ones like the engine and the transformer, that Annie was able to carry it from the shed to the house.

She put it down on the porch, so there would be room to empty the contents, spread them out, and see just what they had.

"What a haul," Annie said. "That was some dumb luck, that lock falling apart."

"I know, right?" said Charlie as he examined the pieces of track and started to arrange them on the porch without connecting them, seeing what kind of configuration he could make.

"Looks like all this stuff has been in the box a long time," Annie said. "Hope the engine still works."

"It will."

"You sound pretty confident. But if it needs oiling or something we can go back to that hardware store where you got the Brasso and—"

"It will work," Charlie said, sounding slightly irritated. "You thought the bike was old and crummy, but *it* worked."

"Okay," she said.

"I can't set it up out here," he said. "I have to do it inside. If it rained and it was blowing it could get all wet."

"What about your bedroom?"

"It's too small. There's a lot of track here."

It was a big house and just the two of them. Annie wondered whether she should let him take over the dining room. But then she hit on a better idea.

"If you don't mind sharing space with me, what about the studio? You could put it on the floor."

Charlie cocked his head at an awkward angle, considering. "Maybe . . ."

It was as big a space as any, and her worktable only took up a fraction of it. There was plenty of natural light, and she didn't know how much work she was actually going to do while they were here, so he'd mostly have the room to himself.

"Okay," Charlie said. "Will you help me get it all up there?"

She did. Once they had everything moved, and Annie had tossed the empty Tide box down into the basement, she came back up and offered to help Charlie put the track together.

"That's okay," he said. "I want to do it by myself."

"You sure? Because it would be fun, a project we could work on to—"

"No," he said firmly, already on his hands and knees, attaching a straight length of track to a curved one, inserting the end pins from one into the openings on the other.

Annie felt as though one of those pins had pierced her heart. She was willing to bet if John were here, Charlie would want his assistance. Who said trains had to be a *guy thing*? She'd have been on the floor, helping him put this layout together, in an instant if he'd let her.

"Okay, then," she said, trying to keep the hurt out of her voice. The last thing she wanted to do was make Charlie feel guilty.

She turned, walked out of the room, and left him to it.

HER HURT FEELINGS aside, the discovery of the trains could not have come at a better time. The day before, Charlie had seemed restless and asked twice about whether his friend Pedro could come up from New York for a visit. Annie had offered that old parental standby: "We'll see."

The truth was, as much as she wanted Charlie to have a good summer here, she did not want Pedro, or any other friend of Charlie's, coming for any extended period of time. Two boys running around made a lot more noise than one, plus there would be extra meals to organize, a different daily routine. Annie felt selfish thinking this way, and if Charlie really wanted his friend to visit, she would find a way to make it happen.

But Charlie's restlessness had been cured with the discovery of the box full of trains. She supposed the novelty might wear off, and he'd return to asking again whether Pedro could come up, so Annie, as John used to say, would jump off that bridge when the time came. For the moment she would just enjoy this special time, having Charlie all to herself.

She went into the kitchen and resumed work on her puzzle. Managed to find all the pieces she needed to make "Yo."

CHARLIE CAME DOWN long enough to eat a grilled cheese sandwich, then bolted back up the stairs. While he was on his last bite, dipping his sandwich into a puddle of ketchup, Annie asked, "How's it going?"

"Almost there," he said, and dashed.

About an hour later, Annie heard a sound. Actually, it was more of a vibration at first, the ceiling above her humming. There was no carpet in the studio. A train running on tracks set up directly on hardwood was bound to make a racket.

She came out of the kitchen and stood at the bottom of the stairs and listened.

Chuffchuffchuffchuffchuff

Her heart swelled. Charlie was right. It worked.

Chuffchuffchuffchuffchuff

She smiled. She wanted to see what he'd accomplished. Pausing halfway up the stairs, she heard another sound drift down to her.

Woo woo!

A whistle! How cool was that?

Seconds later, she was at the studio door. The engine, followed by a series of cars and a caboose, was zipping around a large loop of track. Charlie had not only assembled that, but he had put together all the building kits he'd found in the Tide box. He had lined them up like a street front. A fire station. A bakery. A restaurant. A church. They looked like snap-together kits, which explained how he was able to construct them so speedily.

Charlie sat cross-legged, the transformer in front of him, his hand on the throttle. His head moved with the train, following its every move.

"It's fantastic!" Annie said.

Charlie glanced over his shoulder at his mother and smiled broadly. "I love it!"

Chuffchuffchuffchuffchuff

"It sounds so real," she said. "Make the whistle go again."

Charlie pressed a button.

Woo woo!

Without turning his head, Charlie said, "I need more buildings."

"I don't know where we would get—"

"Where I got the bike," he said. "I saw some there. They were old and kind of busted and stuff, but they'd be good. I need to make the town bigger."

"Okay, then," Annie said. "Why don't we go back there tomorrow. We'll get lunch, make an afternoon of it."

Chuffchuffchuffchuffchuff

"You know what place this is?" Charlie asked.

Annie tried to think like a child. What could a few plastic buildings represent in a kid's imagination?

"Is that New York?"

"Nope."

"Uh, is it the town where we got the bike? Is it Fenelon?"

"Nope."

"I give up. You tell me."

Charlie turned and looked at her. "This is where Daddy lives now."

TWENTY-THREE

It began as an itching in her fingers.

Annie noticed it two mornings later as she was drinking her coffee. It started in her fingers and radiated up her arms and began to spread, ever so subtly, throughout her body. At first she thought it was a caffeine rush, that those coffee pods she was going through at an alarming rate were giving her the jitters, but then she recognized this feeling for what it really was.

She needed to go back to work.

Her body, as well as her subconscious, were ganging up on her, telling her it was time to stop sitting around.

It was time to create.

Annie had suspected this time might come. She was, in the very core of her being, an artist, and an artist could only put things off for so long. She had been through a period of self-recrimination over the death of Evan Corcoran, and moved on from that to an even darker period of grieving John. Not surprisingly, the so-called creative juices had not been flowing during those times, and at least she'd felt no guilt about that. It wasn't just Pierce the Penguin who'd been put up on the shelf. Anything Annie might ever produce was up there next to him.

So when Charlie came down for breakfast the next day, she told him they'd be sharing space. He could keep on playing with his trains, but she was going to be at her worktable.

"Are you going to be drawing again?" her son asked.

"I think I might."

Charlie looked pleased. "Are you going to draw Pierce?"

"I don't know. I guess we'll see. I started something the other day. I might see where that takes me."

That, of course, had been that half-rat, half-wolf creation. She'd been thinking about him lately, wondering whether to direct her talents into this different, gloomier direction. Maybe it was something she had to get out of her system. Considering the kind of year she'd had, was it even reasonable to think that when she put pen to paper she'd draw a cheerful little penguin? She could wallow around in the dark for a while and see where it took her.

"So it won't bug you if I'm in the room while you run your trains?" Annie asked.

Charlie shook his head. "Fine by me," he said, stuffing a spoonful of cereal into his mouth, milk dripping down his chin. "But what about your puzzle?"

Annie said, "That puzzle may be what's driving me back to work."

If she'd had any fears that the toy train's relentless *chuffchuffchuffchuffchuffchuffchuff* would bother her, they were allayed very quickly. While not the same as the city's background din, it served the same purpose. A kind of white noise that allowed her to focus on her work. And Charlie barely said a word. He lay on the floor, on his stomach, propped up on his elbows, and simply watched the train make loop after loop. Occasionally he would slow it down, bring it to a stop in front of the plastic railroad station, let imaginary passengers get on and off, then throttle it up again.

It was a great toy, Annie thought. Better than any video game, where you sat on your butt for hours on end, staring at a screen. With toy trains, you were playing *with* something. But even as she had such positive thoughts, she wondered how long Charlie would be captivated by this activity. How much time could you spend watching an engine, a few cars, and a caboose go around a loop of track?

It did get a bit repetitive.

One thing that had kept him engaged was the addition of several new buildings. The day before, Annie had given in to Charlie's request that they return to the antiques store (still, in her mind, more of a *junk* store) in Fenelon where he claimed to have seen a number of model train kits. Sure enough, he was right. Someone getting out of the hobby must have cleared out their entire stash. Charlie found, some in the original boxes and others in clear plastic bags one would use to freeze pork chops, kits whose pieces could be snapped together to make houses, shops, a switch tower, a radio station, a town hall, and half a dozen common downtown structures. The shopkeeper let them have the lot for twenty bucks. Charlie was so excited by the haul that on the ride home he attempted to build an ice-cream stand and dropped some window parts between the seat cushions that Annie had to dig out later.

He had all of them built, and on his floor layout, within a couple of hours and was very particular about their placement. At one point, Annie had suggested swapping where he had put the town hall and the police station, prompting a curt, "No," from Charlie.

So now Annie was offering no further input. Let him do what he liked. A subject she'd not revisited was what he'd said three days earlier, that this town was where John now resided. She'd been waiting for that other shoe to drop, wondering whether he'd have more to say about where Dad was spending the afterlife. But it had not, so far, come up again, and she had decided it best not to push.

Annie had tucked those sketches she'd drawn a few days ago under the pad of paper and discreetly brought them out for another look. She hadn't decided whether she wanted Charlie to see them.

Maybe she was being too protective. He liked monsters as much as the next kid, but there was something about this new creation of hers that was particularly unsettling.

She took a fresh sheet, taped it to the slanted table, with the intention of taking another run at it. The first attempt had been done with her eyes looking elsewhere, so this would be a more serious effort. She'd never considered, until now, doing a dark graphic novel, something for a totally different audience than she'd appealed to in the past. Unless, she thought wryly, she turned Pierce into an avenging penguin on a campaign to slaughter all the corporate overlords who'd contributed to global warming and the shrinking of the polar ice caps.

For her own amusement, she dashed off a Pierce wielding a machine gun with a word bubble that read, "Take that, motherfucker." She chuckled to herself, took a moment to enjoy it, then crumpled it up and tossed it in the trash.

Back to the rat-wolf.

She started with his head. Concentrated on details. The shape of his snout, the menacing look in his eyes. She did a few quick lines to suggest whiskers. She went back to the eyes, narrowed them to slits. Yeah, that added a new level of creepiness.

"Whatcha doing?" Charlie asked, flipping over onto his back and looking at his mother.

"Nothing much," she said. "Just trying out all these new pencils and markers. Fin set me up very nicely here."

"Do you feel like a snack?" he asked, which actually meant that he felt like a snack, and wanted his mother to get him one.

"Go down and have a look," Annie said. "And could you bring me back a Coke?"

Charlie departed, allowing Annie a moment to sit back and have a look at what she'd done.

"We meet again," she said, shaking her head in wonder. She might have put it out of her mind for years, but she'd not forgotten what she'd imagined seeing through her mental window. The face of that man in Penn Station. His smile. It had seemed so real at the time, but she was a child, with an overly active imagination.

Annie leaned slightly over the table when she heard Charlie coming back. She wasn't ready for him to see this yet. He handed her a can of Coke and nibbled on a chunk of cheese and a handful of crackers he'd found for himself. He flopped back onto the floor and continued what he'd been doing before.

Annie worked on the creature's body for a few minutes until she noticed she was losing her natural light. She glanced up at the skylights. Where had the sun gone? A bank of clouds the color of ink had moved in.

"Looks like a storm coming our way," she said to Charlie.

He looked up. "Whoa," he said. "I'm going outside to look."

He was on his feet in a second and heading for the door. The train continued to run.

"Aren't you going to turn off—"

But he was already running down the stairs. "Stay on the porch!" Annie shouted.

She slid off her chair and considered, briefly, turning off the train, or at least easing back the throttle to slow it down, but it had been running nonstop for a couple of hours without a problem and Charlie would likely be back up here shortly, so she left it alone.

Annie came down the stairs, not at a gallop like Charlie, but one careful step at a time. It had become so dark, so quickly, that she flicked on the front hall lights before she joined Charlie, who had left the front door wide open and was standing at the top of the porch steps, gazing into the dark sky. The wind was picking up and there were flickers of light in the creases of the clouds.

"Lightning!" he cried with excitement, pointing.

And five seconds later, a thunderous clap loud enough to make them both jump.

"*That* was close!" Annie said.

As if turned on by a switch, rain instantly came pelting down. Charlie took half a step back under the porch roof to keep from getting wet.

More lightning and another crack of thunder. Annie slipped her arm around Charlie's shoulder and pulled him close.

"Look!" Charlie said.

He was pointing not at the sky, but down toward the road. It was Daniel's wife, Dolores, who'd spurned Annie's attempt at neighborliness that first day. She was walking down the driveway of their home toward the road, arms hanging down at her side, seemingly oblivious to the rain. She crossed the road without looking, not that there was ever much traffic, but *still*, Annie thought. Dolores moved as if in a trance, reminding Annie of Charlie during his rare episodes of sleepwalking.

"She's getting soaked," Annie said.

"She's looking right at us," Charlie said.

Dolores continued her robotic walk, her arms hanging motionless at her side. The rain had plastered her gray hair to her skull.

There was another bolt of lightning and an almost simultaneous crack of thunder that felt more like an earthquake. Behind her, Annie had a sense the front hall lights had gone off. The storm had kicked out the electricity.

"Mrs. Patten!" Annie cried as the woman got closer. "Is something wrong?"

Dolores's black pants and a gray button-up sweater that she had rolled up to her elbows were as soaked as if she had just come out of a pool, but she gave no indication that the rain was causing her any discomfort. She stopped about ten feet from the bottom of the porch steps.

"Come up here, get out of the rain!" Annie said.

She seemed not to hear. She looked at Charlie, then at Annie, and began to speak.

"What were you thinking?" she asked.

"I'm sorry?" Annie said.

"What were you thinking?"

"*Please*, get out of the rain."

There was another flash, more thunder. Dolores did not move.

"For fuck's sake," Annie said under her breath, and stepped out from under the cover of the porch and closed the distance between herself and Dolores, the rain continuing to pelt down, drenching her almost instantly.

"What were you *thinking*?" the woman asked again, her voice pitched higher this time.

Annie put her arms around her, said, "Let's get you home." But Dolores twisted away from her, and this time raised her right arm and aimed it at Charlie, extending an accusing finger at him.

"What were *you* thinking?" she asked.

As thunder continued to rumble, Annie again tried to coax Dolores to turn around.

"*Dolores!*"

It was Daniel, running across the road, limping with each stride, as though moving his legs that quickly was causing him no small amount of pain. "Dolores!" he shouted a second time. "For God's sake!"

He slipped his arms around her waist from behind when he reached her. She still had her arm extended, pointing at Charlie.

"Come on, honey," he said, rivulets of water streaming down his face. "We're going home."

She turned and looked vacantly into his eyes, as though taking a moment to place him. "What were they thinking?" she asked him.

He got an arm around her shoulder, looked at a drenched Annie, and said, "I'm so sorry."

"It's okay."

"She's having one of her . . . spells. I'm so terribly sorry."

"What can I do?" Annie asked.

Daniel shook his head. "Nothing. I just have to get her home."

And with that, he escorted his wife back to their place. Annie, in no rush now to seek cover from the rain, stood and watched them go. Once they were safely across the road, she turned and mounted the steps to the porch, a troubled Charlie waiting for her.

"What's wrong with her?" he asked.

"Her . . . mind. Dementia. She doesn't always know where she is or who she's talking to."

Charlie did not ask for a further explanation.

Annie glanced down, assessed herself.

"Charlie, can you run upstairs and get my bathrobe? It's hanging on the bottom of the bed."

He was gone like a shot. Annie slipped off her shoes, peeled off her soaking socks. She would wait until she could wrap a robe around her before getting out of her pants and top. When Charlie returned, robe in hand, he told her the lights were all out.

"Yeah," Annie said. "The storm. Don't open the fridge. I don't know how long it might be off."

She unbuttoned her blouse, quickly took it off, then slipped her arms into the robe. Now covered, she got out of her jeans. She entered the house with her clothes rolled up into a ball and took them to the small laundry room off the kitchen. She dumped the clothes into the washer for the time being. With the power off, she couldn't wash or dry them.

Charlie, in the kitchen, asked if he could make a peanut butter sandwich, since all the necessary ingredients were in the cupboard, not the refrigerator.

"Go ahead. I'm gonna put on some dry clothes."

As she climbed the steps, she could hear the train continuing to make its circular journey. The power, she figured, must have just come back on. But when she looked back over her shoulder, she could see the front hall light remained off.

She went into the studio.

Chuffchuffchuffchuffchuffchuffchuff

Annie flicked the switch for the pot lights recessed into the ceiling. They did not come on. Next, she tried the lamp that hung over her desk. No joy there, either.

She walked over to the train layout, her bare toes inches from the edge of the track. She wondered whether the train was battery-powered, but there was the transformer, connected to the wall outlet by a black cord. It *needed* electricity to operate.

Chuffchuffchuffchuffchuffchuffchuff

It made no sense.

Annie knelt down, turned the throttle back to its starting position, but the train continued to run. She shuffled over to the outlet and pulled out the plug.

The train continued on its circular journey.

"Charlie!"

Still in the kitchen, he evidently could not hear her. She would take matters into her own hands. As the locomotive sped past, she grabbed it from above, lifting it from the track. Because the other cars were coupled to it, they all tumbled off the rails, creating a brief racket.

The room was suddenly very quiet. The locomotive in Annie's hand seemed to tingle, sending minor vibrations up her arm and into her shoulder.

Outside, the thunder continued to rumble like a full-sized locomotive bearing down on the house.

TWENTY-FOUR

T hat night, Evan came to visit her again.

It was Annie's standard nightmare, the one that had plagued her for so many nights, but which, for reasons she did not know but was not about to question, had been recurring less frequently.

Tonight, it was back, but this time, with a different ending.

"Evan, come back inside. We're ten floors up. If you step off that ledge you'll be very badly hurt. Your Mom and Dad won't be pleased. They'll be angry. With you, and with me."

"It's okay. I told you. I can fly."

"Six-year-old boys can't fly. You don't have feathers. You don't have wings."

"Yes, I do. I made them."

"Those are cardboard, Evan. Held on with tape. They won't keep you up."

"Pierce Penguin can fly. And penguins aren't supposed to be able to fly."

"He's pretend."

"Pierce Penguin says you can do anything you put your mind to. Mom reads the book to me all the time."

"Evan, what Pierce's saying is, be the best little boy you can be, but it doesn't mean you can turn into a bird and fly or be a fish and live under-water or be a squirrel and climb trees."

"You're wrong. I can fly."

"Evan, just take my hand and come back—"

But then, suddenly, Evan was not Evan. Evan was Charlie.

"Here I go!"

Annie woke with a start.

THE FOLLOWING AFTERNOON, she was sitting on the front porch, reading her Patchett book, when she saw Daniel on the other side of the road, laboriously cutting his front lawn with a gas-powered mower that looked as though it dated back to the sixties or seventies. The yard was probably sixty feet square, and Annie had no idea how much there was to cut out back of the house. It was pushing eighty-five degrees today, and Daniel had to stop every few minutes to wipe the sweat off his brow.

The guy's gonna have a heart attack, she thought.

And he might not be the only one.

Charlie had taken a break from his railroad empire to ride his bike, doing more laps around the house at full tilt. Every time he passed the porch, Annie would look up from her book to check his condition. If he appeared to be on the verge of total exhaustion, she would put a stop to it. But so far—and this was lap . . . sixteen?—he seemed okay.

Her eyes went back to Daniel. She hadn't spoken to him since the storm, when Dolores had confronted them. She wasn't avoiding him; they simply hadn't both been outside at the same time.

Time to end the awkwardness, she thought. And, given that Dolores was not sitting on the porch, this was a perfect opportunity.

She went into the house and got two cold beers out of the refrigerator and—careful not to step in front of Charlie as he made his latest loop—marched them across the road as Daniel was making his final pass across the yard.

He killed the engine—it sputtered a few times in protest, as if it were saying, *Come on, let's keep going!*—as Annie approached, and he took the beer from her without any hesitation.

"Returning the favor," she said, and held out her bottle for a clink, which he weakly accepted. "It's too hot for this."

"Can't exactly leave it till September," he said. "Don't want the neighbors reporting me." He tipped back the beer bottle. "This'll be my one for the day, and it couldn't have come at a better time." He let out a long breath. "Need to get off my feet."

Daniel walked over to his porch steps, sat, and held out a hand, inviting Annie to join him.

"I've been meaning to come over and apologize," he said.

"No apology necessary."

He shook his head strongly. "Nope, it is. Sorry about Dolores coming over and giving you a piece of her mind. That was uncalled-for."

"It's okay," Annie said. "I understand."

"Do you?"

That caught her off guard. "I'm sorry, I didn't mean to presume or—"

He raised a hand. "I just, I don't know how anyone else can understand when I don't, and I live with her twenty-four hours a day."

Annie went quiet.

Daniel looked across the road and grinned. "Look who just ran out of gas."

Charlie had let his bike drop in front of the porch steps and run into the house. "He'll probably drink a gallon of lemonade," Annie said. "I don't know what's got into him. He's either riding that bike like a maniac or upstairs playing with those trains."

Daniel turned his head. "That so."

"I wish there were more kids around. I hadn't really thought about that when I took the place. So far, Charlie seems to be entertaining himself okay, and I like it just being the two of us, but maybe I'm being selfish."

"He's riding that bike hard enough to be training for the Olympics," Daniel said, picking at the beer bottle label with his thumb. "If you don't mind my asking, what was it Dolores was saying to you?"

"I hardly remember. It doesn't matter.'

"Well, maybe not to you, but I'd like to know."

Annie took a breath. "She asked us what we were thinking. A few times."

"Anything else?"

Annie shook her head. "That's all. And, you know, the rain was coming down, and there was thunder, so if she said anything else I might have missed it."

"Okay."

"I'd wondered if she's upset with us taking the place for the summer. Because—I don't know—because of what happened to her there? That she thinks anyone living there is making a mistake?"

"Could be," Daniel said. "You know, when we were talking the other day, I said that this thing what happened to her, that it was like this time bomb in her head, it was gonna go off one day, and it happened to go off when she was over there. Could've been anyplace, but that was where it happened."

"I remember."

"I might not have been totally frank with you about that."

Even with the temperature in the eighties, Annie felt a slight chill.

"I mean, maybe she did have some sort of disposition to something bad happening, but I believe it was triggered by something in that house."

"Christ, what are you saying?" She managed a sardonic chuckle. "That the place is *haunted*?"

"No, no, I'm not saying that. I strike you as the kind of person who'd believe in that nonsense?"

"I haven't known you long enough to make that call," Annie said, an edge to her voice. "My son and I took that house for the summer because we needed to get away, to get our lives back together. Because we've been through some bad shit in the last year, and the suggestion that our place already has ghosts and goblins as tenants, well, that's not helpful."

"The boy who jumped," Daniel said.

The world seemed to stop. Annie stared at him, openmouthed. "What did you say?"

"You told me about your husband, that he'd passed. But there was the boy who thought he could fly. I may look like someone who hasn't moved on since the eight-track tape, but I'm actually hooked up to the *Interweb*." He stressed the last word to make sure she knew he was having her on. "Your name kinda rang a bell and I googled you and I know about the boy. That's a horrible thing."

"It's no business of yours."

"Believe me when I say I mean no offense. What happened to you, that's out in the public. I didn't pry. And I'm very sorry for what you've been through. I'm not going to repeat what I am guessing a hundred people have already told you about blame and responsibility. What I will say is that I think we can all be captive to events that are out of our control."

Annie was still too angry to say anything.

"I want to ask you about that train you said you heard in the night."

"What?"

"I said you must have heard something else, because there's no trains running around here anymore. The A&B went bankrupt. I know the crossing's just up the road there, they still got the signs up, but there's nothing that passes through."

"So I heard something else, then. Or I was dreaming."

"I don't think you were dreaming."

Annie took a breath. She'd grown weary of this discussion. She was sorry she'd brought the beers over. She wanted to get up and go back to her place. She took a final swallow of her drink—the bottle was only half empty—and stood.

"I really should get back to Charlie," she said.

"Did you not hear what I said? I don't think you were dreaming."

"Okay, so I heard a truck, or something. What does it matter?"

Daniel set his beer down on the step and struggled to his feet, putting his hands on his knees for leverage.

"I believe you heard it. I believe you heard a train, even though there's no train to be heard."

Annie didn't know what he was driving at.

And then he said, "Because Dolores heard it, too." He paused. "Last few days, I think even I'm hearing something."

TWENTY-FIVE

While Annie sketched out more versions of Penn Station Man, trying to put the unsettling conversation with Daniel out of her mind, Charlie worked on perfecting his model train village. The loop of track remained static, but what he placed within it changed. He would reposition the buildings on his main street, stand back and look at them like a sculptor, folding his arms and placing one hand to his chin, assessing his creation from afar. Charlie would find some flaw that only he could see, go back, and make some minor adjustment.

Annie watched all this with interest, and without comment. Let him do his thing, she thought.

At one point, he approached her, wanting to borrow a marker and a strip of the masking tape she used to secure her paper to the table. She slid a blank sheet of paper over her work-in-progress.

"What's the tape for?" Annie asked.

"I have to make signs," he said.

With scissors, he cut the tape into short, neat strips and then labeled them. FLOWER SHOP. DINER. FIRE DEPARTMENT. (On that one, the strip of tape he'd cut was too short and the letters in the last half of DEPARTMENT had to be squished together.) He made up several more labels and affixed them to the front of his buildings.

Annie had only one suggestion: "You should have a train store."

Charlie perked his head up. He'd run out of tape, and there was one building left that did not have a sign.

"May I make it for you?" Annie asked.

Charlie's tongue rested on his upper lip while he considered. "Okay."

She cut off a two-inch long strip of tape, stuck it to the table so that she could work on it, took from her coffee can of drawing implements a fine-point marker, and, in a calligraphic style, penned CHOO-CHOO'S TRAINS, adding shading to give the letters a three-dimensional look. Once done, she peeled the tape from the table and attached one end to the tip of her finger, then walked it over to where he sat on the floor.

"How about this?" she said as he delicately took it from her finger.

"That's way better than mine," he said admiringly as he placed the tape above the front display window of his last unlabeled structure.

"Hey, I do this for a living," she said, smiling.

"It's no wonder you picked that name."

"What do you mean?"

"That's where they all come from."

Annie still didn't understand, so Charlie uncoupled the caboose from the rest of the train, brought it over, and turned it upside down so his mother could see the sticker affixed to the underside.

It read: "Choo-Choo's Trains 122 Main Street Lucknow, Vermont." A zip code and a phone number with an 802 area code followed.

"It's on the bottom of all the trains," Charlie said. "You must have peeked."

"I guess I must have seen that and forgotten," Annie said.

Although she couldn't remember when.

IT WAS A little after one in the morning when Annie heard something.

She sat up in bed, expecting to once again hear a phantom train whistle, but that wasn't it. What she had thought she'd heard, in the seconds before she woke up, was a door opening. And not an upstairs door, like the one to Charlie's room, or the bathroom a few steps away.

This had the sound of a heavier door, if that made any sense. One that creaked on its hinges when you opened it.

In New York, she was always hearing something in the night. Ambulances and police cars and fire engines. In the wee hours of the morning, garbage trucks emptying huge Dumpsters. Sometimes even gunshots.

But even in New York—*especially* in New York—if you heard a door open, you might want to investigate. Because that meant someone was coming into your *house*. The world outside could go to shit, but once someone crossed the threshold into your domain, that was cause for fucking alarm.

Annie threw back the covers, reached out to turn on the bedside light, then stopped herself. If there was an intruder, did she want to let them know she was awake? Would she lose the element of surprise? Or was that what she should do? Let whoever had come into the house know she was up and that they better get the hell out.

Charlie.

Whatever plan she might settle on, the priority was to make sure Charlie was safe.

She slipped on her housecoat and crept out of her room and into the second-floor hallway.

There was no one there. No lights on.

She passed the open door to the studio. It was dark in there, save for some moonlight coming through the skylights. For a second she thought she saw a pinprick of light, no larger than the top of a pen, but when she blinked it was gone.

From the top of the stairs, she could see down to the entryway.

The front door was wide open.

Jesus Christ, someone is in the house.

A chill ran the length of Annie's spine. She was certain she'd locked the front door before she and Charlie went to bed. Yes, she was in the country now and security wasn't as big a concern, but old habits die hard. So how did someone get in?

Then it hit her.

Wasn't it possible, even after all these years, that Dolores had a key to the house? She'd cleaned for whoever had lived here years ago.

Crazy Dolores is here.

Okay, that was a bit harsh, Annie knew. The woman was suffering from some form of dementia that she couldn't help. But that didn't mean Annie felt any better about having her in the house.

She went to Charlie's room, found the door already open. The moonlight that was coming through the skylight was filtering through other windows, so rather than flip on a switch and startle him, Annie went right to his bed to wake him.

The covers were turned back. The bed was empty.

Annie tamped down an overwhelming sense of panic. Time for a change of strategy. No more pussyfooting about. She ran from the room, flipped on the hallway lights, and shouted: "Charlie! *Charlie!*"

No answer.

That didn't have to mean he wasn't in the house. She thought back to the sleepwalking episodes after John had died, how a brass band wouldn't have brought Charlie back to the real world. She'd already poked her head into the studio and found it empty, so she checked the bathroom, and when he wasn't there she ran down the stairs, flipping every light on along the way.

That open door did not bode well, and with Charlie missing, several possibilities presented themselves. Charlie had opened it and left on his own, either awake or in a dream state. A stranger had entered the house and Charlie was in hiding. Or someone had entered the house . . . and left with Charlie.

Annie ran through the open doorway and onto the porch, where the light was already on. There, at the foot of the porch steps, was Charlie's bicycle. The thought had crossed her mind that if he could sleepwalk, he might also be able to sleep-cycle. But seeing the bike didn't do much to put her mind at ease.

Again, she shouted: "Charlie!"

Nothing.

She ran inside, checking the kitchen, the basement, calling out her son's name every few seconds. She turned on the outdoor lights that illuminated the backyard and went out there, the cold, dewy grass tickling the soles of her feet. She ran to the shed where Charlie had found the box of trains, opened the door and looked inside, squinted, struggling to see in the dark.

Charlie was not there.

The outdoor lights only illuminated to the edge of the woods. She looked into the dark, foreboding trees and felt a sense of despair wash over her.

I have to call the police.

She ran back into the house and up to her room, where her phone was charging on the bedside table. She grabbed it, hit 911. The moment a dispatcher answered, she said:

"My name is Annie Blunt and I'm at 11318 Scoutland Road and my son is missing!"

The dispatcher wanted details. Annie put the phone on speaker and tossed it onto the bed, trying her best to answer the dispatcher's questions while she got into her jeans, pulled a sweater on over her head, and slipped her feet into a pair of running shoes, not bothering with socks.

She grabbed the phone again and headed for the stairs.

"Where are you going?" the dispatcher asked.

"Looking for him, what do you think?"

"Ma'am, stay at the house until the police—"

But Annie had ended the call.

She grabbed her keys from a decorative bowl on the front hall table and was out the door and in her car in seconds. All she could think to do was drive. Maybe Charlie was sleepwalking along the road, and if he was, she needed to find him before some driver coming home after too much to drink wandered onto the shoulder and—

"Shut up!" she said to herself. "*Shut up shut up shut up!*"

She hit the START ENGINE button on the center console, put the high beams on, and guided the car down the drive to the road. When she reached it, she had a decision to make.

Left or right.

Right would take her in the direction of Fenelon. Left would take her to that railway crossing, maybe half a mile up.

Annie turned left.

She drove slowly, window down, shouting out her son's name every ten yards or so. She scanned the road from shoulder to shoulder.

The high beams caught something. Up ahead, on the opposite shoulder. Where the road rose slightly to meet the railroad crossing.

Something small and blue and moving.

Charlie, in his pajamas, his back to the headlights. He was walking slowly, had almost reached the crossing. Annie didn't hit the gas, didn't want the sound of a racing engine to startle him. Once she was alongside, she stopped the car in the middle of the road, headlights still on and flashers activated, and jumped out.

"Charlie," she said, walking briskly to catch up to him. He was no more than thirty feet ahead of her. "Charlie, honey, it's Mommy."

Charlie had reached the crossing and gone left a few feet, standing between the rails, rusty just as Daniel had said. The ties underfoot were broad, rotted slabs of weathered, rotting wood.

Annie caught Charlie by the arm and knelt before him. She took both his small hands in hers and spoke softly to him.

"Charlie? Charlie? It's me. It's Mommy. You need to wake up."

Charlie, eyes open, seemed to look right through her.

"Come on, sport. You need to wake up and we need to get you home." She gave his hands a squeeze. "You really scared the crap out of me, you know that?"

Charlie said, "It's coming."

"What's coming, sweetheart?"

Still looking vacantly beyond her, he said, "It's coming."

Charlie raised an arm and pointed over his mother's shoulder.

Before Annie turned to look, she could feel a vibration in the ground beneath her. A truck, she thought, heading for the crossing. Her car was still in the middle of the road, but she'd left the lights and emergency flashers on. It was impossible to miss.

But Annie didn't see a truck, or a car, approaching from either direction. She looked back at Charlie and asked, "What's coming, Char—"

And then his face lit up, as though he were on a darkened stage and suddenly hit with a thousand-watt spotlight.

A deafening, primal, earthshaking roar followed, causing Annie's heart rate to skyrocket.

Annie whipped her head around to see what was bearing down on them.

It was a train.

The engine's headlight was so bright, so all-consuming, that it was impossible to see the rest of train it was attached to.

Annie wanted to scream, but there was no time for that. She

figured she had no more than a second, maybe two, to grab Charlie and throw them out of the train's path.

She pulled him in tight and in the moment before she jumped, the light was gone.

The vibrations ended.

The deafening roar ceased.

Slowly, Annie looked over her shoulder again. Save for a few stars in the sky, and the lights from her car, there was only blackness.

Charlie stirred in her arms.

"Mommy?" he said, looking at her as though he really did see her, his voice full of innocence and wonderment. "Where am I?"

TWENTY-SIX

B y the time Annie had bundled Charlie into the car and returned to the house, the night was ablaze with the flashing lights of two police cars. One was sitting down by the road, the other up by the house. Annie brought the car to a stop by the porch, a uniformed officer meeting her as she got out from behind the wheel.

"I found him," Annie told the woman, who identified herself as Officer Standish. Annie opened the back door of the SUV and carried out Charlie, who was groggy but awake. "I'm sorry."

"Not at all, ma'am," Standish said. "Where was he?" she asked.

"Just up the road," Annie said. "By the train crossing."

Should I tell her? Annie thought. *Should I tell her what I saw?*

"How'd your boy get all the way up there?"

Still holding Charlie in her arms, she said, "Just walked. He's had some issues with sleepwalking."

Standish said, "If he's got a history of that, you need to make sure he can't wander out of the house at night." She lowered her voice, as if that would keep Charlie from hearing what she had to say. "This isn't a busy road, but there's still traffic. No telling what could have happened."

Tell me something I don't know, Annie said. She could feel the judgment.

"Of course," she said.

"Just the two of you here?" the cop asked.

"Yes. We've taken the house for the summer."

"Where do you live?"

"In the city."

"Albany? Binghamton?"

"New York."

Standish gave her a look, wrote something down in her notepad. She said she had a few more questions.

"Do you mind if I take Charlie in first?" Not only did she want him back in bed, she didn't think she could hold him much longer.

The cop was agreeable.

She carried Charlie up the stairs, taking him first into the bathroom to wipe the soles of his feet clean with a wet washcloth, then gently placed him him in his bed. He was like a rag doll, letting her do whatever needed to be done. As he laid his head on the pillow, his eyes opened and he smiled.

"You okay?" Annie asked him, and he managed a nod. "Charlie, do you remember anything of how you got to where I found you?"

"No," he said quietly. "I remember going to bed, and then I was on the road with you."

She wasn't sure she could ask, but felt she had no choice. "What did you see when you woke up?"

"I saw you," he said.

"Did you see anything else?"

"Like what?"

"Just . . . anything?"

His head moved back and forth across the pillow.

"Okay," she said, leaning down, kissing his forehead, and pulling the covers up to his chin. She slipped out of the room and closed the door.

She stood a moment at the top of the stairs. She had an answer to that question she was asking herself moments earlier, about whether she would tell the officer what she had seen.

No fucking way.

Once she was back outside, Officer Standish peppered her with questions. She wanted to know Annie's full name, her date of birth, her New York address, a number where she could be reached, who she'd leased the house from.

"Why do you need all this? My son's home. He's okay."

"Just for my report. I think that's everything."

Annie watched as she got back into her cruiser, killed the flashing lights, and drove out to the road. Once she had turned and started driving off, the second car followed.

Something caught Annie's eye.

The lights were on in Daniel's house.

ANNIE PUT IN a call to the leasing agent first thing in the morning.

"Candace," she said, "do you have a handyman?"

She explained that she needed the home's two doors—front and back—to be as secure from the inside as they were from outside. Annie said that if Charlie had another sleepwalking episode, she didn't want him to be able to leave the house. At the same time, she didn't want the place difficult to get out of in the event of a fire or some other emergency.

Candace had a suggestion. "What about a chain on his bedroom door?"

Annie didn't like that. She wanted Charlie safe, but that didn't mean she wanted him to be treated like a prisoner. And what if he had to get up in the night to use the bathroom? But a chain on the front and back doors, mounted high enough that Charlie could not reach it, might be the answer.

"Let me talk to my guy and I'll get back to you," Candace said.

Annie had that call done before Charlie was even down for breakfast. He was more tired than usual, not surprisingly, but other than that seemed no worse for wear. His mother announced that they were going to do something different today. They were getting out of the house. No work for her, no trains for him. They were going to explore.

"We don't have to," Charlie said.

"But we're going to," Annie insisted. "We leave at ten. Got it?"

That gave them an hour before departure. Charlie still had to get dressed and brush his teeth. Annie stayed in the kitchen, reading the news on her tablet, but finding it hard to focus.

I hope I'm not losing my mind, she thought.

How else was she to explain what she'd seen in the night? That train had seemed so real. The roar of the engine. The ground trembling beneath her. The headlight glaring at them.

And then it was gone.

Annie hadn't spoken to her therapist, Dr. Maya Hersh, in some time. She wondered whether she would be available for a Zoom appointment. She used her phone to send an email, asking if she might have time for a session. Today, if possible.

"Ready!" Charlie shouted.

It was a fun afternoon, and good to get out of the house.

By chance, they ended up driving by a small regional airport outside Binghamton and stopped to watch small planes fly in and out for an hour. She and John had taken Charlie out to JFK once to see the big jets come in and take off, so watching smaller passenger planes and private craft land and depart was less dramatic but just as engaging. The airport had a snack bar, where they were able to buy a couple of hot dogs.

Continuing on, they spotted a place where you could pick your own strawberries. Annie asked Charlie if he wanted to give it a go, but he was puzzled.

"I thought strawberries came in little cardboard boxes," Charlie said.

Annie laughed. "And where did you think they were before they ended up in little cardboard boxes?"

"I never really thought about it," Charlie said.

Together, they filled two quart containers. Charlie was eager to pick more, but Annie said you could only eat so many berries and it wasn't like she was going to make a pie.

On the way home, they stopped at an ice-cream stand and bought two chocolate-dipped soft ice-cream cones, and while they were sitting on a nearby bench, Charlie said, "I like your new monster guy."

Annie stopped in mid-lick. "What?"

"The creepy thing you've been drawing. It's scary." But he didn't look troubled. He was intrigued.

"I'm just goofing around, is all," Annie said. "Trying something different while I figure out whether to go back to Pierce. When did you see it?"

"When you went to the bathroom I had a look. I could tell you didn't want me to see what you were working on. Are you mad?"

"I'm not mad. I guess I was worried it might upset you."

He shook his head, licked his ice cream. "Nope."

And that was the end of it.

Within minutes of getting back on the road, Charlie nodded off in the backseat. At least, Annie thought, she didn't have to hide what she was working on from him any longer. That was something of a relief, and their outing had managed to push her various anxieties to the back of her mind.

She'd had only fleeting thoughts about the night before, and had convinced herself she had not seen what she'd thought she'd seen. A brief delusion triggered by stress, she told herself. She'd been in a panic about finding Charlie. Her mind was going places it shouldn't. And when she found him, her relief so overwhelmed her that her brain short-circuited.

Okay, maybe that was something of an oversimplification. Her therapist, whom Annie had yet to hear back from, would have a more clinical analysis, of that Annie was sure. But as she headed home, she wondered whether she even needed to have a session. She felt better. She and Charlie had had a good day.

He woke up when she stopped the car in front of the house. "I think I fell asleep," he said.

"Just a bit."

Charlie unbuckled his seat belt, opened the back door, and slid out. His bike was right there, and he swung his leg over the seat.

"I think I'm going to ride around for a while," he said.

"Okay," Annie said. "But you stay on the property?"

"I will."

She aimed a menacing finger at him. "No riding up the road. Understood?"

"Okay."

"Good. I'm going to do a bit of work."

He pedaled off as Annie mounted the steps to the house, key in hand. Once inside, she looked on the back side of the door to see whether Candace's handyman had been by to install a chain. No joy there.

She set her purse on the hall table, fetched a bottle of sparkling water from the kitchen, and went up to the studio to review her sketches. Now that there was no longer any point in hiding what she was doing from Charlie, she was free to move to the next stage of her creative process.

She would make a three-dimensional version of her rat-wolf man.

Fin had been pretty thorough where it came to stocking her studio with everything she might need, including some packages of plasticine, but she had no wire to fashion into an armature that would serve as the support for her model. But she recalled seeing some white wire hangers from a dry cleaner in her bedroom closet here. She rounded up a couple, but then realized she needed something strong enough to cut the wire, like tin snips or something smaller, and a pair of pliers to twist the wire into various configurations.

Shit.

She could round up Charlie and head back to that hardware store in Fenelon, but that seemed like a lot of trouble. Annie was willing to bet Daniel would have the tools she needed, but their last meeting had not ended well, with Daniel revealing that he knew about Evan Corcoran. Plus, there had been their debate about train sounds in the night. Daniel acknowledging she might have heard them, even though no trains ran on that nearby line, and Annie changing her position, pushing back, saying it could have been a truck.

There had been a development. She'd more than heard a train that wasn't there. She'd *seen* a train that wasn't there.

Was she ready to talk to him about that?

Annie left her studio, went downstairs, and looked out the living room window. There was Daniel, across the way, sitting on his own porch, alone. She went to the front door, opened it, weighed whether to go see him.

No. I can't do it. I can't tell him.

Charlie went flying past on his bike. "Hey," she shouted. "We're making a quick trip into town."

THEY WERE BACK in under an hour. Annie had a new pair of pliers and snippers strong enough to cut through coat hanger wire. Charlie resumed training for the Olympics on his bike as Annie went up to the studio.

She fashioned a wire stick figure in short order, then wrapped crumpled tinfoil around it to build up the body. Next came the plasticine, which she worked up into a torso and limbs and a head. The details would come after she had the basic shape done.

She lost track of time. While she molded her rat-wolf, she reflected on why she was making it. Was she simply working out her demons? Was this anything more than an exercise? Did she really think she'd do a book with something this repellent? If not, what was the point?

What suddenly struck her was how quiet it was.

With Charlie outside riding his bicycle, the trains sat idle. Annie cast her eye at the world her son had created, the town within the large oval of track. The train was parked at the station, where Charlie always stopped it when he was done playing, a kind of courtesy to the imaginary crew, who could go in, use the bathroom, have something to eat.

The steam engine, the attached tender, the various cars, and at the end a caboose, sat there, motionless. The models featured such exquisite attention to detail. Even if Annie wasn't into toy trains, as an artist she could appreciate the work that went into them. The little engineer in the window of the locomotive, his striped hat and red kerchief at his neck, the *chuffchuffchuff* sound it made when under power. The way the doors on the boxcar could be slid open, loaded with cargo, closed again, and—

Hang on.

Something, some small motion, had caught Annie's eye from where she sat at her drafting table.

For a second she thought she'd seen the side door on the red boxcar move from its closed position. It had opened a fraction of an inch.

No, she had to be mistaken. She knew some of the accessories were motorized. A giraffe might poke its head up through the roof of a circus car. A helicopter could be launched from a flatcar. She knew, from looking at an online catalogue, that there was a wide selection of such items, including a cattle car that horses moved into by way of a miniature conveyor belt.

And, given that the transformer, which supplied power to the rails, was not plugged in, that boxcar door should not be moving. So—

It moved again.

Annie was certain this time. The door, no larger than a business card, had slid open another fraction of an inch.

Something long and black, not much thicker than a thread, had worked its way around the edge of the tiny plastic door, pushing it.

"*No no no no,*" Annie whispered.

Then a second thread—no, not a thread, because a thread didn't have joints like, say, a *leg*—emerged to assist, giving the door another nudge, opening it the better part of an inch. And then something larger, something black and round, emerged.

It was a spider. Or, at least, something *spider-like.*

Its body was about the size of a dime, but as its legs fanned out it appeared much larger. It began to extricate itself from the boxcar, its legs like feelers, reaching down for the floor. Finding the smooth surface, it slid out completely and paused, as if looking around, taking in its surroundings.

Annie shivered briefly. She was not a fan of bugs of any kind, but spiders ranked right at the top of the list.

She looked about for a weapon. The pad of art paper was far too big to roll up as a makeshift club. What she needed was a magazine, or a can of Raid she could use to spray the little motherfucker. Her eyes settled on the coffee can filled with markers and pens and brushes, the bottom of it perfect for crushing an unwanted visitor.

But as she went to pick it up, she saw more legs reaching around the edge of the boxcar door.

Another spider came out.

And then another. And another.

Like passengers arriving at their destination, they disembarked and started to head off in all directions. They kept on coming. Dozens at first, and then what seemed like hundreds. Thousands. A section of floor became black with them, an undulating carpet of spiders, moving slowly toward Annie.

How could that tiny car hold so many? How had they gotten in there in the first place?

Annie's breathing became short and hurried. She dropped the can, markers, pens, and brushes scattering across the floor. She had to get out of this room, out of this house, put Charlie in the car without bothering to pack one single fucking thing, and head straight back to New York.

She heard screaming and realized it was her.

She thought, for a millisecond, of Dolores. What had Daniel said?

"Even before I got to the house I could hear the screaming. Never heard a sound like that come out of my Dolores. I get in the house, and she's just standing there at the base of the stairs. Rigid, like she's at attention. Arms at her side, and she's got her mouth open and she's wailing. I'm standing right in front of her, sayin' her name, saying, 'Dolores, it's me, it's Daniel,' and it's like she's looking right through me, like I'm not even there."

Annie continued to scream.

She heard a noise from outside the studio. Someone racing up the stairs.

"Mom?" Charlie shouted. "Are you okay?"

He burst into the room and ran to his mother. "Mom, what's wrong? What's happened?"

Annie stopped screaming and pointed.

"What?" Charlie asked. "What are you looking at?"

Annie continued to point, but then blinked several times, quickly. The floor was clear. There were no spiders. Not a one. The boxcar door was closed.

"Mom?"

Annie pulled Charlie into her arms. "You're shaking," he said, his own voice trembling. "What's going on?"

Her phone, resting on the table, dinged, announcing a new email. Annie let go of her son, picked up the phone, opened the mail app.

It was from Dr. Hersh.

What are you doing now? her note read. **I can send a Zoom link if it's convenient.**

TWENTY-SEVEN

Annie needed a moment to pull herself together first. She told Charlie there was nothing to worry about, just a spider, then sent a quick email to Maya, asking if they could talk in half an hour. That gave her enough time to put together some dinner for Charlie. Mac and cheese from a box. Not her favorite, but that was fine, because she had lost her appetite.

"I've got a Zoom call and I'm going to take it on the laptop in my room," she told Charlie as he ate. "You good down here?"

He shrugged. "I'll watch TV."

She went to her room, closed the door, sat on the bed, and opened up her laptop. She clicked on the link Dr. Hersh had sent, and seconds later, there she was on the screen.

"Hey, Maya," Annie said. Her doctor had insisted she call her by her first name.

"Annie, long time, no chat," Maya said. "How's it going up there?"

"Okay."

"How's Charlie?"

"He's good, he's good. I got him a bike. It's a piece of crap, to be honest, but he doesn't care. He shined it up and he rides around the property like a maniac. We picked strawberries today."

Maya smiled. "Nice. But I'm guessing if everything were perfect, you wouldn't have been in touch."

"Yeah, well."

"What's on your mind?"

"You mean, other than thinking I'm losing it?"

"Talk to me."

Annie hesitated, not sure how to begin. "Did you ever see that old movie *The Rocking Horse Winner*? Or maybe read the story, by D. H. Lawrence?"

Maya thought for a moment. "The movie, I'm pretty sure. Made in the late forties, wasn't it?"

"Yeah, around then."

"Refresh my memory?"

"It's about this boy who has, well, a rocking horse, you know, a wooden toy you sit on and pretend it's a horse. But there's something special about it. It has . . . special powers. The kid rides his rocking horse until he gets visions of which horses are going to win at the track. It's pretty creepy."

"Okay. Not the first movie about a creepy toy." Maya smiled. "There's lots about creepy dolls. Chucky, Annabelle. That more recent one, Megan? That was kind of fun. What was that one with Anthony Hopkins, where he's the ventriloquist? Came out ages ago."

"*Magic*," Annie said.

"That's it. That one freaked me out. So what makes you bring up that rocking horse thing?"

"No judging, right? I tell you something that sounds totally off the wall, you're not going to laugh at me or anything."

"Annie, you know me better than that."

She had to steel herself to tell her. "Charlie found some trains."

"Trains?"

"Some toy trains. Left over in a box up here. An engine and cars and lots of track and some buildings. They were stored in a shed back of the house."

"My dad had trains," Maya said, sounding wistful. "When I was growing up, I thought it was kind of weird and didn't even want my friends to know, but when I got older, I saw that it was good for him. He was a fireman. I ever tell you that? Anyway, it was a good way for him to unwind. It's a big hobby, or was. Not sure how many kids are into it these days."

"Charlie asked if he could set it up, and he did, in the studio where I'm trying to get back to work. Sometimes . . . sometimes when I look at them, I get this kind of vibe off them, like there's something not right with them. Like . . . like they're looking at me, or they run when there's no power hooked up to it, or I see thousands of bugs crawling out of it that aren't really there. And Charlie had a sleepwalking episode last night and wandered up the road to an abandoned rail line, and when I found him I heard the train, saw it coming right at us, and then it was gone." She let out a long breath. "There, I said it."

There was a long silence.

"Jesus, say something," Annie said.

"What do you think's going on here?" Maya asked. "I mean, you're not saying this train set is possessed or something . . ."

Annie didn't say anything.

"Annie?"

"I don't know what I'm saying."

"You are a rational, brilliant woman, so I don't think I need to make the case that in the real world, a doll or any other kind of toy is just that. It might have an emotional attachment, like the stuffed toys we had as kids, but they're not *evil*. They're not possessed. They are not taken over by some kind of spirit. I think what's happening here is more obvious."

Annie waited.

"You're still processing what happened to John, still trying to find a way to deal with the tragedy of that young boy. A mind under stress does some pretty amazing things, Annie. And you're worried about Charlie. Your anxiety surrounding him is manifesting itself in ways that are hard to understand."

"Maybe so."

"And Charlie has found something he really likes. He's found a focus. These trains are probably a great way for him to think about something other than losing his father."

"He says John lives in his little town."

"Ah, I see. But, you know, it sounds like he's dealing with it, in his own way. And you need to let him."

"I don't know."

"Annie." Maya's tone said everything. *Pull yourself together, for fuck's sake.*

"You're probably right," Annie said.

"Do you need your prescription renewed? I can phone it in to a local drugstore for you if you let me know which one."

"I still have some," Annie said. "If I run out, I'll be in touch."

"You going to be okay?"

"I'm going to be okay," Annie said. "Thanks for this."

They said their farewells, and Annie slowly closed the laptop, thinking, *She's wrong.*

Across the road, Daniel was clearing the kitchen table of their dinner plates and asked his wife, "Can I interest you in a piece of pie?"

Dolores turned her head slowly to look at him. "What kind of pie?" she asked flatly.

"Peach. Got it in Fenelon. Your favorite place."

"Do we have any ice cream?" she asked.

"There was some vanilla, but we might have used it all up." He set the plates on the counter by the sink, went to the fridge. The freezer compartment took up the lower third. He gave the handle a firm tug and peered inside. "Here we go," he said. He brought out a carton and peeled off the top. "Just enough."

"Okay, then," Dolores said without enthusiasm.

Daniel opened a cardboard bakery box and slid out the pie, carefully cut out two slices and placed them on plates, then dug out the last of the ice cream. There was enough for a good-sized scoop for Dolores's slice. He put a small scoop next to his.

He brought the plates back to the table and sat down.

Dolores broke off a piece of pie with the edge of her fork, added a bit of ice cream to it, and put it into her mouth. If it gave her any pleasure, she showed no indication.

"Good?" Daniel asked.

"Yes," Dolores said, finishing a bite and swallowing. "It's very good, Daniel. Thank you for getting it."

He smiled, took a bite from his own plate. "That is a damn good peach pie they make."

"Yes."

"Their cherry is good, too. I think the last time I was there, I got cherry."

"Yes, I believe you did."

"But I'm gonna have to make sure we've got ice cream before I get another one," he said.

"Yes," Dolores said. "I like ice cream with my pie."

"What would you like to do tonight, hon?" He always asked her this, even though he knew the answer was always going to be the same.

"Whatever you want to do," she said.

"I was thinking we'd watch some TV."

"Okay."

Dolores finished her slice first, ran her index finger through some melted ice cream, and licked it off. "You do love your ice cream," Daniel said.

"She's going to come over," Dolores said.

"Is she, now," Daniel said.

He didn't have to ask who Dolores was referring to. He'd also been thinking Annie Blunt would be paying them a visit in the near future. There'd been quite the to-do over there last night. Two police cars. Daniel had been in bed but was wide awake and noticed the flashing lights coming through the curtains in their bedroom. Dolores was awake, too, but she chose to stay in bed when Daniel got up to see what all the fuss was about.

By the time he'd pulled on some clothes, he saw Annie's SUV turn back up the drive and come to a stop out front of the house. Daniel took a stroll out to the cruiser that was parked on the main road. A young man behind the wheel powered down the window.

"What's up?" Daniel asked.

"Boy went missing," the cop said. "But the mom just found him, brought him back."

"Oh, that's good," Daniel said. "Where'd he get off to?"

The cop pointed a thumb back over this shoulder. "Up that way."

Daniel looked. Not that there was anything to see this time of night, but he knew that up that way was the derelict railroad crossing. For a moment he considered heading up to the house to tell Annie that if there was anything he could do, let him know, but their last meeting had not ended well, so he went back inside.

When he got back under the covers, Dolores asked, "Did she see it?"

"I didn't speak to her. The boy wandered off, but she found him."

"For now," Dolores said, then rolled over and closed her eyes.

Now, sitting at the dinner table, she said, "Any time now."

"You took your meds? Don't want a repeat of what happened during that storm."

Dolores said, "I took them. Maybe you should make some coffee."

Daniel said, "I'll clean up, make a pot."

He started the coffee first, then rinsed off the plates and loaded the dishwasher. He was putting in the last fork—the one Dolores had used to eat her pie, and there wasn't a single crumb on it—when there was a knock.

Dolores pushed back her chair and went into the living room as Daniel closed the dishwasher and went to the front door.

Annie stood there on the porch, looking apologetic.

"Hey," she said.

"Hi, Annie. Come on in."

"Thanks," she said, but before accepting the invitation, she turned and said, "You just wait there."

"Okay."

Daniel peered down the porch steps and saw Charlie sitting there.

"He's welcome, too," Daniel said.

"He's fine."

He opened the door wider for her and led her into the living room, where Dolores was sitting in a recliner, staring at the television, which was tuned in to *Jeopardy!*, but the sound was muted.

"Would it be okay," Daniel asked, "if I took Charlie out a piece of peach pie? I'm afraid there's no ice cream left, but the pie is delicious."

"That would be . . . that's very kind of you. Charlie would love that."

"You have a seat and I'll be right back."

Daniel vanished into the kitchen, while Annie sat down on an angle from Dolores. "Good evening," Annie said. "I'm sorry to drop in on you like this."

Dolores, not taking her eyes from the TV, said, "I was expecting you."

The front door opened and closed. Annie could hear Daniel offering Charlie some pie, and a quiet, "Thank you very much," in reply. Seconds later, Daniel reappeared, offering coffee.

"Yes, that would be nice," Annie said. "A bit of milk."

"On it."

He brought out a cup for her and one for himself. "Dolores doesn't like coffee this late. Keeps her up."

He sat and said, "I'm sorry if I offended you the other day, bringing up that business."

Annie waved it off. "I was being oversensitive. What happened to me, it's no secret. It's out there."

"I'm glad Charlie is okay. I spoke to one of the officers last night, wondering what had happened. This was after you brought him home."

"He gave me a scare, that's for sure." She dropped her head, paused, then looked up, first at Daniel and then at Dolores. "I feel . . . a little foolish coming here tonight."

"Don't be silly."

She focused more on Dolores. "I don't want to bring up a difficult subject, but Daniel had mentioned to me something that had happened to you in that house," at which point she nodded in that direction, "that precipitated an . . . event." She looked worriedly at Daniel. "I hope I haven't made a mistake, saying that you told me about it."

"Not at all."

"The thing is," Annie continued, "there've been some . . . unusual things happening lately. And the latest . . . a few hours ago, it really affected me."

Dolores slowly turned her head to face Annie more directly. "You were scared."

"Yes, I was scared."

"And you screamed."

"I did."

"Because you saw something."

Annie nodded.

"Do you want to say what it was?"

She thought about that. "I don't know. Let's just say, it was awful. And it was very real. And then it was gone." A pause. "And there was something last night, too. It appeared, and then it was gone. I've been wondering whether I'm losing my mind."

Dolores, still in a monotone voice, said, "I did lose my mind. A part of it. Like losing a finger. It doesn't grow back." She paused, added, "My mind got scared away."

Annie leaned forward. "What frightened you? What did you see?"

"That's mostly in the part that's gone," Dolores said, and for the first time almost managed a smile. "I suppose that's a blessing."

"Do you remember what you were doing at the time?"

"I was cleaning."

"I mean, specifically."

Dolores went very quiet and her focus shifted, away from Annie to something undetermined.

"It's okay, honey," Daniel said. "You don't have to think about this if you don't want to." He turned to Annie and said, "We have these moments, sometimes, of clarity, but they don't last all that long."

Dolores said, "They weren't a happy family."

"Was this the photographers?" Annie asked.

Dolores shook her head slowly. "Long before them. The Andersons. They had a son and a daughter. Jeremy. And Glynis. She was a nasty child. Her hand was funny."

"What do you mean?"

"She lost a finger and they stitched it back on, but the doctors did it wrong and it always looked like she was giving you the finger." Dolores almost smiled. "They did a couple more operations on it but never did get it right. I wonder what ever happened to her." Her speech had taken on a dreamlike quality. "Her brother wasn't much better. Jeremy. Something wrong with him. Something wrong with all of them. They moved away."

"When was that?"

Daniel stepped in. "A few months into 2002, I think it was. Not long after Dolores had her episode."

"They didn't take it with them when they moved," Dolores said. "They figured it out."

"Didn't take what?" Annie asked. "What did they figure out?"

"I was cleaning," she said, ignoring Annie's quest for clarification.

Annie opted not to press. She waited.

"The boy's room . . ."

Dolores's eyes rolled upward, her pupils half-hidden by her eyelids.

"On the floor . . . it was all set up . . ."

Her eyelids started fluttering.

"What was set up?" Annie asked. "His trains?"

"Went to move them . . . touched them . . ."

She was starting to shake. Worry crossed Daniel's face. "This is worse than usual," he whispered to Annie. "I think we should stop before—"

"Fire in their lungs!" Dolores screamed. "All of them burning from the inside out! They can't breathe! *Can't breathe!*"

Annie recoiled, horrified. "I'm sorry," she said to Daniel. "She can stop. I don't want to put her through—"

"Everyone dying!"

Daniel had squeezed himself next to his wife and put his arms around her, trying to stop her trembling.

"Mom, come see! It's beautiful!"

Annie was on her feet. Daniel said, "You should go."

"I'm so sorry."

"Just go."

Annie backed out of the room, unable to take her eyes off the woman as Daniel encircled her in his arms, whispering to her that he was there, that everything would be fine, that the lady from across the road was going home.

Annie found Charlie where she'd left him, on the bottom porch step. He held out the plate, which had been scraped clean of peach pie. "That was really good," he said.

Annie took the plate from him and weighed whether to leave it on the porch railing, or discreetly go back into the house and leave it in the kitchen sink.

I can't go back in there.

Annie, sitting on the porch, had arrived at a decision.

She couldn't say that it was rational. She couldn't say it made any sense. But she was going to get that Tide box from the basement, pack up those trains, and return them to that shed. And if that padlock was broken, she would buy a new one.

Annie didn't know how she would explain it to Charlie. All she knew was that since he had found that box of toy trains, things had not been right around here. Whistles in the night, phantom trains running on an abandoned line, spiders coming out of boxcars.

She had an even better idea.

She'd tell Charlie they were going to spend another day exploring, and while she was away, she'd have Candace's handyman, if and when he ever showed up to put chains on the doors, pack up the trains and take them away. Forget putting them back in the shed.

Get rid of them.

She would tell Charlie the previous occupants had been in touch. When they'd moved, they had forgotten that Tide box, and could its contents kindly be returned to them?

Yes, that would work.

Or—and maybe this was the best idea yet—they could go home.

Getting away from it all, spending the summer in the country, was not the panacea she had hoped it would be. She could have them packed up in an hour. She'd feel bad, given all the work Finnegan had gone to. Annie would say Charlie missed his friend, that living up here had felt too isolating.

She heard the front door open, and Charlie walked out onto the porch.

"Hey, sweetie," Annie said. "I've been thinking, we had so much fun today, going to the airport, picking strawberries, that I thought we'd head out again tomorrow in a totally different direction. See what we might find. Or, and just hear me out here, we could go back to the city. If you feel like we're running out of stuff to do here, we could to that, too. What do you think?"

Charlie showed no reaction to the proposal. In fact, he had looked annoyed from the moment he'd walked into the room.

"I don't want you playing with my stuff," he said. "I like it the way it is."

"What are you talking about, Charlie?"

"I like the track the way it is. I don't want you taking it apart and making it into something different. It's just the way I like it."

Annie got up. "Show me."

They went back in, up the stairs, and into the studio. Charlie stopped and pointed.

"That," he said.

It took Annie a second to realize what had happened. Charlie had, from the beginning, put the track sections together to make a large loop. Two long straight sides, curved at each end, not unlike a horse-racing track.

The track pieces had been reassembled to make a figure eight. Annie stared disbelievingly.

"And you moved all the buildings around, too," Charlie said. "I'm going to hafta put it back the way it was."

TWENTY-EIGHT

Finnegan Sproule had been thinking about a surprise visit for several days.

Drive up to see Annie and Charlie and bring some New York with him. Now, lots of foods that were identified with the city wouldn't travel well. He couldn't bring a slice from Joe's Pizza or a dirty water hot dog from a street vendor or a fresh-off-the-grill steak from Smith & Wollensky, not when there was a drive of several hours involved, but he could arrive with a variety of bagels and some babka from Ess-a-Bagel. Maybe some cronuts from that place down on Spring Street, fruit tarts from Le Pain Quotidien. If he brought along a cooler and some ice packs, he could treat them to some cheesecake and some sliced pastrami.

And wine. Definitely wine.

He'd also wander some of the other divisions of the publishing empire he was part of, grab a few advance copies for Annie to enjoy. A Grisham that didn't come out for another five months, or another novel from actor Tom Hanks. Some books for Charlie, too, who Finnegan knew to be a reader.

His motives were not entirely altruistic. He could use a break from the city. It had been a hot, humid week and there wasn't much relief unless you wanted to run through a city-run splash pool with a bunch of grade-schoolers. So he decided to get his twenty-year-old Porsche Boxster out of the garage and give it a good run.

He had packed an overnight bag and booked a bed-and-breakfast for two nights not far from where Annie and Charlie were living so he could make a weekend of it. Finnegan did not have a partner—it was just him. He'd had a few boyfriends over the years, but there'd never been a relationship serious enough that he wanted to share accommodation, and he was okay with that.

He set out in the morning, after the worst of the rush hour was over, although rush hour was never really over in New York. But by eleven he was clear of the city and hitting the open road with the top down and AC blowing out of the vents.

The Porsche had no navigation system, but he had his phone hanging from a bracket on the dash to assist him with directions. Stopped along the way twice for coffee and bathroom breaks, and by midafternoon, he was closing in on the place.

It occurred to him Annie and Charlie might not be there when he arrived, and if that happened, what was he to do? Especially considering he was bringing some food that would need to come out of the cooler and go into a fridge. He put in a call to Candace, with whom he had arranged things, and asked whether she could leave a key in the mailbox for him if Annie and Charlie were out. He explained he wanted to surprise them.

She said she would be happy to oblige.

So when Finnegan arrived, and did not see Annie's SUV in the driveway, he was glad he had planned ahead. He parked out front, then walked back down to the road to the mailbox, where he found a key inside an envelope.

Just to be sure Annie wasn't home, he rapped hard on the door several times. When there was no response, he unlocked the door and opened it wide.

"Wow," he said under his breath. "Do I have excellent taste, or what?"

He didn't want to be overly intrusive. He decided he would just bring in all the goodies that needed to go into the fridge then wait on the porch for Annie and Charlie. He made two trips out to the Boxster, emptying the front trunk. He set the baked goods, like the cronuts and bagels, on the kitchen island where they couldn't be missed. He made two small stacks of books. One for Annie, and one for Charlie.

He was heading for the front door when he heard something.

Chuffchuffchuffchuffchuffchuffchuff

What the holy fuck was that?

Whatever it was, it was coming from upstairs. He froze, held his breath, waiting for the sound to repeat.

Chuffchuffchuffchuffchuffchuffchuff

It was a noise that took him back. If he wasn't mistaken, it sounded like a toy train he'd had as a kid. A Lionel train his father would set up around the tree at Christmas.

He had no business snooping around the house when no one was here, but then again, if that was a toy train, then maybe there *was* someone here, and they hadn't heard him banging on the door earlier.

"Annie?" he called out. "Charlie? It's Fin! I brought treats! You guys home?"

Chuffchuffchuffchuffchuffchuffchuff

Evidently not.

Finnegan found curiosity getting the better of him. He had to know what that sound was. He went slowly up the stairs, hand on the railing, and when he'd reached the second floor he stopped, not sure which way to go. The noise had stopped.

He went right, found what was clearly Charlie's room. The Spider-Man bedspread, the Harry Potter posters on the wall. He returned to the top of the stairs and went the other way, poking his head into the master bedroom, and then he found the door to the studio.

Finnegan opened the door, stepped inside, and smiled.

There was the drafting table, set up just the way he'd asked for it to be. And from the looks of things, Annie had been doing some work. He walked over, looked at a drawing she was in the middle of, as well as a sculpted figure to match.

"Jesus, Annie," he said aloud. "What the hell is this?"

A creature that looked like a cross between a rat and a wolf, but standing upright, like a person. Its eyes narrow and menacing, its teeth sharp.

"Annie, baby," he said under his breath, "this is no Pierce the Penguin."

He took in the rest of the room. On the floor was a miniature village made up of plastic building kits that Finnegan, again, thought he recognized from his childhood. Model train accessories.

But where was the train? Or the tracks?

Chuffchuffchuffchuffchuffchuffchuff

The noise seemed to be coming from the hall.

Finnegan went back out but didn't see anything. Maybe the sound hadn't been coming from upstairs, as he'd originally thought, but from the first floor, or even the basement.

He made his way back to the top of the stairs.

Took a step.

Chuffchuffchuffchuffchuffchuffchuff

He glanced down. Right there, spanning the top of the stairs, was a train track, and on it, a speeding locomotive with several cars behind it.

It was impossible.

It hadn't been there a second ago. He was sure of it. He'd come up these stairs two minutes earlier. There was no way he could have missed it.

But now it was here, and his foot had caught the edge of the track, knocked the red boxcar off, and now he was falling headlong. He reached for the railing but missed, and down he went, step after step, rolling and rolling until he reached the foot of the stairs, not moving, his neck snapped like a stick of celery.

TWENTY-NINE

Annie was sitting in the kitchen with the same police officer who had come the night Charlie had disappeared. Standish, her name was. Annie had sent Charlie to ride his bike around in the backyard. She couldn't send him to his room without having him step over Finnegan Sproule's body, which remained at the foot of the stairs as the police continued their investigation.

Standish asked for a glass of water. Annie ran the tap, filled a glass, and then Standish suggested they both take a seat. Standish asked, "Where did you and Charlie go today?"

"Just . . . driving. We'd talked about heading back to the city, but Charlie didn't want to, so we settled on an outing."

"Why were you thinking about going back to New York?"

Annie took a moment. "Just . . . Charlie misses his friends."

"So tell me about this outing."

"We went into Fenelon and had lunch and then kind of explored. We did that the other day, found an airport and a pick-your-own strawberries place, and today we went in another direction."

"When did you get home?"

"Just after four." She bit her lip, her eyes looking up toward the ceiling. "I saw the car in the driveway and recognized it, I said to Charlie, oh, look who's here. He didn't know, because he'd never seen Fin's car, but I explained. And since Fin wasn't sitting on the porch or hanging around outside, I figured he must have been inside."

"He had a key? Or had you left the house unlocked when you went out?"

"It was locked. I'm only guessing, but you should call this Candace person? The leasing agent? Fin arranged all this—setting me and Charlie up with this place for the summer—so he might have called ahead, asked her to let him in or to leave a key somewhere. So he could . . . surprise us."

Annie thinking, *He sure did that.*

"And so, since the house was probably open, once Charlie was out of the car he ran in fast as he could, and . . ." Annie stopped, struggling to regain her composure. She took a couple of deep breaths, and continued. "He was inside and he starting shouting and I ran in and there he was."

"At the bottom of the stairs. You didn't touch him or move him."

Annie said, "I didn't move him. But I got down and put my hands on him and I guess I was shouting his name, but . . ."

"Okay, I understand." Standish took a sip of water.

"I didn't want Charlie to see. I told him to go back outside and I called 911. And then I came out to the porch until you got here."

"He didn't call ahead? Let you know he was coming?"

Annie shook her head, glanced at the counter. "I guess he wanted to surprise us. He brought some of our favorite things. Bagels. Some wine and pastrami in the fridge."

"Your relationship with Mr. Sproule is a business one?"

"He's my editor." Annie had explained what she did for a living, that Finnegan had booked her this place as a kind of retreat to help her unwind before starting her next project. "Oh God, there's so many people that need to be called."

"Was he married?"

"No," Annie said. "No spouse, no children. But there must be other family. And everyone at the house will be devastated."

"House?"

"The publishing house. The people he worked with. This is so horrible." She put her head into her hands for a moment before asking, "What do you think happened?"

"That's what we have to determine," Standish said. "Did he have any health problems that you know of?"

"No. I mean, maybe he did, but he didn't share them with me. Do you think he had a heart attack?"

"That's something the coroner will have to determine. It appears he broke his neck. And he was at the bottom of the stairs. He might have tripped coming down them. Or maybe he did have a heart attack, or blacked out, or something, when he was at the top of the stairs, and then when he fell he suffered an additional injury."

"Why would he have gone upstairs?" Annie asked.

"I don't know. I was about to ask you."

Annie, puzzled, shook her head. "I could see him coming into the house when we weren't here to put things here in the kitchen, but I don't think he'd go snooping around upstairs,"

"Maybe to use the bathroom."

She pointed toward the rear of the house. "There's one back there."

"So he'd have had to go looking for it. Maybe it was easier to find one upstairs, and when he was coming back down, he tripped."

"Or maybe . . ." Annie was thinking. "Maybe he brought something for Charlie. Or he put something in my studio."

Standish put a finger in the air. "Give me a second. I'll be right back."

She left the kitchen. Annie could hear her exchanging words with people in the front hall. There was a commotion of some kind. A couple of minutes later, she returned.

"They've moved Mr. Sproule from the house," she said. "Why don't we go upstairs and have a look."

Slowly, Annie rose from her chair and followed the officer. At the foot of the stairs she stared briefly at the spot where her friend and editor had been found, and stepped over it as though he were still there. She went up the steps deliberately, hand gripped on the railing, and when she reached the top she needed a second, as if to orient herself to the house for the first time.

"I don't see what he could have tripped on," Annie said, looking down at the top of the steps. "There's no carpet or anything."

Standish nodded thoughtfully. "That's true," she said. "You didn't bring a pet from New York, did you? A dog or a cat? Something that might have darted in front of him?"

Annie shook her head.

"Any visitors to the house? Someone else who might have been here?"

"Candace was going to send a handyman around to put chains on the front and back doors."

"Was there some concern about someone getting in?"

"For Charlie," Annie said. "The other night? When he was sleepwalking and let himself out? I didn't want that to happen again. If the chain was mounted high enough, he wouldn't be able to reach it."

From where she stood, Standish could see the front door. "I don't see any chain."

"He still hasn't shown up." Annie sighed. "I guess he takes his time getting to these things."

"You know his name?"

"No."

"I can check with Candace," Standish said. "I know where to find her. Can ask her about the key, too." She appeared to be thinking.

"What?" Annie asked.

"Maybe he was here when Mr. Sproule was. Maybe they had a disagreement of some kind."

"And, what? Fin was *pushed* down these stairs?"

"I'm not saying that. I'd just like to talk to him, that's all." Standish smiled. "Just dotting the *i*'s and crossing the *t*'s. Show me your son's room."

Annie led the way, pushed the door wide open.

"You see anything out of place here? Anything that's here now that wasn't here before?"

Annie stepped into the room, walked about. "No."

"You're sure?"

"I'm sure."

"You said he might have left something in your studio?"

"Possibly."

Annie went back out into the hall, making a brief comment as she passed the bathroom—"I suppose he could have come up here"—and then entered the studio. The room was filled with light. Standish looked impressed.

"What a great place to work," she said. She pointed to the drafting table. "That's yours, of course."

"Yes."

"And that's quite something," Standish said.

Annie saw that she was looking at the train layout on the floor. "That's Charlie's setup."

"He's made a little town and everything."

They both stood there, neither speaking, until Standish finally asked, "So, you see anything different in here? Something Mr. Sproule might have left for you? Something that's not like it was before?"

"Nothing."

Although that wasn't entirely true. She did see one thing, but it hardly seemed worth mentioning to the officer.

There was a break in the loop of track. Two sections had come apart from each other. If the train were to be engaged, it would derail. And the wheels of the red boxcar, the one from which Annie had imagined seeing all those spiders emerge, were off the track.

Outside, Charlie pedaled his bicycle.

He went around and around and around the backyard. Pumping his legs as hard as they would go. Lap after lap after lap. Sweat running down his forehead and stinging his eyes. But neither that, nor the pain he felt in his calves and thighs, would slow him down.

His mother's friend's accident was a terrible, terrible thing. But it was also a sign. Things were coming to a head. Charlie had to be ready. He knew he would have to go soon.

I'm coming, Dad.

THIRTY

Annie had made up her mind for real, this time. She and Charlie were going home.

For all she knew, given what had happened today, he'd be ready to pack up and get the hell out of here, too. But she wasn't going to spring her decision on him until the following day, not until she was ready to put all their stuff into the car and hit the road.

Annie had spent the rest of the day, after Finnegan's body had been removed and the police had departed, dealing with the fallout. She first made calls to people Finnegan worked with in the publishing office, but it was getting late in the day and many had left. But she had several email addresses, and sent out a joint communiqué, explaining that Finnegan had come up to see her and that there had been a terrible accident.

She was, in effect, putting the ball in their court. They would know whom to reach out to about making the necessary arrangements. Someone else could take the lead here. Annie felt guilty, not volunteering to be that person. Finnegan was a good friend. He'd discovered her, launched her, and she owed so much of her success to him. But he had always been a very private person, telling her very little about himself, and, while Annie felt that was probably not a sufficient excuse not to get involved, she simply was not up to it.

It didn't take long before she received responses to her group email. Texts, emails, and a call from the publisher herself, Finnegan's superior. "We've got this," she said. "You do what you have to do. We'll handle it."

Finnegan had a brother outside of Boston, she told Annie, and she had already been in touch with him. If he had any further questions, he was to get in touch with the local authorities, not Annie. The keys to his Boxster could be left with them; the brother would figure out what to do with it, how to get it back to the city or Boston or wherever.

"Thank you," Annie said.

And, while Annie was glad to be relieved of those responsibilities, she was still feeling traumatized, and worried Charlie was as well. After all, he'd found Finnegan. Later that evening, she sat down with him in the living room, the TV on in the background but the sound off.

"How you doing?" she asked, sidling up next to him on the couch and slipping her arm around him.

"I'm okay," he said.

"I'm really sorry about what you went through."

"I've never seen a dead person before," he said. "Except on TV. I've seen lots of dead people on TV."

"But it's not the same."

"One's pretend," Charlie said. "And one's real."

"Yeah. You have any questions? You want to talk about it?"

Charlie shrugged. "I don't know."

"You must be wondering how it happened."

"Not really," Charlie said.

That gave Annie pause. "Nobody can figure out how it happened."

"He must've tripped," he said, like it was simple.

"Well, yeah, he did, but how he tripped is kind of hard to figure out."

"Sometimes people just trip."

"That's true. I just want to be sure you're okay. I'm worried you might have bad dreams or something."

"I'll be okay."

"Why don't you bunk in with me tonight."

"I'm not a baby."

Annie wasn't sure whether to feel hurt or relieved. But if her son was strong enough to deal with this, well, that was a good thing, wasn't it? And considering what he'd already been through in the past year, maybe he was tougher than she gave him credit for.

"If you change your mind, that's okay."

He glanced at the muted TV. "Can we watch a movie?"

"I guess. Was there one in particular you wanted to see?"

"Doesn't matter." As she went to pick up the remote, he said, "What are we going to do?"

"What do you mean?"

"Are we going home?"

She put the remote back down on the coffee table.

"I . . . I don't know. What do you want to do? Do you want to go home? Because if you'd like that, that would be okay."

Make it seem like his idea, she thought, *even though I'm ready to leave right this second.*

"I don't know," he said. "Let's talk about it tomorrow?"

"Sure. We could do that. Sleep on it."

Charlie nodded. "And can I take home the bike?"

"Uh, let me think about that."

"And the trains?"

Annie thought about the lie she had been formulating earlier. About how to get rid of those fucking toy trains.

"I don't think we can do that," she said.

"Why not?"

"I had a call. The people who used to live here. They didn't call me, but they called the lady, the one we got the place from? And then she got in touch with me. When those people moved out, they forgot to take that box of trains with them. So we're going to have to pack them up so they can be shipped to wherever they live now."

Charlie stared at her.

"What?" she said.

"They really said that?" he asked.

Annie wondered whether she had a tell. A facial tic, something Charlie could read in her expression that would give her away, that he would spot and know she was lying.

"Yes," she said.

He nodded slowly. "Oh well," he said. "They were fun to play with while I had them."

Annie smiled. "When we get home, we'll look into replacing them. A brand-new train set. What do you think about that?"

"I guess."

If he was excited, Annie thought, he was doing a good job of hiding it. But at least he didn't fight her. She believed that by tomorrow he'd be on board with leaving. If it weren't for the fact that she hated driving at night—even if Sherpa would be happy to guide her— she'd pack up the car and go right now.

She'd just put Charlie to bed when she heard a car pulling up to the house. When Annie went out onto the porch, Candace was getting out of her car.

"It's just so awful," Candace said, standing at the foot of the porch steps, then stepping up onto the first one.

Annie did not feel inclined to invite her in and stood at the center of the top step, as though blocking the woman's path.

"Yes," Annie said.

"The police came to see me. It's all my fault."

Annie waited.

"Mr. Sproule was in touch, asked me to leave a key in the mailbox in case you weren't here when he arrived." Her chin quivered. "I shouldn't have done that. I had the best of intentions."

The road to hell, Annie thought.

"He was so excited about coming to see you, to bring you some New York treats. If I had known, if I'd had any idea—"

"It doesn't matter."

"And I came to tell you that I'm so sorry that Bert—he's my handyman—hasn't been by to install the chains, but he got swamped with some other projects and has promised to come by tomorrow, and—"

"We're leaving."

"You're what?"

"First thing tomorrow. We're packing up and going home."

Candace nodded slowly. "I can't blame you for that. I wish things had turned out differently."

There was something in the back of Annie's mind, something she had been meaning to ask Candace about.

"The photographers," Annie said. "The ones who were here last."

"Yes?"

"Why did they leave?"

Candance looked uncomfortable. "Sometimes people want a change."

"I'm betting there was more to it than that."

"It doesn't matter, anyway. You've decided to leave, so leave."

"What were their names?"

"I really don't—"

"Names. If you don't tell me, I'm betting Daniel will know. But I'd really rather not bother him right now. His wife's not well. Is it Smitherton? That's the name still on the mailbox."

Candace sighed, as though admitting defeat. "Yes. Graham and Steph. Short for Stephanie."

"Where'd they move to?"

"New Haven, I think. They were from there originally. Look, I'm really sorry how things turned out, but if you ever—"

"Good night," Annie said, turned and went back into the house.

It didn't take her five minutes of Google-searching on the laptop in her bedroom to find a Graham and Stephanie Smitherton in New Haven who ran a photo studio. Their website offered a variety of services, from simple things like passports to more ambitious projects like weddings. There was a phone number, but when Annie called it went straight to voicemail. It was late in the day, and their business hours were nine to five.

There was an email address. Annie dashed off a quick message, identifying herself not as someone who lived in their former residence, but as the children's book author and illustrator. (She hoped they might recognize her name.) She said she had an urgent request, and would they be good enough to call her when they received this email?

She hit SEND.

While she awaited a reply, she set about getting Charlie and herself ready to leave. She went downstairs, eyed the unfinished jigsaw puzzle. Only the border and most of *The New Yorker* masthead were finished. She took the open box, held it under the edge of the table, and swept all the pieces—those that had not yet been placed and those that had—into it, slid the lid back on top of it, and gave it a shake. She held the box a moment, as though wondering in what bag she'd place it for the trip home, then opened the door to the cupboard below the sink and shoved it into the garbage bin.

Annie took a look in the fridge and the pantry, assessing what, if anything, she might take home with her. She would need to make a lunch for the trip, something they could eat in the car. She didn't want to stop on the way for anything but gas and bathroom breaks. She wanted to put this place as far behind her as quickly as she could.

Her eyes went to the bag of bagels Finnegan had brought, and teared up.

Problem solved.

Her cell phone, which she had left by the kitchen sink, rang.

"Hello?" she said.

"Ms. Blunt?" a woman asked.

"Yes. Is this Stephanie Smitherton?"

"Call me Steph."

"And please, call me Annie."

"I can't tell you how excited I was to hear from you. I'm a real fan, and we don't even have kids. I love your work, and I can't even imagine why you're calling me. What can I do for you?"

Annie hated to burst the woman's bubble. "I'm afraid I wasn't entirely up-front in my email. I have something unrelated to my work to ask you about."

Steph said, "Oh?"

"My son and I have been staying in the house you used to live in. The place near Fenelon."

Silence on the other end of the line.

"Steph?"

"I'm here." Her voice, friendly a moment earlier, was now cold. "What is it you want?"

"I wanted to know why you left this place."

"I don't know what business that is of yours."

"Something's not right here. I'm reluctant to discuss it with anyone, but as a former resident, maybe you wouldn't think what I have to say sounds so crazy."

"I don't think I want to know."

"But if I were to tell you strange things have been happening to my son and me, would you be surprised?"

After a few seconds, Steph said, "No." There was a pause, and then she said, "You went to the garden shed."

"My son did."

"You won't be able to get rid of them," Steph said. "We tried. We put it out for trash pickup one day, but the next time we went into the shed, it was still there. We took it into Fenelon and threw it into a Dumpster behind a pizza place, and that didn't work, either. The box always returned."

Annie felt a chill.

"What sort of . . . phenomena . . . did you experience?" Annie asked.

"I *really* don't want to talk about this. We've tried to put it behind us. But we couldn't run our business there. It wasn't possible."

"Why?"

"None of the photos we took were usable."

"Why was that?"

More silence. Then, "This is just an example, but one you can see. A couple came in with their six-month-old son, hired us to do a family portrait. We had a setup in the studio, a nice backdrop, perfect for that kind of thing. But we couldn't get a good picture. None of the shots taken there could be used. See for yourself."

"How?"

"In the basement. There's a big kind of worktable there, with drawers."

"Right."

"There's a couple of pictures left in one of them. I threw all the others away, but I saved those. Like proof, you know? But when we moved, I just left them there. You might have to stare at them for a few seconds to understand what I'm talking about. Please don't contact me again. I've nothing else to say about this. I'm sorry."

"What should I be looking—"

"Goodbye."

Steph ended the call.

Annie put down the phone, stupefied. She took barely a moment to collect her thoughts and headed for the basement.

She went to the worktable, started sliding open the drawers. Two of them were filled with old screws and clamps, one was empty, but the last one had a couple of what Annie thought of as eight-by-ten glossies. She whipped them out.

Two pictures of a black couple, late twenties, sitting close together, dressed sharply, their baby boy sitting across both their laps, looking anywhere but at the camera. The tot was dressed up in a tiny suit, a small bow tie at his neck. The parents look frustrated, no doubt because the baby was distressed, his face in a grimace. The fact that Steph had this shot printed suggested the others were even worse.

Behind them was a blue velvet draping that ran over the seats they were perched on, and on down to the floor.

"I don't get it," Annie said to herself.

It was far from an ideal family portrait, given how uncooperative the little boy was, but other than that, what was the problem? What was it Steph expected Annie to see? There was nothing ominous about—

Oh fuck.

Steph had been right. You had to look at the picture for a moment. It was like those so-called 3D "magic eye" posters from the nineties, where if you stared at them long enough you saw a hidden image.

It was like when her inspirational pane of glass would appear.

Only the edge visible at first, but then the glass began to turn. And Annie saw something take shape in the folds of the backdrop fabric.

For a second, and then it was gone. She would blink a couple of times, and it would reappear. Then vanish. She'd squint, and it was back again.

A face, but not human. More like a rat, or maybe a wolf. Or a combination of the two.

Annie knew this face.

She shoved the pictures back into the drawer and slammed it shut.

Dawn, she thought as she went upstairs to her bedroom. *At dawn, we are getting the fuck out of here.*

THE NEXT MORNING, when she got up, Charlie was gone.

THIRTY-ONE

Annie had one of the worst sleeps of her life, woke up for good at five, and shortly before six decided to jump out of bed and get moving.

Before heading downstairs, she showered, dressed, and packed up her clothes. Filled the two suitcases she'd brought for herself, gathered up all her items in the bathroom. Stripped the sheets from the bed, tucking them into a pillowcase, and threw the cover back on. Candace could put on a fresh set when she rented this place out to someone else—if she even did.

Then she entered the studio. Her work area had been set up by Finnegan before her arrival, so much of what was here duplicated what she had at home. And yet, it seemed wrong to leave everything here. What were the odds Candace would find another artist/illustrator to take the place? And wasn't it borderline disrespectful to Finnegan to let all this stuff be pitched? She would have to think about this. There were some empty grocery bags in the kitchen to pack up some brushes and paints and whatnot.

She had a moment's hesitation about taking home the illustrations of her latest creation, as well as the six-inch tall figure she'd made of it. In the last couple of days, she had put the finishing touches to it. Detailed the trench coat, perfected the hairy, claw-like paws or hands extending from the sleeves and pant legs. Worked on those menacing eyes, the sharp teeth.

If anyone had asked her the day before whether she would take this work home with her, she wouldn't have hesitated.

But this morning, the memory of what she'd seen in that studio portrait haunted her. And not because she was seeing it for the first time, but because it reinforced what she had seen before. Years ago, when she was a child, and then again, years later, since coming to this house. Why was this Penn Station rat-wolf eating its way into her brain? Was it something intrinsic to this house? Did it have something to do with the trains? And would packing this representation she'd made of it be like taking home a memento of a nightmare?

She concluded, finally, that leaving it behind wouldn't erase it from her memory. She'd made it with her own hands, for Christ's sake. *It was a part of her.* To toss it was to admit her fear of it. Well, fuck that.

She would pack it.

Despite wanting to leave early, she wasn't going to wake Charlie at this hour. His door was closed, and she would let him sleep. Stealthily, she brought her two suitcases down the stairs and set them inside the front door. In the kitchen she found some bags that would hold everything she wanted to bring home from the studio.

But first she decided to prepare some food for the trip. She took the bag of bagels Finnegan had brought. She was thinking he'd brought an entire dozen, but there were only six. Still, plenty for the trip home. She put just butter on three, and cream cheese on the other three. She would have put peanut butter on at least one of them, but she couldn't find it in the cupboard. She put the bagels into the small cooler Finnegan had brought, along with an ice pack, mainly for the ones slathered with cream cheese. There were several different bottled beverages in the fridge that she'd add just before they left.

Back to the studio she went with several bags. She packed up everything she wanted to keep, and took extra care with the figure, wrapping it in some paper before placing it in a Bloomingdale's canvas tote with the words MEDIUM BROWN BAG printed on the side.

She cast her eye on the train layout on the floor.

"Goodbye," she said.

And she could have sworn, for a split second, the headlight on the engine flicked on and off. She stared at it for several seconds, willing it to flash once more, but it did not. She was leaving everything there as it was. She was not going downstairs for that Tide box and packing it up. Let Candace do it.

She went back down to the front hall, grabbed her car remote, went outside, and hit the button to open the tailgate. She put everything in. The only stuff left to pack was what was in Charlie's room.

He had asked about taking the bicycle home, a question she had dodged. She didn't want to take it, didn't want him riding around the streets of New York. And even if she were to change her mind, she would want to get him a better bike.

All of which was moot if she couldn't fit it into the back of the car with the rest of their stuff. To gauge its size, Annie walked over to the side of the porch where Charlie'd been parking the bike.

It was not there.

That gave Annie a brief start, but then she remembered that when the police were here, she'd instructed Charlie to ride it out back of the house. So she rounded the corner, walked down the side, then into the backyard.

The bike was nowhere to be seen.

Annie had a bad feeling.

It could have been stolen, of course. Not as likely here as in New York, but possible. Someone driving by could have seen the bike up by the porch, run up, and taken it. Except it would have been after dark, and the bike would have been hard to see from the road, and who would want a shit bike like that anyway?

Annie ran back around to the front and into the house, no longer making any effort to be quiet. She bounded up the stairs and pushed open the door to Charlie's room.

The bed was empty.

"Charlie!" Annie shouted loud enough, she believed, to be heard back in New York.

No answer.

Maybe he was in the basement. Why, she couldn't imagine, but if he was, he might not have heard her calling for him. Seconds later, she was down there, shouting his name every few seconds.

Had he gone sleepwalking again? Had he taken the bike, pedaling madly in a trance-like state?

She ran back out front. If he'd gone the same route as last time, he could be at the defunct railroad crossing. She got in her car, fired it up, and, kicking up gravel, sped down to the road and hung a left. She tromped down on the gas and was at the crossing within a couple of minutes, but there was no sign of Charlie, or his bike.

Daniel.

Would Charlie have gone over there to talk to Daniel or Dolores? Craving another slice of peach pie? It seemed unlikely, but he had to be *somewhere*. She did a wild three-point turn and sped back, this time turning into Daniel's place instead of hers, hitting the brakes so hard the SUV did a short skid.

Daniel, evidently an early riser, was at the door before Annie reached it.

"What's wrong?" he asked.

"Have you seen Charlie?" she asked breathlessly.

"Charlie?"

"He's gone. His bike, too."

Daniel shook his head. "No. You been up the road?"

She nodded.

"Both ways?"

Annie blinked. "No."

"Maybe he went to Fenelon," Daniel said.

That would be a long bike ride, Annie thought, but Charlie had to have gone someplace, and Fenelon made as much sense as anything else.

"Would you do me a favor?" she asked. Daniel waited. "Will you go to the house, in case he comes back? I'm gonna go up the road a few miles."

He nodded.

Annie ran back to her car—she'd left the engine running—and took off in the other direction.

She'd driven nearly three miles when she pulled over to the side of the road. How far could Charlie have cycled, realistically? If, in fact, that was what he'd done? Just because the bike was gone didn't mean Charlie had ridden it. Someone could have grabbed the bike independently of Charlie embarking on another sleepwalking adventure. Or Charlie could have sneaked out of the house and gone on a midnight ride, and—

Oh Jesus.

He could have been hit by a car. Some drunk driver could have strayed onto the shoulder. A careless driver could have been looking at his phone. Annie might already have driven past him. Charlie and the bike could be in a ditch.

She got out her phone and called 911 for the third time this week.

"Do you have any idea when he might have left?"

Officer Standish, once again. Asking questions, and Annie at a loss to answer them.

"I don't know," she said, standing out front of the house. "I didn't hear a thing. His door was closed when I got up around six."

"And you don't think he went sleepwalking this time."

"I just don't know. Could he do that on a bike?"

"I am aware of incidences of people doing complex tasks while in that state," Standish said. "People have prepared meals, eaten, even driven cars while in a sleepwalking state."

"Oh God." Annie put a fist to her lip, pressed. "Someone could have . . . not paying attention . . ."

"We've got police going up and down the road, walking it, looking on both sides, in case something like that happened. Your neighbor Daniel? He's out with them, helping. So far, nothing." She paused, then asked, "Could this have anything to do with what happened to Mr. Sproule?"

Annie said, "How?"

"Only hours after Mr. Sproule's death, your son is missing. That's a lot to happen in less than twenty-four hours."

"I don't understand . . . how could they be connected? I mean, yes, Charlie was the first to find him, but . . ."

"Was he pretty upset about that?"

"Of course he was upset! Who wouldn't be upset?" But even as she said the words, Annie thought back to the night before when she was having her heart-to-heart with Charlie, and how he was less traumatized by what had happened than she might have expected. But that didn't have to mean anything.

"Upset enough that he'd feel he needed to get away?" Standish asked.

"I don't know," Annie snapped, growing exasperated. "He's not *here*. Can't we just focus on *finding* him? Does it matter why he left? Does it matter whether he was sleepwalking or freaked out by what happened to Fin? Shouldn't we just find him?"

"You seem very upset," Standish said, keeping her voice even.

"For fuck's sake, you think?" Annie shot back.

"Maybe we should go in and sit down, take a minute." She put a hand on Annie's shoulder, getting ready to guide her into the house.

"We're wasting time, standing here," Annie said, pushing Standish's hand away and heading for her car.

"No, Ms. Blunt, I'd like you to stay here. I have more questions."

"About what?"

"Well, frankly, I'd like to ask you a few questions about your state of mind."

"I'm sorry, what? I'm fucking scared to death, that's my fucking state of mind."

"And I totally understand that, I do. But right now we've got lots of people looking, and if we could talk through a few things, that would help. Please. Could we take a seat?"

Standish tipped her head toward the porch. With some reluctance, Annie agreed to walk away from her car and sit down on one of the porch chairs. Standish took the next closest one to her.

"I understand this has been a very difficult year for you," the officer said.

"Christ," Annie said. "First Daniel, and now you. Everyone's googling me. I'm starting to feel like I'm *trending*."

"You lost your husband, and before that, all that controversy about the boy who thought he could fly."

Annie bit her lip and look away. "I don't need reminding."

"And now your son's missing not even a full twenty-four hours after this man, Mr. Sproule, died in your house."

"Make your point."

Standish hesitated before making it. "There has been an inordinate amount of trouble for people in your orbit."

Annie slowly turned her head and narrowed her eyes. "Are you saying that I'm somehow responsible?"

"It's an observation. Not necessarily responsible, but somehow at the center of things."

"I didn't know that boy. Evan Corcoran. I'd never met him. But, believe me, even though that book sold hundreds of thousands of copies, and there were no other similar incidents, his death weighs on me every day, and no matter what anyone says, I feel responsible. So, yeah, that one's on me, I suppose. He was in my orbit, as you say. And John? That was a hit-and-run. He walked out into the street looking at his phone and some son of a bitch ran him down. So, another one in my fucking solar system."

Standish pursed her lips thoughtfully. "As I said, it was an observation. And a sympathetic one, whether you choose to believe that. The stress, the grief, it must be incalculable."

Annie said nothing.

"Are you under any kind of care?" Standish asked.

"Am I what?"

"A counselor? A therapist? A psychiatrist?"

Annie slowly rose out of the chair. "Get out," she said.

Standish remained seated. "Please, Ms. Blunt, I mean no offense. I'm simply—"

"Get out!" Annie said again, and this time Standish stood. "Is this how they do things here? When your son goes missing they accuse you of having something to do with it?"

"I've made no such accusation."

"Well, there's a fuck-ton of insinuation in the air."

"We're going to go through the house now," Standish said matter-of-factly.

"What? I've been through the house. Charlie's not here! I've looked. His bike is gone! Why are you—"

Standish raised a hand. "You'll stay out here while we take a look." She waved one of the other officers over, directed him with her thumb to head inside.

"You have no right to—"

"I'm not asking."

With that, Standish turned and followed the other officer into the house, leaving Annie standing there, shell-shocked.

It was the longest day.

Police from neighboring counties came in to join the hunt, which was expanded from roadways to nearby forests. Once the police were done with searching the house—Annie could only assume they believed she'd killed her own son and were looking for, if not his actual body, some evidence he'd died on the premises—they allowed her to come back inside.

Standish insisted she stay on the property and allow others to conduct the search. At one point, a van with ACTION NEWS emblazoned on the side was parked down at the end of the driveway. From the porch, Annie could see Standish being interviewed by a young woman with big hair who was accompanied by a cameraman. When the reporter failed to come up to the house to get a quote from her, Annie could only assume Standish had not permitted it. Didn't want the media interviewing their prime suspect, Annie guessed.

Okay, *sure*, there *had* been a lot of shit happening in her fucking *orbit*, Annie conceded. But this—this was just lazy police work. Without any evidence, they were zeroing in on her because it was *convenient*. And whatever energy they were focusing on her wasn't being directed toward finding Charlie.

Oh, John, I wish you were here.

By late afternoon, as the search continued, Annie began to feel faint and realized she'd eaten nothing all day. For reasons of pure survival, she went into the kitchen and ate one of the bagels she'd put in the cooler. That, and a coffee, gave her some strength, but to do what? She wanted to be out looking for Charlie, too, but what area would she search that hadn't already been combed over by the police?

She had to think about this in a different way. The question wasn't where Charlie was. The question really was: Why had he left? Maybe Standish was right. Charlie's motive for leaving was critical.

If she believed Charlie was still alive—and she simply *had* to— and that he had not been abducted but left on his own accord, where would he go?

Back to the city? He might want to, but on a bicycle? It was hundreds of miles, and he'd be spotted somewhere along the way. A kid that little, pedaling on an interstate highway?

If not the city, then—

"Ms. Blunt?"

She put down her bagel and turned to find Standish in her kitchen. There was nothing in the officer's expression that suggested good news.

"We're scaling back the search, for the moment," she said, "but that doesn't mean we're done. We're short of people. We're in the process of bringing in more teams. We have someone coming with tracking dogs. There are still going to be some people on this tonight. We're bringing in a plane first thing in the morning that can pick up heat signals, so if Charlie is lost in the woods somewhere, we have a good chance of finding him that way, provided he's . . . We could find him that way. I want you to know we're not giving up. We're throwing everything we have at this tomorrow. Plus, we've got media coverage. A lot of people, just regular folks, are going to be checking their own property to see whether Charlie might be there."

Annie said, "Okay."

"And you have my card. You can call me. Doesn't matter when."

Annie said nothing.

Standish started walking backward from the room. "So, tomorrow, then."

And then she was gone.

A moment later, Annie walked out to the porch and watched the various police and other emergency vehicles depart. Feeling weak, she settled into a chair until the last of them was gone.

It was suddenly very quiet.

Annie bowed her head and began to weep. She was long overdue for a meltdown. She owed herself one. She cried and cried and cried.

"Oh, Charlie," she said under her breath. "Charlie, Charlie, Charlie, where the fuck have you gone?"

She cried some more. And then she heard something over the sound of her own weeping. Something from inside the house.

Chuffchuffchuffchuffchuffchuffchuff . . .

THIRTY-TWO

*C*harlie's home, she thought. *He's upstairs playing with his trains.*
Annie shot out of her chair and entered the house and ran up the stairs to her studio. "Charlie!" she shouted. "Charlie!"

Somehow, she figured, he had to have been home all this time, hiding so well that even the police had been unable to find him. Could he have been in the attic? Did this house even *have* an attic? If there was an access to it, she'd failed to discover it in the time they'd been here.

She burst into the studio, expecting to find her son on the floor, hand on the throttle of the transformer, guiding his train around and around the loop.

Charlie was not there.

"*Stop it!*" Annie cried. "*Just stop it!*"

But the little steam engine kept on going. In fact, rather than slowing down or stopping, the train began to move even more quickly. It was whipping around the loop and the village Charlie had made with greater speed than Annie had ever seen it go before, faster than she would have thought possible. It was traveling so swiftly that it was becoming a blur, as though it were a floor-level jet.

It was a wonder that the cars weren't being flung from the tracks as they went into and out of the curves. And then that was exactly what happened.

A rail disaster on a small scale. The engine and the tender, as well as the various attached freight cars and caboose, became uncoupled from each other and scattered, the centrifugal force sending them across the floor in all directions. The steam engine hit one of the legs of Annie's drafting table and broke into several pieces. The red boxcar from which Annie had imagined seeing spiders emerge hit the baseboards on the far side of the room and broke apart.

The caboose flipped over onto its side and skittered across the floor and came to an abrupt stop when it hit the toe of Annie's shoe.

She stared down at it.

Positioned as it was, she could see the sticker affixed to the bottom bearing the name and address of the store from which it had originally been purchased.

Annie bent over and picked up the caboose. She read aloud what was on the sticker.

"Choo-Choo's Trains, 122 Main Street, Lucknow, Vermont."

She thought back to what Charlie had said one day while playing with this train.

"This is the place where Daddy lives now."

And then Annie recalled something else Charlie had said to her. When he had worked up a sweat riding his bike around and around the house for so long. Why was he doing that? she had asked him.

"Just in case I ever had to ride somewhere far one day."

Annie put the caboose down, took out her phone, opened up the map app, and looked up Lucknow. If it was in Vermont, then it could be relatively close, depending on what corner of that state it was in. She found it in seconds, saw that it was in the southwest. A hike, to be sure, but could a determined little boy, desperate to find a father he refused to believe was dead, get there on his bicycle?

"He could," Annie said to herself. "I believe he could."

She looked at the caboose resting on her table, at the remains of Charlie's trains scattered across the floor.

"You were trying to tell me, weren't you?" she said.

The train was silent.

There was no point in calling Standish. First of all, Annie was sure she viewed her as a suspect. And second, if Annie told her she believed she knew where Charlie was, and how she'd come to this conclusion, the officer would have her committed.

Annie was on her own here.

She ran down the stairs, grabbed her car keys, and was gone.

Part IV

HARRY

THIRTY-THREE

Chief Harry Cook couldn't find anyone who claimed to have seen Gavin Denham in the last five days.

He hadn't been at his usual morning station, the bench out front of the Lucknow Diner, since the Friday before, and it was Wednesday. His old pickup truck remained parked a couple of blocks off Main Street, where Harry had found it the morning of the sidewalk sale. He had left under the windshield wiper what might have looked at first like a parking ticket, but was actually a note from Harry that read: "Gavin, when you see this, come find me. Best, Harry."

Ordinarily, someone like Gavin going missing would not set off too many alarms. He was a down-on-his-luck guy, homeless, unless you counted his pickup truck as a residence, and was known to like the bottle more than he should. But this town had already seen two men go missing—one of whom had been found without much of his skeletal structure, the other still unaccounted for—so Gavin made three, and that had Harry concerned.

He hadn't made a big deal about it yet. The department was yet to issue a news release asking for information as to Gavin's whereabouts, although Harry had asked Mary to get one ready. He had not made a call Rachel Bosma, the reporter for the *Lucknow Leader*, suggesting she do a story.

He'd put that note on the windshield Monday morning, and when he drove past it today, it was still there, untouched. He stopped his cruiser next to the truck, got out, walked around it, checked to see whether the vehicle was still locked, which it was. Harry decided it was time to get inside, see whether there might be anything that would offer a clue as to where Gavin might be. This wasn't an emergency, like a kid trapped in a car on a hot day, so he didn't want to break the window. On the Lucknow Police Rolodex was a locksmith by the name of Gertie they got in touch with whenever they needed her services, usually for nothing more serious than someone accidentally locking their keys inside their vehicle.

Gavin radioed into the station and asked them to get Gertie out to his location, and within twenty minutes she was there.

"This is Gavin Denham's truck, isn't it?" she asked.

Harry said it was.

"That sad bastard," she said. "Came to me one day, looking for work, and I didn't have anything for him. Truck been sitting here a few days, you say?"

Harry said yes.

"So what's happening with that guy Hillman? You found him yet? We got another guy disappeared into thin air?"

"Could you open the truck, Gertie?" Harry asked. Gertie could be chatty.

She had the door open in under a minute. Harry thanked her and told her to bill the department. He waited until she was gone before hauling himself up behind the wheel to begin his search.

Some of what was in here Harry had been able to see through the window. A couple of blankets, a pillow. Behind the seats, a plastic grocery bag with a wadded-up tube of toothpaste and toothbrush, a comb, half a bottle of Jameson, and some Preparation H, which was about when Harry wished he'd slipped on a pair of rubber gloves. There were two worn and yellowed paperback novels that looked to date back to the seventies. A Donald Hamilton novel about his Matt Helm character called *The Ambushers*. Harry could remember reading some of those when he was in his teens. The other book was an 87th Precinct novel by Ed McBain called *Fuzz*.

Under the seat were some empty paper coffee cups, a Big Mac container with a few traces of lettuce and special sauce, a Subway bag. Harry leaned over and popped open the glove compartment. He found the vehicle registration and a long-since-expired insurance slip. No big surprise there. Some road maps for Vermont, New York, Massachusetts, and Connecticut, all of which Gavin had failed to fold back up correctly, making them twice as thick as they should have been. A flashlight and some loose batteries, a package of tissues.

Nothing that one might call a clue jumped out at Harry.

He got back out of the truck and closed the door. Without a key he couldn't lock it, but he didn't feel there was much in there to interest a thief, unless it was a crook with hemorrhoids who'd be delighted to find some remaining ointment in that tube.

He drove the few blocks back into the center of town and parked out front of the diner. Once inside, he sat himself on a stool and waited for Jenny to bring him a coffee. He never needed to ask. He had out his notebook, reviewing things he had jotted down over the last few days.

He'd checked Wendell Comstock's alibi. He had, in fact, been to Brattleboro to help a friend seeking his opinion on a possible house purchase. Wendell had been nowhere near his home when Nadine had died in the bathtub from electrocution, courtesy of that toy train transformer. There was no evidence to suggest her death was anything other than suicide, although it bothered Harry that Wendell had not believed his wife to be seriously depressed. Harry had spoken to her doctor, whom she had seen within the last four months when she'd felt a lump in her breast. Tests had shown that she had nothing to worry about. If she was feeling at all despondent, she had not made that known.

Sometimes you just didn't know what was going on inside people's heads.

If only Gavin had been Harry's only worry of late. Lucknow seemed to be losing its mind.

The radio clipped to Harry's belt crackled, and then a voice came through. "Chief?"

He grabbed it off his belt, brought it to his mouth, pressed the button, and said, "Yeah?"

"Report of shots fired over on Guildwood."

Harry headed for his car.

Guildwood Street was in the town's north end. Harry was making good time, pedal to the floor, until he approached that Albany & Bennington double-track mainline. It cut across the town along an east-west axis, dividing north Lucknow from south Lucknow. Harry saw the crossing gates begin to lower, the lights start to flash.

He thought, for a moment, he could gun it, cross the tracks before the first of three blue linked Conrail engines rumbled into view. Great big roaring behemoths clipping along, and the odds that Harry could slip through the crossing without getting hit—and killed—were slim to none.

The engineer hit the horn and held it, a deep-throated warning that echoed across the landscape and chilled Harry to the bone.

The front end of his vehicle was on the first set of tracks when the diesels flew past, missing the SUV's bumper by inches.

"Shit shit shit!" Harry cried, his foot pressing down so hard on the brake it was a wonder it didn't go through the floor. He put the vehicle into reverse and rolled back to safety, off the first track and ahead of the gate, where he should have stopped in the first place.

It was a long train, a mile long at least.

"We got anyone north of the tracks?" he barked into the receiver, shouting to be heard over the racket made by the passing train.

Dispatch came back: "Bloodworth."

That would be Officer Ben Bloodworth. Stick.

"Get him to Guildwood!"

Harry scanned the freight cars, his frustration growing with each one that passed. A long line of tanker cars, linked together in the middle of the train, rumbled past. Going way too fast, Harry thought. A freight train barreling through the center of town should be required to slow down. A derailment of those cars, carrying God knows what kind of deadly chemicals, would be a catastrophe.

The end of the train was in view. Harry got ready. When the last car rolled by and the gates began to rise, Harry floored it.

When Harry reached Guildwood Street, he saw another Lucknow Police Department car was already there. Stick had beat him to the scene.

The front door of the house, a stately two-story that had likely been built in the last couple of years, was wide open. Harry screeched to a stop and got out of his car. He heard no gunfire, but that didn't mean the situation was under control. Hand resting atop the firearm at his side, he proceeded up the driveway and was almost to the front door when Stick walked out, holding a gun, the barrel pointed toward the ground.

From where Harry stood, it looked like a Smith & Wesson CSX, one of the smaller handguns on the market.

Stick looked stricken.

"Stick?" Harry said.

"Situation's under control, Chief," he said, working to control his voice, keep it from shaking. "No civilians hurt. Don't need the paramedics."

Harry said, "Whose gun is that?"

He held it out to Harry, who took it from him and put it into his jacket pocket. "Belongs to Mrs. Wilford. Betty Wilford. She's inside."

"Anyone else in the house?"

"Her son. Tyler. Upstairs. He's seven, home from school today because he's got an upset stomach."

"What happened?"

"Mrs. Wilford shot Dougie."

"Dougie?"

"The dog. Big one. A Lab. Five shots. Dougie was moving fast. First two missed him."

"You go stay with the son. I'll talk to Mrs. Wilford."

He found her in the kitchen, but not before seeing Dougie, motionless on his side on the gray broadloom next to the coffee table in the living room.

Mrs. Wilford, a dark-haired woman in her mid-thirties, dressed in black slacks and a black silk blouse, a strand of pearls at her neck, sat at the table, staring into space. Harry took a seat, introduced himself.

"Why don't you tell me what happened."

"Dougie went crazy. He's the kindest, gentlest dog in the whole world. Never bit a soul. We could always trust him with Tyler. I don't . . . I can't understand how he could . . . he turned into a wild animal, snarling and baring his teeth and oh God Trevor loved him so much and I don't know what I'm going to tell him."

"Trevor?"

"My husband. He's in Boston on business. He won't believe me when I tell him. Tyler was upstairs—he's home today, he woke up with a funny tummy, but he got over it once I said he didn't have to go to school, you know how kids are—and he was playing, and

Dougie was down here, and he started growling and barking and coming after me. Look."

She pushed back her chair and extended her right leg. Her pants were torn below the knee, and there was blood on her calf.

"You need to get that tended to," Harry said.

"He was chasing me around the living room and into the kitchen, and I jumped up onto a chair and he leapt up, and that's when he bit my leg."

"Tell me about the gun."

"Trevor bought it for me. Protection for when he was away. I keep it up there." She nodded toward the kitchen cabinetry. "Above the microwave."

"So you managed to get to the gun, and then?"

"I started firing. I was scared Tyler would come downstairs, or Dougie would go up there, after him. I didn't know what else to do."

Her eyes welled up with tears. "I missed a couple of times. He jumped right at me, baring his teeth. I though he was going to kill me. When Tyler heard the shots he came running down and I screamed at him to stay in his room. How could something like this happen? I just don't understand."

Harry gave her arm a squeeze. "I'm going to go up and check on Tyler and see if Officer Bloodworth can do something about getting Dougie out of the house."

The woman nodded.

As Harry left the kitchen, he heard a sound from upstairs. A sound that should have been innocuous enough, but gave him a chill when he heard it.

Chuffchuffchuffchuffchuffchuffchuff

Harry climbed the stairs and poked his head into the room where the sound was coming from. Stick was sitting on the floor with the boy, Tyler, watching a toy train go around an oval of track. Stick got to his feet and said, "Tyler here was showing me his awesome new train set."

Harry pulled Stick aside and said to him quietly, "Get Dougie out of the house."

Stick nodded and slipped out of the room. Harry took a knee and smiled at Tyler.

"Hey, Tyler. You mind if we slow that train down for a second? I want to talk to you."

Tyler eased back on the transformer throttle. The train came to a stop and went silent.

"I'm real sorry about what happened to your dog."

The boy's lower lip extended and he said, "Mom said he must have got rabies or something."

"You never saw him act like that before?"

Tyler's head went back and forth.

Harry laid a hand on his shoulder. "Anyway, I just came up to see how you were doing, and let you know your mom will be okay but she's a little upset." He took a moment to admire the train set. It consisted of a steam engine, a gondola car with three large canisters that looked like milk jugs, a flatcar with a load of barrels, a coal car, and a caboose.

"That's a pretty nice setup you have there, Tyler."

Sadly, the boy said, "I guess."

"Why don't you turn it back on, show me how it works."

Tyler turned the throttle on the transformer and the train started to go around the loop.

"I love the sound it makes," Harry said. "That choo-choo sound."

"It's supposed to have a whistle, but it doesn't work." To demonstrate, Tyler pressed a red button on the transformer labeled WHISTLE. The engine did not make a sound.

"See?"

"Let me try it."

Tyler took his thumb off the button. Harry shifted over, pushed down on it with his thumb.

Felt a small tingle.

Held his thumb there for several seconds. Harry could hear nothing out of the engine but the *chuffchuffchuffchuffchuffchuffchuff* sound it had been making all along.

But then he thought he did hear something.

"What was that?" he asked Tyler.

"What was what?"

Harry took his finger off the button, listened. He didn't hear what it was he'd thought he'd heard a moment earlier.

"Do your neighbors have a dog, too?"

The boy nodded. "Scruffy."

Harry got up, went over to the window, and raised it open far enough to feel a cool breeze blow into the room.

"Tyler, hit the whistle button again and hold it."

Tyler did as he was told.

Next door, a dog began to howl and bark furiously.

THIRTY-FOUR

As his stay in Lucknow continued, Edwin Nabler could not have been more pleased with how things were going.

Since opening his shop here he'd sold nearly two dozen train sets, and results were trickling in. Best to go slow. Not a good thing to attract attention too quickly, and he felt he was just riding the edge of that. But there had definitely been some successes.

You had to take your time with these things. Just as good food took time to prepare, enabling chaos was something to be embraced artfully. And again, to follow that analogy, some foods were made for elaborate feasts, and other were designed to be appetizers. Every set that went out the door had a different level of potency. It wasn't so much a quality control issue. Nabler didn't let anything leave the store that wasn't top-notch. But just like if you ran a deli, sometimes a customer left with nothing more than a wedge of Brie, while the next guy ordered a Smithfield ham. They catered to different appetites but both had to be delicious.

So one train set, once it had been set up in a household, might spark nothing more than a flooded basement or a nasty argument or maybe a bird flying through the window and landing in a bloody, feathery heap on the dining room table. But a set with a little more oomph to it, well, who could guess what kind of mayhem would ensue? Explosions? Missing limbs? Decapitations?

Suicides?

That woman in the bathtub was a nice one. Hit that right out of the park, Nabler thought, giving himself a mental pat on the back. Perhaps, of all the toys he had prepared, that one had the most life—or death?—in it. He didn't think that little set was done yet. It had potential, even if that dead woman's husband was packing up the engine and cars and track and hoping to hand it off to someone else when the opportunity arose.

Nabler had been working through the night on the layout in the back of the shop. He had little use for sleep. Occasionally he would sit down for a spell, and there was no doubt his work was taking a toll, but closing his eyes and tuning out for seven or eight hours at a stretch had never been part of his routine. Yes, it was about time he found someone else to take over.

But in the meantime, Edwin Nabler was determined to give it his all, and that was exactly what he had been doing. The progress he had been making back here was impressive, if he did say so himself, and Gavin's contributions to the project had been most welcome.

His hair, once dyed green and brown and cut into short lengths, was used to create a grassy field. His rib cage, once draped with plaster-soaked paper towels and painted green, had served nicely to make a small mountain. And his teeth, once extracted and filed down, came in handy when Nabler set his mind to making a little rock garden in the miniature town square.

Nabler had also been consumed with putting down more track. The longer the route, the more opportunity for a train to absorb the qualities of that through which it passed. What Nabler was creating was a nurturing nest, the loops of track akin to the small sticks and blades of grass a bird collected and stitched together. To enter this area behind the shop was to immerse yourself into a literal web of tracks. Visitors—and there would surely be more of those who would get to see his handiwork *once*—would have to duck and weave to work their way to the center of it, not unlike some jungle explorer navigating a pathway obstructed by vines.

What a beautiful thing it was.

And there were always trains running. A cacophony of sound that might be annoying to the non-enthusiast, but it was a glorious medley to Nabler. There were multiple loops of track that allowed him to run eight, nine, ten trains at any given time. The chorus of metal wheels traversing metal track was a symphony.

ChuffchuffCLICKETYCLACKclicketyCLACKwooWOOchuff CLICKETYchuffCLICKETYchuffWOOchuggachuggaclackclickety CHUFFCHUFFclicketyCLACKwooWOOchuffCLICKETYchuff CLICKETYchuffWOOchuggachuggaclackclicketyCHUFFCHUFF clicketyCLACKwooWOOchuffCLICKETYchuffCLICKETYchuff WOOchuggachuggaclackclicketyCHUFF . . .

It was a good thing he'd found a way to surreptitiously tap into the town's electrical grid.

His current favorite train consisted of three blue Chesapeake & Ohio diesels pulling a long line of tanker cars. It clickety-clacked past on one of the upper tracks, roughly eye level for Nabler. He squinted as it sped by, imagining it was a real train hurtling toward some yet-to-be-realized catastrophe.

So, what next?

While there was always more to be done on the layout—and to accomplish that, Nabler would need more *material,* including not just actual people, but their personal items—it struck him as prudent to ease up for a period of time. Lucknow's rate of calamities was on a noticeable upswing. Nabler believed it highly unlikely anyone would connect the dots—even if someone did, they'd question their own sanity suspecting that a toy train somehow played a role—but it didn't hurt to play it safe. That meant turning out product that was a little less, well, high-voltage. Dial it back some. Once things settled down, he'd do some modifications to the production process and re-sume selling sets with a high level of chaotic potential.

It was good to have a plan.

Over the din, Edwin heard a sound.

The bell.

"Ah!" Nabler said. "A customer."

THIRTY-FIVE

Harry sat in the diner, nursing a coffee and rereading his notes, going back not only to the disappearances of Tanner and Hillman—what struck Harry as the starting point of Lucknow's recent troubles—but to more recent events, including one that happened only that morning.

After that incident two days earlier—the adorable family dog that had gone feral—he didn't think anything could top that. Then he got the call about trouble over on Braymor Drive.

"Woman says her son's choking to death on a pack of cigarettes," the dispatcher said.

"What?"

"Tried to get her to tell me more, but she wasn't making sense, said he was trying to turn himself into a chimney, and then she started screaming, and—"

"Ambulance and fire on the way?"

"Yeah."

As Harry brought the cruiser to a screeching halt at the address, he realized he had been here before. The red Ford Torino in the driveway was something of a clue.

This was where Delbert Dorfman, the racist dickhead who had spray-painted OSAMA LOVER GO HOME on the window of Ahsan Basher's convenience store, and later thrown a rock through it, lived.

Harry jumped out and ran toward the house, and stopped briefly when he saw what was happening on the roof. There was a man in his mid-twenties up there, on his back, staring into the sky, barefoot but wearing a pair of jeans and a white T-shirt. There was smoke billowing up from his face.

It was, Harry was pretty sure, Dorfman.

Harry noticed a TV tower at the side of the house, figured the man had gotten onto the roof by climbing it rather than using a ladder, since there wasn't one in sight. Partway up the tower was a heavyset woman Harry guessed to be in her fifties, screaming.

"Stop it!" she shouted. "Come down here right now, Delbert!"

But Delbert was giving her no mind. He was busy having a smoke.

Or, more accurately, smokes.

From where Harry stood, the man, jaw wide, appeared to have the contents of an entire package of cigarettes—a good twenty of them, if not more—jammed into his mouth, and every one of them was lit. It was as bizarre a sight as Harry had ever seen, like something an onstage comic would do to provoke a laugh, or a magician might attempt before disappearing in a cloud of smoke.

Delbert lay there spread-eagled, and even though he appeared to be struggling to breathe, and despite his chest going up and down in clear distress, he made no attempt to spit out the cigarettes wadded into his mouth.

"Delbert!" the woman cried. "What are you doing?"

Given her size and age, Harry was thinking, that woman was not meant to be climbing a TV tower. She had one arm looped into a metal brace and appeared to be struggling to get her breath. Harry hadn't met this woman when he had come here before to warn Delbert off his harassment campaign but was guessing it was his mother.

"Mrs. Dorfman," Harry shouted. "Get down from there!"

She looked at him and said, "He's gone crazy!"

Harry wanted her off that tower for more reasons than her own safety. Once she was off it, he could scramble up there himself, get onto the roof, and save Delbert from his own insanity. If Harry couldn't get up there, they'd be waiting until the fire department arrived with scaling equipment, or simply shot water onto the roof to douse those cigarettes.

Harry could hear fire engine sirens in the distance and was betting they were still two or three minutes away.

At the house next door, a second-floor window had been raised and a girl who looked about the same age as Harry's son, Dylan, was watching the show unfold with great interest. Where the fuck were her parents? Harry thought. They needed to get her away from the window. But the kid was the least of his worries.

"Get down!" he said again to the woman, who had not moved.

There was so much smoke emanating from the man's mouth and trailing out of his nose that his head was becoming lost in the cloud.

"Delbert!" Harry shouted. "Delbert, it's Chief Cook! Stop what you're doing! Spit out those cigarettes!"

The woman was now working her way down the TV tower, one horizontal brace at a time. Harry headed that way, ready to start his ascent. He nearly pushed her off when she had one rung to go.

Harry grabbed a metal bracing above his head, got his boot on a lower one, and up he went. The braces on the tower were a good foot apart, broader than on a ladder, but Harry scaled the tower quickly. As he reached the roof—it wasn't a steep slope, easily navigated provided you paid attention to what you were doing—and was putting his first foot onto it, he got a better view of Delbert.

All the cigarettes clustered together were like one Marlboro four inches long and three inches wide. The tips, red and glowing, began to meld. Ashes, mixed with still-burning flecks of tobacco, drifted onto his shirt, the skin of his cheeks and neck, and into his hair.

"Shit," Harry said under his breath, and began to make his way across the roof.

Delbert's hair began to catch fire, and a few seconds later his head erupted into flames.

"Christ!" Harry shouted, closing the distance between Delbert and himself, peeling off his sport jacket and throwing it over the man's face in a bid to put out the fire.

"He never moved," Harry had told his wife, Janice, when he got home much later that evening. "He just lay there."

"You did what you could," she'd said.

Harry was thinking about that now, sitting at the diner counter in a fresh jacket. Had he done all he could? Maybe, if he hadn't had to wait for Mrs. Dorfman to get down off that TV tower, if he'd gotten up there ten seconds sooner, he might—

"Any sign of our friend?"

Harry was shaken out of his dark reverie. He looked up from his notebook to see Jenny filling his porcelain mug with coffee.

"Say again?"

"Gavin," Jenny said. "Found him yet?"

Harry shook his head regretfully. "No."

Jenny leaned in close so that no one else would be able to hear what she had to say. Harry could smell bacon in her hair.

"People are on edge, Harry. Don't know whether you've noticed, but everyone's kinda freaking out."

"Say it ain't so," Harry whispered back. "Suggestions?"

"Harry, my area of expertise is putting enough bacon and eggs and hash browns into people so that one day they clutch their chest and drop dead of a heart attack but they're still smiling when they go because we serve the best breakfast within fifty miles. It is *not* trying to figure out why everyone in Lucknow is losing their shit. That's *your* job."

"I'm workin' on it."

"Workin' on it, he says," Jenny said dismissively, and went off to deal with another customer.

Harry went back to studying his notebook. He'd written down something Delbert's mother, June, said as his body was being loaded into the ambulance.

"He didn't even smoke," she told the chief.

THIRTY-SIX

B ack when Edwin Nabler opened his very first shop—where was it, now? Cleveland? or was it Scranton?—there was a thrill surrounding the first customer of the day. Who would it be? A serious shopper? A browser? (There weren't many of those. Nabler had a gift when it came to salesmanship. They might not buy on the first visit, but they always came back.)

But he had to admit, that thrill was gone.

It was still a pleasure to welcome the first person to open the shop door. He still had the strength for a "How are you today?" or a "What fine weather we're having, wouldn't you say?" or "Is there anything special you're looking for?" But that charge he used to get at the start of his business day had dropped to a lower voltage.

Still, he managed a smile for the woman who had stepped into Choo-Choo's Trains on this sunny morning. When he emerged from the back room, he closed the door quickly so as to muffle the sound of those multiple trains chugging their way around his layout.

He walked up to the cash register and flashed the woman a smile as she looked his way.

"What fine weather we're having, wouldn't you say?" he asked. As good an opener as any from his repertoire.

"I love the fall," the woman said.

"We won't have these colors for much longer," Nabler said. "It all seems so fleeting. The beauty of the changing season is here, and then it's gone."

He put her in her late thirties. Slim, attractive, dark hair. The ring on her finger told him she was married, and a mother in all likelihood, given that she had entered what some would derisively refer to as a toy store. (How he hated that, but they were called *toy* trains, so what could you do?) But part of the workforce, too, he thought, judging by her professional attire. A simple blue dress with long sleeves, two-inch heels, just the right amount of makeup.

"I've never been in here before," she said. "I must have walked past it, but somehow it escaped my notice."

Nabler smiled. "I hear that a lot."

"Been here long?"

"A while. But we're more of a specialty shop. It's not like you need a model train every day. We're not like the diner across the street, where if you don't get your daily cup of joe you're not going to be any good to anybody."

She chuckled. "Isn't that the truth."

"So, you're into the hobby? A collector, perhaps?"

"Oh no, not me. I'm thinking this might be a perfect Christmas gift for both my husband and my son. Something they could enjoy together."

"And get them out of your hair," Nabler said.

The woman laughed. "That's not my intention, but you might be right about that."

She was wandering down the far aisle, looking at sets and packages containing individual engines and cars. "You have some beautiful stuff here."

"Thank you. I do all the detailing on the cars myself."

"Really? But the trains themselves, are they made in America? Overseas?"

"They're manufactured right here in the good ol' US of A, but you know the way things are going. I think we're going to see much of the work move to China. But even when it comes to that, when the trains arrive here, I do extra work on them in the back, so that anything you get from Choo-Choo's is essentially an exclusive product."

"Nice to hear. What sort of extra work do you do to them?"

Nabler smiled. "You know, there was this restaurant I used to go to. A very swanky place, and they had the best scrambled eggs I'd ever had in my life. And I thought, they're just scrambled eggs. We all know how to make scrambled eggs, right? But these had something extra about them. So one day, I asked the waiter if he could ask the chef what he put into the eggs that made them so extraordinary. So he went off to see the chef and came back, and you know what he said?"

"What did he say?"

"The secret ingredient is *love*."

"Oh come on!" the woman said, laughing. "I thought you were going to say cheese or mayonnaise or onions or something. So that's it, then. You put *love* into your trains."

"What can I say? I hate to toot my own horn." He waited to see if she would laugh at that. When she didn't, he said, "That was a train joke. Toot? Horn?"

"Ah," she said.

Nabler smiled sheepishly. "We train nerds aren't particularly noted for our wit."

"Tell me about this set," she said.

"Oh, that's a good one," Edwin said, coming around the counter and checking out the woman's choice. "A Southern Pacific steam engine, four-six-two, a—"

"What does four-six-two mean? The number on the side is zero-four-three."

"Okay, so, you see all the drive wheels? Four small wheels at the front, then six big wheels in the middle, and two small wheels at the back end. Four-six-two."

"Oh."

"Maybe that's more detail than you need. So, a Southern Pacific steam engine with matching tender where the coal would be, a cattle car, a missile-launching car, and—"

"Like, a military missile? A rocket? Why would a train be carrying a missile?"

"There's an element of whimsy with these sets. They're designed more for fun than realism. The roof opens down the middle and a missile pops up and fires. Just don't aim it at anyone's eyes."

"It fires? You're not serious."

"Ma'am, I would never kid about something as serious as a missile car. It has been a mainstay of the toy train lineup since the early sixties."

"Sorry. I guess I'm a bit of a literalist."

"Not a problem. So, a cattle car, a missile car, this one carries a giraffe, and then there's the matching Southern Pacific caboose. And it comes with track and a power pack, or transformer, to make it run."

"It's perfect. I can see it under the tree now."

"If I may make a suggestion," Nabler said hesitantly, "why not give it to them now as opposed to waiting another couple of months till Christmas? And if they get the bug—"

"A bug? Is that an accessory?"

"The *bug*. As in, they get caught up in the hobby—then you'll want to come back to get more boxcars and buildings and scenery for them for Christmas. So that they can build their empire."

The woman smiled. "Aren't you the clever salesman."

He raised his palms innocently. "It's only a suggestion."

"An empire," she said thoughtfully. "Do *you* have one of those?"

"I do, in fact. In the back of the shop. I wouldn't be cut out for this line of work if I hadn't caught the bug myself."

Her eyes brightened. "Would I be able to see it? I mean, is it available for public viewing?"

It was then that he fully appreciated how nice her hair was. Long and flowing, and once dyed, it would be ideal for a field or a lawn. And there were hints of a fine bone structure in her face and, presumably, her entire body. Given her petite stature, she would be easy to prepare. He could fillet her like a perch, extract her delicate frame in no time.

He felt an itch, wanting to make her part of his process.

But no, he'd already had this debate with himself. Time to take a bit of a breather. Although this particular set she had her hands on, it would pack a punch, he believed.

"I'm sorry," he said. "It's a bit of mess at the moment. Before I show it off, I have to work out some of the kinks in the track. Don't want to be running a train and have any embarrassing derailments."

"Of course. Forgive me if I was being pushy, there."

"Not at all."

"Anyway, I'm sold. I'm going to get this."

She went to lift the set off the shelf, but Edwin intervened. "Allow me," he said, and carried the package over to the counter. He slipped behind it as the woman approached and opened her purse.

She suddenly shook her head, as though she had forgotten something. "I'm so rude. I haven't even asked you your name."

"Edwin," he said, extending a hand. "Edwin Nabler. And you are?"

"Janice," she said.

"Janice. Nice to meet you."

She laughed. "I'm buying this for my husband, Harry, and our son, Dylan. Harry's the chief of police here, in Lucknow. Chief Cook?"

"Yes, yes," Nabler said, nodding. "I do believe we've met."

THIRTY-SEVEN

Harry had put in another call to Melissa Cairns, his friend who worked at the FBI. He'd gotten in touch with her briefly after the discovery of Angus Tanner's body, wondering whether the bureau had ever come across any cases where a victim's bones had been removed from the body. She'd made some mention of a case in Des Moines, had said she would get back to him, but he hadn't heard from her.

So he'd left a message for her after Delbert Dorfman stuffed a pack of cigarettes into his mouth and set himself ablaze. There'd already been a couple of very dark jokes around the station in the wake of that, something about how maybe the anti-smoking lobby might want to make that dude their "In Memoriam" spokesperson, or how a picture of his flaming head might be best placed on every pack of smokes as a deterrent.

Harry hadn't laughed.

Melissa was originally from Lucknow, and she and Harry had been in some of the same classes at the local high school. Harry could still recall sitting at the back of his history class, admiring the way Melissa, in her short skirt, one row over and three desks ahead, would sit slightly sideways and cross her legs, dangling one shoe. Pretty much drove him out of his mind. Didn't dare walk out of that class without holding a binder in front of him.

As he headed for his office, Mary waved a couple of yellow

message slips in the air and said, "Rachel Bosma called, and there's some TV reporter from Montpelier who wants to do an on-camera interview about Tanner and Hillman."

Harry took the messages, crumpled them, and tossed them into the closest wastebasket.

Mary, nonplussed, said, "If they call again I'll say you have no comment at this time but that you are aggressively pursuing various leads."

Harry filled a mug with coffee from the machine in the break room, went into his office, and closed the door.

He needed a minute.

Harry kept thinking about how when he depressed the whistle button on that toy train transformer, the dog from next door started barking and howling. When he took his finger off the button, the dog went quiet. He hung out in young Tyler's bedroom for a few more minutes, repeating the experiment. Every time he held the button down, that mutt nearby went nuts.

The whistle, Harry concluded, *did* work, but was not producing a sound that could be heard by human ears. It was operating at a much higher frequency, one that could only he detected, at least in this case, by dogs. The toy train version of a dog whistle.

The Lucknow department did not have a canine unit, but the state police did, its so-called K-9 unit. Harry had brought them in in the summer of 2000, more than a year ago, when a five-year-old boy got separated from his family during a camping trip. The tracking dogs were brought in and the boy was found within twenty-four hours. Cold and hungry and covered in mosquito bites, but he was okay.

Harry went to his Rolodex, found the number he'd called in, and made a call.

"John Garfield, K-9."

Yes, it was true. The head of the canine unit's surname was the same as a famous cartoon cat. And yes, he also had the same full name as a once-famous movie star who'd died at the young age of thirty-nine. But the cat connection was funnier.

"Harry Cook over in Lucknow."

"Hey, Harry. You got another lost kid?"

"No, nothing like that today, thank God. But it's good to know your dogs are at the ready next time we're in a fix like that."

"What can I do for you today?"

"I want to talk to you about dog whistles."

"Dog whistles? What, you getting a dog? Training him?"

"No, nothing like that. I wanted to know what effect a high-pitched whistle could have on a dog."

"Uh, well, as you know, people can hear sounds above twenty thousand hertz, but dogs hear in the range of forty-seven to sixty-five thousand hertz."

"I've no idea what that means, John. Are you saying dogs hear way better than we do?"

"Yeah. At way higher frequencies. You know when a dog tilts its head when it looks at you, all cute? He's probably hearing something you can't hear and moving his head, trying to make it clearer. It's got nothing to do with thinking you're adorable."

"Okay, so let's say you could make a sound that was way up in that higher range. Something no person could hear. Would that hurt a dog?"

"Hurt him? Might make him a little uncomfortable, but it wouldn't hurt him," Garfield said. "Although, yeah, it'd be like if someone blew a regular whistle super-loud right by your ear. It would startle you, might damage your eardrum. So, yeah, high enough frequency, duration, it might damage a dog's ability to hear. If you don't mind my asking, Harry, the fuck is this about?"

"Ever see a dog lose his shit because of a whistle?"

"What do you mean, lose his shit?"

"Become violent. Like, a mad dog. Vicious, attacking. A dog that up to that moment had always been gentle, a dog you could trust with kids. But it was like a switch got flipped, the dog goes crazy."

"Never seen anything like that. What the hell's going on in Lucknow?"

Harry managed a chuckle. "I wish I knew. We had this—"

One of the other lines on his phone lit up. "I got another call I gotta take, John. Thanks for letting me bend your ear."

He ended the one call and answered the other.

"Cook."

"Hey," said Melissa. "Sorry not to get back to you sooner."

"I was just thinking about calling you."

"I did a little checking. On victims with their bones removed. I was thinking there was something like that in Des Moines, but turns out it was Duluth. But it was a long time ago, Harry. We're talking back in the seventies, nearly thirty years ago. One case. A homeless guy, early forties. Police believed some sort of satanic cult or something did it, but they never got anywhere with it. And at the time, they were aware of another case they'd got wind of, in Nashville, but that went all the way back to '55. We're talking close to half a century, Harry."

"Huh," he said, making some notes.

"This guy you found at the side of the road, I don't see how it could have anything to do with those other homicides, so I'm sorry if I got your hopes up, thinking there was a pattern. For it to be the same perpetrator, you're looking at someone who's been active for nearly fifty years. Even if he—and we always assume it's a *he*—started off in his late teens or early twenties, we're talking someone who'd now be in his seventies. Doesn't fit any pattern that I'm familiar with."

"Look, I appreciate this. I really do."

"If you had any other commonalities, I could see whether there was anything that jumped out."

Commonalities, he thought.

Harry had been looking for commonalities between his one homicide and any others that might have happened. But maybe that wasn't where he needed to be looking for things in common. They had been occurring elsewhere, in events that were in no way related to the death of Angus Tanner.

Unless they were.

"You there?" Melissa asked.

"Yeah, sorry. My mind was wandering there for a second."

"How's Janice?" she asked.

"She's good, she's great. And Dylan's getting taller every day."

"Kids have a way of doing that."

Harry knew that Melissa had two children of her own, two girls, and that her husband, Albert, also worked for the FBI.

"You take care, Harry, and if there's anything else you want to bounce off me, let me know."

Was there a hint, Harry wondered, of condescension in her voice? Like she was the big federal agent, counseling the small-town chief who stayed behind because he didn't think he could make it in the big leagues? Or did he hear that tone because that was exactly how he felt? He was in over his head and knew he couldn't handle this on his own?

"Thanks, Melissa," he said. "Best to the girls and Albert."

He hung up the phone and took a sip of his cold coffee.

Commonalities.

Darryl Pidgeon died when his barbecue blew up in his face. Not a murder. An accident.

Nadine Comstock died of an electrical shock in her bathtub. Not a murder. A suicide.

Delbert Dorfman smoked himself to death on the roof of his house.

Betty Wilford shot her dog dead when it went crazy and attacked her.

Four unrelated tragedies.

But at least three of them had something in common.

"This is nuts," Harry said under this breath. "Totally nuts."

When Darryl Pidgeon died, there was a train.

When Nadine Comstock died, there was a train.

When Betty Wilford shot her dog, there was a train.

And in each case, he was willing to bet, they had come from a shop run by Mr. Edwin Nabler. But none of these events had anything to do with what had happened to Angus Tanner.

Hang on.

Harry thought back to the night Angus Tanner's body had been found. He'd knocked on the door of one Darrell Crohn and asked him whether he had seen or heard anything in the night. Maybe a car stopping by the side of the road, someone getting out and dumping a body.

Crohn hadn't heard or seen anything. At least, nothing like that.

But there was the sound of that train in the night that brought him out of a deep sleep. Harry had dismissed it. Even Crohn had to admit he might have imagined it. He'd had quite a bit to drink before nodding off.

After all, it simply wasn't possible. There wasn't a rail line anywhere near there.

THIRTY-EIGHT

A few days passed.

Harry sat in his office, leaning back in his chair and throwing darts at a board hanging on the wall, ruminating.

He had been thinking about a famous serial killer whose day job was as an installer of home security systems. This allowed him to gain access to private residences, install locks and alarms, and in the process gain the trust of the individuals who had engaged his services. The killer would select his victims from those he had met in his job, and when it came time to break in and snuff the life out of one of them, he had the technical know-how to bypass whatever security measures he'd installed.

So what if, Harry thought, this Mr. Nabler had personally delivered the toy train sets to the homes where these tragedies had occurred? Assembled the track, carefully taken the trains from their packaging, did all the wiring that connected the power pack to the rails and an electrical outlet, gave everything a test run to make sure it was working. Then Nabler would have gained a familiarity with the workings of the household. Know that they had a barbecue, a liking for baths, a normally friendly dog.

And?

Suppose he *had* been in those homes. Did he sabotage the barbecue? Put that poor woman in the tub and drop in a live transformer?

Drive a dog mad? How the fuck was he supposed to have done *those* things?

And yet, there was something about him that got under Harry's skin. The fact that one day, his store was just *there*. Like he'd come out of nowhere. How these tragedies had all happened since his arrival. The fact that he was, well, at least judging from the couple of times Harry had met him, kind of fucking weird.

Not what Melissa Cairns would call hard evidence.

Maybe, Harry thought, he was so ill-equipped to solve Angus Tanner's murder and Walter Hillman's disappearance that he was grabbing at fantastical straws. There had to be logical answers to the questions he was puzzling over. He just lacked the smarts to come up with them.

These weren't *commonalities* that meant anything. They were *co-incidences*, plain and simple. Maybe these families struck by tragedy all went to the same grocery store. Maybe they used the same toothpaste, dined at the same restaurants. And plenty of families could have made purchases at Choo-Choo's Trains. Nabler was doing a brisk business the morning of the street sale. Who knew how many trains were chugga-chugging away in homes across Lucknow?

Take Delbert Dorfman. Harry had been in that house later, after the man's body had been removed from the roof and taken away in an ambulance. He had spoken with his mother, who had been at a loss to explain his behavior. Her son had no history of mental illness, was not depressed, did not use, so far as she knew, hallucinogenic drugs. He was not in the care of a psychiatrist. Sure, Harry thought to himself, he was a racist asshole, but that would seem to have no bearing on how he had taken his own life.

Baffling, like the other recent events. But that was the only commonality. The Dorfmans had not spent any money at that new shop in town, so far as Harry knew, which kind of shot to hell his theory that Nabler was behind *all* these occurrences.

Unless Harry missed something.

It wasn't like he'd actually searched the house. Why would he have? On what pretext?

This was going to nag at him. He had to *know*.

But as he got into his car, he had two other stops before going back to the Dorfman house. The first was at the Pidgeon home. Darryl's wife, Christina, came to the door after Harry rang the bell, opening it only a few inches.

"Oh, Chief Cook," she said, opening the door wider upon seeing who it was.

"Ms. Pidgeon," he said, nodding his head. "Forgive my coming unannounced."

"It's okay. Come in."

He followed her into the living room, where they both took a seat. There was no longer a train setup on the dining room table. He managed a quick glance through the kitchen doorway and saw a sheet of plywood where the sliding glass door once was.

Christina caught him looking and said, "The new door goes in tomorrow. It had to be ordered. It was some special kind of glass that takes a week or more to get. The insurance people were a problem at first, but that got ironed out."

"How's Auden doing?"

"He's back at school. Everyone's been very supportive. His teacher's been great and the kids have been pretty decent. But"—and she clenched her fists, digging her nails into her palm—"he's pretty devastated."

"Of course. I had a couple of quick questions."

"Um, okay."

"Did they find out what caused the accident? Why the barbecue ignited?"

She sighed. "The fire department looked into it and the insurance company had an investigator come out, and whatever might have been wrong with it, they can't guess what it was. And it was relatively new. Darryl bought it only three or four months ago and he was always very careful with the gas connections and everything. It doesn't make any sense."

"Had there been someone here to service it?" he asked.

"No. Not since they brought it from the barbecue place."

"Okay. Anyone else been in the house lately?"

"Like who?"

"Service people? Someone to fix a washer or dryer or the furnace or anything like that at all?"

Christina thought for a moment. "No."

"Maybe that train set of Auden's? Did someone come to the house to put it together?"

"Oh no. Auden and his father did that. It wasn't very complicated." Her eyes glistened, and she looked away momentarily. "What makes you ask?"

"It's routine. Whenever there's an accident and the cause is undetermined, we like to know if there's any likelihood that it could have been tampered with, improperly maintained, anything like that."

She shook her head.

"Those trains . . . I don't see them on the dining room table this time," Harry said.

"After what happened to his father, Auden didn't want to play with them anymore. We boxed them up and put them in the garage."

"Maybe you could return it."

"I don't know," she said. "The man I bought it from, he was so nice. Auden might want to get it out again someday."

"Well," Harry said, putting his hands on his knees and pushing himself up. "I wanted to drop by and see how you were doing. I won't take up any more of your time."

She saw him to the door and closed it softly behind him as he went to his car.

So much for that theory, he thought, keying the ignition. Edwin Nabler hadn't set foot in the Pidgeon house. But that didn't mean he was ready to abandon his hunch quite yet.

When he got to Wendell Comstock's house, there was a moving van backed into the driveway. Two men were walking a couch up the ramp and into the back of the truck when Harry wandered through the open door of the house. Save for a couple of chairs, the living room was empty. He found Wendell in the kitchen, using a tape gun to seal a large cardboard box, one of several on the counter. The table and chairs were gone, making the room seem larger than it normally would have.

"Mr. Comstock."

The greeting startled the man. He turned, and when he saw the chief he put down the tape gun. "Oh, hello," he said.

Harry waved a hand at the boxes. "I see you've made some big decisions."

"I can't be here any longer. Got a sister across the border in New York State, a lead on a job there in Fenelon. Need to put some distance between me and this place. Something I can help you with?"

"Not . . . really. Bit of a follow-up."

He asked Wendell basically the same questions he had asked Christina Pidgeon. Any service calls? Workmen in the house? Deliveries?

No, no, and no.

"Those trains that were set up in the basement? Someone do that for you?"

Another no.

"What are you getting at?" Wendell asked. "You think someone who'd been in the house came back and killed Nadine?"

"Not suggesting anything. Just asking."

"Because they ruled it a suicide. That's what the coroner said. You saying something different?" Wendell became agitated. "Because if you think something different happened, then I have a right to know!"

Harry shook his head definitively. "No, Mr. Comstock. I have *no evidence* to suggest that."

"Then what the fuck are you doing here?"

Harry raised a palm. "I'll let you get on with what you were doing."

As he walked out of the kitchen, he stepped aside to make way for one of the movers coming up the steps from the basement, carrying a cardboard box with TIDE printed on the side. When they were outside, Harry heard one of the movers say to the other, "I think he said that wasn't going, but . . . you know what, just throw it in the truck."

NEITHER THE PIDGEONS nor the Comstocks had been visited by Nabler. This so-called commonality wasn't proving to amount to much.

Harry had one last stop planned. He parked out front of the Dorfman house. There was, on the roof, a slightly darker patch on the shingles where Dorfman's body was immolated.

His mother, June, looking like someone who'd not slept since Harry's last time here, came to the door after he rang the bell.

"Oh, it's you," she said, and began to cry. "Thank you for trying to save my son."

She invited him into the kitchen and asked if he would like a drink. Scotch, a beer, vodka?

"Glass of water would be nice," he said.

June ran the tap until the water was cold, held a glass under it, and put it on the table in front of Harry, then poured two fingers of scotch into a tumbler. Harry had the sense it was not her first drink of the day.

"Carvers say there's nothing they can do," she said.

One of the two funeral homes in Lucknow. Carvers & Sons. Always had struck Harry as an unfortunate name for an undertaker.

"Closed casket," she said. "There was nothing left of his face."

She knocked back half the drink, her eye going back to the bottle on the counter. "His father's not even coming, the son of a bitch. He's over in Nigeria or Ghana or some other fucking place in Africa. He's an engineer."

"He's away a lot?"

"Gone since January ninth, 1993, when he walked out that door and said he'd had enough, but you'd think the bastard would come back for the funeral of his own son."

"Must be tough, dealing with all this yourself."

"You think?"

"Tell me about Delbert." Harry already had his own opinion of the man.

The woman's eyes appeared to glaze over, as though trying to recall whom she'd just been asked about. "I know he had a run-in with you. He told me about that. You accusing him of hassling that man who runs the gas station. But he was a good boy. Always good to me. He'd have moved out a long time ago but didn't want to leave me on my own like his son-of-a-bitch father did. Did you know he made me tea every morning?"

"I didn't."

"A boy who makes his mother tea in the morning has good in him, Chief."

"You have any idea why Delbert did what he did?"

"What would make *anyone* do that?"

Harry had no answer.

"Did Delbert have friends?" he asked. "A girlfriend?"

"Not . . . really."

"What'd he do in his off time? Interests? Hobbies?"

"I guess that car of his was the closest thing he had to a girlfriend. Always cleaning and polishing it. He watched a lot of movies. On his VCR downstairs." She leaned in, lowered her voice to a whisper, even though there was no one else there. "He had a lot of, you know, sex tapes. He didn't think I knew. So when he was down there, I didn't disturb him, if you know what I mean."

"Sure," Harry said.

June downed the rest of her drink, pushed back her chair, and went for a refill. She was unsteady on her feet. "I need to sit down in the living room," she said.

"Okay," Harry said.

He led her out of the kitchen and settled her onto a sofa. She took a sip of her drink, set it on the coffee table, then rested the back of her head on the top of the cushion.

Harry said, "Would you mind if I looked around?"

Her eyes closed, she waved a hand and said, "Whatever."

The basement seemed like a good place to start. There was a couch, a rowing machine, bookcases loaded with old sets of encyclopedias, a large TV, and the videocassette recorder June had mentioned. Atop the TV was a stack of VHS tapes. Three *Die Hard* movies, some James Bond flicks, and a number of cassettes that had been used to tape programs. Labels taped to the side indicated, in marker, what shows had been recorded, including *Buffy the Vampire Slayer*, *The X Files*, and *Beverly Hills 90210*. In a box tucked behind the set Harry found the porn stash.

No trains.

He came back upstairs, checked in on June, who was snoring, and went up to the second floor to find Delbert's bedroom. There wasn't much there Harry wouldn't have expected to find. Some *Penthouse* magazines, a few paperback novels based on *Star Trek*, clothing, shoes, a stack of textbooks in the closet left over from high school days.

And again, nothing that might have come from Choo-Choo's Trains.

Harry told himself he shouldn't be surprised. His theory was too outlandish to be serious. What Lucknow had endured, he was coming to accept, was a series of bizarre, tragic events that had nothing to do with one another.

There was a door to the garage off the kitchen. In there, Harry found the red Torino and a VW Golf, presumably the mother's car. He hoped she wasn't doing any driving these days, considering how hard she was hitting the bottle. He made a mental note to keep an eye out for the car when he was driving around town.

Harry gave both vehicles, which were unlocked, a quick search. Not a caboose to be found.

He checked in on June before leaving. She was out cold, snoring, her head resting at an awkward angle on the cushion. He quietly slipped out the front door.

Harry was getting back into his car when he noticed something. *Smoke.*

It was rising from a basement window of the house next to the Dorfman residence. The base of the window, which consisted of two panes with a bar down the middle, was at ground level. One pane had been slid behind the other, and the smoke was wafting out through the screen.

It wasn't a lot of smoke. But for all Harry knew, if this was the early stages of a fire, those wisps of smoke would soon turn into billows.

He ran first to the window, went down on one knee, and peered inside, but it was too dark to make anything out. But he did hear something.

Chuffchuffchuffchuffchuffchuff

"Hello!" he shouted.

There was no reply. Just more:

Chuffchuffchuffchuffchuffchuff

He stood, ran around to the front door, and banged on it. When there was no answer after ten seconds, he banged on it again, this time shouting: "Police!"

A startled woman swung open the door. Before she could say anything, Harry pushed past her.

"How do you get to the basement?" he asked.

"What is this?"

"The basement. Something's burning."

"There!"

He was, it turned out, standing by the door that led downstairs. He opened it and was down the steps in seconds, finding himself in a finished rec room, wood paneling on the walls, a pool table, a TV set, and a couch. At the far end of the room, near the slightly opened window, was a child sitting cross-legged on the floor.

He stopped short, quickly assessing that there was no fire.

A little girl was sitting within a large oval of toy train track, and whizzing around her at high speed was a steam engine pulling three cars. Whiffs of smoke were puffing continuously from the locomotive's chimney, much of it drifting upward and out the window. In the girl's hands was a small plastic bottle, about the size of a container of nasal spray. On the side were the words TOY TRAIN SMOKE FLUID.

Harry recognized her as the child who'd been at an upstairs window when Delbert Dorfman was smoking himself to death. She stared straight ahead, rocking her body slowly frontward and backward. She was oblivious to Harry's arrival.

The woman came up behind him. "There's no fire," she told him.

He turned slowly. "I'm sorry. I saw smoke outside."

The woman rolled her eyes at him. "It's just pretend. It's some special stuff that goes into the engine. It's not toxic or anything. I checked. Allison loves it when the train puffs out the smoke. She finds it calming."

Harry glanced back at the girl, then said to the mother, "She's, like, in a trance or something."

The woman sighed, annoyed. "She has autism. Don't they teach you police anything?"

Harry sighed. "I'll let myself out."

As he moved past the woman, he stopped and asked, "When did you get those trains for her?"

"A week ago," the woman said. "That new shop in town."

"He seems to be doing a bang-up business," Harry said.

THIRTY-NINE

Something was up. Edwin Nabler could always tell.

While he couldn't accurately predict what his products would trigger when he sent them out into the world, he liked to stay on top of what they'd set in motion. It was much more than idle curiosity, or taking pleasure in one's work. He wanted to know the trains were doing what they were designed to do, which amounted to so much more than bringing a smile to a little boy or girl's face.

Nabler had never been a student of chemistry, but he understood the principle of an activating agent. Something that when introduced into a situation exacted a change onto whatever it came into contact with. But chemistry was rooted in science, and Nabler considered his talents as more metaphysical, something beyond the realm of human understanding, given that he operated within the sliver. He wasn't so much an activating agent, or a change agent, to use the more popular current terminology, but an agent of chaos.

He'd hardly be the first. Such agents were the stuff of myth and folklore, like the coyote-like trickster common to the cultures of many North American indigenous tribes, or the conniving Anansi spider from the African fable of the Ashanti people of Ghana, or even the mischievous gremlin believed to be behind aircraft malfunctions. They even appeared in the pages of comic books. What was Batman's nemesis, the Joker, if not an agent of chaos? Nabler fancied himself much like them, except he presented himself to the masses in a ridiculous engineer's cap and a stupid vest peppered with railway logos. He liked to be as original as the circumstances allowed.

There were plenty of others like him in the sliver, some with similar methods, others more fantastical. The work ethic they all stuck to was simple: insinuate yourself into a host, which could be an individual or a group setting, and ensure that bad things happened to good people. (It was acceptable if a bad thing happened to a bad person, too, of course, and Nabler was not unhappy with how things turned out for Delbert Dorfman.)

Nabler employed an iconic, much-loved toy to work his magic. Others made use of everyday appliances from toasters to televisions, the latter being especially useful for transmitting subliminal messages. Nabler knew of one in the sliver who used automobiles. That fellow who wrote about a homicidal Plymouth Fury with a girl's name would be astounded to learn how close he'd come to the truth. Nabler heard tell of another colleague who did amazing things with Royal Doulton figurines. How many little old ladies had choked on their Jell-O while one of those porcelain doodads looked on from a nearby shelf?

Some even used common house pets, although adapting a living organism did present challenges. Nabler's trains could *affect* pets, but that wasn't the same as a cat or a dog or an adorable little bunny that was chock-full of mayhem from the get-go.

As for the more fantastical, well, Nabler was willing to admit he envied those who engineered the crashing of jumbo jets, the careening of overloaded buses off cliffs, the capsizing of ferry boats, the plunging of elevators.

He had a grudging admiration for the ones who'd executed the events of September 11. Those were actual *people* intent on chaos and disruption. Pulled it off all on their own without any help from the Edwin Nablers of the sliver world. You had to tip your hat to them. Enough types like that would put Nabler and his ilk out of business.

Thankfully, there were not.

That didn't mean he didn't have his work cut out for him these days. So many safeguards! Smoke detectors, seat belts, childproof outlet plugs, playgrounds with padded ground cover, parents who drove their moppets to school instead of letting them walk, the goddamn Food and Drug Administration, for Christ's sake. No one worried about any of this forty or fifty or sixty years ago. It all made the work that much more important.

How did Nabler know something was up?

When a man blew himself up at a barbecue, a woman killed herself in the tub, a dog went mad, it was as though Nabler were *there*. His trains were his receivers, his eyes, transmitting information back to him, and not through some sophisticated surveillance software.

On top of that, Nabler himself had special gifts. When it suited his purposes, he could make those within his sphere of influence see and hear things that were not there. Whistles in the night. Creepy-crawlies. Lost loved ones. He could present himself as he wished to be seen, and often sensed what they were feeling.

Which was how he was so confident that someone was sniffing around. It was his own fault, getting lazy with Tanner, leaving his boneless carcass to be found. He'd run into a temporary glitch with the mini-cremation machine he had tucked into a secondary room back of the shop. Worked fine for Hillman, but then Nabler briefly lost his surreptitious hookup to the local power grid.

But it was more than that. His successes in Lucknow had been, if he could say this to himself modestly, a bit splashier than he might have hoped for.

Chief Harry Cook's interest had been piqued.

Nabler would have to exercise greater caution. What worked in his favor was that if and when the chief started putting it together, he'd doubt himself. When the evidence led him to a theory so outside the realm of the possible, he would discount it. He would think he must be wrong, that there had to be some other explanation.

Nabler certainly hoped so. He'd grown weary of moving. There was still much he could accomplish here in Lucknow and environs. He could attract customers from as far away as Bennington and Montpelier and Burlington and Middlebury, even from some towns across the border into New York State. Spread the mayhem far and wide.

But if he had to pull up stakes, so be it.

Nabler was ready.

It would be interesting to see whether Chief Cook could think beyond whatever investigative techniques he'd learned back in his police academy days.

And if he could, if he ended up at Nabler's door, well, the man did have a decent bone structure.

FORTY

Harry was thinking about a cartoon he watched as a kid.

Bugs Bunny has conned gangster Rocky into thinking his moron henchman, Mugsy, has been tormenting him. Mugsy's tied up in a closet while Bugs cuts a hole in the floor under Rocky's chair. Rocky plunges into the basement, and when he finds Mugsy, there's a saw planted into his bound hands, courtesy of Bugs.

And Rocky says, before giving Mugsy a whoopin': "I don't know how ya's done it, but I know ya's done it!"

Which was exactly how Harry felt about Edwin Nabler. Except where Nabler was concerned, not only did Harry not know how he'd done it, he wasn't entirely sure what he'd done.

But in each of those households where tragedy had struck recently, there was a train set from Nabler's store. It was more than that. There were, at least in some of these instances, freakish parallels. While Auden struggled to make his new Santa Fe train run, his father could not start his barbecue. As Delbert Dorfman smoked himself to death, a toy train pumped out smoke only a few feet away. A dog went wild when a whistle button was depressed on a transformer at the Wilford home.

If Harry had felt in over his head over the Tanner murder, he was now at the bottom of the pond with these new developments.

So who was Edwin Nabler?

As a law officer, Harry had access to numerous government databases. If he wanted to know whether someone had a police record, he entered a name and a date of birth and a Social Security number and waited to see what popped up. And if this grand and glorious Internet that everyone was so excited about turned out be everything it was cracked up to be, the day would come when Harry could find out even more personal information on someone.

And in the wake of September 11 and the Patriot Act that President George W. Bush had pushed through Congress, getting details on a suspect faced fewer roadblocks than in the past, especially if you dropped even the slightest hint that said suspect might be involved in a terrorist act.

Harry didn't have Edwin Nabler's Social Security number or date of birth, but he did have something to start with. He had wandered the alley that ran behind the Main Street stores. It was there he found a van with CHOO-CHOO'S TRAINS printed on the side. He made a note of the letter and numbers on the green Vermont license plate.

A good place to start.

Back at the station, he logged in to the Vermont Department of Motor Vehicles and entered the plate from Nabler's truck.

And nothing came back.

Harry wondered whether he had copied it down wrong. Did he mistake a lowercase letter *l* for the numeral 1? No, he hadn't, because the plate contained neither. He had written it down clearly, legibly. So he entered the plate into the system again.

And again, nothing came back.

He put in a call to someone he knew at the DMV. "I got a plate that when I enter it I'm coming up with nothing," he told the woman who took his call after identifying himself.

"Let me try it," she said. He could hear her tapping away on a keyboard. "Chief, there is no such plate."

"Yes, there is. It's on the guy's van." Harry had encountered stolen plates plenty of times, but never ones that were outright fake.

"Well, there's no plate that's been issued by the state of Vermont that matches what you've given me. You sure it was a Vermont plate?"

Harry sighed. "I can read. It said Vermont on the plate. I've done this before. And to the best of my knowledge, there's not another state in these United States of America that has green plates like Vermont's."

"You don't have to get snippy, sir."

"Forget the plate. Run a name for me. I want to see if this guy I'm looking at has a driver's license more legit than his plate."

"Go ahead."

"Edwin Nabler." He spelled it.

"Middle name or initial?"

"Don't know."

More tapping in the background.

"There's no one in Vermont with a driver's license by that name," the woman said.

Harry said nothing.

"Chief?"

"Thanks," he said, and ended the call.

He tried some non-vehicle-related databases, entering the name Edwin Nabler. When one came up short, he tried another, and then another.

Until he gave up. As best Harry could tell, there wasn't a single governmental agency in the US that knew one damn thing about Edwin Nabler, because Edwin Nabler did not exist.

If he wanted to nail Nabler for something, all he'd have to do is spot him driving that van around town one day, pull him over, ask for his license and registration, and when he couldn't come up with anything, bring him in. Ask him who the fuck he really was.

Harry could do that.

But it wouldn't get him any further ahead in trying to figure out how—and if—Nabler was linked to those bizarre events. Harry couldn't move precipitously. He needed to watch the guy first, see what he was up to, learn his routine.

He'd like to enlist Stick's help, or maybe Nancy's. A twenty-four-hour surveillance couldn't be conducted solo. But what would he give for a reason? What would Harry say when Stick asked whether Nabler was a suspect? Yeah, well, maybe. And what was it he was suspected of doing?

It would be a short conversation.

Nor would Harry get authorization to tap Nabler's phone. Not when all he had was a gut feeling that was impossible to articulate. Harry was going to have to do this alone, at least for now. And there wasn't a damn soul he could talk to about this, not even Melissa, because instead of trying to help him out, they'd be picking up the phone and calling the guys in the white coats to take him away.

Harry was going to have to do this on his own. He'd start tomorrow.

THROUGH THE DAY, keeping tabs on Edwin Nabler was simple.

When his shop was open, he was there. He had no employees, so it wasn't like he could take off for a couple of hours without closing.

In the morning, Harry went into the diner for a take-out coffee and sat on the bench where Gavin had once been a fixture. He'd wait until the OPEN sign came on in the window of Choo-Choo's Trains, finish his coffee, and then go about his duties, checking back occasionally to make sure Nabler hadn't closed early or taken a long lunch.

What struck Harry was that Nabler didn't come from some other location when it was time to open up. The man was living in his store, sleeping in his store, presumably in some room at the back. All he'd need, Harry figured, was a bed, a bathroom with a shower, a mini-fridge, and a hot plate. The question was why Nabler chose to live that way.

A man that age—and now that Harry thought about it, he really had no sense of how old Nabler was—would at the very least have an apartment, wouldn't he? It was true some people chose to live frugally. They were not concerned with material things. Maybe Nabler was like that. There was no sign of a significant other. He had what he needed, and no more.

Nabler's shop had been open for fifteen minutes and, so far, had attracted no customers. Harry drank the last of his coffee, tossed the paper cup into a nearby trash bin, got in his car, and backed out of the angled spot. Rather than head to the station, he opted to patrol. Drive around with no particular goal in mind, although he was always hoping he might come upon Gavin, that maybe he'd been on a bender, had busted into a vacant house, taken a few days to sober up, and finally decided to rejoin the world. But in his gut, Harry didn't expect to see Gavin again. Not alive, anyway.

After half an hour of wandering, he made it to the station and dealt with the paperwork piling up on his desk. Figured out the next three weeks' worth of schedules for the staff. When it got to be eleven, he walked down the street to the deli and bought a tuna sandwich with a dill pickle on the side and a Diet Coke and brought it all back and ate lunch at his desk.

At half-past the hour, he got back in his car, found a parking spot on Main Street, and found a spot on a bench across, and a little ways down, from Nabler's shop.

Just as he put his butt on the bench, the sign at Choo-Choo's went from OPEN to CLOSED.

Hello.

If Nabler was closing for lunch, was he staying there to eat it, or heading out? Harry got back into his car, backed out of the spot, drove a block, and turned around, waiting to see whether Nabler's van would appear from the alley that separated his business from Featherstone's next door.

After two minutes, the front of the van nosed out onto the street, made a right, and drove up Main. Harry followed, staying well back. He wasn't too worried about losing Nabler. This wasn't like tailing a car in New York City—not that he'd ever done that, but he could imagine. There wasn't dense traffic in Lucknow. There weren't stoplights every block.

Nabler made a right, heading north. Harry stopped for a moment at the turn, waiting for Nabler to get far enough ahead that he wouldn't notice Harry in his rearview mirror. Nabler's van rumbled over the same railroad crossing where Harry had been delayed the other day. This time, Harry made it through without having to take any chances. But as he crossed the tracks, he glanced to the west and saw the distant headlight of an approaching freight. Once he was through, he heard the familiar clang and, looking into his driver's-door mirror, saw the lights begin to flash and the gates descend.

Up ahead, the white van's right blinker had come on. Nabler steered the vehicle into the parking lot of the Lucknow Community Center and Arena, a multifunctional municipal structure where everything from bake sales to hockey games to day care took place.

What the hell was he doing here? Or was he using the parking lot to turn around, see whether he was being followed?

Harry kept on driving. As he went past, he saw Nabler getting out of the van and heading for the front door. Another hundred yards on, Harry slowed, did a U-turn, and idled on the opposite shoulder.

Fifteen minutes passed before Nabler's van reappeared, during which time a multi-engine freight train of mostly tanker cars passed by up ahead. The van headed back in the direction it had come from. Harry followed. Nabler drove back down the alley to the rear of his shop. Harry waited until he saw the sign go back to OPEN, then turned around and went back to the community center.

At the office he found someone he recognized, a woman in her forties named Pam, sitting at an electric typewriter.

"Hey, Pam."

She looked up and smiled. "Hey, Harry. What's up?"

"You had a guy in here a little while ago? Engineer's hat, railroad patches all over his vest?"

"Yeah, right. He met with Susie." She pointed a thumb over the shoulder. Susie Mince was the general manager. "Just go on in. She's not doing anything so important she can't be interrupted." She flashed a sly grin.

Harry made his way past Pam's desk and rapped on the open door of Susie's office. She looked up from the latest edition of the *Lucknow Leader* and smiled when she saw who it was.

"Am I under arrest, Harry?" she asked.

"Dunno. What'd you do?"

"Put someone else's parking ticket under my windshield so I wouldn't get one." She smiled mischievously.

Harry considered that. "Left the cuffs in the car. Back in a sec."

Susie grinned. "And why are you darkening my door today?"

"That guy who came in to see you? Nabler?"

"That train nut?"

Harry smiled. "That'd be the guy."

"I could see wearing a getup like that in your store, but going out in public? It's like having an I'M A NERD flashing sign on your head. You know, last year we rented the arena to an organization holding a huge model train flea market. That was an interesting group, let me tell you. Mostly old men with questionable fashion sense. Tables set up selling everything from old Lionel and American Flyer trains to electronics to books full of railway trivia. I thought they could have done with just one vendor offering deodorant."

"You mind my asking what Nabler wanted?"

Susie nodded. "I guess I can't make fun when he's well-intentioned."

"How so?"

"He was talking about making a contribution, being a sponsor, something like that. Buying new jerseys or skates or sticks, say, for the Bobcats." The Lucknow Bobcats, the local kids' hockey team. "And putting an ad on the jerseys, or maybe one on the boards."

"Oh," Harry said.

"Kind of goofy, but nice of him. He was saying he's relatively new here and wanted to make a contribution, be more involved in the community."

"What'd you decide on?"

"Nothing yet. I said I'd think about it, see where whatever funds he wanted to donate could be put to the best use. Truth be told, this whole place could use a coat of paint. I keep telling the mayor and his band of numbnuts we need more funds for upkeep, but they've got their heads so far up their asses it's like trying to explain France to a chicken. Why?"

"Why, what?"

"Why you asking me about the train geek?"

Harry smiled. "He's been putting other people's parking tickets under his wiper so he won't get one."

"Bastard," she said.

HARRY SPENT MUCH of the afternoon going through the annual budget he would present to the town. The community center wasn't the only municipal operation looking for more money. Harry wanted to hire another person to keep the station running smoothly, plus one more officer. They were stretched too thin to cover the town's needs twenty-four hours a day.

When it got to be close to five, Harry left the station and returned to his Main Street bench. Choo-Choo's Trains closed at five. What did Nabler do once his workday was over?

Harry sat there, glanced at this watch: 4:55 p.m.

Waited. Looked again: 4:58 p.m.

The sign in the window of Choo-Choo's Trains went from OPEN to CLOSED.

Harry looked at his watch. Exactly 5:00 p.m.

Game on.

FORTY-ONE

As Harry got off the bench, he used his Nokia cell to call Janice and tell her he'd be late getting home this evening.

Standing next to their bed, using the extension that sat on the bedside table, Janice said that was a shame, because she had a surprise for him. A surprise? What kind of surprise? he wanted to know. His thoughts immediately leaned toward matters of an intimate nature. With all the stress he'd been under these last few weeks, he knew he hadn't exactly been the most attentive partner, and maybe Janice had something in the works to get him back on track.

But then she offered one hint. It was a surprise for both him and Dylan. Well, so much for *that* theory.

"I might be home after he's gone to bed," he said.

"Then we can do it tomorrow. What are you working on, anyway?"

He almost told her he was going to be on a "stakeout" but didn't want to sound like he thought he was in an episode of *NYPD Blue*. But he wanted to tell her something, and she was about the only one he *could* tell. And even then, he wasn't about to get into specifics. Not that he actually had any.

"There's this guy I'm keeping my eye on."

"Oh?" Janice said, intrigued. It wasn't very often, in a town like Lucknow, that Harry had to conduct a surveillance. "Can you say anything?"

"Not really. I haven't got enough to get a wiretap or a search warrant. What I do have is so out there, I'd get laughed out of a judge's chambers. But there's something just wrong about this guy. So I'm gonna sit on his place tonight."

"Be careful, will ya?"

"In this town?"

It was their private joke. A snippet of dialogue from early in the movie *Jaws*. Chief Brody laughs off his wife's concerns as he heads to work. Amity was like Lucknow, a place where nothing big happened.

Of course, this was before the shark showed up.

Harry wondered what kind of shark was in his future.

"I'll be home when I get home," he said.

"I'll save you some dinner."

"I might grab something. Gotta go."

Janice placed the cordless receiver back in its cradle and hung up the phone and looked at the large gift-wrapped package resting on the bed.

Inside the box, something stirred, as though it had been listening.

THE ALLEY BEHIND Main Street was lined with Dumpsters and garbage cans and bundled cardboard. The odd rat scurried by. Cats wandered, hunting for them. There were service doors to all the businesses, and where there was enough room, merchants' vehicles hugged the walls so others could pass.

Among them was Nabler's white van.

Harry was keeping an eye on it, but not from behind the wheel of his cruiser. It would have attracted unwanted attention. Instead, he was a few businesses away from Nabler's, perched atop a stack of old cinder blocks around the corner of a Dumpster. If Nabler emerged from the back of his shop, Harry would hear either the door open-ing and closing or the engine of his van turning over when he keyed the ignition.

Harry was counting on the fact that if Nabler left his shop, he wouldn't come out the front door. Once the CLOSED sign was on, the door locked, he'd leave by the back door because his vehicle was here. If he came out at all.

If he did drive off, Harry would run flat-out to his car, parked across the street, and trail Nabler before he was out of sight.

And where did Harry think he might go? What would be the point of following him?

Harry had no idea.

He sat on the cement blocks and waited. And waited. Did this guy ever go out for groceries? Hit the drive-through for a Big Mac and fries? Go to the lumber store for more shelving?

And damned if Harry hadn't forgotten to pick himself up a sand-wich before embarking on this mission. By half-past six, his stomach was growling so loudly he was worried he'd give away his hiding spot. He had his phone, but what was he supposed to do? Order a pizza to the alley?

He heard a door open.

Harry poked his head out around the edge of the Dumpster. Someone was coming out the back of a business a couple of doors beyond the train store. Len's Bakery, he thought. An woman in her sixties appeared, hunting in her purse for the keys to a silver Kia Sportage. She started up the car and began slowly making her way up the alley to Harry's position. Not wanting to alarm her, he moved back and crouched down next to the Dumpster until the little car had rolled past. The woman had her eyes focused straight ahead, hands gripping the wheel at ten and two, and did not notice him.

The evening dragged on. Shortly before eight, he realized he had to take a leak. He turned in close to the wall, unzipped, and did what he had to do. Good thing there wasn't a cop around, he thought. Might have gotten arrested for indecent exposure.

He kept glancing at his watch, wondering how much longer he could do this. By nine, it was completely dark. If Nabler wanted to conduct some nefarious business, this would be a good time to get to it. But the door never opened, and the van never moved. Harry was coming to the realization that this stakeout (he did kind of like that word) was a waste of time. Whatever Nabler might have been up to, maybe he'd finished. And anything that might incriminate him wasn't to be discovered by following him.

It might well be in his shop.

What Harry really needed was to get in *there*. And if he wasn't going to be able to get a warrant to search the place, he might have to bend the rules somewhat.

A plan began to formulate in Harry's mind. He would need to enlist an accomplice.

JANICE MET HARRY when he came through the front door shortly before ten.

"I forgot to eat," he said.

There was some leftover lasagna that she popped into the microwave while he took off his jacket, put his service weapon in the top of the front hall closet, then went to the fridge for a cold beer.

"How'd it go?" she asked.

He shrugged. "Gonna have to come at this another way." Harry looked at her as he took a long pull on the beer.

The microwave tinged. Janice slipped on an oven mitt to bring out the plate, peeled off the plastic wrap, and put it on the table. "Thanks," Harry said, sitting down. "I'm gonna hoover this."

Janice took a seat across from him. "I'm worried about you."

"I'm fine," he said, blowing on a forkful of pasta before putting it into his mouth.

"You're exhausted. This Angus Tanner thing is wearing you down. Can't you get help from, I don't know, the FBI?"

He shrugged. "I've called. Everything's taking a backseat to anti-terrorism. First all those planes, then everybody losing their shit over those letters that maybe were loaded with anthrax. You think anyone outside of Lucknow cares about one murder and a couple of men still missing, one who was pretty much the town drunk? The things keeping me up at night, I don't even know how to explain what the hell they're about."

He shoveled more lasagna into his mouth, washed it down with more beer. He set the bottle down, rested the fork on the side of his plate, and went quiet.

"Talk to me, Harry."

"For a long time, I wondered if maybe I made the right decision, about never moving away, staying in the town where I grew up, becoming a cop, working my way up to chief. Did I settle? Doesn't everybody have to go someplace else to become something? Could I have been more?"

Janice smiled sadly. "You've been talking to Melissa."

Harry sighed. "Busted."

"You think you'd have been happier working for the FBI, having to go all over the country, being transferred to North Dakota, dealing with a massive bureaucracy? Is that what you would have wanted? Don't ever, ever discount what you do for the people of Lucknow. You make a difference here." She put her hand over his for a moment. "That's what matters. You help folks, one-on-one, and I could not be more proud walking the streets of this town knowing you're my husband."

He looked off to one side. "Yeah, well." He got the last piece of lasagna onto his fork, popped it into his mouth, and finished off the beer. He was picking up the plate to take to the sink when Janice grabbed him by the wrist. She stood, took the plate from his hand and put it on the table, slid her arms around him, pulled him close to her. She tilted her head up and put her lips on his.

"Take me upstairs," she said.

Once they were undressed and under the covers, it was as special as it had ever been, and Harry found himself thinking fate was a wonderful thing, that somehow he had met this woman and fallen in love with her, that they had made a life together and this union had blessed them with a terrific son, and it didn't matter how much shit got thrown his way as Lucknow's chief of police, he was still the luckiest son of a bitch in the whole world.

FORTY-TWO

I promised you a surprise," Janice said the following morning in the kitchen.

"That was a pretty good one last night," Harry said, taking a bite out of a slice of toast. For the first time in weeks, he had slept well.

"When Dylan gets down here," she said, giving him a smirk, "all will be revealed."

Their son showed up five minutes later. It was a school day, but aside from getting up earlier than he would have on a weekend, there was no sense of urgency in his actions. He wandered in, opened the fridge and got himself a glass of orange juice, poured some corn-flakes into a bowl, and added a splash of milk.

As he took his first bite, Janice said, "Gentlemen, if I might have your attention for a moment."

Harry leaned back in his chair, arms folded, a sly smile on his face. Dylan looked up from his cereal.

"What?" he said.

"I know it's not Christmas yet," she said, "but I got a little something for the two of you to work on together, and decided to give it to you now."

"What, like a puzzle?" Dylan asked.

"Better," she said. "Stay right there."

She ducked out to the living room. Harry and Dylan exchanged puzzled glances. "What is it?" Dylan asked.

His father shrugged.

Janice was back in under ten seconds, bearing a wrapped package in her arms. She set it on the table. "You can fight over who opens it."

Harry gave his son a nod. "All yours."

Dylan put down his spoon, found a spot where the wrapping had been taped together, and tore into it. His eyes went wide and a broad grin took over his face as what lay hidden by the paper was exposed.

"Oh, cool!" he said.

Harry said nothing.

"This is awesome," Dylan said. He raised the box up onto its side so that his father could see the steam engine and various boxcars displayed through clear plastic windows.

"That Southern Pacific steam engine?" Janice said. "That's a four-six-two. That means it has four small wheels in the front, six big ones in the middle, and two little ones at the back." She smiled broadly. "I just learned that. And I know some of the cars seem a little silly—that one there, a giraffe pokes his head up out of a hatch in the top of the boxcar—but I saw it and I thought of you guys and how you could set it up and, I don't know, have some fun."

She could see so far Harry had no reaction, which was, in itself, a reaction.

"What?" she asked. "It's got a missile car. Roof opens up and it fires a rocket or something like that, and—"

"It has to go back," Harry said.

There was a moment of stunned silence from Janice and Dylan.

"I'm sorry, but it has to be returned." He looked at Janice. "I can take it back. You don't have to do it. I know where you got it."

"Why would I take it back?" she asked. "Dylan likes it. What's your problem?"

Harry was slowly shaking his head. "I'll deal with it. Don't worry about it."

Dylan looked at him, wounded. "You don't *want* to set it up with me?"

"No, it's not like that," Harry protested. "I'd love to do something with you. Just not—just not this."

"Can I talk to you?" Janice said quietly, giving her head a tilt.

Harry got up and followed her into the dining room, but not before pointing at Dylan and saying, "Do *not* open that."

Once in the other room, with the door to the kitchen closed, Janice got up close to his face and said, in a heated whisper, "All I wanted to do was find something you guys could do together. You've hardly been around for ages, you don't have much time for either of us, and, okay, I can deal with that, I get that you're under a lot of pressure lately, but your son? He misses his dad and I saw that fucking train set and thought, hey, I bet they'd *love* this, but instead you just took a huge dump on the whole thing."

"We have to get it out of the house," Harry said evenly.

"What? You think I'm spoiling him? When's the last time I did anything like this?"

"You're not—look, all I'm saying is, we have to get it out of here."

Janice rolled her eyes. "Is it wired to explode?"

Harry thought that was closer to the truth than he wanted to admit. "Please just trust me on this. Look, it was a wonderful thing you did. I love the idea of doing something with Dylan, something we can build or make together. But it can't be that."

Janice's look of anger had shifted to one of bafflement. "I don't know what the hell is going on with you."

Harry rubbed his forehead, and dropped his voice lower. "You know that guy I was watching last night?"

She waited.

"It's that shop owner. Where you bought this."

Her eyebrows sprang up. "What?"

"Yeah. I've been keeping an eye on him. I can't really say what it's about."

Janice was trying to read between the lines. "It's stolen merchandise, right? Is that what's going on? The stuff in his shop is hot?"

Harry liked that, and nodded. "Something like that."

"Shit, I can't believe I bought stolen goods. He seemed like an okay guy. Oh my God."

"Yeah, that's what everyone—"

They heard the front door slam. Harry ran, opened the door in time to see Dylan reach the sidewalk, his backpack slung over his shoulder.

"Hey!" Harry called out. "Wait up, pal!"

Dylan didn't look back, kept on walking. Harry ran after him, grabbed him by the shoulder, and turned him around despite his son's resistance.

"I have to go to school," he said sullenly.

"Look, I'm sorry about the trains. It's hard to explain."

"I understand. You don't want to do stuff with me. And you made Mom feel like shit."

Harry took a knee. "I'm going to let you off the hook on using that kind of language this one time. And, yeah, I did make Mom feel bad, and I'm sorry about that. And even sorrier about how I've made you feel. The truth is, we can't have anything from the store where your mom got that. You have to swear to me that you'll never say a word about this to anyone, but I think the guy who runs that store is a bad man."

"What did he do?"

Good question.

"I'm working on getting answers to that. Can't say anything more. But your mom's right that I haven't made enough time for you lately, and I'm working on that. Maybe we can do something this weekend. You pick. Whatever you want, that's what we'll do."

Dylan appeared to be thinking. "Pancakes."

"Pancakes?"

"At the diner."

Harry smiled. "Saturday morning. Pancakes at the diner. It's a deal." He extended a hand and they shook on it.

"Okay, get to school."

He spun Dylan around, gave him a soft swat on the butt to launch him on his way, and watched his son until he turned the corner.

Harry would never see him again.

FORTY-THREE

H arry had no intention of taking that set back to Choo-Choo's for a refund. But he knew he didn't want Janice doing it. If either of them were to ask for a refund, it might arouse Edwin Nabler's suspicions. Why, out of all his customers, would the chief be unsatisfied? Were the boxcars broken? Did the transformer not come to life when plugged in? If everything was in perfect working order, why return it?

Because you're some kind of fucking freak.

That wasn't going to fly.

But Harry definitely wanted it out of the house. It didn't matter what Janice had paid for it. That set was never going to be opened, never going to be played with. After Janice went to work, Harry put the set in the trunk of his cruiser and drove straight to the Lucknow Municipal Waste Facility, which was a fancy name for a dump. It sat five miles out of town off the road that led to Bennington.

He came up to the manned gate, flashed his badge at the attendant so as to give the impression that he was here on official business and avoid the fee, and entered the facility. When he was out of the attendant's sight, he stopped, got out, opened the trunk, and picked up the box, all the pieces still carefully packaged inside.

While birds circled overhead, Harry walked it over to the edge of an enormous pit of trash and, swinging this arms three times to work up some momentum, pitched the set into the air. It sailed in a long arc before dropping into the middle of dozens of green garbage bags. Harry wanted to be sure it was too far away to tempt anyone to wade in after it. The box had landed face down, hiding the plastic windows revealing the treasures within, so it wouldn't be obvious to any dump scroungers what it was. Soon all this would be bulldozed over. Harry slapped his palms together, as though he'd actually had to touch some of that trash, returned to his car, and drove out, feeling a weight lifting off his shoulders as he got back onto the highway and headed for the Lucknow Community Center, stopping for take-out coffee and donuts along the way.

"Ooh, a cream-filled," Susie said, reaching into the box. "I don't know what kind of favor you're looking for, but if there's also a lemon one in here, and you want me to sleep with you, the answer's yes."

"Last I heard, Susie, you were playing for the other team," Harry said.

"Doesn't matter. We're talkin' donuts here. What is it you want?"

She and Harry were sitting at a picnic table out back of the community center. Harry had dropped by and suggested they leave her office to discuss a proposal.

"That Mr. Nabler who came to see you about doing something community-minded? Buying uniforms for the kids or whatever?"

"Yeah?"

"I think you should have some further discussions with him about it."

Susie's eyes narrowed. "Okay," she said, drawing the word out. "And why would I do that?"

"As a favor to me. And I'd like you to suggest he come out around, say, seven this evening. He closes his shop at five. That gives him time for dinner, and then he could come out here."

"And I'm supposed to say what, exactly?"

"How much detail did you get into when he came out the first time?"

"Not a lot. I told him I'd give it some thought."

"Have you done that yet?"

"Nope."

"Think you could?"

"I could pull together some prices for him. Like, if he wanted to spend a thousand, we could do this, and if he wanted to spend five thousand, we could do that. Something along those lines."

"That sounds perfect," Harry said.

"Uh, Harry, why are you trying to stick it to a guy who's showing an interest in making a contribution? Dude wants to give back and you've got a problem with that?"

"I think it's an act. He's burnishing his image. Wants to look like a fine, upstanding citizen."

"But he isn't?"

"That's what I'm trying to determine. Look, if this guy's really on the up-and-up, no one'll be happier than me."

"What do you think he's done, Harry?"

He just smiled.

"How long you want me to keep him here?"

"Think you could charm the pants off him for an hour?"

"Well, for sure *that's* not happening, unless he brings donuts, too." She made a face. "No, he's too weird. Not even for a lemon-filled."

"You wanna try him now, see if he'll take the bait?"

Susie studied Harry for a moment. "Okay."

He followed her back into her office, sat on the other side of her desk while she looked up the number and dialed. Waited. Suddenly she raised her index finger, signaling that someone had picked up at the other end.

"Hey, Mr. Nabler, it's Susie at the community center . . . Right,

Edwin. I was pulling together some numbers for you, Edwin, and wondered if you had some time this evening to come out and have a look at them."

She nodded, listened. "Terrific. How's around seven? I gotta work late tonight, setting up for a flower show they're holding here on the weekend. Okay, good."

Susie hung up.

"This guy's not, like, a serial killer or something, is he?"

"I do not know him to be a serial killer, for certain," Harry said, dodging a direct answer.

Susie spotted some lemon filling on her pinkie finger and licked it off.

"These donuts aren't going to cover it. You owe me."

A SKILL HARRY had picked up over the years was how to pick a lock. He'd once arrested a break-in artist who'd agreed to show him the tricks of his trade. They'd even become friends after, and every once in a while Harry took him out for a beer in exchange for a refresher course.

But even then, it was never as easy as it looked on the TV shows, where someone whipped out an array of lock-picking tools and broke into a secret government installation in under twenty seconds. Real life was not an episode of *The X Files*.

Harry didn't know whether he'd acquired sufficient skills to get into Nabler's shop through the alley access. If he couldn't, he might have to resort to using a blunt instrument, like a rock through the front window when no one was looking. Then, as a trusted officer of the law, he could enter the premises as part of an *investigation* into an act of vandalism. But that was definitely Plan B.

He once again phoned and told Janice he would be late getting home.

"Same thing as last night," he said.

"Roger that, over and out," Janice said.

God, he loved her.

He muted his phone, slipped it into his pocket, then settled into the spot he'd used the night before, perched on the cinder blocks by the Dumpster. He was there when, at fifteen minutes to seven, the back door of Choo-Choo's Trains opened and out walked Edwin Nabler.

Good ol' Susie, Harry thought.

Harry watched the man double-check the lock, then walk around and get into his van. Harry slipped off the blocks and crouched down low as the van wheeled by him.

Seconds later, Harry was at the shop's rear door, taking the lock-picking kit from his pocket. He knelt down and had a close look at the lock, wondering which pick his burglar buddy would choose.

Even before inserting the first pick, he thought he could hear something on the other side of the door. A mechanical sound of some kind. A chorus of metal spinning on metal. And something else. Something faint.

A muted *chuffchuffchuffchuffchuffchuff*.

Harry knew Edwin left a train running all the time on a loop in the front window of the shop, but it wasn't likely that he would be able to hear it all the way back here.

He gently worked one wire, then another, into the slot where a key would normally go, moving it one way and then another, feeling a little like a surgeon performing a delicate operation.

It took him just under five minutes. The lock disabled, he opened the door, holding his breath, hoping an alarm wouldn't go off.

None did.

But the sound he'd heard earlier was now louder, closer to a din. Much more than a *chuffchuffchuffchuff* and more like—

ChuffchuffCLICKETYCLACKclicketyCLACKwooWOOchuff
CLICKETYchuffCLICKETYchuffWOOchuggachuggaclackclickety
CHUFFCHUFFclicketyCLACKwooWOOchuffCLICKETYchuff
CLICKETYchuffWOOchuggachuggaclackclicketyCHUFFCHUFF
clicketyCLACKwooWOOchuffCLICKETYchuffCLICKETYchuff
WOOchuggachuggaclackclicketyCHUFF . . .

Harry slipped into the building, closed the door behind him, then turned to see what was making all the racket.

"Oh my God," Harry said.

FORTY-FOUR

For all her talk about Harry still owing her for doing him this solid, Susie was excited to be involved in whatever he was up to. She started looking at her watch at six thirty, knowing Mr. Edwin Nabler would be arriving soon.

The Bobcats were having a practice, so the rink echoed with the *whooshing* of skates on ice, a sound Susie had always found particularly soothing, as well as slap shots and sticks tapping the ice and a coach's whistle and the general vocal pandemonium a bunch of teenage boys created. She walked the perimeter of the arena once, then popped into the snack bar that was doing a reasonable business with moms and dads waiting for their kids to finish up. Harry had been wise to bring coffee and donuts from outside when he'd come earlier. The snack bar stuff was shit, especially those hot dogs that had been spinning on that rotisserie since Bobby Orr played for the Bruins.

She had no idea why Harry was interested in Nabler, but that didn't stop her from coming up with possible reasons. Given the current fucked-up state of the world, maybe he was one of those sleeper agents. Someone from an unfriendly foreign power who'd infiltrated American society, posing as a native, waiting for his orders to carry out a mission years in the planning stages. While that one gave Susie a bit of a thrill, she realized it was more likely someone like that would be the target of an FBI, CIA, or Homeland Security sting. No slight against Harry, but come on. He was the local chief of police.

The most likely scenario? Edwin Nabler had a thing for kids. What a perfect cover for someone who was a pedophile, running a business that catered, although not exclusively, to young boys. Yeah, Susie was putting her money on that one. And while she kept Nabler busy, Harry was probably searching his place for proof. Incriminating magazines and videocassettes.

Ick.

It was nearly seven.

Susie had come up with several pitches. And they were *real* pitches, because if it turned out Nabler was not up to anything nefarious, and if he really did want to make a contribution, well, why not give it a shot? He could buy a huge banner advertising his business that could be hung from the rafters over the ice. Every hockey game, people would see it. If he wanted to buy an ad for the boards, she could arrange that, too.

Seven o'clock.

She didn't want to be hanging around the entrance. Didn't want to look too needy, too desperate.

When it got to be five minutes past seven, Susie didn't give it much thought. Anybody could be five minutes late. And even when it was 7:10 p.m., she wasn't particularly worried. Anyone coming out this way had to cross the tracks. All it took was one lone freight train to make someone late for an appointment.

At 7:15, Susie got out from behind her desk and strolled to the entrance, stepped outside, and checked the parking lot.

No Mr. Choo.

She gazed down the road in the direction from which he would be coming. From here, she'd be able to see and hear a train passing through town, but there was no sign of one. No sign of Nabler's van, either.

The guy was a no-show.

Shit, Susie thought.

She ran back into the community center to make a call to Harry's cell phone.

FORTY-FIVE

It took Harry a minute to comprehend what he was looking at, and even then, he couldn't quite get his head around it. He'd never seen anything like this in his life. He had no basis for comparison.

The space he was in was larger than it would have seemed from the alley. The ceiling was a good fifteen feet over his head, and the space between him and the wall that was presumably the back side of the public area of the shop was filled with more . . . whatever this was. It was like trying to peer through a jungle.

That was the word that came to mind: *jungle*. Not long ago, he'd been to the local Blockbuster to rent for Dylan that Robin Williams movie *Jumanji*, and there was that point where the house was overrun with so many vines and tree trunks and branches that you almost couldn't tell you were *in* a house, and that was what it was like in this room. But instead of vines and branches, ribbons of toy train track, attached to narrow strips of planking and supported by a network of wires that hung down from the ceiling, were everywhere. Helixes and loops and straight sections, too many to even attempt to count.

And on all of them: trains. Dozens of them.

They weren't resting on the track, as if on display. They were *running*. Every last one, and at maximum speed. Whipping past one way and the other. Steam engines and diesels and freight trains and passenger trains. A train consisting of nothing but green boxcars chugged past only a foot or so above the floor. A red and silver Santa Fe diesel flew by at chest level on another track, sped past pulling at least ten passenger cars, the interiors illuminated, little silhouettes of riders in the windows. And then, catching Harry by surprise as it came from a different direction, on a stretch of track that ran right past his left ear, a trio of Albany & Bennington diesel engines pulling a line of tanker cars that seemed to go off into infinity.

And the noise. God, the noise. It was close to deafening. An incessant din.

ChuffchuffCLICKETYCLACKclicketyCLACKwooWOOchuff CLICKETYchuffCLICKETYchuffWOOchuggachuggaclackclickety CHUFFCHUFFclicketyCLACKwooWOOchuffCLICKETYchuff CLICKETYchuffWOOchuggachuggaclackclicketyCHUFFCHUFF clicketyCLACKwooWOOchuffCLICKETYchuffCLICKETYchuff WOOchuggachuggaclackclicketyCHUFF . . .

It felt to Harry like being inside a power plant, as if all these trains were turbines, cranking out enough electricity to light a city. Why had Nabler built such an elaborate apparatus? What on earth could be the point of all this? And why would he leave it running even when he wasn't on the premises?

As Harry ducked and weaved his way through the tracks, he found there was even more to see. At the center of all this, and along the walls, were scale-model re-creations of towns and hills and tunnels and bridges that the trains were passing through continuously. As he got closer, he could make out the details more clearly.

At first glance, what Nabler had made looked like a typical model village. Stores and houses and trees and anything else one might expect to find on a typical American street. But Nabler had incorporated what an artist might have referred to as "found objects" into what would have otherwise been fairly realistic scenes. That chimney atop the pickle factory was clearly a lipstick tube. Those electrical wires strung from pole to pole were brown shoelaces. That manhole cover on the street was a button from a shirt. The building labeled OPTOMETRIST had a real pair of reading glasses sitting atop it. The store with a LOCKSMITH sign had a set of actual car keys dangling from it.

Harry remembered that day when a woman came back into the diner looking for her lipstick.

There was a wide stretch of road about two feet long that, unlike a normal section of highway, curled up at each end. Harry reached down, ran his hand over its surface, felt the rough texture, almost like sandpaper. And it was then Harry realized this was the deck of a skateboard that had been worked into the layout.

Harry thought back to when Dylan had told him he'd lost his skateboard. One second it was there, the next it was gone.

"Jesus Christ," Harry said under his breath. Wasn't this what witches did? Made a brew consisting of items from people they wanted cursed? Or was that the specialty of voodoo practitioners? Take a lock of hair from someone they wanted to die and attached it to a doll before they stuck pins into—

Speaking of hair.

That grassy field, at the base of the mountain that a train had just vanished into through a rocky portal, looked particularly silky. Hesitantly, Harry ran his fingers through the grass, and, while he knew a more forensic examination would be called for, it sure felt like hair. Was it human hair? Was it a goat's?

One of the small model houses had a garden in the front yard that was edged with stones. But they did not look like stones to Harry. He ran his finger over the top of them to confirm his suspicion. The stones were teeth.

A small tree drew Harry's attention. No more than six inches tall, with a slender trunk that fanned out into branches onto which had been glued green clumps of sponge. Harry took hold of the base between his thumb and index finger and wiggled it back and forth until he had pried it off the layout. He brought it up close for a better look. He used a fingernail to scrape off some of the brown paint on the trunk. Underneath, it was white. He picked off the green clumps of sponge and had a look at the branches, one of the narrowest ones snapping off.

Fingers. The branches were finger bones.

Tests would confirm. But that grass looked like human hair, that tree appeared to be made of bone, and, holy shit, that rock outcropping.

He brushed away some of the fake vegetation until he saw what the outcropping was.

A skull.

A train came barreling out of a tunnel. Once it had passed, Harry leaned over, looked into the dark opening, and saw a latticework structure. Strips of material in a crisscross pattern, overlapped for strength to hold up the mountain above.

Harry decided to see just how strong it was. He dug his hand into the tunnel opening, grabbed the top of the portal, and gave it a good yank, revealing what was underneath.

More bones.

A conventional model train buff would probably use chicken wire and plaster to make his mountains, but not Edwin Nabler. No, he had a very different technique. He used *people*.

Okay, Harry thought. *We know what Nabler is now. He's a psychopathic killer who uses stolen items and body parts to build his creation.* But the larger question remained: *Why?* Was there a purpose to all this? Was something *happening* to these trains as they circled at high speed through his macabre setup?

Now that he was here, now that he could see what Nabler was

up to, Harry gave himself permission to think, as they liked to say these days, outside the box. What was going on in this room defied any kind of scientific, rational explanation. What Nabler was doing very likely defied the most basic laws of physics. Nabler had found a way to infuse these trains with some kind of malevolent force, some strange brand of evil intent, and once they found their way into the home of an unsuspecting family, that darkness was unleashed.

I'm losing my mind.

No, he told himself. He wasn't. From the beginning—okay, maybe not when Darryl Pidgeon had died in that barbecue explosion, but when Nadine Comstock had died with the help of a toy train transformer—Harry had felt that there was something that connected Edwin Nabler to an inexplicable depravity in Lucknow.

Now he was closer to understanding that connection. Once he left here, would anyone believe him? Would his unlawful entry into the premises derail (*Ha!* Harry thought wildly. *Pun intended*) his ability to get a search warrant? Would it foul up any potential prosecution and conviction?

Harry believed he had landed in a situation that was outside the bounds of conventional law. Search warrants and suspects' rights be damned. This was a crime scene of unimaginable proportions, and he'd ensure it was preserved and Nabler, that sick fuck, exposed.

That guy would never see the outside of a prison for the rest of his life. Lucky for Nabler that Vermont abolished the death penalty nearly thirty years ago, so he'd never—

What was that vibration in the front pocket of his jeans?

Harry's phone, of course.

He'd muted it before coming in here, and even if he hadn't, he might never have heard it ring over the din of the trains. He dug the phone out, saw that it was a call from the community center. But before he could answer it, he heard a voice.

"What do you think of my trains?"

Harry jumped, dropped his phone, spun around. What he saw standing there, for no more than a fraction of second, was a figure, six feet tall or more, wearing a long dark trench coat, a face featuring a snout and whiskers and pointed ears, almost like a dog or a coyote or a rat, and then Harry blinked—

And now it was Edwin Nabler standing there, wearing a big grin, as well as his usual garb. The vest with the railway patches, the stupid engineer's cap.

"Please don't say cute," Nabler said. "I hate it when people call my trains cute."

FORTY-SIX

Y our little trick didn't work," Nabler said. "I drove out of the alley, parked down the street for a bit, and then came back. That was very naughty of you. And very naughty of Susie. How stupid did you two think I am?"

Harry had not yet been able to find any words. He hadn't fully reconciled what he'd found in here. The horror of it.

Nabler smiled. "And, while I'm annoyed with you, I'm still inclined to do you a favor. I'm going to give you the opportunity to be part of something larger than yourself. Not very many people get that kind of chance."

Harry managed to part his lips, to speak, as a passenger train sped past him.

"What *are* you?"

"I am Mr. Choo. I bring joy and delight to young and old."

"The fuck you do." Harry shot a quick glance at the miniature town, not wanting to take his eyes off Edwin for long. "Who's in there?"

"I'm sorry?"

"Gavin? Are parts of him in that? And Walter Hillman? The bones you took out of Angus Tanner. Are they what hold up the mountain? Those his teeth in the garden? That's my son's goddamn skateboard, isn't it? How many personal trinkets have you lifted off people and folded into this shit? And a fucking goat?"

"So many questions," Edwin said, raising his voice to be heard over the din. A steam engine pulling a dozen cars barreled past his shoulder on a ribbon of suspended track. "I have one for you."

Harry waited.

"Who knows you're here? Other than that dyke at the community center, who I'll deal with later."

"Plenty of people."

"You're lying."

Harry shook his head. "You're the focus of a large investigation. I've been talking to state and federal officials. The net's closing in on you, Nabler."

"I see. And that's why you recruited Susie to help you. Because of her extensive background in Homeland Security." His grin grew broader, almost unnaturally so, exposing a mouthful of gleaming teeth. "You're on your own."

Harry began to think there was little point in denying it.

"And I'll tell you why. Because even you couldn't believe what you thought I was up to. If you weren't sure, how would you be able to convince anyone else?"

"But I'm right, aren't I?"

"I don't know. What is it, exactly, you suspect me of? Beyond killing a few people and pets for my project here." He tossed that last part off as if he were confessing to speeding in a school zone.

"The sets you sell," Harry said, starting off slowly. "They . . . make people do things. Make things happen. I don't know how, but I think this is where you prep them. Running them through this monstrosity, filled with personal items and body parts. But it's more than that. It's *you*. There something about *you*. Some power you possess. You're the secret ingredient. And you're not . . . a real person. You're something else."

"Close enough," Nabler said, nodding while another train circled around both of them.

"What I don't get is why."

Nabler sighed. "I get tired of explaining myself. I went through all of this with your friend Gavin. Suffice it to say that I'm one of those working in the sliver who restores things to a natural order, creating balance in a world where the frequency with which bad things happen is dropping."

Sliver? Harry thought. But what he said was, "I guess you don't get CNN."

Nabler waved a dismissive hand. "Three thousand dead here, three thousand there, they seem like major events, but they are but a drop in the ocean. The population continues to soar. Resources are dwindling. It can't go on like this forever. My kind are buying you some time. Spreading out, doing our work in countless locations in a multitude of ways, working, as you might say, under the radar."

"So you're, what, some sick force of nature, like a pandemic? Keeping the population in check?"

Nabler sighed. "I've been at this a long time, in different places, and you've figured it out as well as anybody. Not bad, for a two-bit cop in a two-bit town." He paused, reflecting. "And now I may have to move on. It's always a pain, and I was hoping this was a place where I could settle down."

The trains continued to swirl and race around them.

"Can we pull the plug on these things?" Harry asked. "Your electric bill must be through the roof."

It was then he remembered something Janice had told him. How, in her work for the town's electric company, there'd been a power drain they'd not been able to account for. Harry figured he was standing in the middle of it.

Enough, Harry thought.

Time to take out his gun, put the handcuffs on this sick fuck, and take him in, whoever and *whatever* he was. Linking him to recent bizarre deaths like Darryl Pidgeon's or Nadine Comstock's would never be possible, but there was plenty of physical evidence in this room to convict Nabler on charges of being a serial killer. There'd been huge advances in DNA technology in the last few years. Forensic experts would be able to match these ghastly remains to the deceased, or their relatives.

Harry pulled his weapon. "I'm taking you in," he said.

"Oh my," Nabler said. "What do they say? The jig is up?"

All but one of the trains maintained their frenzied loops around Harry and Nabler. One train slowed to a stop not far from where they stood facing one another. A steam engine with several cars attached, including one very special gray boxcar.

"Turn around and put your hands behind your back."

"Perhaps we might discuss this further first."

"Shut up and turn around."

Slowly, Nabler started to turn his back to Harry, who had pulled a set of handcuffs from his jacket and reholstered his weapon so that he might grab first one arm and then the other to link Nabler's wrists together.

The roof of the gray boxcar split along a center line, then the two pieces slowly retracted down the side of the car. From inside, a small red projectile rose up on an angle. Ready to fire.

A missile car.

And suddenly it launched with the swiftness of a dart thrown at a wall-mounted board, but it was not aiming for the wall, it was aiming for Harry.

He never saw it coming, not even when it struck him in the left eye.

"Jesus fuck!" he shouted, dropping the cuffs before he'd had a chance to attach one to Nabler's first wrist and throwing both hands over his injured eye. "Goddamn it!"

Nabler moved very quickly.

He went into his pocket for the scalpel-like instrument that had served him so well, but this was not the time for a precise incision. Gripping the knife as firmly as he could, he drove it into Harry's stomach.

Harry screamed. And continued to scream as Nabler thrust the knife into him a second time, and then a third.

Harry moved his hands to his gut, blood already seeping through his clothes and between his fingers. He looked down with his one good eye and saw what was happening to him. In a moment of clarity, realizing he had very little time to get out of this alive, he reached for the gun that seconds ago—had it even been half a minute?—he had tucked back into the holster at his side.

But when he reached for it, he discovered it was gone.

"Looking for this?" Nabler asked, waving the gun in front of Harry's face, taunting him.

"You son of a . . ."

"You have a mighty fine bone structure, Chief. A true model train enthusiast will tell you the layout is never finished. You think you're done, but then you go back to a completed section and think, *I want to take another run at that. I think I can make it better.* Kind of like highway projects. You think that stretch of the interstate is done, and then they rip it up and do it all over again. The layout is always evolving, always hungry, if you will, for new material."

The train to which the missile car was coupled began to move once more. Soon it was keeping pace with all the other ones that continued to race around the room.

Harry was slowly sliding toward the floor, clutching his stomach. Nabler knelt, synchronizing his descent so his mouth stayed close to Harry's ear.

"They will never find you. The parts I don't use I will burn. I was careless with Tanner, but I won't be with you."

Harry was almost to the floor.

And then, with his last dying breath, he shot himself forward, throwing his arms around Nabler in a half-assed tackle that, while hardly worthy of a linebacker, was enough to throw Nabler off balance. Nabler managed to shove Harry off him, and when the chief hit the floor he did not try to get back up.

Nabler staggered as he regained his balance and threw an arm out instinctively to steady himself. His hand came down hard on one of the ribbons of track five feet above the floor, suspended by wires that went to the ceiling. Nabler hit it hard enough that the track and the thin strip of wood to which it was nailed down buckled sharply. A second before one of Nabler's many trains was approaching. The engine hit the gap, jumped the rails, and plummeted to the floor, hitting it with a splintering thud, bits and pieces of its plastic-and-metal shell scattering everywhere.

What really mattered, however, was not the engine but what came down in its wake.

Coupled to the engine was a long trail of tanker cars. At least twenty of them. Detailed replicas of the freight cars that carried hazardous chemicals from one side of the country to another, often passing through the heart of Lucknow.

One car hit the floor and practically disintegrated. Then another, and another, and another, and before Nabler could catch even one of them, they had all landed on the concrete and shattered into hundreds of pieces.

Nabler worked his way through the jungle of tracks to the control panel that powered everything and shut it down. For the first time, the room went eerily quiet.

"What a fucking mess," he said, looking at Harry's body, the blood on the floor, the busted trains scattered helter-skelter.

He took a long breath, dreading the tasks ahead. Sure, the chief's remains would make an excellent addition to the layout, but slitting open his torso and limbs to retrieve what he could best make use of was not something he felt up to at the moment. And he was going to have to repair that broken stretch of track if he—

Nabler heard something.

A distant rumbling. Minor at first, but then it began to build. Nabler could sense it coming up through the walls and the floor, and if he didn't know better, he would have thought Lucknow was in the throes of an earthquake.

But Nabler did know better, and had a strong suspicion that this was not an earthquake, which were not common to this area of Vermont, anyway. What he believed he was hearing was, potentially, something far more serious.

He left the back room, made his way through his shop, turned back the front door lock, and stepped out onto the sidewalk. The rumbling persisted, and it was coming from the direction of the rail line that ran straight through the center of town.

Nabler thought about all those mangled toy tanker cars on the floor, and the fact that this was often the time in the evening when a large chemical train made its way through town.

Some of his trains had more chaotic agency than others. The tanker cars that hit the floor clearly packed a punch.

Nabler said, "Oh shit."

FORTY-SEVEN

D ad promised we'd go out for pancakes Saturday," Dylan said.

He was in his bedroom, doing math homework, when his mother checked in on him. She rested a hand on each of his shoulders, looking at the exercises he was doing in his notebook.

"That'll be fun," Janice said. "We haven't done that in a while. The diner?"

Dylan nodded. "You like their coffee."

"Oh yes, I do."

She took her hands off his shoulders and sat on the bed. "Put your pencil down. I want to talk to you."

Dylan did as he was told and turned in his chair so he could face his mother.

"I hope you're not mad at your father."

Dylan shrugged. "I guess not."

"It was my fault, what happened. I should have discussed it with him first, buying that train set. If I had, we wouldn't have had that scene this morning."

"It was just a train set. Aren't you allowed to do things without asking Dad?"

"Well, yes, of course. But some decisions we should make together, and that turned out to be one of them. It's hard to explain, but your father had a good reason for us not keeping it."

"He said the man who runs that store is a bad person."

"He doesn't know that for a fact, but he thinks he might be, so we don't want to give our business to someone like that, do we?"

"I guess not."

"Your father's a good man, you know."

"I know."

She smiled. "In case you were wondering."

"I wasn't."

"I should let you get your homework done. You have much more?"

"Just this."

"When you're done, you want to come down and have some ice cream? There's two cartons in the freezer with a tiny bit in each one, and I'm going shopping tomorrow so I want to make some room. So, you know, you'd be doing me a favor."

Dylan smiled. "Okay."

"Five minutes?"

He nodded.

It only took four. He was down the steps and coming into the kitchen, where his mother had set up two bowls and was scooping out the ends from two Ben & Jerry containers, when the entire house began to shake.

Janice said, "What the—"

The vibration was enough to prompt Dylan to reach out and grab the counter to keep from falling over.

"Wow!" he said. "Was that an earth—"

The house shook even harder.

Dylan turned and started running. "Gonna see what it is!"

"Dylan! Wait!"

But he was already gone. She heard the front door open and slam shut.

Dylan ran to the end of the driveway. He was far from the only one. People up and down the street were streaming out of their houses, wondering what was happening.

Everyone looked to the west, where the heavens were turning orange. Great balls of flame leapt up into the sky.

Dylan glanced back at his house, saw his mother coming out the front door.

"Mom, come see!" Dylan cried. "It's beautiful!"

FORTY-EIGHT

O ver the weeks and months that followed, the National Transportation Safety Board, or NTSB for short, would conclude, although not conclusively, that the Lucknow Disaster, as it would come to be known, was caused by a "hot box."

A "hot box" was in actuality a lubricated journal bearing on one of the tanker car's wheels. It was believed that the lubricant had leaked out, which caused the bearing to overheat. Sparks from the overheating would have progressed to fire, and before long the axle would break, causing one of the car's wheels to fall off. These so-called "hot boxes" were all supposed to have been phased out years earlier, but clearly some cars were still equipped with them.

Once the wheel fell off, that car—the forty-third in a ninety-two-car train that was being pulled by one Albany & Bennington and two CSX diesel engines—slipped off the rails. And given that it was coupled at each end to other tanker cars, they were yanked off the tracks. And so on, and so on, until more than half the cars that made up that freight had derailed before it came to a stop.

When the cars crashed into each other, some of the them exploded. In a chain reaction effect, almost every car that exploded would set off one or both of the cars to which it was coupled. Those cars contained such chemicals as styrene, propane, caustic soda, and, most critically, chlorine.

Many people were reminded of an incident north of the border, near Toronto, more than two decades earlier, when several chlorine-filled cars derailed. Chlorine gas, being heavier than air, displaces oxygen. People exposed to chlorine gas would be unable to breathe, and the gas they inhaled would burn the lining of their lungs.

And they would die.

Fearing an explosion was imminent, authorities back then ordered a mass evacuation, and in the end the cars did not blow up, and no one died.

Lucknow would not be so fortunate. As the residents would soon discover.

The first car derailed at 7:48 p.m. The others that ran off the rails did so in quick succession. The explosions were immediate. Two propane cars that blew up almost simultaneously sent dark clouds billowing nearly a mile into the air. Smoke was seen from as far away as Brattleboro.

There was blast after blast, likely leading many to believe, at first, that there was an earthquake.

(In its report, the NTSB used the word "likely," given that there were no survivors to recount what thoughts might have been going through their heads at the time.)

Many of the homes situated close to the rail line were effectively vaporized by the explosions, and those living within them would have died instantly. In retrospect, they were the lucky ones.

Those who ran outside to view the spectacle faced a different fate, and more quickly than individuals who remained in their dwellings. Investigators were able to conclude that the number of people who did this was very high, given how many bodies were found in yards and on sidewalks and in the middle of streets across Lucknow.

But remaining inside only bought people some time.

The chlorine cloud that settled onto the town like a smothering pillow quickly worked its way into all structures through ventilation systems, open windows, people throwing open their doors to see what was happening.

Regardless of how quickly the chlorine gas reached the good citizens of Lucknow, death came to them all. There were many, of course, who were not in town at the time. Some were on vacation. Some worked evening shifts in areas outside of Lucknow. But, as this was evening, and most people were home after spending a day at schools or jobs, the toll was high.

Initial symptoms would have been coughing and irritation to the eyes and nose. Those symptoms would quickly have escalated to a complete constriction of the air passages, and a burning sensation in the lungs. Many would have died within a few minutes, some would have taken up to thirty.

Of the 4,386 people residing in Lucknow (according to the latest census, of course) only 295 survived, because they were out of town.

The authors of the NTSB's report were hesitant to say with absolute certainty that a hot box was the cause, but it seemed the most likely. Much of the wreckage was so charred, it was as though it had been through a nuclear blast. There was a degree of speculation about what had caused the incident.

Not surprisingly, no one came up with a theory that was even remotely close to the true cause—the derailment of a string of toy tanker cars on a layout created by something inhuman and unholy.

In retrospect, perhaps one of the lucky ones that evening was Lucknow police chief Harry Cook, who had bled to death from the wounds inflicted on him by Edwin Nabler before the first tanker car's wheels had jumped the track. His death was undoubtedly painful, but perhaps not quite as horrific as not being able to breathe and feeling as though your lungs were on fire.

His body was not found in the back of Choo-Choo's Trains. It was surmised that Chief Cook must have been one of the first to rush to the scene, as his body, later identified by a badge that had survived the fire, was found in the wreckage of the tanker cars. His remains were so severely burned that the doctor performing the autopsy did not find, nor think to look for, a number of stab wounds.

Having perished when he did, he was spared the knowledge of what had happened to those who meant the most to him.

Because Janice was dead. She died on the street with their son, Dylan, holding him in her arms as he struggled to breathe and the chlorine cloud enveloped them.

Stick and Nancy, from police headquarters, died on the way to the scene, the gas filling the car through the air vents.

Jenny, sitting at home with her feet up, watching *Jeopardy!* after a long day at the diner, had drifted off to sleep and woke up, briefly, with a horrific burning in her lungs.

Those still mourning recently lost loved ones—Auden Pidgeon and his mom; the Tanner and Hillman families, Delbert Dorfman's mother—mourned no more.

Wendell Comstock caught a break. He had already moved away.

The only one in the town at the time of the disaster who did not die was the owner and manager of Choo-Choo's Trains.

Before choosing to lie low for a while, Nabler took a stroll about the town before hundreds of emergency responders descended, and marveled at what had happened. Bodies everywhere he went. Unparalleled devastation.

Those who operated within the sliver, the ones who'd brought down jets and caused dams to burst and set entire apartment buildings on fire, well, Edwin Nabler felt he could hold his head up with the best of them now.

He would have to think about how to move forward. For anyone else in the sliver, this would be a crowning achievement, no doubt about it.

But Nabler was not done yet.

Part V

FORTY-NINE

At first, Annie thought it would be impossible.

Once she was on the road, having thrown some of Charlie's things into a bag and tossed it into the back of the car, she asked Sherpa for help finding the fastest route from where she and Charlie had been staying the last couple of weeks to Lucknow, Vermont. What came up was a route that would take her north to Syracuse, where she would catch I-90 east, which would eventually take her through Albany before reaching the New York–Vermont border. Once she was into Vermont, Lucknow wasn't that far, but in total, her navigation system was telling her it was more than a four-hour drive.

Annie went to her phone to see how long Google Maps calculated it would take to do that journey on a bicycle: *twenty-two hours*. And that was probably an estimate of how long it would take an *adult* to ride that distance. On a decent bike. Not a kid on a crappy bicycle found in the back of a junk shop.

There was no way.

Even if she accepted the premise that Charlie could actually ride his bike all the way to Lucknow, someone his age traveling along one of the interstates would attract attention. Charlie would get picked up. Annie would be notified. He would have to take secondary roads to avoid detection, and that would take even longer.

So there was no way he could be there yet.

In which case, Annie thought, she would be able to catch up with him. If he'd left in the middle of the night, he had a good twenty- to eighteen-hour head start, but in her SUV, she could be where he was in a couple of hours.

Except which route did he take? Sherpa offered only a couple of choices to get to her destination in a hurry, but there were a hundred less direct ways to go. Charlie could have taken any one of them.

If she went straight to Lucknow, the odds were good she'd be there well ahead of Charlie. She'd check out the train store, and if he wasn't there, she'd start doubling back, intercept him on the most likely route at the end of his travels.

Unless, of course, she was just *wrong* about all of it.

Suppose Charlie wasn't even headed to Lucknow? Annie had rolled the dice and come to the conclusion that that was his intended destination because of the sticker on the bottom of a toy train. What had persuaded her was the manner in which that information had been delivered to her. The train spinning around and around that track on the floor of her studio, going so fast that the cars were scattered, one ending up at her foot with the address of Choo-Choo's Trains in full view.

It *had* to be a message. How else could she interpret it? Annie was already convinced there was something very special—and not in a good way—about these trains Charlie had found in that shed. Annie had already seen things she could not explain. So when that address presented itself, she was ready to see it for what it was.

An *invitation*.

So now here she was on I-90 east, having put Syracuse in her rearview mirror, driving into the night, struggling to keep her eyes open.

She'd slept poorly the night before. Finnegan's death had hit her hard, and she'd spent much of the night staring at the ceiling. She clearly had fallen asleep at some point. Otherwise, she would have heard Charlie get up and try to slip out of the house. She'd have caught him in the act.

So it was little wonder that in the early hours of the next morning, she was having trouble concentrating on the road ahead. Twice her eyes closed for an instant, the SUV drifting toward the shoulder. Luckily, it was one of the newer models that sent a vibration through the steering wheel when a driver wandered off course.

Despite wanting to get to Lucknow as quickly as possible, Annie knew she wasn't going to be much help to her son if she ran her car into the ditch and killed herself. On top of that, the car was down to less than a quarter tank. Once she had passed Herkimer, she promised herself she'd stop at the next service center along that stretch of the New York Thruway. She didn't have long to wait.

She hit her blinker and exited. She parked, went inside and hit the bathroom, then bought herself a large coffee, black. Maybe that would keep her awake. She got back in the car, pulled ahead to the pumps, and filled the car up with premium unleaded. When she got back behind the wheel, she took a sip of her coffee, and keyed the ignition. But she had only driven a few car lengths when she began to feel woozy. She steered over to the far side of the lot, put the car in park, and took another drink from her take-out cup.

Could be the coffee wasn't going to do the trick.

While she debated whether to surrender to sleep, even for the shortest of naps, she got out her phone and did a search on "Lucknow." For a while now, she'd been thinking that the name of the town rang a bell, that it was known for something, but she couldn't recall what. But she thought it had to be some time ago, when she was younger and paying as much attention to the six o'clock news as she was to her parents telling her what to do with her life.

Only a few hundred stories came up.

All of them were, in one way or another, about the "Lucknow

Disaster," a catastrophic accident almost two months after the September 11 terrorist attacks. Annie scrolled through a few stories that laid out the basics of what had happened but zeroed in on a story from the *New York Times* that had been written in only the last few months.

Under the headline LUCKNOW EXPLOSION FALLOUT CONTINUES AFTER 23 YEARS was a lengthy story by a reporter named Carol Hannigan. It began:

> Nearly two and half decades after a freight train on the Albany & Bennington line derailed in Lucknow, Vermont, killing more than 4,000 people when a cloud of chlorine gas descended on the town, lawsuits continue to drag their way through the courts.
>
> Several investigations conducted since the accident have cast doubt on whether the train went off the tracks because of an overheated bearing on one of the tanker cars, and have instead focused on whether defective track issues were at the heart of the catastrophe. But given that the Albany & Bennington railroad company went bankrupt in the wake of the disaster, just whom to sue and hold responsible for the damages, which run into the billions of dollars, has remained elusive.
>
> What is not in question is the fact that Lucknow remains a ghost town. When the train went off the rails and several tanker cars exploded into a mushroom-type cloud that could be seen and heard miles away, a large number of homes situated near the event were destroyed. But even people who lived blocks away died from exposure to the chlorine gas.
>
> The homes remain empty to this day, reminding many

of the fallout from the Love Canal disaster, near Buf-
falo, when an entire neighborhood had to be abandoned
after 20,000 tons of chemical waste and pesticides
leaked into homes and—

Annie stopped reading.

"Ghost town," she said under the breath.

Lucknow was a ghost town. No one lived there. The place had
been abandoned. There was, according to what she read, nothing
there.

No. No, that wasn't possible. What was the point of Charlie heading to Lucknow if there was nothing there to go to?

Annie rested her head on the top of the steering wheel and began
to shake.

FIFTY

C harlie could not recall ever being this excited.

When he went to bed, he knew this would be *the night*. He would have to be very quiet not to wake his mother. He didn't just have to get dressed and slip out of the house unnoticed, he needed to prepare. That meant going down to the kitchen and packing up as much food as he could carry in a backpack. It was too bad about what happened to his mother's friend, Finnegan, but the good news was he'd brought lots of good stuff for them to eat from New York, especially the bagels. He grabbed six. Charlie didn't want to take the time to cut them and put peanut butter on them. He'd pack that stuff, and a knife from the kitchen drawer, and take it with him.

He wished he could tell his mother he was going. Then they could take the car, which would not only be faster, but would take a whole lot less energy than would be required to ride a bike all the way to Vermont. But he knew that if he told his mother that they had to go Lucknow because his dad was there, she'd be all, "Oh, Charlie, no one wants your father to still be alive more than I do, but I'm sorry, he's no longer with us."

Other mothers might have said he was in heaven now, something along those lines, but Charlie's mother had never been a very religious person. You were alive, or you were dead, simple as that. But Charlie knew different.

Charlie could have told her he'd been talking to his father, that his dad had shown him how to get the key to the shed, that his dad had told him he was living in the real town that was the inspiration for the one Charlie had made on the floor of his mother's studio, but what was the point? Some days you just couldn't talk to her.

Which left Charlie with no choice but to leave without telling her. He didn't know where, exactly, Lucknow was, but he wasn't worried about that. His father would guide him, tell him which roads to take. All Charlie knew for sure was that it was a *very long way*, which was why he had been riding his bike so much, around and around the house, building up his strength, so that when it was time to go, he'd be up to it.

He figured his mother would be all worried when she woke up and found him gone, because mothers were like that. She'd be mad, too. But when he found his father, and when he brought him back, and they were a family again, he was pretty sure his mother would forgive him.

AFTER ONLY TEN miles, or at least what he guessed were ten miles, since he didn't have any way to accurately measure distance, he was exhausted.

The sun was coming up ahead of him, and while he had no real idea where he was, the sun rose in the east, and Vermont was east, or so his father had told him. The sun was a reassuring sight, but holy moly was he tired.

It was time for a break.

He came to a stop, hopped off the bike, walked it down into the ditch and up the other side, and leaned it against a large oak tree. He sat down, his back up against the rough bark of the tree, and dug into his backpack for breakfast, which consisted of a plain bagel with gobs of peanut butter on it. The knife he'd brought was not a sharp one, and he would have needed a flat surface on which to slice the bagel in half, so he simply piled the peanut butter on top of it and went at it, one bite at a time.

He'd also brought three bottles of water with him. He would have brought more, but they were heavy, and he figured water was something he could get along the way.

Charlie finished the bagel and washed it down with half a bottle of water. Needed to conserve. He wasn't sure how long this trip would take, but he knew it was a long way.

He went around the back of the tree for a pee, zipped up, and hopped on his bike, first checking to make sure there was decent air pressure in the tires, and continued on. After another hour, he was feeling especially weary. He hadn't had much sleep and had been pushing himself hard. Up ahead he saw a barn set close to the road and thought he might find a spot there where he could recharge. He whipped off the road and pedaled to the side of the barn that faced away from the farmhouse so as not to be spotted, tucked his bike behind some rusted barrels, and squeezed through the barn doors to get inside. He found a convenient mound of hay, settled into it, and tried reading a couple of pages from the Ray Bradbury book his father loved so much that he'd thought to bring, but he wished his dad could be reading it to him. Soon enough.

And then he was asleep.

He guessed he had slept three or more hours. When he poked his head outside, the sun was at its highest point in the sky, so early afternoon. He drained the other half of his water bottle, slipped the backpack over his shoulder, and hit the road again.

Charlie was passing through a small town two hours later and his hunger pangs were getting pretty serious. He spotted a small park, sat down at a picnic table, and went into his bag for another bagel. The bagel was dry and stale, and, even with peanut butter on it, was not very appetizing.

A block ahead he saw a Denny's sign towering over the sidewalk. He had some money in his pocket. He'd been sneaking a dollar or two a day out of his mother's purse the last week, so he had enough for at least one good meal. Maybe he was closer to his destination than he thought. Maybe his dad was already preparing a meal for him for when he arrived, so if he spent all his money now on a restaurant meal, it wouldn't matter.

He pitched the bagel and the container of peanut butter into a nearby trash can and got back on his bike, hiding it behind the Denny's where it wouldn't be stolen, then went around and in the front door, taking his backpack with him. He slipped into an empty booth.

After five minutes, a waitress approached and said, "You alone, kid?"

"No," said Charlie. "My mom's in the bathroom."

"Okay," she said skeptically. "Want some water?"

"Yes, please. A glass for me and a glass for my mom."

The waitress disappeared for a moment and returned with two glasses of water. "Your mom still in the bathroom?"

Charlie nodded. "I think she's constipated."

The waitress nodded. "Well, that's no fun. When she comes back I'll take your or—"

"I know what she wants. She just wants coffee and some toast. She's not a big eater. And I'll have the Super Slam."

"You can eat all that? It's a lot of food."

Charlie nodded. "And a chocolate shake."

The waitress made a note. "Super Slam, chocolate shake, coffee, toast. How's your mom take her coffee?"

"She likes Nespresso."

The waitress gave Charlie a blank stare. "She want milk or cream? The sugar's on the table."

"Just whatever way it comes. You don't have to worry. We have money." Charlie dug some bills out of his pocket and dropped them onto the table, flashing a reassuring smile.

The waitress did not return it. "You might want to hit the bathroom yourself. Wash up."

He looked at his grimy hands, making him wonder what the rest of him looked like. "When my mom comes back."

The moment the waitress walked away, Charlie guzzled down both glasses of water. When the waitress returned with the coffee and dropped a couple of creamers onto the table, she eyed the empty water glass across from him but didn't mention it.

"Your Super Slam is coming up."

She brought it to the table two minutes later, along with the chocolate milkshake. "I'll hold the toast and coffee till your mother gets back."

Charlie pounced on the meal, shoveling pancakes and eggs and hash browns and sausages into his mouth like it was the last meal he'd ever have. It was, he concluded, the *best* meal he'd eaten in his entire life. He sucked down the milkshake so quickly he got a brain freeze, and had to wait a moment for it to pass before he continued.

When he had finished everything, he felt gloriously full and ready to continue on his journey.

While he was wiping his mouth with a paper napkin, he noticed the waitress talking to the man behind the cash register. He had a feeling they were talking about him, because they kept glancing in his direction while trying to act like they were *not* looking in his direction. Charlie knew they were probably starting to wonder just how bad his mother's constipation might be, and whether they should call an ambulance for her.

And then he thought, no, that wasn't what was going on. If they were worried about his mom, the waitress could have gone into the ladies' room and asked if she was okay, and then they'd know that there was no mom.

The man nodded to the waitress and picked up the phone next to the register.

The waitress came over to his table, and for the first time was smiling sweetly. "How was everything?" she asked.

"It was really good," Charlie said. "Please give my compliments to the chef."

"I'll be sure to do that. Shall I finally bring your mom's toast and coffee now?"

"Uh, you know, I don't think she's even going to want it."

The waitress nodded, glanced back at the man on the register, who gave her a nod. "Well, why don't you take your time, let your food settle, and I'll come back in a minute in case there's anything else you want."

"Okay," Charlie said.

He might only be a kid, but he had a feeling something was going on. And that feeling was confirmed when he looked out the window and saw a police car turning into the parking lot.

He didn't know exactly how much his meal was going to cost, so he put everything he had on the table and slid out of the booth, grabbing his backpack as he did so.

The waitress, taking an order at another table, spotted him and called out anxiously, "Can I get you something?"

"I'm going to the bathroom!" he said, and as it turned out he could have benefited from the visit, but was afraid if he took the time he wouldn't be able to get away before the police came into the restaurant.

There had to be a back way out.

He ran past the door that said MEN's and pushed open one that said STAFF ONLY. That took him into the kitchen, where two women and a man were busily preparing meals.

"Hey, kid!" the man shouted. "Can't come back here!"

Charlie ran. He spotted another door and aimed for it, hoping it would lead outside. He turned the knob and pushed and he was out back of the restaurant, and there was his bike, right where he'd left it.

He hopped on and took off as fast as he could.

EVEN A SUPER Slam lasted for only so long.

By dusk, Charlie was getting hungry again, and now that he was out in the country somewhere, between towns, there was no place to get something to eat. There were still some stale bagels in his backpack if he got really desperate. And now he had to start thinking about where he would spend the night. It wasn't like he could check into a motel. He didn't have enough money for that. He was starting to wonder if he hadn't thought this through as well as he could have.

Especially when the chain on his bike broke.

He'd been going along pretty good when suddenly the pedals offered no resistance and he could hear something clicking and whacking down by his ankles, and he looked down and saw that the chain had snapped.

And I put out eight bucks for this thing, he thought.

Charlie wobbled the bike to the shoulder, got off, and inspected the damage. There was no way he could fix this. The bike was toast. He let it fall to the gravel shoulder.

He was in the middle of nowhere and in another hour it would be dark.

For the first time since embarking on this adventure, Charlie was scared. He didn't know what to do. He had to get to Lucknow. He'd come too far to give up now. Would he hitchhike the rest of the way? No, he couldn't do that. No one was going to pick up a kid unless it was to take him to the police station.

Or something much, much worse. Charlie was a kid from New York. He knew the stories.

Maybe someone *nice* would come along and take him and the bike to a repair shop. Except they'd all be closed now, and anyway, Charlie didn't have any money left.

He started to cry.

Up ahead, he could hear a vehicle approaching. There hadn't been a lot of traffic on this road, and there was no telling when the next car might go by. Should he take a chance and flag it down, ask for help? He knew there were risks doing something like that.

So, no, he wouldn't flag down the car, which had almost reached him. He'd find another tree to sleep under and in the morning contemplate his next move. Wasn't that something his mom would say to him sometimes? "Things will look better in the morning."

The driver of the car must have spotted him, because it was slowing down. And as it got closer, Charlie could see that it wasn't a car, but a white van.

The van pulled over to the shoulder on the other side of the road and the driver powered down his window.

"You okay, kid?"

Charlie stopped crying long enough to say, "I'm okay."

"Your bike broken?"

Charlie nodded.

"You a long way from home?"

Charlie didn't say anything.

"I get it. You're not supposed to talk to strangers."

Charlie nodded again.

"But I'm not really a stranger," the man said, "if I know your dad."

Charlie felt an uncertain swelling of hope in his heart.

"I'm betting you're on your way to Lucknow," the driver said. It was at this point Charlie noticed the man was wearing a funny engineer's hat and a vest with patches all over it.

"Yeah," Charlie said. "That's where I'm going."

"Well, that's where I'm going, too. Actually, it's where I'm coming *from*, but I can turn around right here and head back. It's not that far. You've come a long ways."

Charlie was wondering how the man would know that. He hadn't told him where he'd started out from.

"Truth is," the man said, "I was expecting you, and then I started to worry that even for a boy like you, who's been training so hard on his bike, it'd be a long haul, so I decided to come meet you along the way. Now, I understand if you're worried about getting in the van with me. I bet your mom's told you not to do something that dumb, but we're not really strangers if I already know your name, right, Charlie?"

Charlie smiled. The man had a point.

"Hop in and I'll take you to Lucknow. Your dad can't wait to see you."

Charlie had stopped crying, but now he was ready to start again. Only this time they'd be tears of joy running down his cheek. He could feel himself being drawn toward the van. This guy knew him, knew where he was going and why. And he couldn't have come along at a better time.

"I guess . . . it would be okay," Charlie said, and grabbed the bike by the handlebars, getting ready to wheel it across the road.

"You can leave that," the man said. "You're not going to need it anymore. You won't need that backpack, either."

Charlie paused, looked at the bike that had served him so well up to now. But it really had reached the end of the road. He let it fall, then flung his backpack into the ditch.

"Come around and hop in."

Charlie hardly needed to since there were no other cars on the road, but out of habit looked both ways before he crossed, ran around the front of the van to the passenger door, reached up for the handle, pulled it open, and climbed in.

"Nice to meet you, Charlie," the man said. "My name is Edwin."

"Hi, Edwin," Charlie said.

"You know what would be fun? You try to name all the railroad patches I've got on my vest."

Charlie grinned. That did sound like fun.

FIFTY-ONE

Annie had decided it didn't matter whether Lucknow had become a ghost town. Just because there was no one there didn't mean Charlie wouldn't still consider it his destination. When he left, he probably didn't know any more about that place's history than she had before reading about it on her phone.

After an hour's sleep at the service center, she continued on, and was traveling some secondary roads north of Albany, asking Sherpa how much longer it would take to reach Lucknow as dawn began to break.

Her cell phone rang.

Her heart leapt. The first thing she thought was that it would be Charlie, but Charlie did not have a cell phone. But it could have been someone calling on his behalf, a Good Samaritan who had found her son and was trying to reunite them.

She thumbed a button to accept the call.

"Hello?"

"Ms. Blunt?"

"Yes?"

"It's Officer Standish."

Annie said nothing.

"Hello? Are you there?"

"I'm here," Annie said, suddenly thinking that her trip to Lucknow was pointless, that maybe Standish had news. And that it wasn't good. "Have you found Charlie?"

"I'm sorry, no, but we're back out this morning. Where are you, Ms. Blunt?"

"I'm out looking for my son."

"And where is it that you're looking?"

"Just around."

"I came by your place last night and you weren't there, and you're not there this morning. What is your location?"

"I'm kind of on the move."

"I would ask that you return, Ms. Blunt. Your presence is necessary as we continue our investigation."

It struck Annie that Standish might be able to track where she was through her phone. And if she could, wherever Annie happened to be, Standish might send the police after her and bring her back.

Anne couldn't allow that to happen.

"Okay," Annie said. "I should be back in half an hour, tops."

"That would be good," Standish said, unable to hide the skepticism in her voice. "I'm holding you to that."

"Of course," Annie said. "Talk soon."

She hit the button on her steering wheel to end the call, then pulled over to the side of the road so that she could take her phone from her purse and shut it down completely. Once that was done, she tossed it back into her bag and hit the road.

She was clipping down a country road and sped past something that caught her eye for a millisecond. She glanced in her mirror, hoping for a better look, but whatever it was could not be determined from a distance. She hit the brakes, careful to make sure no one was behind her, put the SUV into reverse, and backed up about a hundred yards. She put the car in park, got out, and walked over to the shoulder to see what had drawn her attention.

A bicycle on its side.

She knew instantly that it was her son's. A girl's bike with the sloping center bar, the banana seat, the angle handlebars. She felt her legs go weak and then she went down, gravel digging into her knees and one palm as she grasped one end of the handlebars for support.

"Oh God, oh God," she said.

And there, in the ditch, was her son's backpack. She gasped for air, wondered whether she might faint.

Hold it together.

This did not have to be bad news. The abandoned bike showed that Charlie had somehow made it this far. Aside from a busted chain, the bike was more or less intact. It wasn't mangled, as it would have been if Charlie had been hit by a car while riding it. There was no blood. Not on the bike, not on the road.

She managed to get to her feet and edged her way down into the ditch to get the backpack. She looked inside, found a bottle and a knife from a cutlery set and not much else. She surveyed the landscape in all directions and shouted: "Charlie! *Charlie!*"

No reply.

Annie tried to think it through. The bike broke down. Charlie had decided to start walking, and didn't want to be weighed down by the backpack, so he pitched it. It was possible. And if that was the case, he might be up ahead somewhere.

She got back into the car, kicking up gravel from all four wheels as she hit the gas.

"I'm coming, Charlie. I'm coming."

Looking for more upsides, she told herself that she'd been right all along. Charlie really was heading to Lucknow. She'd interpreted the message from that upturned toy train correctly. The invitation had been real.

But for the first time a question that had been lingering in the back of her brain moved to the forefront.

Why?

Why did Charlie want to go to Lucknow? Did he imagine his toy train world to be that town? He had told his mother that this was where his father now lived. When he'd said that, Annie had written it off as the wishful imaginings of a heartbroken child. But what if he hadn't so much imagined it, as the idea had somehow been implanted in him?

What if Charlie, and now Annie, was being lured to Lucknow? And if that was true, by whom, and for what possible reason?

It didn't make any sense. But so many things that had happened lately fell into that category. After a while, you almost started to get used to it. In fact, there was a small comfort in believing she and Charlie were being drawn to Lucknow for an unknown reason. It meant that something was looking out for them, that Charlie was okay.

SHE HAD JUST crossed the New York–Vermont state line when Sherpa informed Annie that she was nearly to her destination, and that the exit was ahead on her right.

She saw a sign that said LUCKNOW 6, but nailed over it was a narrow yellow strip with black letters reading CLOSED. She took the right anyway, and a mile later she found the road barred by a ten-foot-high stretch of chain-link gate from which similar fencing ran off in both directions, into the forest. More than the road to Lucknow was closed off. There'd clearly been a perimeter fence established around the entire town.

There were several signs attached to the gate.

KEEP OUT

NO TRESPASSING

VIOLATORS WILL BE ARRESTED AND PROSECUTED

BY ORDER OF THE VERMONT STATE POLICE

Annie hadn't finished reading that piece in the *Times* she'd found on her phone, but she was willing to bet the entire town was an environmental no-go. While the chlorine gas in the air would have eventually dissipated, whatever liquids had leaked out of those derailed tanker cars could have leached down into the ground and poisoned the town's water supply.

All of which suggested that there was nothing going on in the town's center, and no reason for Charlie to be there. Would there have been a way for him to have made it through this barrier? Maybe there were gaps somewhere, or access into the town from another direction.

Annie left the engine running as she got out of the car and walked up to the gate. It was secured in the middle by a chain and lock. Annie gave it a tug, on the off chance it hadn't been secured, but there was no luck there.

She went back to the car and took a look at the map on the dashboard navigation screen. She moved it around with her fingers, looking for another way in. There were two other roads that led into Lucknow from the other side, and it would take a long time for her to get to them, only to find that they'd be padlocked, too.

Annie took a deep breath. She could think of only one way to get this done.

She didn't want to set off the car's airbags by hitting the gate with the front end of the car, so she did a three point-turn so that she was looking at the gate in her rearview mirror. She wanted to get a good run at it, so she drove forward about twenty yards, stopped, moved the gearshift from forward to reverse, grabbed hold of the steering wheel as firmly as she could with both hands, lining the car up with the center of the gate, took her foot off the brake, and tromped on the accelerator.

The car's wheels squealed, the engine roared.

Gritting her teeth, preparing herself for the impact, Annie had the car doing at least thirty miles per hour by the time she hit the gate.

Her scream was drowned out by the sound of the chain snapping, the two halves of the gate swinging back and scraping along the pavement, the car's bumper and tailgate taking a hit. For half a second, Annie wondered whether her insurance would cover this, and she almost laughed. She'd had her eyes locked on the mirror, but now she looked forward to a view of the buckled gate from the other side.

"Fucking-A," she said to herself, hitting the brakes and bringing the car to a stop.

Any other time, she might have gotten out and had a look at the damage she'd done to her car, but right now she didn't give a shit.

She turned the SUV around and headed into downtown Lucknow.

FIFTY-TWO

Annie was thinking, the cliché's always *It looked like something out of a movie*. But damned if it didn't look like something out of a movie.

She and John had watched a lot of movies and TV together, and end-of-the-world shows were a favorite. Films like *Dawn of the Dead*, *28 Days Later*, *I Am Legend*, *The Road*, television fare like *The Walking Dead* and *The Last of Us*. Empty streets, at least until the zombies came out from around a corner.

Who needed zombies? Annie thought. What had really happened here was scary enough.

She was driving into a town where history stopped twenty-three years ago. More than four thousand souls had once lived here. Grown up, gone to school, fallen in love, raised families, headed off to work every morning. Made friends, got drunk, bickered, shopped, had sex in the back of cars, played Frisbee, met over coffee. Four thousand people who together made up a community, a complex living and breathing organism.

And in a matter of minutes, it was all over.

But unlike, say, if a nuclear bomb had been detonated, the structures remained, except for those closest to the derailment. The town was intact, but had endured more than two decades of neglect.

As Annie drove slowly through the streets, the evidence was everywhere. Front yards that were once well tended were now essentially fields, lawns that had grown into two-foot-tall grasses and weeds. Some houses were hard to distinguish because they'd become completely overgrown with vines and moss, cocooned. Shingles were curled up or missing from rooftops. Weeds sprouted through pavement cracks in the middle of the road. Bits and pieces of trash blew about.

Windows were boarded up on some homes, but smashed in on others, shredded drapes still hanging from the rods, drifting idly in the breeze. Annie saw a mangy dog leap out of one home's glassless picture window, a rabbit between its teeth.

Off to the side of one house, a child's swing set was nearly swallowed up by tall grass. Annie surmised the city was without power, given the number of dropped lines that crisscrossed the roads, the absence of any working traffic lights.

"Christ!" she shouted, and hit the brakes.

In the middle of the road, directly ahead of her, was a moose.

The beast was unruffled by Annie's presence. It gave Annie a disinterested look, then strolled majestically past her car, its left antler passing within a couple of inches of her window.

What Annie might have expected to see more of were abandoned cars—if this were a real disaster movie, they'd be all over the place—but there were relatively few. Those were probably reclaimed by extended family or insurance companies, although she did see an old pickup truck parked at the curb as she started coming into the downtown business area. Who would want to buy a used car from a town where everyone died? Annie supposed if the price was right . . .

She could see a more dense cluster of buildings ahead, what would most likely be the downtown area. But she wasn't going to be able to get to it in her car, as a once-towering oak tree that must have been downed during a storm sometime since 2001 blocked her path.

She'd have to go on foot; there was a gap between the road and the tree she'd be able to duck under.

So she stopped the car, killed the engine, and, with more than a little trepidation, opened her door and got out.

What struck her was how quiet it was. Other than the rustling of some leaves in trees that were still standing, there was barely a sound. When she closed her car door, several blackbirds she'd not previously noticed took flight from a nearby yard, making her heart skip a beat.

She stooped to get under the downed tree, then walked slowly toward the downtown stretch. Even though there was no one around, she did not feel safe. What if another moose showed up? Would that dog with the rabbit in its mouth see her and consider a change in its dinner plans? Annie'd never been much for guns, but she wouldn't have said no to one now if someone offered.

She found herself standing in front of the Lucknow Diner, the windows all smashed in, the door open. She took a step inside, shook her head in wonder as she stared at the empty stools and booths, cushions ripped apart, stuffing pulled out by birds and animals looking for material to make their nests. A sign above the counter read YOU CAN'T BEAT OUR COFFEE!

Annie could have gone for a cup right about now.

She emerged from the diner, looked about. A dry cleaner, an optometrist, a card shop, a florist.

It all seemed strangely familiar.

And then it hit her. This was how Charlie had arranged and labeled the buildings on his train setup. Everything was in the same place here as it had been on the floor of Annie's studio.

Charlie had been building Lucknow.

If Charlie was here, she believed he had to be nearby.

"Charlie!" she shouted as loudly as she could, hands around her mouth in a makeshift megaphone. "Charlie, I'm here! It's your mom!"

Her voice echoed down the deserted street.

And then she saw something that was, at least for this street at this time, incongruous.

An illuminated storefront window, across the main street from the diner. Something in the display area was moving. Annie looked up, read the sign above the window:

CHOO-CHOO'S TRAINS.

Unlike the abandoned businesses, this storefront looked as well kept as it would have the day it opened. No missing letters in its name, the sidewalk out front swept, the window glass not only intact but clean.

Slowly, she crossed the empty street, and as she got closer she saw that there was a train running continuously on a loop of track on the other side of the glass. In the window, a lit sign:

OPEN.

FIFTY-THREE

Annie was trembling.

This was the place to which she had been summoned. This was where she knew Charlie had to be. She was sure of it. He was inside this shop.

And he was not alone.

Someone—some*thing*—was here with him, and the only way she was going to get Charlie back was to go through this door and confront whatever it was.

She walked up to the door, turned the handle, and pushed it open.

A bell rang, announcing her arrival. As she stepped into the shop, someone said:

"Ah! At last! I was afraid you'd never get here."

The words were spoken by a short man standing behind the cash register. He wore a silly engineer's cap and a vest covered with the patches of numerous railroad companies. He was flashing a warm smile and there was something of a twinkle in his eye, as if in his spare time he moonlighted as a leprechaun. But despite his offbeat, quirky—even nerdy—appearance, there was an air of menace about him. It wafted off him like a bad smell.

"Where's my son?" Annie said, pushing down her fear and struggling to fill her voice with authority.

He raised his palms in a gesture of reassurance. "Please, please, come in and let me—"

"Where is my son?" she said, her voice rising. "Where is Charlie? Tell me right now, or God help me I'll take that stupid hat off your head and shove it down your goddamn throat."

The man's smile grew smaller and the eye twinkle vanished. "If you don't show some civility, you'll never know."

She was about to repeat her demand at an even louder volume, but something told her to hold back. If she followed through on her threat, if she choked this man to death, she might never find her son.

In a more restrained tone, she said, "I've come all this way for him. I have to know he's okay."

"He is. He's absolutely fine. And you'll see him shortly. But there are a few matters I need to discuss with you first, if you'll permit me. Allow me to introduce myself. My name is Edwin Nabler, and you, of course, are the amazing Annie Blunt." His smile came back. "I can't begin to tell you what a fan I am." A small grin. "Not, perhaps, in the way you might think, but I'll get to that."

"Who are you?"

"I told you. I'm Edwin Nabler, and this is my shop." He waved his arm. "As you can see, I carry a wide assortment of toy trains for the beginner and the enthusiast. Back in the day, when there were still people here, my clientele was made up entirely of Lucknow residents. After the . . . catastrophe . . . it might have made sense to relocate. In fact, even before, I was sensing I might need to pull up stakes once again. But that unfortunate incident—I'm sure you're familiar with it—occurred at about the same time as the Internet's reach began to expand. So I decided to stay, take orders online." Nabler smiled proudly. "We ship all over the world. I can't tell you what a godsend these technological advances have been for someone in my line of work."

"You mean, as a toy train merchant, or something else?"

Nabler came out from behind the counter and raised a finger

in the air. "Very perceptive. But I would imagine that some of the things you've experienced lately have persuaded you that there are . . . what's the word? Forces? That there are forces at work with which you have been, up until recently, unfamiliar?"

"You could say that."

"Forgive me if I sound boastful, because that's not my intention, but I have to take the credit for that."

"What are you? Some sort of magician?"

Nabler pondered how to reply. "That's not a bad way of putting it. I don't know that there's any way I could explain it to you that would be adequate. I've tried with others in the past and they're always left a little overwhelmed. Those of us who operate in the sliver have our own set of natural laws that are difficult to articulate. You know how it's hard to imagine space going on forever?"

Was this an actual question, or rhetorical? But Annie said, "I think so."

"You think, well, it has to end somewhere, right? But then, if it did, what would be beyond *that*? You see what I mean? Explaining myself would be like that. Beyond your ability to comprehend. No offense intended."

"Why am I here? What do you want with Charlie and me? Because that's what you've done, isn't it? We've been summoned. There was no direct invitation, but we were manipulated, conned into coming here."

"Yes," Nabler said without hesitation. "You could not be more correct."

"Why us?"

"The question is, why *you*. And I want to get to that. It's my intention to be much more forthcoming with you than I've been with anyone else outside the sliver. Explaining my role. Have you heard of those . . . what is it they call them in the business world? Head hunters? People who match the right person to the right job?"

Annie said nothing.

"Anyway, I've been acting as my own head hunter for some time now. You see, I've been at this for longer than you can imagine, and not just in this location. Been many, many places. Set up shop, stay awhile, then pack up my tent and move on to the next venue. Name a town, I've probably been there."

Annie wasn't sure she was actually supposed to play this game, so she continued to say nothing.

"There's a perception in the culture that someone like myself lives forever. Not unlike that Dracula myth, not that I bear any resemblance. Anyway, that's fiction, and this is the real world. I'm tired, and I'd like to pass the torch."

"What the fuck are you talking about?"

"Ah, she speaks. One of the amazing things about living as long as I have is getting to see the wired world. The World Wide Web. A great time-saver. Saves on shoe leather."

"Please just tell me where my son is."

"He's closer than you can imagine. I promise you, he's fine, having a wonderful time, even. You'll be with him soon. But first, there's something I would like to show you." He pointed his thumb toward the back of the shop. "Something I've been working on for years in one place or another."

Some sort of fucking torture chamber, Annie thought. *I won't go back there. I can't go back there. Unless that's where Charlie is . . .*

"I swear to you, you won't be harmed. This will help me explain what it is I do and how I do it, and then we can discuss how to make the necessary reconfigurations. Come."

He started walking between two aisles of toy train merchandise, beckoning her to follow him. He reached a door at the back of the shop and opened it, and Annie was almost knocked back by the din.

ChuffchuffCLICKETYCLACKclicketyCLACKwooWOOchuff CLICKETYchuffCLICKETYchuffWOOchuggachuggaclackclickety CHUFFCHUFFclicketyCLACKwooWOOchuffCLICKETYchuff CLICKETYchuffWOOchuggachuggaclackclicketyCHUFFCHUFF clicketyCLACKwooWOOchuffCLICKETYchuffCLICKETYchuff WOOchuggachuggaclackclicketyCHUFF . . .

"I know, it's a bit noisy, but you get used to it after a while. Like white noise."

Nabler held the door for her, and as she entered the back room her jaw dropped. Her reaction was not unlike that of those who had come before her. Trains whipping around the room on tracks that hung in the air on strips of wood suspended by wires. A toy train jungle, ribbons of steel that twirled through the room like spaghetti. Along the far wall, an immense diorama featuring a town and mountains and rivers and bridges, but none of them quite right. Outcroppings of rock that looked more like skulls. Grass that looked like hair, tree trunks that had the look of bone.

"What . . . what is this . . . ?"

"This is where the magic happens," Nabler said. "This is where all the trains are given that extra special something. Like that train set Charlie found in the shed out back of the place where you were staying. The quality of that set was top-notch. Very potent. Look how it held its resonance more than two decades after I ran it through the process. One of my very best, if I do say so myself."

Annie had weaved her way through some of the suspended tracks to get closer to the miniature town. A long passenger train's diesel horn sounded as it whipped past her head, startling her. She stood before Nabler's handiwork, a town with various shops and services and a park and even what looked to be a town hall with a clock tower.

Something about it caught her eye, and she gasped.

It was the clock set into the top of the building. It wasn't a regular clock. It was a Marvin the Martian watch.

FIFTY-FOUR

A nnie looked at Nabler and opened her mouth to scream, to say something, anything, but the words caught in her throat.

All she managed was, "That's . . . that's John's . . . how did . . ."

"I'll give you a minute," Nabler said.

"*You*," she said, finding her voice. In a voice that was no more than a whisper, she said, "You ran John down. You ran him down and you stole his watch. You murdered my husband." She gazed upon his creation. "For this."

"Not for that," he said. "Not exactly."

Annie wanted to summon the strength to lunge at him, tear him to pieces with her bare hands, and she was on the verge of doing it when something caught her eye.

That pane of glass that came to her in moments of inspiration and clarity.

No more than a foot square, crystal clear, as though someone had Windexed the bejesus out of it, catching light from the overhead fluorescents as it turned slowly in the air. It found its way between Annie and Nabler, closer to her, so that when she looked through it, she saw all of him.

And saw him for what he was.

The goofy hat and the vest with all the badges faded away, and Nabler was no longer his short, pixieish self, but six, maybe seven feet tall, with an elongated snout and whiskers and large, pointed teeth and ears that stuck up straight and hairy hands with long, dark nails.

Her rat-wolf man from Penn Station.

Smiling.

And just like that, the pane of glass was gone, and Edwin Nabler, toy train proprietor, was back.

Annie froze in disbelief. She'd been holding her breath, speechless. Nabler was not oblivious to the change that had washed over her.

He said, "You saw something."

Annie shook her head. "No, I didn't see anything."

Nabler smiled. Annie knew that smile. "We've crossed paths before, haven't we? A long time ago?"

"I don't believe so," Annie said.

He was studying her, looking at her differently than he had when she'd first arrived. "This is all starting to feel more preordained than I could have imagined. There are a few . . . what I would call civilians . . . who can sometimes catch brief glimpses into the sliver. Creative types, usually. You're definitely one of the special ones."

Annie took several quick, deep breaths, in and out, in and out. She needed her wits about her. As bizarre as her circumstances were, she needed a clear head.

She asked, "Why did you kill my husband? It *was* you, *wasn't* it? You ran him down in the street. You ran him down and ran back and stole his watch. Why?"

"It was integral to my objective."

"Which was?"

"I need someone to take over, and I'd like it to be you."

Annie blinked. "What?"

"There will be fair amount of work to handle the transition. I'm not kidding myself on that score. Much to be done, a retrofit of the facilities. But I think it's all doable, and you strike me as the most likely candidate. Even more so now that I have a hint of your abilities. It was a hell of a job getting you here, but it wasn't as if I could simply ask. I had to make you *want* to come here. I had to make it in your *interest*. And that meant settling you someplace where I could pique that interest. That house near Fenelon, where one of the best sets I ever made was sitting in that shed waiting for you to arrive."

"How . . ."

"So, first, John had to die. You would have to mourn, and for a period of time you would want to forget. To forget, you would need to leave the city. And that house near Fenelon was still there, that Tide box full of trains in the shed, waiting to be found. Made a couple of trips into Manhattan—my God, the traffic, I don't know how you stand it—first, to kill John, and then again, later, to put the idea of sending you here into your editor's head. Waltzed right in, pretended to have a job there, struck up a chat with him. They really ought to tighten up security."

Annie listened, trying to get her head around what he was telling her.

"You killed Fin," she said under breath.

"I wasn't present, but I did make it happen." He shrugged modestly. "You know, that was one of the first sets I sold from this location. This Wendell Comstock fellow was quite taken with it the moment he saw it. Had some unfortunate business with his wife and decided to move away, and lucky for him he did, or he'd have been here for the big event. You know, he told the movers not to pack up the trains, but they ended up in the truck anyway." He smiled. "Funny how these things happen. Anyway, a splendid set, that one. Gotten a lot of mileage out of it."

"Why? Why did Fin have to die?"

Nabler shrugged. "Sometimes these things just happen. It's not like he was a loose end, that he had even an inkling of how he'd been manipulated. But you have to admit, it ramped up the pressure on you. Am I right? And once Charlie got it in his head that he had to come here, you had no choice but to chase after him. You felt compelled. And now you're here, and we can talk about succession plans."

Annie blinked, dumbstruck for a moment.

"You're out of your fucking mind," she said finally. "Thinking I'd take over from you? I don't even understand what the fuck you do, but I know it's nothing I want to be part of."

"While you're not part of the sliver, we can work on that. We've recruited before. You've already demonstrated since you arrived that you have certain talents. Under my tutelage, before I'm gone, you'll be running the show as efficiently as I was. But it won't involve any of this." He waved his hands about the room. "Toy trains are not your milieu."

Annie gave her head a slow shake and, wiping a tear from her cheek, said pleadingly, "Please let me have Charlie back."

"In time, in time! I told you. And, honestly, he's closer than you think, having the time of his life."

Two more trains went whistling past. A freight train with a long string of boxcars and a Santa Fe passenger train consisting of several gleaming silver cars, including one with an observation dome on top.

"I promise you, you'll see Charlie as soon as you let me finish explaining to you what all of this has been about."

Annie stayed silent.

"First, you have to understand how I operate. In simplest terms, I make bad things happen." He smiled broadly. "I know that sounds wrong, but it's all part of a larger purpose, to keep order and balance in the world. How can there be joy without sorrow? How can there be success without failure? How can there be happiness without tragedy? Sometimes, the balance gets out of whack."

Nabler took a breath, then said, "My trains make the difference. An innocent, beloved toy, rich with history. Who doesn't love toy trains? When they leave my shop, when they insinuate themselves into a household, that's when they do what they're designed for. A kind of Trojan horse, you see. And what they are capable of, it's nothing short of amazing. But kids don't love trains now the way they used to. Oh, they're too *sophisticated* for them. No more trains or Silly Putty or cap guns. It's all computer games and social media, although I dare say, that last one might end up doing the kind of damage I could only dream of. But here's the thing. Even if parents aren't buying trains for their kids anymore, you know what they *are* buying? If they're good parents and they care about their youngsters' intellectual development?"

Annie felt a sense of dread washing over her.

"Ah, I can tell by your face you know what's coming. It's *books*."

Annie felt a chill.

"You know I mentioned how the Internet has changed things? Sitting here, taking orders for what train sets I still have, delivering mayhem to unsuspecting families from here to Timbuktu, I also spend a lot of time reading the news. Online, of course. Once I found a way to tap into a nearby power source—everything in town here is dead—I arranged an Internet connection and I've kept up on what's happening, and while doing that I've always been on the lookout for someone who could take over."

He smiled. "And I saw a story about you." He paused. "And Evan Corcoran."

"No," Annie whispered.

"His parents bought that book you wrote about Pierce the Penguin? The one where he decides that nothing is going to hold him back, that he might only be a penguin, but he was still a bird, and damn it, he was going to fly. And little Evan Corcoran found that book so inspiring that he—"

"Shut up! Just shut up!"

Annie had placed her hands over her ears, but Nabler kept on talking, as if he knew his words would get through no matter how she tried to block them.

"So inspiring that he went out onto the balcony and jumped. When I saw that story, and the ones that followed, I thought to my-self, *Edwin, your search is over. You've found the person you're looking for. What an accomplishment.*"

Nabler smiled, took the engineer's cap from his head, and bowed. "You killed a child with a seemingly innocent little book. I doff my hat to you."

FIFTY-FIVE

T hat's not how it was," Annie said after taking her hands away from her ears and composing herself. "I mean, I blamed myself for a long time, it's true. I told myself that, yeah, I had killed that child, but in my wildest dreams I could never have imagined such a thing happening. There was never any intent to harm that boy."

Nabler gave her a smile that bordered on the sympathetic. "It must have been very hard for you."

"Not as hard as it was for Evan's parents."

"Anyway, your intent is irrelevant," he said, his look of empathy fading. "It is a distinction without a difference. That incident showed what a book could do. But to me it was, if not proof, then evidence of potential."

"I don't understand."

"You have an untapped power."

"I can draw, and I can write. That's it."

"Now you're just being modest. Or maybe you really aren't cognizant of what you can do. There are a great many books designed to inspire youngsters to reach for that higher rung, to be more than they believed themselves capable. But how many of those books inspired any child to do what Evan Corcoran did? None. But yours, *yours* was special."

"I hate you."

Oblivious to her loathing, Nabler was already engaged in how they would move forward. He gazed about the room, imagining its transformation, as the trains continued to circle with their incessant din.

"What we'll have to do is convert everything over from trains to a printing operation. Or, you could continue to have your books printed in their current location, but before distribution we bring them here and put them through the process. We'll need fresh material, and given that there are no longer people here in Lucknow we'll have to do some scouting in Bennington or Montpelier, or we'll head west to Albany. Lots to choose from there, no question."

"Fresh material?"

"I'm sure you already noticed some of the scenic elements on the little town there are not what you would find in a more traditional hobby shop. The bones, the teeth, the hair, that kind of thing. Your husband's watch. It's what gives the project its zing. With books, I'm thinking we might take a different, more direct approach. Did you know that around 150 BC, in Pergamon in West Asia, parchment was made from animal skin? So there's no reason to think it can't be made from human skin. Just a page or two, that's all we'd need. Slip it in somewhere, and—"

He cut himself off and laughed. "Those loonie politicians trying to ban books in schools and libraries? They might be on to something without even knowing it."

"I won't do it," Annie said.

"Yes, you will."

"No, I won't have any part of it."

Nabler gave her a smile one might offer a naïve child. "I'm amused that you think you're in a position to bargain. Have you forgotten someone?"

"Don't hurt my son."

"I would certainly hate to do that. He seems like a lovely young man. He was very tired and hungry when I found him. I had my doubts he'd make it here on his own despite his best efforts, so I met him along the way."

"I found his bike."

"I knew you would. Bread crumbs."

"Please, I'm sure he's tired and hungry. I have his things in the car. A change of clothes. Just give him to me and we'll go to the car and then we can talk."

Nabler rolled his eyes. "I know this getup is a bit ridiculous, but tell me I don't look that stupid."

Annie shook her head. "I just want my son."

Nabler went on as if she hadn't spoken. "You know what surprised me after the big event, when everyone died? I felt lonely. I never would have expected that. Up until that time, I kept my interactions with people to a minimum. Dealt with them when I had to, tolerated them. But when they were all gone, I was a little regretful."

"Regretful?" Annie said. "You made it happen? You killed four thousand people?"

Nabler sighed. "The way things work is that in many cases there's a kind of symbiosis between what the trains are doing and what happens to those in their orbit. A mirroring, if you will. There was an incident in this room. The local chief of police, getting a little too close to the truth, and in our back-and-forth, a few tanker cars were knocked off the tracks and hit the floor and made quite the mess."

"That . . . triggered the derailment?"

Nabler nodded. "It wasn't planned, but it was without question a high point for me. Perhaps a case of be careful what you wish for. I've been ready to retire ever since."

"Where does some unspeakably evil thing like you retire to?"

Nabler shrugged. "Florida."

There was a moment of quiet between them. Annie was assessing her situation, and Nabler felt it was only right to give her some time.

Finally, she said, "I won't agree to anything until I see Charlie and know he's okay."

Nabler nodded slowly. "That seems reasonable."

"Where is he?"

"He's been with us this whole time. I thought you might have noticed by now."

Annie looked about the room. "Where the hell is he?"

Nabler raised a palm and waved it slowly in front of him, as if clearing a space on a frosted window. As he did so, one of the trains that had been circling around the room slowed to a stop next to Annie on a track that was slightly below eye level.

It was the passenger train.

"The dome car," Nabler said.

She focused her attention on the streamlined car with a glass bubble on top, the place where, in a real dome car, passengers would sit so that they might have a more spectacular view during their journey.

Inside the bubble was a scale figure, no more than an inch tall, but detailed enough that Annie could see how it looked remarkably like Charlie.

But then the figure waved its arms. It was not a representation of her son.

It was him. Shouting something she could not hear because they were separated by the dome's glass.

But she could make out what he was saying nonetheless.

"Mommy!"

FIFTY-SIX

C harlie!" Annie shouted. *"Charlie!"*

Before she could reach out and lift the passenger car off the track, Nabler had waved his hand again and the train began to pull away. Charlie pressed his palms to the glass and continued to call out silently to his mother.

"It's not him!" Annie said to Nabler. "It's not possible! You're playing some trick on me! You're making me imagine it!"

"Am I?" he replied.

"Like hearing trains in the night. Or when I saw that train bearing down on us at the crossing. It was there, and then it wasn't. Or like the spiders. It's all a hallucination!"

Nabler nodded thoughtfully. "If that's what you think, then I suppose you can refuse to help me."

Annie began to shake again. She wanted Charlie back. And she was weighing what she was prepared to do to make that happen.

She asked, "You can make him big again?"

"Of course."

"If I do what you want, what happens to Charlie?"

"Nothing."

"Would you turn him into the same thing you'd turn me into?"

"What do you think I am, Annie? Some kind of monster?"

"I've seen what you are."

"I wouldn't do that to Charlie. We formed quite a bond on the way up here. As I said, he's a fine boy."

"What will happen to him?"

"I'll see that he gets home, back to the West Village, back to your place on Bank Street."

"But without his mother."

Nabler sighed. "Yes. But there is extended family, is there not, who will take him in? And a substantial estate by now. You've had a very successful career. The boy will be well provided for. No worries there."

"What will the story be? I'm just missing? Presumed dead?"

"Mere details. Don't trouble yourself with them."

"Will he remember? Won't he know what happened here, what happened to his mother?"

"No."

"What do I . . . become?"

"Something so much bigger than yourself. I can help you with that. I've never brought anyone into the sliver before, but it's been done. And once it is, you'll wonder why you ever had any objection."

"What will you do to him if I refuse?"

"Well, in that case, it will be the status quo around here, even if the market for toy trains isn't what it once was. The layout needs some freshening." Nabler thought a moment. "His fingernails would make excellent patio stones."

Annie said, "Okay. I'll do it."

FIFTY-SEVEN

B ut I want a moment with Charlie first," Annie said. "And not some miniaturized version of him. I want my real son." She paused, bit her lower lip. "I want to be able to say goodbye to him."

Nabler nodded in agreement. "Of course."

"You'll see that he gets home?"

Nabler crossed his heart. "Hope to die."

Like that means anything. She did not expect him to allow Charlie to survive this, but felt she had to make Nabler think she did. She had one hope in the back of her mind, and she would need Charlie's help if she were to make it happen.

"And how do I . . . turn into what you want me to be?"

"It's a rather . . . intimate procedure." He could see the horror in Annie's expression. "Not quite that. Don't worry. I have no need for that kind of pleasure. There will be a closeness. And you won't feel a thing."

"Will Charlie have to watch?"

"Probably better that he doesn't."

"Get him out of that train. Make him his real size again."

"Already have. He's right there."

Annie whirled around. Standing by the door that led into the shop stood Charlie, the *real* Charlie, full size and rubbing his eyes as though waking up from a nap. His clothes were dirty, his hair a

matted mess. Annie maneuvered her way through the various ribbons of track in her path, ran to him, dropped to her knees, and
threw her arms around him.

"Oh, Charlie, Charlie," she said, burying her face in his neck and
squeezing him to her. "I was so scared for you."

When she pulled back to look him in the eye, she saw that as many
tears were running down his face as there were running down hers.

"I'm sorry I ran away," he whimpered. "I thought I had to. The
man tricked me." He was looking at Nabler over his mother's
shoulder.

"He made me think he was Dad. He was in my dream one
night and showed me where the key was to open the shed, so I
could get out the trains. He made me think Daddy was here." His
chin crumpled. "But when we got here, Daddy wasn't here."

"I know, sweetheart, I know."

She recalled that night John spoke to her, warning her not to
leave the city. That was the real deal, she thought. Not Nabler
working his black magic.

Charlie said, "I kept thinking, if there was a chance, if maybe
Daddy was really alive, I had to come here and get him. And when I
found him I'd bring him back and you'd be so happy."

He tightened his arms around his mother's neck, and she could
feel the tears running down into her collar.

Charlie put his lips to his mother's ear and whispered, "He killed
Daddy."

"I know."

"And he wants you. Everything was a trick to get you here."

"I know that, too, Charlie."

"One time when I looked at him, he was different. Just for a
second. Like the thing you were making."

"I saw that, too. We're in a tough spot here, but I want you to know I love you more than anything in the whole world."

"I love you, too, Mommy."

Nabler tapped his wrist. "Tick-tock," he said.

Annie turned and looked at him. "You said he could get some fresh clothes?"

"Yes, but you should say your goodbyes now."

Annie said to Charlie, "The car's just down the street, past the tree that fell down. It's unlocked. All our stuff's packed in the back. You'll find some of your clothes there. I packed real fast, so I might have missed some things. And I brought back my stuff, even some of the things I'd been working on."

"Okay."

She put hand on each shoulder and looked at him very directly. "Mr. Nabler here wants me to help him with what he does. I don't want to do it, but we've kind of made a deal. I help him, and you'll be okay."

"We get to go home?"

"*You* get to go home. It looks like I'll be staying here."

He started to tear up again. "I don't want to go home without you."

"Mr. Nabler's giving me a real once-in-a-lifetime opportunity. I'll be able to use my talents to do some amazing things. He's been explaining it all to me. When you were in the train, circling around us, did you hear him talking about it?"

"A little, yeah," he said, and sniffed.

She spoke slowly and deliberately. "About how when something happens with the trains, it makes something like that happen in the real world? Did you hear him talking about that?"

Charlie nodded.

"Don't you think that's interesting? And the way I understand it, it doesn't always have to be with trains. Like, you know that saying when you're walking on the sidewalk, step on a crack, break your mother's back?"

"I would never do that."

"I know, but you know the saying?"

Charlie nodded.

"It's kind of like that. When you hurt something that's pretend, it makes the real thing feel the pain. I just wanted to be sure you understood."

"I guess I do."

"And you're going to find just what you need in my Bloomingdale's bag. You know the one? That says MEDIUM BROWN BAG on it?"

"I know the one you mean."

"Okay. I love you, Charlie. We're a great team, always have been."

She gave him another hug, and a kiss, and then stood. Charlie looked at her and then at Nabler, not sure if he was supposed to leave now or not.

"Go on, now," Nabler said. "Get your stuff. I know your mom doesn't believe me, but I *am* going to take you home. Soon. I hold up my end. And don't be thinking of doing anything stupid, like running off without me, because if you do that, I'm not going to give your mother that once-in-a-lifetime opportunity she was telling you about. I'm going to be sending her to join your dad. You understand me?"

Charlie nodded.

"Then get going. You go through that door, takes you through the shop, you head out the front. Got it?"

Another nod. He took one last look at his mother.

"Bye, Mom," he said.

His mother tried to smile, with a quivering chin.

"Bye, Charlie. You be good."

Charlie turned away, opened the door to the shop, and disappeared.

Annie stood there a moment, collecting herself, before turning around to face Nabler.

"Shall we begin?" he said.

FIFTY-EIGHT

Charlie walked through Choo-Choo's Trains as though still emerging from a dream. He remained so exhausted from his hours of nonstop bicycling that the enormity of what had just happened had yet to sink in. His legs ached, his chest hurt with every breath he took, even his arms were sore from holding on to those raised handlebars. Looking back, he realized that bike ride had been similar to one of this sleepwalking episodes. Had he actually been awake as he pushed on those pedals, or under some kind of spell from Mr. Nabler?

He'd been functioning while under a delusion, that was for sure, thinking that his father was alive. He knew that wasn't true now. But other facts had not quite come into focus. Had he really been inside that toy train, looking at his mother through the top of that dome car? Had his mother really said goodbye to him? Was she really staying here to help that bad man and sending him, Charlie, away?

Or had she been trying to tell him something?

He walked through the store, paying little attention to the boxed train sets that lined the shelves. They no longer held any interest for him. If he never played with trains again in his entire life, that would be just fine.

Charlie came to the front door of the shop and stepped outside.

Whoa.

He hadn't seen any of this when he got to Lucknow. After he had hopped into the van with Nabler, and not long after he'd managed to guess which railroads were represented by many of the patches on his vest, he had fallen asleep, and it wasn't until the van was parked in the alley behind the shop that Nabler had said, "We're here!" They had entered through the rear of the store, so the first thing Charlie saw was Nabler's bizarre model railroad, and at first, he had to admit, he thought it was pretty cool. Totally weird, but cool.

And then he saw the watch.

That was when Charlie knew he'd been tricked.

So as he came out the front door of Choo-Choo's Trains and stood on the sidewalk, he stared openmouthed at what must have been, at one time, a vibrant street. It didn't take him long to notice that the various businesses were just as he had arranged them, albeit rather crudely, on the floor of his mother's temporary studio. In his mind, he'd already been here, but when he imagined Lucknow, it wasn't deserted like this. The stores weren't boarded up, didn't have their windows smashed in. There certainly wasn't a moose walking down the middle of the street.

He took a moment to get his bearings, then looked left, saw the downed tree, and beyond it his mother's car. He started running toward the car, slipping quickly under the downed tree like he was sliding into home plate, then back on his feet.

He went around to the back of the car, intending to open the hatch, but the bumper was all smashed in, the glass shattered, and the liftgate damaged to the point that when Charlie hit the button to activate it, it would not budge.

No problem.

He went to the back door on the passenger side, opened it, and crawled in. His booster seat was there, and he got onto it on his knees and leaned over the top of the backseat so he could reach into the cargo area.

Supposedly he was out here to get some fresh clothes, although he also suspected his mother didn't want him to see something bad that was about to happen between her and Nabler. He didn't think it was the sex thing, which he knew plenty about, and what kid didn't in this day and age, but it was definitely something not nice and maybe even a little scary.

And, again, he wondered if she had been trying to get some message across to him without sounding like she was.

Like that bit about how when you step on a crack you break your mother's back? Which made him wince at the recollection, because he'd lied to her, saying he'd never rattled off that rhyme. He'd said it while skipping along the sidewalk on Bank Street, but he'd done it without thinking about the words or what they meant. It was a silly rhyme, that's all.

His mother must have already packed a lot of stuff before finding out that he had slipped out of the house in the night. And, pushing the various bags around, he found his mother's clothes and the books she had brought up and her things from the studio. And, just like she'd said, there was a bag with some of his things in it. Some jeans and shirts and underwear. He pulled out one of each, and a pair of socks. Should he get changed here, in the car? He felt a little funny about that. Or he could do it outside of the car, right next to it. No one was going to see him. There was no one left in Lucknow, by the looks of things.

He stopped thinking about putting on fresh clothes and instead recalled something his mother had said. What was it, again?

When you hurt something that's pretend, it makes the real thing feel the pain.

Charlie began to look through the other bags, at items that were not his. Things that belonged to his mother.

And then he saw the bag his mother had specifically mentioned. The one from Bloomingdale's, with MEDIUM BROWN BAG printed on the side.

When he looked inside, Charlie understood what it was his mother had been trying to tell him.

FIFTY-NINE

L et's start with a drink," said Nabler, who no longer looked like Nabler. He had transformed into the creature Annie had seen for an instant moments earlier, allowing himself to be seen as he truly was. He was pouring a greenish liquid into a long-stemmed glass.

"What is that?" Annie said.

"If you're going to have questions every step of the way, this is all going to take a very long time."

"It looks like a smoothie."

"Sure," Nabler said, the whiskers on his snout twitching. "Let's call it a smoothie."

She accepted the offered glass, brought the drink up to her nose, and gave it a sniff. Fruity, not half bad, but that didn't mean it was going to taste good. She took the tiniest sip and made a face.

"Think of all the times you've made Charlie swallow something he didn't love," Nabler said. "Like broccoli or peas, or maybe a medicine he didn't much care for. You told him it was good for him, or would make him all better."

"This isn't good for me and it won't make me all better."

"You say that now, but you wait."

She took another sip, grimaced, drank some more. Taking her time. She didn't know how long it would take Charlie to find it, if he found it at all. And even if he did, would he know what to do? Everything was a long shot now. All guesswork. The odds, she knew, were not in her favor.

"That's it," Nabler said. *"Over the lips, past the gums, look out stomach, here it comes."*

Very slowly, she drank the contents of the glass and handed it back to Nabler.

"How does it feel?" he asked.

"Very . . . cold. It wasn't cold when I drank it, but now that it's inside me, there's like this freezing that's spreading all over the place."

Nabler nodded. "That's good. That's what you're supposed to feel. Do you feel sick to your stomach at all?"

Annie thought a moment. "No. Just cold."

She was feeling something more than that. A clarity of vision, as if all her senses were slowly sharpening, becoming heightened. It was ever so slight, but she was becoming aware of every part of her body, right down to her toenails. The din of the running trains—

ChuffchuffCLICKETYCLACKclicketyCLACKwooWOOchuff CLICKETYchuffCLICKETYchuffWOOchuggachuggaclackclickety CHUFFCHUFFclicketyCLACKwooWOOchuffCLICKETYchuff CLICKETYchuffWOOchuggachuggaclackclicketyCHUFFCHUFF clicketyCLACKwooWOOchuffCLICKETYchuffCLICKETYchuff WOOchuggachuggaclackclicketyCHUFF . . .

—lulled her into an almost trance-like state.

"Let's give that a minute to work its magic," Nabler said. "I have a little of that every day." He grinned. "Not available at Costco."

There was a lightness, too. Was this how it would feel if you were on the moon? Annie thought. Not weightless, but as though there was less of you than there was before.

"Okay," Nabler said. "Come to me."

"What?"

He opened his arms wide. The vest filled with railroad patches was gone. It was hard to tell whether he was actually wearing anything at all now. Was there a trench coat, as she had imagined? If there was, it was melding with the thin, bristly fur that covered him. She took note of his leathery hands, the long fingers with black nails.

"It's okay," he said. "It's just a hug. No more and no less. Don't worry."

She allowed herself to drift into his arms, and as her body touched his she felt overwhelmed with the stench. That fruity potion she could handle, but as he slowly folded his arms around her she was reminded of that first apartment she and John shared. There were rats in the building and the super had put out poison. The creatures had feasted on it and then died in the walls, the stink of their decaying corpses coming through the drywall and the paint, and there wasn't enough Air Wick in the world to get rid of it.

Annie began to gag.

"It'll pass, it'll pass," Nabler said reassuringly. "Think about what's to come. Think about the powers you'll have."

She could feel it happening as the nausea began to fade. A wave working its way through her, almost like a sexual peak that was slowly growing. She wanted to fight it, but at the same time, she was surrendering. Not because it was pleasurable, although it was, but because she believed she needed to become what he was, up to a point. But she couldn't go past it. There had to be a sweet spot, where she had some but not all of his power. A stage from which she could return to her real self.

It all depended on her son.

Come on, Charlie.

"It's wonderful, isn't it?" Nabler said. "Think of what you'll be capable of when everything is up and running. When you start sending your books into houses all over the world. It'll be a bit hit-and-miss at the beginning, getting the balance just right. I wasn't hitting my prime with the trains until the fifties. I'll help you get started before I take my leave."

"You'll come back after you take Charlie home?"

"Well, about that," Nabler said quietly. "I think you're already far enough along to handle the truth about Charlie."

Sleepily, Annie said, "What do you mean?"

"I can do a lot of things, Annie, but I can't make people forget. That's not in my repertoire. And I'm afraid Charlie can never leave here knowing what he knows, having seen what he's seen. I'm sure you're coming to understand that."

Had they lifted off the floor? Was that possible? Annie moved her feet, as if they were hanging off the end of a chair. She and Nabler, in their embrace, had levitated. Just a few inches, she reckoned, but floating just the same.

"I didn't want you to hurt him," she whispered. "But I suppose you have to do what you have to do."

"You see? You coming around that way, it's already started, but we have a ways to go yet before you're there. You're a soufflé, Annie, rising to perfection, but one misstep and you'll completely collapse."

She thought she sensed a door opening and closing, although it couldn't be heard over the trains.

Yes, yes, she was right. There was someone in the room with them.

"We have company," Nabler said softly. "It's okay. Whatever sad little trauma he might experience watching this won't be with him for long." And then, annoyedly, he said, "He still looks like the mess he was before."

"Maybe he came inside to change his clothes," Annie said dreamily, although she was still hanging on, part of her still in the real world.

"Hi, Mom," Charlie said, taking a few steps closer. "You're floating."

"I know. It feels really strange."

"I wanted to say goodbye again."

"Oh, sweetie," Annie said. "I'm so glad you did. Reach up and let me give your hand a squeeze."

As Annie lowered her hand toward him, he raised his up and their fingers touched.

Charlie placed something in Annie's palm.

He did it, she thought. *He got the message. And he might never have figured it out had Nabler not revealed himself to Charlie, however briefly.*

She moved the object about in her hand, confirming that it was what she hoped it would be. The small sculpture she had made from plasticine. The rat-wolf figure that stood on its two hind legs that had come to her as a vision when she had sketched it out on a sheet of paper, and then created in three dimensions.

Why am I making this? she had wondered at the time. Now she knew.

"Thank you, Charlie," she said, and then, with the last scintilla of free will in her possession, she swiftly brought the figure to her mouth and bit off its head.

SIXTY

S he wasn't able to bite through the wire armature, of course. But her teeth sank right into it, and then she pulled away, tearing the molded head off the way one might rip the meat off a barbecued rib.

And then she spat it out.

Annie and Nabler dropped to the floor, their elevated embrace having come to an abrupt end.

She hit the floor on her side and rolled, while Nabler landed on his feet—or, more accurately, ratty paws—with his hands clutching his throat, a bluish-green liquid spilling out between his fingers. He let rip with a scream that drowned out the trains still stampeding about the layout.

A few tendrils of viscera, a brain stem, were all that linked his head to his body as he staggered about the room. Those tendrils gave way, and the head landed on the floor with a plop. But what amazed and horrified Annie was that he continued moving, the proverbial chicken with its head cut off.

Nabler wasn't done.

Even without eyes, his body sensed where Annie was and came for her. She was still reeling from the fruity potion and Nabler's embrace and was unsteady as she scrambled to her feet.

The timing, she believed—and hoped—was just about right. Charlie had shown up when she'd needed him most. She'd acquired enough power so that when she bit off that head, the so-called "mirroring" effect kicked in. But, judging by Nabler's headless lunging in her direction, it hadn't quite been enough.

She looked to her hand, to see what else she could do to the figure, but it was not there. In her fall, she had lost her grip on it.

ChuffchuffCLICKETYCLACKclicketyCLACKwooWOOchuff CLICKETYchuffCLICKETYchuffWOOchuggachuggaclackclickety CHUFFCHUFFclicketyCLACKwooWOOchuffCLICKETYchuff CLICKETYchuffWOOchuggachuggaclackclicketyCHUFFCHUFF clicketyCLACKwooWOOchuffCLICKETYchuffCLICKETYchuff WOOchuggachuggaclackclicketyCHUFF . . .

Annie jumped back as Nabler came at her, swinging his arms like Frankenstein's monster in some old black-and-white horror movie. He might be missing a head, but if he managed to get hold of her, she had no doubt he could crush the life out of her.

Where the fuck was the—

"I have it!" Charlie cried.

He waved it in the air, briefly, his eyes wild. The figure, headless. But he didn't take more than a millisecond to figure out what he had to do. He ran for one of the closest tracks that was at a level he could reach. A mighty steam engine was furiously approaching.

Chuffchuffchuffchuffchuff

Charlie placed the figure across the rails, straddling them, one hand on the feet, the other on the upper torso, holding it down firmly so that it wouldn't simply be tossed aside when the train reached it.

Chuffchuffchuffchuffchuff

The real dismembered head, on the floor in a puddle of blue-green blood, shouted, its eyes still open: "*Nooooooo.*"

The train hit the figure square on, its wheels slicing through it at the knees and stomach, striking with enough force to sever the inner armature.

The headless Nabler, lunging forward to grab Annie by the

throat, suddenly fell apart, as if someone with a great sword in each hand had slashed him across the body in two places.

The three remaining chunks of him fell to the floor and moved no more. The eyes on the head drifted shut.

Chuff . . . chuff . . . chuff . . .

All the trains stopped.

The only sound left in the room was the frantic panting of both Annie and Charlie. She slid down to her knees and Charlie ran into her arms and the two of them clung to each other like they would never let go.

And for a moment, Annie saw John giving her a thumbs-up.

SIXTY-ONE

Annie had hoisted Charlie up into her arms as they walked out the front of Choo-Choo's Trains. He was no baby anymore, and she felt the strain on her back, but he had his arms wrapped around her neck and that was taking some of the load off.

"I saw a moose before," Charlie said.

"I saw one, too."

As they reached the fallen tree, Annie set Charlie down so that he could scoot under it. It was more of a struggle for her, getting down on her knees briefly to get to the other side.

"The back of the car is all smashed in," Charlie said, running ahead to show her.

"I know."

She was astonished to realize she was thinking about Pierce the Penguin. She was ready to return to him, to share him with the world again. A story was forming in her mind, but she couldn't see it yet.

"Mom, look."

Charlie was pointing back to the train shop. She turned and saw smoke was rising above the building. Moments later, there were flames.

"It's like he's getting rid of the evidence," Charlie said.

Not him, Annie thought. *The sliver, whatever it is. It's stepped in to clean up after him.*

"I don't think anyone's going to be coming to put that out," Annie said.

And just as well. Let it all burn. Let it all burn to the ground.

She got Charlie settled into the backseat. For a moment, she thought about letting him sit up front with her, so she could reach over and touch him and squeeze his knee, even though airbag deployments were said to be risky for a child his age, figuring if they could survive what they'd just been through, they could survive anything.

But her motherly instinct overruled her. Now was not the time to take chances. They'd come this far, don't fuck it up now.

"Are we going back to that place?" Charlie asked.

"No, sweetheart. We're going home."

Not that there wasn't some unfinished business back there in Fenelon. She'd have to let Standish know she'd found her son. She'd need a good story to explain how she knew where to look, and why he had run away. But she was a writer. She'd use her imagination, come up with something good. Wait for that pane of glass to materialize.

It was a noisy drive, what with the back window gone, so Annie drove with a light foot. She wanted to be able to hear Charlie over any wind noise.

At one point, Charlie asked, "Mom, did all these things really happen?"

She wasn't sure how to answer, because she wasn't sure herself. "I think so, but it might be best if we never told anyone else about it. It's our story. But I'll tell you one thing."

"What's that?"

"Your dad's so proud of you."

"You mean, he *would* be proud of me?" Charlie said.

She smiled. "Both."

They were quiet for a long time. Charlie had his eyes closed for a while, and Annie hoped he would be spared any nightmares. But they were coming. She knew they'd be inevitable.

When they got onto an interstate heading south back to New York, Charlie stirred and broke the silence. He had a question he'd been wanting to ask his mother for some time.

"Mom," he said tentatively.

"Yeah?"

"When we get home, and everything kind of settles down . . ."

"Yes?"

"Could you get me a decent bike?"

She looked at him in the mirror and smiled. "No," she said.

Charlie didn't think it was worth arguing about. At least not now. Maybe after a couple of weeks. There'd be plenty of time to work on her then.

Daniel thought he smelled smoke.

He had dozed off, sitting in his chair in the living room. The whiff of something burning drifted up his nostrils and woke him. He got up, walked out the front door, and stared in wonder at the house across the street.

There were flames coming out the skylights on the roof. Just above the studio, he was thinking. The fire spread quickly, blowing out windows on the second floor, flames billowing out.

Daniel was wondering whether he should put in a call to the fire department, then decided against it. Something told him he should let it burn.

Within minutes, the entire structure was fully engulfed.

Daniel sensed someone coming up behind him, and when he looked down, there were Dolores's hands, fingers laced together across his belly. He felt her head press up against his back.

He shifted around, put his arms around her, and his lips met hers as she tilted her head up to him.

"I love you," he told her.

She smiled. "I'm back."

They went inside, arm in arm, as the house across the street burned to the ground. They couldn't say for certain, but they thought they heard a dying whistle.

ACKNOWLEDGMENTS

First, I'd like to thank you, the reader, for following me down a different path with *Whistle*. I hope you enjoyed it, because this might not be my last time exploring an even darker world. A grateful nod to booksellers, too, for embracing *Whistle*.

In the UK, I am in debt to the team at HQ: Charlie Redmayne, Lisa Milton, Kate Mills, Claire Brett, Alvar Jover, Sophie Rosewell, Joanna Rose, Georgina Green, and Anna Derkacz.

At HarperCollins Canada, a big shout-out to Lauren Morocco, Cory Beatty, Neil Wadhwa, Brennan Francis, Shamin Alli, and Melissa Brooks.

At William Morrow in the US, thanks go out to Liate Stehlik, Tessa James, Jennifer Hart, Emily Krump, Christopher Connolly, Laura Brady, Jamie Csimbok, Kerry Rubenstein, and Dave Cole.

I am grateful to Steve Fisher at APA, the Marsh Agency, Jemma McDonagh, and, especially, Helen Heller for representing my interests.

For this and that, thank you Tien Le, Rose Rillo, Jean Debos, Charles Heller, Tom Straw, and Leonard Szymanski.

Finally, a special thank-you to Stephen King, who read the first draft of *Whistle* and was encouraging from the get-go.

 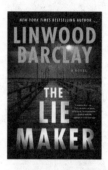
 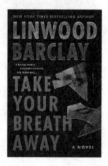
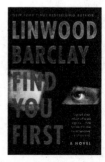 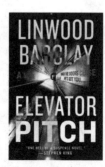 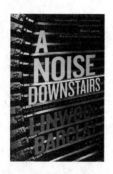